BOOKS BY RICHARD B. WRIGHT

Farthing's Fortunes   1976

In the Middle of a Life   1973

The Weekend Man   1971

FARTHING'S FORTUNES

FARTHING'S
FORTUNES

—

RICHARD B. WRIGHT, 1937–

New York **ATHENEUM** 1976

This edition of this book is not for re-sale in or export to Canada.

*The author wishes to express his gratitude to the Canada Council
for an arts grant which materially assisted him during the
writing of this book.*

Library of Congress Cataloging in Publication Data

Wright, Richard Bruce, 1937–
    Farthing's fortunes.

    I. Title.
PZ4.W9516Far [PR9199.3.W7]   813'.5'4   76-11860
ISBN 0-689-10756-0

THIS BOOK IS FOR MY TWO SONS

_____

You can't get justice in this world.
It doesn't grow in these parts.

The Horse's Mouth

The first hundred years are the worst.

Old saying

CONTENTS

Contents

PUBLISHER'S FOREWORD

IT MIGHT BE fitting to preface these remarkable memoirs with a few brief words indicating how the author came to our attention. Last autumn we were pleased to publish the latest addition to our *Days of Yore* series. I'm referring, of course, to Hector McCoy's autobiography *All Our Yesteryears*, a sensitive and revealing portrait of a man who taught elementary school in a small Ontario town for half a century. To celebrate the publication of Mr. McCoy's book we thought it might be appropriate and rather fun to have a party for him and his friends at Sunset Manor, the senior citizens' home in Craven Falls, Ontario, where the author now resides.

The party was a splendid success save for one jarring note. It was during an informal sing-along around the piano that a small elderly man in tan pants and blue shirt appeared at one end of the room and provoked an incident by calling Mr. McCoy a fake and a humbug. These were demonstrably false charges, but they had the effect of dissipating the festive atmosphere of the day. Three nurses were immediately dispatched to quiet the man, but he proved singularly nimble and contrived to lock himself in a small closet in the hallway. From there he raised a considerable din by repeating these base accusations. Mr. McCoy, a tall, genial man in gray slacks, blue blazer, and bow tie, was visibly distressed, as were several ladies, two of whom required a generous application of smelling salts to restore consciousness.

You may easily imagine my surprise when it was revealed to me by Sunset Manor's able administrator, Mrs. Kirby-Allison, that the elderly gentleman, a Mr. Farthing, would come out and be quiet only if I promised to have a few words with him in his room. Needless to say, I agreed. I have been importuned by many an aspiring author in my time and am not unfamiliar with their sense of urgency. I did, however, take the precaution of inquiring whether this Mr. Farthing was dangerous, for though he was a very old man he appeared extremely fit. Mrs. Kirby-Allison assured me that while his temperament could be described as generally peevish, he was quite harmless. She ascribed these outbursts to pressure on the brain occasioned by the insertion of a silver plate in his head, the unfortunate result of an old war wound. Mr. Farthing was then in his ninety-fifth year, and although he had been at Sunset Manor for two decades, he was still considered difficult and not particularly well liked.

I subsequently visited his room, where I found him sitting in a chair with his feet up on a hassock. He was smoking an unfiltered cigarette and sipping from a glass of amber liquid. On the table next to him stood a bottle of Canadian Club rye whiskey. I will not try to reproduce our exact conversation, for as you may appreciate, what talents I possess are of a critical rather than creative nature. "Come in and take a load off your pins" was, I believe, Mr. Farthing's initial remark to me. "Have a drink!" he said. "It's better than the cake and buttermilk those Presbyterians are serving downstairs."

He was a refreshingly eccentric old character, and to humor him I readily accepted the libation. It also gave me an opportunity to study his physical person. He was small and lean with vivid blue eyes. Although his hair was still thick, the years had left their silver trail. His face was remarkably unseamed and indeed he didn't look a day over seventy-five. He then said to me, "That book of McCoy's is a load of bullshit. The farthest he's ever been is bass fishing over at Spider Lake. No, wait a minute. I think he once took a busload of kids down to Niagara Falls. But he hasn't been anywhere to speak of. He hasn't done anything. I doubt if he's ever met one interesting person in his life. What the —— are you bringing out his memoirs for?"

I patiently pointed out to him that Mr. McCoy's autobiography was laden with the rich ore of a usefully lived life. Or words to that effect. He drained his glass and muttered an oath that is becoming increasingly popular in our permissive society. He then said, "I'm not an educated man, mister, but I've been places and seen things that I'll bet most people haven't. I once knew a fellow named Findlater. Damnedest character you've ever seen. We went through the Klondike gold rush together. Traveled all over this continent. I was in the First Great War too. At the Battle of the Somme. There was a —— up! I once tried to kill General Douglas Haig. I don't care who knows it now. They can come for me if they like. I'll be ninety-five next July 1. If you want a story, I can give you a good one."

This was familiar. Everyone wants to write a book at some point in his life. I rose to leave, and Mr. Farthing leaped from his chair. "They told you I got a plate in my head, didn't they? Well, I haven't. I made that up so I'd get away with things like drinking this whiskey in my room. I've drunk a lot of whiskey in my time. Smoked cigarettes by the carload and had a weakness for red-headed women. As a matter of fact, there's a cute little number downstairs that just moved in. She can't be much more than sixty-five. I wouldn't mind a crack at her either, but those damn doctors reamed out my prostate gland twenty years ago when I first came here. Those bastards can't wait to get the knife in you. Have another drink."

"I think not," I said. "And now if you'll excuse me, I must be on my way."

At this he reached into a drawer and withdrew a sheaf of papers and letters. "I've got the first chapters of my memoirs here and you can give them a look. It's a helluva lot more interesting than that stuff by McCoy." He pushed these papers towards me with such fierce determination that, Mrs. Kirby-Allison's remarks notwithstanding, I feared physical violence.

It was some two weeks later that I actually perused them. It was during one of those noisy and smoke-filled cocktail parties that are the bane of a busy publisher's life. At one point I retreated to an unoccupied room, the better to gather my wits. There was no reading matter readily available, but by chance I did discover in the inside coat pocket of my gray herringbone Mr. Farthing's opening chapter. Thinking to while away a few moments, I began to read. I was struck at once by the note of authenticity which runs through the book like a bright thread. Clearly the material was unsuitable for our *Days of Yore* series, which is aimed at a family market. But something lively and strong was nevertheless there. Call it a publisher's instinct if you will. I subsequently sent one of our bright young editors up to Craven Falls to visit Mr. Farthing.

Over the course of the next several months Mr. Farthing spoke about his life and times into a Klear-Tone 132 tape recorder. What you are about to read are his actual words. We have eschewed fastidious editing in the hope of capturing the texture and color of the man. This has resulted in obvious contradictions, which may trouble some readers. At times, for example, Mr. Farthing is perfectly grammatical, even coping with the difficult subjunctive mood. On other occasions he violates good usage and commits the most obvious solecisms. But such is the paradoxical nature of the man!

Many readers may regard these memoirs as exceedingly coarse, but it must be borne in mind that the author was privileged to meet people from all walks of life. And it will be immediately apparent that many of them were of dubious quality. In trying to recapture their essence, the author is merely subscribing to the writer's age-old responsibility of creating verisimilitude. An interesting departure from this adherence to naturalism is the author's insistence that a common four-letter word be represented by a dash. We are at a loss to explain this curious streak of puritanism in a man not conspicuously virtuous, but we have complied with his request. Thus an expression such as "fuck you" which is common enough nowadays will be seen rather quaintly on the page as —— you!

Publisher's Foreword

There are other readers who may feel that, like his native country, Bill Farthing is destined to play second fiddle, as it were, to his remarkable American companion Findlater. I can only say that each reader must judge for himself whether this is true. But whatever conclusions you arrive at, it remains that Farthing is the one who lives to tell the tale. Here, then, are the adventures of a colorful old Canadian: a man who, though he traveled to many countries and met myriad characters, remained to the very end a loyal son of the true north, strong and free.

Toronto, Canada

FARTHING'S FORTUNES

1

DOWN ON THE FARM

———————

I WAS BORN on July 1, 1880, in a farmhouse about a hundred and thirty miles northeast of the city of Toronto in Ontario, Canada. My mother died giving birth to me and they buried her two days later in the Anglican churchyard here in Craven Falls, not a hundred yards from where I'm sitting at this very moment.

After my mother's funeral my father got drunk and stayed that way for the better part of a year. A few people, mostly his drinking cronies at Plumb's Hotel, thought that was fairly remarkable but the rest of the town considered it disgraceful and claimed to feel sorry for us children. However, it didn't keep them from telling their children to stay away from us Farthings.

Besides my father there were three brothers and a sister. With the exception of Tom, who was next youngest to me, they all more or less blamed me for my mother's death. After all, my mother had been useful around the house. She was always cooking meals and sewing on buttons. Or pumping water and gathering firewood. Now she was gone and there I was, crying and messing my pants and making a general nuisance of myself. None of my family was any too bright but they could see the unfairness of this exchange and they resented it. It didn't take me long to learn what a kick in the arse felt like.

Our farm wasn't much of a place and my father just picked away at it. He knew next to bugger-all about farming. He'd only settled in these backwoods after the Canadian government gave him two hundred acres of stones and swamp in recognition of "his valorous contribution to the Canadian militia which materially assisted Her Majesty's forces in repelling the enemy during the recent Fenian invasion." Or so said the scroll which my father took out every second day of June on the anniversary of the Battle of Ridgeway, where he had

3

received a wound in the foot. This wound flared up whenever my father went into town for groceries or whiskey. So he'd limp down the concession road, looking like a preacher in his dark swallow-tailed coat and pipestem trousers with a derby on his head and a volume of Henry Wadsworth Longfellow's poetry under his arm. He was proud to have been one of Booker's boys, and he loved to tell of how they had put the run to the heathen Irish and sent them back to the States where they belonged.

Years later I read a book about the Fenian raids and it told a different story about the Battle of Ridgeway. And the gist of it was that Booker's boys saw a couple of Irishmen coming at them on horses and, thinking it was a cavalry charge, broke and ran. This was pretty much the way it was described to me by a man who claimed he was there. I had a conversation with him in the saloon bar of the Walker House Hotel in Toronto. That would have been in the spring of 1914, but he was still sore as hell about it. "I'll tell you something about that battle," this old blister said to me. "That was the goddamnedest mix-up you ever saw in your life. No food to speak of and half the boys had no ammunition. Things could have been worse if those Irishmen had had more sense. But most of them were drunk as a fart and couldn't see to shoot anything. If they'd been sensible they could have walked right into Upper Canada and taken her over lock, stock and barrel. Most of our boys had never fired a gun before. When they saw those drunken dogans comin' across the field laughin' and hollerin' and singin', they nearly crapped their pants. Why, there was one little fellow, an Englishman and a snotty little bastard too. He'd only been in the country a few years but he's givin' orders left and right and claimin' to be some kind of aristocrat. Tellin' us how his uncles fought at the Battle of Waterloo, and all the rest of it. Well . . ." The old bastard looked pretty grim and drank some beer. "When this little Englishman sees this gang of drunken Irishmen comin' across the field, he gets so excited he fires his gun and puts a bullet right through his goddam boot. Can you beat it? We had to carry him off the field, and what a commotion he set up! Saucy little devil he was too! I think his name was Farmington or Farthington or something. I sometimes wonder what became of him."

Well, what became of him was not much, though it wasn't really his fault. You see, my father's nature was all against him being success-ful in nearly anything he tried. He was a poet at heart and had this idea of being another Henry Wadsworth Longfellow. He was crazy about *The Song of Hiawatha* and knew the damn thing word for word. The same with *The Courtship of Miles Standish*. One of my earliest memories is of my father standing by the kitchen table with a glass of Bullseye whiskey in one hand reciting Longfellow. It was a helluva in-troduction to poetry, and I've never felt comfortable with it since. The trouble was that my father didn't appear to be suited for anything else. He had good manners when he was sober, wasn't bad-looking, and had a little of what you might call personality. The ladies liked him and

4

he might have made a living as a yard goods drummer or something along those lines. But he had no head for business, couldn't add a column of figures with any precision, and anyway felt that such work was beneath him. And since he was but slightly built, even a shade frail, and had no way with his hands at all, he was a poor risk as an immigrant in a raw land. But he had to leave England. My grandfather got tired of having him moon around the house all day, writing poems about red Indians and fancy sunsets he'd never seen. So he told him to get out to Canada or Australia and make something of himself.

My father was twenty-six years old at the time, had been to Oxford University, but hadn't done a day's work in his life. Like me he was the youngest in his family, there being an older brother and two sisters. His brother Rodney was exactly opposite in temperament and inclination, being a sober-minded man, full of business arithmetic and Methodist ire. He followed my grandfather into the family sweet-meat business. Any reader who was a child in England seventy or eighty years ago can probably remember Farthing's Fancies and Assorted Fruit Centers. They used to sell for a farthing a dozen. Fancies for a Farthing! Get it? The business was sold to a Dutch chocolate firm in 1920.

But my father had no interest at all in boiled sweets. Somehow he persuaded my grandfather to pay for the printing of a volume of his poetry, which he called *Pine Smoke at Evensong*. Don't ask me why! My grandfather quite rightly thought this was a pretty foolish idea but he agreed on condition that if the book didn't do a respectable trade, my father would have to emigrate. They printed three hundred copies and my father went to London and tried to interest the booksellers. Naturally no one took any notice of him. Bad poets have always been common as houseflies. He also joined two or three literary societies and got hold of their membership lists and tried a mail order campaign. In the end he sold ten or twelve copies. I heard the whole story when I visited my two aunts in England during the First World War.

Aunt Laura and Aunt Lucy were twins, prim little spinsters in lace and long skirts. They smelled of caramel and had bad teeth from a lifetime of sucking hard candy. Mind you, they were in their eighties then and perhaps it's a miracle they had any teeth at all. They didn't get along with Uncle Rodney, who had inherited the family home after my grandfather's death. So my aunts lived in this fancy old apartment house in Cheltenham. They were tickled to see me and made quite a fuss over me being as I was dear Jack's youngest son. And then too I was in uniform at the time and cut quite a dashing figure. Sugar was scarce during the war and in fact the family business was in poor shape, but the old girls had plenty of sweet stuff around and they were always shoving bowls of toffee and licorice under my nose. They'd felt so sorry for my father when his book of poems didn't sell and they cried for weeks after he left for Canada. Later they took me into this long, carpeted room and showed me an entire wall of *Pine Smoke at Evensong*. But the green cover with its gold lettering on the spine was familiar enough to me. My father had brought a trunkload of these books with him when he came out to Canada in 1861.

I suppose his general idea was to get away from civilization for a while and go native. This used to happen quite often to overeducated Englishmen. Anyway, in a Toronto saloon he had a drink with a trade goods salesman who traveled throughout northern Ontario and met plenty of Indians as a matter of course. On his next trip my father went along and they visited an Algonquin village. Well, this drummer unloaded a few dollars' worth of junk and I suppose my father just scribbled away in his notebook, all excited about being in the wilderness. The upshot of this visit was that my father persuaded the chief to let him stay. So they gave him a tent and a couple of skins to sleep on and he settled in. But he wasn't used to the Indians' manner of looking at life. And the stink and general squalor of the place was so bad that he found he couldn't keep his beans down let alone have any stomach for writing poems. So, bitten to death by mosquitoes and black flies, he returned to civilization.

When he got back, the American Civil War was going full blast and my father decided to fight on the side of the Confederacy. I don't think he necessarily believed in slavery, but I've heard him say more than once that Jefferson Davis was a gentleman. He crossed the border at Buffalo, where he got drunk in a hotel and called Abraham Lincoln an ignorant lout. He was smartly arrested on suspicion of being a spy and there was talk of a hanging. In the end they just deported him with a warning never to set foot again in the United States of America. That was all right with my father, because he just couldn't see that country. He was sure their republicanism would get them into trouble one day. Besides, the country was filled with heathen Irish. And my father held a prejudice against the Irish all his life.

Back in Toronto he worked in a bookstore for a few years. At night he labored on his poems, dreaming, I imagine, of some kind of fame, hoping perhaps for an honorable death, for he was always going on about "death's welcome embrace" and similar foolishness. When the Fenian invasion came along, he marched away and put a hole through his foot. After that he lived in a boarding hotel in Toronto and there he fell in love with a chambermaid, a big, strapping girl with a bad temper. This was my mother. I don't know what they saw in each other. Maybe she thought my father was something special, and probably he was. He must have presented a raffish exterior, scowling and limping around the hotel, reciting his poems in a fancy accent. Anyway, they took a shine to each other and the result of this was she got pregnant. So they got married. My father used to sing a little song about it:

> *She was one of the early birds*
> *And I was one of the worms.*

1. *Down on the Farm*

They decided to homestead this government land near Craven Falls. But this half-assed farm didn't work out. My mother kept having babies and my father just picked away at the stones and cleared a little cedar brush off the land. Mostly, though, he sat at the kitchen table with his derby hat on his head, drinking Bullseye whiskey and reading Longfellow. Or cursing Canada and Canadians and waiting for the check which my grandfather sent him each month. Around Plumb's Hotel he was known as the remittance man and was good for a touch when he had the money. I don't remember much of those early years, of course, but my sister Annie told me something about them later. Annie was the oldest and after her there were my twin brothers Ned and Fred and then Tom, who was three years older than me. A couple of others died in childbirth and another brother, George, succumbed to meningitis before I was born.

After my mother's death Annie took care of us, though she was only twelve years old. But she was tough and wouldn't take any nonsense from anyone, including my father, who was often in a black humor on Saturday nights when he came back from Plumb's Hotel, cursing his fate, as he liked to call it. Annie was all right at times but she had a wide mean streak in her and if you caught her on a bad day she could make your life damn miserable. She liked me at first because I was the baby, though that doesn't mean she let me get away with much. She was a strong, slim girl with big work-reddened hands, built along the lines of my mother, if old photographs are anything to go on. By the time she was sixteen she was half a head taller than my father and broader through the shoulders too. I remember when I was about eight she caught Tom playing with himself in the outhouse. That day she was in a grim mood to begin with and when she caught poor Tom she fetched him such a clout across the side of the head that his left ear started to bleed. It took a long time to stop and for a while we thought we might have to go for the doctor in town. After that Tom never did hear properly from the left side and he was always complaining of headaches.

I was sorry about that, for Tom was certainly my favorite member of the family even though he was a gloomy little fellow who always looked on the dark side of things. I'm inclined that way myself, though I've never been as pessimistic about life in general as poor Tom. The fact is we were quite a bit alike in many ways, though he was a good deal more mannerly and genteel. The local kids were rough on him because he was smart at his lessons and wouldn't fight when you told him so. The truth is he didn't know how to fight and wasn't a bit interested in learning. The kids called him pickle-ass because of the queer way he walked. He sort of flounced along like a girl and it used to drive them wild with rage. Ned and Fred weren't much better than these local louts. They were always teasing Tom about the size of his pecker and such things.

Tom and I both enjoyed reading, and in fact it was Tom who

taught me to read. I liked geography and travel books, but Tom could never get enough of those romances that Annie would bring home from the lending library and never finish. And he read the Bible a lot too and was always going on about Jesus. He also learned to play the violin that my father brought with him from England. My father couldn't play a note on it, but he was fond of violin music of the more serious type and was always after Tom to practice. This meant that Tom didn't have to do nearly as much work around the place as the rest of us, and Ned and Fred and Annie would get sore about that. Tom got pretty good on the fiddle and for a few weeks one year he went into town and took lessons from some fellow who rented a room above the Mercantile bank and played the organ in the Presbyterian church. My father sold off some firewood to pay for the lessons because he thought maybe Tom would make something of himself with the violin. Tom used to tell me how this teacher would pinch his backside when he played a wrong note and squeeze it when he played the right one. But that joker didn't last long. As I recall, he got into some kind of trouble with the minister's wife and had to leave town in a hurry. But he was good. And he taught Tom quite a bit.

On Saturday nights, as I've said, my father would come home drunk. He'd sit at the kitchen table and for a while he'd quote some Longfellow. Then the gloom would settle over him and he'd go on about how we'd all ruined his chances to be a great poet and he'd curse us. By and by, though, he'd calm down and ask Tom to play something quiet and mournful. So while the rest of us sat around bored and fidgety Tom would play "I Dreamt I Dwelt in Marble Halls" or "A Mother's Prayer for Her Son." And soon my father would start to cry like an infant and tell us how he would make it up to us one day. Some nights when he was feeling particularly low and Tom's playing seemed sweeter than ever, my father would talk about ending what he called this sorry journey. There was an old Henry revolver in the cupboard and when my father started talking like that, Tom would nod at me over the fiddle and I would sneak the revolver out to the shed and hide it behind the woodpile. None of us ever believed my father would shoot himself, but we weren't going to take any chances.

As Tom sawed away, my father would grow more and more tired and pretty soon his head would droop way down and his derby hat would fall to the floor and roll under the table. With his arms folded across his chest and his hands tucked up into his armpits, he'd fall asleep like a bird on a branch. Then Annie would get up with a sigh, for she was fond of my father deep down, and she'd take him under the arms while Ned and Fred each took a leg and they'd carry him into the bedroom and throw him on some old quilts like a sack of meal. Ned and Fred would then help themselves to a few shots of Bullseye whiskey from the jug on the table. When the whiskey went to work, they'd get frisky as hell and start to whoop a bit, dancing on one leg, cutting farts and grabbing each other by the root. They'd wrestle around, knocking over chairs and just as often giving Tom and me a

1. Down on the Farm

punch on the arm, until they got on Annie's nerves and she'd drive them from the house with the broom. They'd take off across the dark fields, laughing and hooting, heading for the Millers, who lived on the next concession and had a half-wit daughter who would let you screw her for about three cents or maybe an old piece of colored string. I never had her myself, but that's what I was told.

After they left Annie always closed the kitchen door and stood in front of the old cracked mirror primping herself up a bit. She'd wash her face and soap her armpits and sometimes bend down to swab out her parts. Tom and I always watched through a knothole in the door. She'd then put on her one good dress; it was black and shiny across the arse like my father's suit. Then she'd sprinkle some of his bay rum over herself and slip out the back way to meet a fellow who'd be waiting for her down by the old mill stream. Usually it was one of Dan Landry's boys or maybe Charley Skinner, who was called Snake for reasons I won't mention to anyone under twelve years old.

After she'd leave, Tom would fill one tumbler with whiskey and another with well water and we'd take turns sipping from each until we were feeling pretty mellow. Sometimes Tom read me a story from one of Annie's romances, some tale about a young girl locked up in a drafty castle somewhere in Germany or Bohemia. And she was always surrounded by bats and spiders and was always trying to keep out of the clutches of some wicked old count who was keen to get into her pants. None of them ever did, as far as I can remember. After the story Tom would check on my father, make sure he was covered up and comfortable. Then we'd climb the ladder to the loft where we slept. I can still see it. Ned and Fred had one corner and Tom and me took another. Besides our beds, the only furniture was a beat-up chest of drawers and an old stump table which my father carved up with a broadax when he'd first arrived in the township and was still full of bullshit ideas about conquering the frontier and living off the land, etc. etc.

After we'd been lying in bed for a while, just letting the whiskey sing away in our blood, Tom and I always fell into the same conversation. It used to go something like this. He'd say, "Do you miss your Momma, Billy?"

"No," I always replied. "I don't really think I do, because I can't remember nothing about her."

"Anything, Billy?"

"Eh!"

"You can't remember anything about her?"

"That's right. That's what I mean."

"But I don't think that really matters. You can still miss having her around, can't you?"

"Well, yes. I suppose I can. But there's Annie."

Tom always laughed bitterly at this. "Annie is a cow on two legs. She has no true feelings."

"Oh, I wouldn't go that far, Tom," I'd say.

But Tom would just sigh and say nothing for a minute or two. And all we'd hear was the wind stirring the poplar leaves outside the window, scraping them against the roof. With the whiskey and the wind and sometimes the howl of a neighbor's dog, I'd get sleepy and only half hear Tom, who sometimes liked to talk religion about this time. "It's a lonely old road we must travel, Bill. Have you ever thought about that?"

"Well, yes," I'd say. "I guess so . . . Sometimes."

"We must learn to love each other or perish. That's in the Bible."

"It makes sense, Tom."

"We need comfort and succor through the long night. Do you agree with that?"

"What's succor, Tom?"

"I can't hear you very well, Bill," he'd say, "because you're whispering and I have my bad ear towards you. So come over here now close to me and don't worry about a thing. Don't worry about Papa and his drinking. Or Annie and her temper. Or Ned and Fred or any of the Miller boys. Just don't worry about any of them, because I'm going to look after you. Do you believe that?"

"I believe it, Tom, except that they're all bigger than us."

"Well, don't worry, little brother. Jesus will help us. I pray to him every night. I'm praying to him right now."

"Right this very minute?"

"Right this very minute." Then Tom would pull me closer to him. "I love you, Bill. Do you mind me saying that?"

"No . . . I don't mind."

I didn't either. Nor did I mind when he put his arm around my neck and held me as gently as ever woman held a child.

2

TRAGEDY

WHAT HAPPENED NEXT was one of the most tragic events of my life. It was the middle of the summer and I was fifteen at the time and things were going moderately well for us Farthings. To start with, there was my father's change of habits. That spring, after years of hard drinking, he had been persuaded to take the pledge. This miracle was performed by a local maiden lady, Miss Elsie Boswell. She also set my father to work on his poetry again. I remember her as a stout, cheerful woman with short legs and a tremendous bosom, all laced together with straps and stays and smelling powerfully of lavender. She ran the millinery shop in Craven Falls and was active in the Methodist church. Everyone spoke highly of her and a lot of people must have wondered what possessed her to take up with my father. But she did, and they began to court like youngsters.

On Tuesday and Thursday evenings my father hitched up the buggy and drove into town to accompany Miss Boswell to the temperance meetings. On Sunday afternoons they went driving along the township roads with my father reading his latest poems while Miss Boswell, who was a capable woman in every way, handled the reins. I'd never seen my father so contented and altogether agreeable. He kept referring to Miss Boswell as a lady of taste and refinement, one of the few persons in that meager community who appreciated the finer things of life. Through the week he spent most of his time shut away in his room writing poems.

When my grandfather's check arrived, he no longer grabbed his derby and hurried off to Plumb's Hotel. Instead he made a ceremony of handing the check across the kitchen table to Annie, telling her to buy some clothes for herself and Tom and me. He claimed to need very little to sustain himself and would gravely raise a hand over Annie's objections. "My art is my life," he would say. "That and the love of a good woman is all I need." Then he would drink a glass of water and make a sour face before heading back to his room. Sometimes he talked about sending Tom and me away to school in Toronto. He told us this would happen when he got his poems together and sold them to a publisher. As I say, he was in pretty good spirits, and that meant that Annie was too. With Annie, though, there was more to it than my father's reformed way of life. What was making her smile that summer was the fact that she was getting ready to marry a prosperous young farmer named Rufus Talbot.

The Talbots were the best farmers in the township and just about the only people in that neck of the woods who made a decent living off the land. Old Lazarus Talbot had shrewdly chosen the only four hundred acres for miles around that wasn't swamp or Christmas trees. And he'd worked hard over the years and had several big healthy sons to help him. Rufus was the youngest, just turned nineteen, strong as a plow ox but a bit weak in the head. Not crazy, mind you, or even foolish, but just a little slow on the rebound. Still and all he was a considerable cut above the likes of Snake Skinner or any other of Annie's old beaus.

I liked Rufus. He was a big, loose-jointed fellow with a pile of straw-colored hair that he kept shyly pushing out of his eyes with a hand the size of a pie plate. It was hard to get a word out of him when he'd come to visit. He'd just sit in a corner and fix a pair of big calf eyes on Annie as she stood by the stove frying him maybe half a dozen eggs and a pound of bacon. He just couldn't keep his eyes off her. Probably Annie gave him his first piece of tail and he was still caught up in the wonder of it all. He certainly looked humble and grateful sitting there watching her as she stood by the stove with that little swell of belly already showing. Annie was then in her late twenties and she knew it wasn't any too soon to be settling in with a husband and kids.

The Talbots, however, were straight-laced, church-going people and they weren't all that keen on joining forces with us Farthings. I suppose they felt that Rufus had been taken advantage of by an older experienced woman, and I have no doubt they were right about that. At first there was some talk of making trouble. But my father fixed all this. As soon as Annie gave him the news of her condition he sent Tom across to the Talbots' with a message that we'd be calling on them Sunday afternoon.

On Sunday my father, Annie, Tom, and me, dressed in our best clothes and brushed up well, drove over to the Talbots' behind our old fleabag mare Neptune. My father had even brushed her up a little and made me polish the buckles on her harness. I may have already remarked on my father's gift for looking and acting dignified when the occasion demanded it. But it bears repeating, for he could, as they used to say around Craven Falls, put on the dog when he felt so inclined. When we got to the Talbots' he doffed his derby and helped Annie down from the buggy, taking her big red hand and treating her as though she were some piece of delicate china. Holding on to her arm, he escorted her past the chickens and a yapping yellow dog to the farmhouse door, where I could see a lot of dark figures standing behind the curtains. Tom and I stayed in the buggy. The yellow dog came back and stood there looking up at us, barking his foolish head off until I gave him a few licks with the buggy whip and he slunk away to the barn like the coward I figured him to be. After he'd shut up and left we could hear voices coming through the open window. Mostly it was one voice—the voice of a cultivated English gentleman who knows how to use the Queen's language and isn't a bit uneasy with expressions like "the ravaging of an innocent young woman" or "a young Christian gentleman's moral responsibilities."

After an hour or so of this kind of banter with some flat-sounding backwoods Canadian muttering thrown in between, the front door opened and my father came out into the sunlight followed by Annie, who had her hands behind her back and was looking down at the ground, almost scuffing her feet like a scolded schoolgirl. And then came Rufus, grinning with a face as red as a Macintosh apple and looking, to tell the truth, like the village idiot with his high bone collar half choking him. Next came his brothers, all giants of men in their Sunday suits. And they stood around like little boys while old Lazarus himself came out, all white whiskers and dark coat, looking like some old prophet from the pages of the Bible. Well, old Lazarus and my father shook hands as though they'd made a deal and then my father took Annie's arm and brought her along to the buggy, helping her up as though she were Queen Victoria herself. Then he tipped his derby to the Talbot boys, who were standing there with their mouths agape like a bunch of rubes at a tent show, and we set off for home. As we passed an open side window I saw a woman weeping and holding a handkerchief to her eyes.

Driving along, my father cast an appreciating eye over the Talbot farm with the fields waist-deep in ripening grain and the fat cattle lying out under the trees. I remember him saying that a gentleman could live very well off the fruits of those fields and it was a fortunate man whose daughter married well. Then he cleared his throat and said, "What a time for a little celebratory libation!" Or words to that effect. But he shook his head sternly and flicked the reins. "Homeward, Neptune," he said. "I have some lines to pen on self-discipline. Miss Boswell will understand."

Now perhaps you're wondering why I haven't said a word lately about my twin brothers Ned and Fred. Well, they weren't around anymore, you see, and that was another reason why things were going so well that summer. The fact is that those two jokers had gone down to Belleville in the spring and got themselves jobs in the cider factory. So they weren't around to torment Tom and me, and we had the loft to ourselves. Tom spent a lot of time up there, musing or writing in a notebook that he carried with him all the time and wouldn't show anybody. He was usually so inside himself with his notebook and his daydreaming that he wouldn't even bother to come fishing or frog hunting with me. He didn't go for much of that stuff anyway, but he came along sometimes if only to lecture me on cruelty to animals. He couldn't stand to see me skewer a frog on a hook with a bit of the gut hanging out and the frog dancing in misery. Whenever he saw something like that he'd shudder like a young girl and say, "Must you do that, William?" For some reason he'd taken to calling me William just like my father.

Tom was acting very queerly in other ways too. For weeks you couldn't get a word or a smile out of him. Then, suddenly, for no reason you could think of, he'd come out of this shell and be friendly. In these moods he'd talk about his plans for becoming a great man of literature or maybe a famous concert hall musician. When he went on about these things he could lift your spirits and sweep you along with his dreams. Then, just as suddenly, he'd fall into the sulks again and sit up in the loft staring at the wall or playing some damn mournful air over and over on the violin until it nearly drove you crazy. Then Annie would bellow up from the kitchen and tell him to put a stopper on that wailing. Then the two of them would hurl insults at each other, with Tom always getting the best of it because he kept cool and was good with words while Annie could only bluster and slam pots and pans on the stove lids.

Although Tom was then eighteen, Annie could easily have flattened him with one punch or broken his nose with a backhander. She did that once to a fellow—at a dance over near Irish Mills when this drunken bog-trotter tried to slip her a feel when she wasn't in the humor. But having in mind her future as Mrs. Rufus Talbot, she was trying to act the lady. Nevertheless, these encounters with Tom must have been a burden on her blood pressure, for her face would smolder dark red, especially when Tom pulled his favorite trick and cupped a hand to his bad ear, saying to her at the same time, "What, ma'am? I can't hear you, ma'am. You see, I have this bad ear." That used to put Annie in a state of total frenzy and she'd call Tom a lazy good-for-nothing little bastard with no balls in his pants. This kind of outburst always brought my father from his bedroom and he'd stand in his shirtsleeves and his vest with his hair all stirred up and on end and his eyes dark and sunken from no sleep. He'd wave a piece of paper at them and shout, "How can I write my poetry in this atmosphere of animosity and rancor?"

But when things settled down and Tom was feeling sociable and Annie and my father were in their own little worlds of love and literature, then everything in the household seemed to be going well. In fact, things were going along too well. I haven't lived nearly a hundred years without learning a few lessons. And one of the lessons I've

2. Tragedy

learned is that when things are going too well—watch out! Something bad is going to descend upon you just as a thunderstorm is duty bound to follow a stretch of fair weather. It's a corker how long it takes you to learn this. Anyway, the tragic thing that happened that summer of '95 was this—Tom killed himself one Sunday afternoon in August.

It was a hot, still day with the cicadas screeching away in the pine trees and a dull heat shimmer lying over the fields. I remember sitting against the side of the house, trying to keep cool and whittling something or other with an old broken jackknife. Besides Tom, I was the only one home. Annie was over at the Talbots', putting the finishing touches to the wedding plans, and my father and Miss Boswell had just left on their weekly buggy ride. I was sitting there, already bored with the whittling and thinking maybe of putting some flies and claw beetles and a spider in a glass jar to see who'd win the brawl, when I heard this loud crack followed by a bumping sound. It all came from overhead and I jumped to my feet. Then everything was still again and the cicadas started up once more and I had the feeling pass through me that something terrible had happened and my life would be changed forever.

Now you may say, what the devil, he heard a gunshot, of course something terrible happened. But I will tell you now that up to that moment I had never heard a gun fired. No sir, not even by someone hunting, since there was no wild game to speak of around the homestead. And to you people who think you know what a gunshot sounds like because you hear it every night on your televisions, I will only say this. Those actors are firing blank rounds and real gunfire doesn't sound like that at all. On that August Sunday afternoon over eighty years ago, what came down to my ears was a hard, flat noise, like slamming the palm of your hand against a barn wall.

So I didn't put anything together at first, though as I say, I experienced this feeling that something terrible had come to pass. What I did then was, I got up slowly and went into the house. Then I smelled this burnt air, an evil smell that I became all too familiar with in later years. And I called out, "Hey, Tom! What are you doing up there? What are you fooling with now? You want to come down and read me a story?" That usually got to him, because he loved to read stories aloud. But of course there was no answer. So I climbed the stairs, and not in any particular hurry either. Then I poked my head through the opening into the loft. The old Henry must have been dirty, for the smoke was still just clearing away, drifting up slowly in the shaft of sunlight coming through the window. The smell was so strong that it clung to your nostrils like ammonia. Then I saw Tom. God Almighty, I'll never forget it if I live another lifetime! He was lying on his back with one leg hooked over the stump table and his arms stretched out. Just as though someone had struck him a helluva blow. I suppose he'd put the muzzle into his mouth, for the shot had taken off half the top of his head and already the flies were buzzing and settling. I've

15

seen some godawful sights in my time, including plenty of raw guts and scattered brains at the Somme in July of '16. But the picture of poor Tom's torn head still enters my mind on bad nights.

Now, I just didn't know what to do. So like most people in similar situations, I did something senseless under the impression that I was doing something important. I couldn't figure it out at the time, of course, but I was stricken more by anger than by grief. I was mad as hell at everybody and everything because I was put into a situation I couldn't handle. So I kept saying it isn't fair, it isn't fair, and why me? why me? All of which is pretty foolish, because if some Higher Power is overseeing such events he is just as likely to reply, why not you? Or what makes you think you're so special that calamity can walk right around you and shake hands with the next fellow in line. So I stood over Tom's body, carrying on like a fool, crying and cursing and trying to shoo the damn flies away from him with my hand. Which was crazy, because the heat and the mess was drawing them up from downstairs by the dozens.

After maybe five minutes I climbed down the ladder and went outside and puked in the long grass by the side of the house. Then I drank a lot of water and started running down the lane to the concession road. The water was a mistake, because it gave me pains in the gut and I had to stop and puke some more. There wasn't a soul around, just heat shimmer and grasshoppers and a burning blue sky. It didn't seem natural that fifteen minutes before Tom had been alive. Now he was dead, already decomposing with the flies, and yet everything was going on just the same. It struck me as peculiar at the time, though I know now that the death of an ordinary mortal means sweet —— all to the natural world.

When I was feeling a little better, I started to run for town. There was only one other farm between us and the town and that was the Coulsons', but we didn't get along with them. There'd been some dispute over fencing years before and my father and old man Coulson weren't on speaking terms. As I ran by their place I could see old lady Coulson sitting on their front stoop fanning herself with a newspaper and one of her brats rolling a hoop around the yard. But I didn't feel like telling them anything so personally tragic as Tom's death so I ran on into town, which was another half mile further along.

The main street was absolutely deserted except for a couple of stray dogs lying in the dust by the feed store. When they saw me they came running and barking. God Almighty, I can't stand a dog that barks at everything passing by. But then, to make matters worse, one of these mongrels, a black-and-white collie bitch with a long wet snout, took an instant dislike to me and began to nip at my heels. It was all too much. My brother's death and the flies and the heat and the ——ing dogs! I must have gone berserk, for I started to bawl and roar and went after the dogs, kicking at them and calling them every blessed name I could summon. Taken by surprise, they retreated a little. Then they hunched up their backs and showed their long yellow teeth and the fight was on.

The three of us raised such a commotion that I don't see how anyone could not have heard us, yet no one, so far as I could tell, came to their windows or doorways to see the spectacle of a maddened boy fighting two mean street dogs. I was winded from running and the dogs were getting the best of me. The collie bitch had already sunk her teeth blood-deep into my right arse and I was beginning to think I might be chewed to death right on the main street of Craven Falls. I thought of my poor father. Going home to find one son with most of his head blown away. And then to find another gnawed to pieces in the dust of the street. How could a man be expected to go on after such tragedies?

Well, I plucked up my last bit of wind and started to run. The dogs, now smelling victory, stayed close behind. What I was looking for was a tree to climb or a door to enter. Then a miracle happened. Not twenty yards away a woman stepped out the front door of a house. I say a miracle because that's what she looked like to me at the time. She was wearing a long white dress and from her wrist dangled a little white bag and on her head was a tremendous wide hat with flowers on it. She looked so cool and beautiful standing there that I started to cry even harder. When you're losing a fight or just being generally humiliated, especially by something as low in the scale of creation as two stray mongrels, then the sight of someone relaxed and composed only makes you feel worse.

But the woman in white took control of things very nicely. What she did was, she stepped forward and clapped her hands and said to the dogs, "All right now . . . Beat it, you bastards." She might have been talking to a pair of kittens on the window sill. And the dogs paid attention too. They stopped in their tracks, shut their ugly mouths, and just trotted away with their tails between their legs. Then this woman in white says to me, "Why, you poor kid! Aren't you one of John Farthing's? What's the matter anyway? You come and tell Mary Jane." That's when I collapsed in tears against her beautiful white bosom, inhaling the smell of orange blossom and feeling long cool fingers on the back of my damp neck. And that's how I came to meet Mrs. Fletcher!

3

MR. AND MRS. FLETCHER

I COULDN'T HAVE BEEN luckier if I'd chosen my own rescuer, for Mrs. Fletcher was the wife of the local undertaker. As a matter of fact my meeting with Mrs. Fletcher was the start of a new life for me, as I will now relate. That Sunday afternoon she led me into the house, past a long dark room filled with coffins and into a parlor where everything was bright and cheerful-looking. And a good deal classier than anything I'd ever seen. When I finally got around to blurting out the news of the tragedy, Mrs. Fletcher took me once again to her bosom and actually rocked me in her arms, saying over and over, "You poor kid. Oh, you poor kid!" Huddled up against her sweet-smelling chest I didn't ever want to surface and the awful thing was that Tom's death seemed somehow remote, though it was less than an hour since I'd laid eyes on his poor fly-covered head.

A few moments passed and then Mrs. Fletcher left me sitting on the horsehair sofa while she went upstairs to rouse her husband, who was having a Sunday afternoon nap. I'd seen Phineas Fletcher before, sitting behind his big dappled mare in the driver's box of the dead wagon. I didn't care for his looks. He was maybe fifty, a tall, thin man with sparse gray hair combed flat against his head and large powerful hands. After a bit he came down the stairs in his pants and shirtsleeves, rubbing his eyes and slipping suspenders over his shoulders. When he heard the news he was all business and began to rub those big hooks together. His voice was peculiar, soft as a young girl's. "Was it a shotgun, boy?" he asked. "Did your brother use a shotgun? My word, that can leave a mess to clean up. And it takes a bit of doing to make them presentable afterwards too."

Mrs. Fletcher was standing near the stairs with her hands on her hips. She'd thrown the flowered hat onto a chair and she was glaring at her husband. "For Christ's sakes, Phineas," she says. "Will you get out to the Farthings' and see what you can do? And stop scaring this boy half to death."

Mr. Fletcher tucked some loose shirttail into his pants. "I was only suggesting, my dear, that in my profession a man needs the delicate skills of a surgeon and the resolve . . ."

"Oh —— your profession!" cried Mrs. Fletcher. "Get the hell out there and do your job."

I have to say I was shocked to hear language like that coming from such a well-dressed lady, even in a rough-and-ready town such as Craven Falls was back in the nineties. But her husband only said "Tut-tut" and, pulling on a long white duster, left the room. Through a window I saw him heading for the stable behind the house. After he left Mrs. Fletcher went to the cabinet and took out a fancy cut-glass decanter and poured some whiskey into two small glasses. She knocked one glassful back and poured herself another before coming across the room. "Here," she said, offering this thimble-sized glass to me. "You look old enough to handle this but sip, don't gulp, or you'll burn your gullet." I did as I was told, even though whiskey was no stranger to my throat after those Saturday evenings with Tom.

Mrs. Fletcher sat down beside me and smiled. Up close she wasn't as beautiful as I had first thought. There were plenty of living lines by her mouth and crow's feet around her eyes. But she had a beautiful head of chestnut-colored hair, regular features, and a good full figure, so she was still a fine-looking woman. I figure she must have been about thirty at the time. She told me she knew my father slightly. She said that whenever they met on the street he always tipped his hat and wished her a good day. It sounded like the sort of thing my father would do. Mrs. Fletcher went on to say that so far as she could tell, my father was the kindest and most considerate gentleman in that whole godforsaken corner of a godforsaken country. I noticed that she spoke with an accent. It wasn't quite like my father's but a bit similar, so I judged her to be English.

There were two things about Mrs. Fletcher that bear noting. One was her strong laugh. The sort of braying laugh you sometimes hear from certain women in certain taverns. Say late Saturday afternoon, an hour or so before the bottles start flying. And then Mrs. Fletcher was also one of the foulest-tongued women I've ever met. Nor did she seem to care who knew it. It was as though she didn't notice herself, for she never appeared the least embarrassed, and when I got to know the household a little better, I discovered that old Fletcher, for all his religious ways, didn't appear to mind either. He seemed to take her cursing as you might tolerate another person's farting or belching. Or maybe he just feared his wife's tongue more than the wrath of God.

Mrs. Fletcher was also very interested in my father and asked me where he was. I told her he was out riding with Miss Boswell, and Mrs. Fletcher pulled the end of her nose with thumb and forefinger.

"What in hell does a man like your father see in that old sow? She's too fat. And she's bloody fifty if she's a day!"

"Father says she's refined," I said.

Mrs. Fletcher brayed at that. "Shit. She's about as refined as my bare nubbins. She's only a hat rack in a twopenny town. Her and her Methodist friends. Too bloody good to say hello to a person on the street. A bunch of bloody hypocrites, that's what they are."

About this time my buttock started to heat up with pain from the dog bite and I must have winced, for Mrs. Fletcher said, "Say, are you hurt? Did those bloody dogs take a chunk out of you, Billy?"

"Yes, ma'am," I said. "It feels like one of them did."

"Well, let's have a look then," she said, standing up. But being just fifteen and naturally shy about such things, I wasn't too eager to bare my backside to a woman. However, Mrs. Fletcher had already gone to the cabinet. "Where did the bastard get you?" she asked, filling up her glass again and returning with the decanter. From the way I was sitting she must have guessed, for she laughed her strong laugh and said, "The dirty buggers. Nipped you on one of the cheeks, eh! That's nasty. Let's have a look." I stood up but remained stock still, rooted there like a tree. Mrs. Fletcher had taken out a clean handkerchief and was spilling whiskey on it. "This'll clean it up." Still I didn't move, and she snorted again. "Say," she said, "you're not embarrassed to show me your other end, are you?" My face was flaming, for she smiled and went to the window and drew the curtains. "For a start we better keep the ——ing neighbors from entertaining the wrong ideas. Wouldn't want them to think I've got you in here to have my evil ways with you. And that's just what the bastards would think too. Well, never mind, we'll get you fixed up here."

I swallowed the rest of my whiskey fast and then she came back from the window and told me to drop my pants. "Let's have a look now, luv," she says, kneeling down beside me. "And don't worry about showing yourself to me. Mary Jane Hinks has seen a lot of men's backsides in her day. Front sides too, if you want to know the truth, so you're not going to show me anything I haven't seen before." With that she unbuttoned my pants and, pulling them down to my ankles, proceeded to dab the wound with the whiskey-soaked handkerchief. "This'll smart a bit but it don't look too bad," she says.

It was just about this time that Mr. Fletcher walked into the room. He stood there looking at us, stroking his jaw with one of those huge mitts of his. "Whatever are you doing there, Mary Jane?" he asks in this mild, pleasant voice.

Mrs. Fletcher stopped and looked over at him. "What in hell does it look like I'm doing, Phineas? The boy has been bitten by a dog and I'm cleaning the bite."

"A dog, you say?" says Fletcher slowly, and then shakes his head. "Well, that's unfortunate. I was bitten by a dog once. On King Street in Toronto. Minding my own business. Walking along the street . . ."

3. Mr. and Mrs. Fletcher

"Yes, yes, yes," says Mrs. Fletcher. "Who bloody cares? Are you going out to the Farthings' or not?"

"Well, I just wondered if the boy here wanted to come back with me. The horse is ready."

"The boy will stay here for a bit," says Mrs. Fletcher. "He's in no condition to go back out there now, for God's sakes!"

"I see," says Fletcher. "Well, maybe you're right about that." He stood there watching us for a moment, the room quiet except for a tall clock ticking in the hallway. Then finally he says, "Well, I'll be off then."

"Yes, yes," says Mrs. Fletcher. "Get on with it."

"Have a care, boy," says Fletcher.

"Yes, sir," I says.

And he left the room on his big quiet feet. Then through an open window we heard him say, "Now, horse," and the dead wagon moved off with a sound like creaking boards.

After Mrs. Fletcher cleaned up the dog bite she helped herself to more whiskey. I was wishing she'd let me have another belt but she didn't offer and I didn't like to ask. Then she sat down next to me and, leaning forward, told me I was the spitting image of my father. "Yes," she said, looking me over closely, "you look enough like your old man to be his younger brother. And that's a compliment, kid, because your father's a handsome gent. And if you can't get the father, then the son will have to do parley-vous, parley-vous." She laughed and slapped my knee. "That's what these French girls used to say, Bill. In this guest house where I worked. There were two of them. Now what were their bloody names? Georgette was one. That's right, for we used to call her Georgie. A nice kid. But I'm ——ed if I can remember the name of the other one. Well, it don't matter anyway."

She leaned back and hiked one leg across her knee like a man. "We met a lot of proper gents in those days, Bill. Some of them was real dukes and earls, mind you. Sometimes the fathers and sometimes the sons. And sometimes both." She took another snort. "Do you know where London is?" she asked. I told her it was across the ocean. I'd learned that much geography. "That's right, my duckling," said Mrs. Fletcher. "And what I wouldn't give to hear those lovely ——ing bells, ringing away on a nice gray Sunday morning with the rain fallin' on the cobblestones and half a dozen friends to talk to, all of us just lying about in our petticoats with a bit of gin and bloody nothing to do all day but talk and drink till the first guests turn up." She belched. "And here I am in this wilderness! Surrounded by cowshit farmers and Irish navvies. That's why every time I see your father, Bill, I'm reminded of happier days when my favors were appreciated by gentlemen."

She then proceeded to tell me her life story, which I pass along for what it's worth—though I've shortened it a good deal and cleaned up the language. I don't believe half of it now, but I did at the time and it helped to hurry along the hours of a frightening and miserable day in my life.

Mrs. Fletcher was a Londoner. Her family was poor and at ten years of age she was peddling flowers in Covent Garden, where she worked for several years, just scraping by but enjoying the free life of a street urchin. Then one night she was stopped by a young handsome gentleman out on the town. He gave her a long, soulful look, bought all her flowers, and said goodnight. Next day he was back and soon he was coming every evening to see her. Then he sent her a note confessing his love. She could hardly read but a friend helped her make out the gist of it. Mary Jane Hinks, for that was her maiden name, was barely sixteen at the time and didn't know what to make of all this. But the young gentleman was kind and mannerly and so she allowed herself to be set up in rooms. Soon her gentleman friend was coming around to visit with fancy clothes and bottles of scent and little geegaws. They'd sit on the love seat and eat pigs' knuckles and drink German wine while he read her the poems of Lord Byron. Of course he debauched her along the way and in a few months she found herself pregnant. When she told him the news he was on his knees, covering her with kisses. That night while she was sleeping he left a purse of gold sovereigns under her pillow and slipped out the door and out of her life.

Naturally she was heartbroken and cried for weeks. But time heals wounds and gold sovereigns help too, so when she finally realized he wasn't coming back, she settled her mind into making the best of it. Unfortunately the child was stillborn and Mrs. Fletcher told me that this was why she took to drink. To support herself she went to work in what she insisted on calling a guest house. Here she spent a number of years until she met a fellow named Bloggs, who promised to make an honest woman out of her. Bloggs was a Canadian (he did something in railway building) and he was over in London on business. That is, when he wasn't visiting whorehouses. He seems to have been an honest, solid sort of a man, short on imagination and horny as only certain middle-aged bachelors who have spent a lifetime with ledgers and accounting books can be. He persuaded Mary Jane to accompany him out to Canada, where they would marry after he introduced her to his family. As Mrs. Fletcher put it to me that afternoon, "If only we'd married before we left England, Bill. If only I'd insisted on that. But if . . . if . . . if . . . What's the use of iffing? If the Queen had balls she'd be the ——ing King!"

Bloggs lived in Toronto but he had some business in New York City, so the two of them put up at a fancy hotel there and had the time of their lives. Bloggs wasn't exactly lavish with money but he learned how to spread a little around, and for her part Mary Jane did her best to make the railwayman forget his worries about land surveys and rolling stock. They were both as happy as honeymooners and they moved on to Buffalo, where Bloggs had further business. In order to

3.   *Mr. and Mrs. Fletcher*

avoid the louts and the general run of riffraff common to those border towns, they put up at the best hotel. But even here trouble pursued them in the guise of a tall handsome stranger in a cream-colored suit and a broad hat. He spoke with a southern drawl between puffs on a black cheroot cigar. This ex-riverboat gambler took a liking to Mary Jane and made himself objectionable and unwelcome at their table in the dining room. Squat and solid Bloggs made it clear that the stranger's leers and open advances were in poor taste and a nasty situation developed in which the southerner challenged Bloggs to a duel at daybreak. Mary Jane begged him not to go, but Bloggs, to give him his due, was no coward. The next morning at dawn Bloggs and the southerner met in a deserted park and walked off their paces. Mrs. Fletcher wasn't there. She stayed at the hotel walking back and forth, twisting her handkerchief into a little ball. When a man arrived at her door with the news, she fainted dead away. The news was that both Bloggs and the southerner had fired at exactly the same time and with the same accuracy. Both perished instantly with bullets through the left eye.

Mary Jane Hinks, twenty-one years old, was left friendless and alone. She moved on to Toronto with Bloggs's body in the baggage car, thinking his family would understand and be sympathetic. But his family turned out to be one tall, skinny, sharp-nosed spinster sister with a railway spike for a heart. Bloggs's sister pitched the immigrant out into the street. The result of all this misfortune was another session in a guest house, this one on Lot Street in Toronto. Here she met Phineas Fletcher. Fletcher traveled down to Toronto a few times a year to order caskets, and in those days, before he got religion, it was his habit to refresh himself at one of these guest houses. Each time he came he asked for Mary Jane. He was well-spoken and quiet with reasonable manners, and she took him for a gentleman. He told her about his prosperous business and of life in the clear pine-sweet air around Craven Falls. So she married him only to find herself stepping off a train into a bush town with mud alleys and board buildings, the Saturday streets filled with half-breeds and Irishmen who tossed off crude remarks as you walked by.

At home she discovered that Fletcher wasn't quite the gentleman she thought he was. He picked his teeth with his fingers and wiped his mouth on the back of his sleeve. There was always a musty smell clinging to his clothes. And then a couple of years after they were married he got religion and now belonged to some sect which was stricter than the Baptists. What bothered her most, however, was that he never got mad. No matter how she abused him, he never got upset or swore at her but always turned the other cheek. And it was driving her crazy. As for what she called nuptial obligations, he couldn't get it up half the time. And when he did it wasn't worth much anyway. And all the ladies in town snubbed her and ever since she'd set foot in the place she'd suffered with a nervous stomach.

Mrs. Fletcher told me all this that afternoon and she was still talking when her husband returned with my father and Miss Boswell. Mrs. Fletcher had been helping herself to the decanter through all this and was feeling no pain. She remained seated, for I don't think she was any too steady on her pins. Fletcher quietly excused himself and left to attend to poor Tom. My father stood at the entrance to the parlor, looking drawn and pale as milk in his dark Sunday coat. Miss Boswell, all white bodice and flounce and pink round cheek, held tightly to his arm and didn't bother to hide the notion that she was slumming here in Mrs. Fletcher's parlor. My father, who was always a courtly man, even in distress, bowed and said, "Mrs. Fletcher, this is a sad day for the Farthing family. And I'm most grateful to you for looking after my youngest."

"Not at all, Mr. Farthing," said Mrs. Fletcher, sitting up straight-backed and measuring out each word, determined not to stumble in front of Miss Boswell. "I'm very pleased to be servicing a gentleman."

Miss Boswell smiled her butter-sweet smile at me. "Come along, William. We'd better be on our way."

Mrs. Fletcher had leaned forward at such a dangerous angle that I thought she might topple right off the sofa. But she straightened up and said, "Can I offer you a small glash of something, Mister Farting?"

My father scratched his cheek and looked at the whiskey decanter. Now I've seen plenty of longing in my day. In the winter of '32 I saw plenty of men looking through restaurant windows at hamburg steak and potatoes. But not one of them ever looked at a plate of hamburger and potatoes with half the hunger or longing that my father summoned up in his eyes on that August afternoon in '95 when he looked at the whiskey decanter in Mrs. Fletcher's parlor. "Well," he said after scratching his cheek again, "perhaps a small one might be in order."

But Miss Boswell's smile had turned a little rancid at the corners and I could tell she was working hard just to keep it on her face. "Do you think that's wise, dear?" she says to my father. Then she turned to Mrs. Fletcher. "Mr. Farthing no longer uses alcohol. We don't think it's necessary in a full Christian life. Do we, dear?"

"Ah . . . no," said my father, stroking his nose. "But it was kind of you to offer, Mrs. Fletcher."

"Anytime at all," said Mrs. Fletcher, finishing off another glass. "Any old time at all." Then she squeezed my hand. "Thish is a fine boy you have here. A real little gentleman. Just like his father."

"I thank you for that," said my father, bowing again.

"I won't see you to the door," said Mrs. Fletcher. "My rheu-matishm is acting up today. There must be rain in the air."

"Ah yes, rain," said my father. "A pathetic fallacy we might all devoutly pray for."

Outside my father helped Miss Boswell into the buggy and she fluffed herself down on the seat like a hen on an egg. I climbed in behind. "I do believe that woman is drunk," said Miss Boswell. "And on the Sabbath too. Really. She is an affront to respectability."

3. Mr. and Mrs. Fletcher

My father said nothing but flicked the reins and Neptune started forward. Behind us through an open window we heard Mrs. Fletcher say, "I can't undershtand what he sees in that ——ing old cow. She's fifty if she's a day." Miss Boswell flushed and gasped and we drove away.

THE MAN IN THE BOAT

MY FATHER took Tom's death hard. Tom had always been his favorite and he'd once had high hopes for Tom's musical career. Oddly enough, Annie took it hard too. At home she was reduced to such a state that she could only sit at the kitchen table and cry. She did this for three days with Rufus Talbot always standing by her side, his long arms hanging down and his naturally sad face just right for a funeral. I don't remember him saying a single word during all that time. He just stood there watching Annie with his big calf eyes. I hadn't expected Annie to carry on like that over Tom, but it's a fact that his death just took her apart. She wasn't good for anything around the house and that just opened the door for Miss Boswell, who walked right in and took charge. I suppose it was a good thing, because there was a lot to do. Aside from the meals the house had to be tidied up and our Sunday clothes cleaned and pressed. Somebody had to get in touch with Ned and Fred down in Belleville and also arrange matters with Fletcher. Miss Boswell did all this and she did a good job too.

Ned and Fred arrived next day on the afternoon train, looking faintly idiotic in identical cheap-looking moss-colored suits and yellow shoes. They must have had a jug with them on the train for they smelled ripe, and Miss Boswell set her mouth in a grim line. Fletcher brought Tom's body back to the house and set up the casket in the front room. The top was nailed down, which must have been a disappointment to the people who came by that evening for a look and a piece of cake. Those stump-pullers loved deaths and funerals. It gave them somewhere to go in the evening. A few people from town came too, including Mrs. Fletcher, sober and beautiful to me in her long dark dress and veil. She made me feel better too. The full weight of Tom's death had finally settled over me and I was feeling as low as

I've ever felt in my life. But Mrs. Fletcher squeezed my arm and I remember her whispering, "Now you cheer up a bit, luv, because your brother's sleeping now. He's peaceful at last and a bloody sight better off than the rest of us." Then the preacher said a few words and Miss Boswell told everybody it was time to go home.

Ned and Fred were down in the barn with a few of their boyhood cronies, mostly young Irishmen from around the township. They were passing around a jug of whiskey. Ned and Fred were turning out to be a couple of bad eggs. Or so I judged in my puritanical fifteen-year-old head. Besides drinking they now chewed tobacco and played cards and you could tell the way they swaggered about in their yellow shoes that they moved with a fast crowd down in Belleville. But this didn't stop Miss Boswell from marching right down to the barn and putting the run to their friends before escorting Ned and Fred back to the house.

Then she did a remarkable thing. She sat the two of them down at the kitchen table and lectured them for over three hours on the evils of drink and card playing. At the end of it she reached over and plucked a deck of cards from Ned's vest. "This, Edward," says Miss Boswell, "this is the devil's picture book. And I'm of the opinion that you might more profitably spend your leisure time in the company of Messrs. Matthew, Mark, Luke and John." Then like a magician, she flipped back Fred's coat and pulled out a hip flask. In a trice she'd emptied the contents into a rusty chamberpot under the stove. "And is it your intention, Frederick," she asked, standing over him, "to end your days as a poor despised derelict? An everlasting shadow on your poor father's name? Your poor father whose brave example is there for you to follow." Next she produced pledge cards and buttons for the Band of Hope and the Workingman's Temperance Association and damn me for a liar if she didn't sign them both up on the spot, even writing down the name of the secretary of the Belleville chapter. As I say, a remarkable performance, but then she was a determined woman.

The next day we buried Tom in the midst of a thunderstorm. Afterwards my father and Miss Boswell stood around for the longest time talking to the Fletchers. Then we left for the railway station and there Miss Boswell planted herself out on the platform in the downpour and lectured my two brothers on their future conduct. Their cheap green suits were turning a sickly lime color in the rain and so they stood there like a pair of miserable fleeced peacocks with the rain beating on their heads and the people moving around them to get aboard while Miss Boswell sounded like old Polonius in Shakespeare's play *Hamlet*, dishing out the advice before the boys hit the road. She had to shout above the fierce cracks of thunder and you could catch a sentence or two here and there. For instance, I remember her saying, "You both might find Sunday school teaching a rewarding experience." I can tell you they were both damn glad to get on that train.

About two weeks later I had a conversation with my father that changed my life forever. It wasn't really a conversation, for he did all the talking, and I'll try to reproduce it as best I can. By this time Miss Boswell was spending a good bit of her time at our place. She'd more or less taken over things. Annie and Rufus were married in a small private ceremony right in the Talbots' parlor a week after the funeral. I didn't go but Annie sent me a piece of wedding cake and a few books of romantic stories which she said she wouldn't be needing now that she had the real business. So on this particular day I was called up from the barn, where I'd been fooling around, mostly moping. I walked into the kitchen and there was my father in his best coat and vest, sitting in his usual Longfellow-reading place at the kitchen table. And standing right behind him with her hands on his shoulder was Miss Boswell. I'll tell you, they looked like they were posing for one of those old brown photographs you sometimes see in family picture albums.

Although my father still looked like a man in need of a drink, he'd cheered up a little in the last couple of days and now he made an effort to smile at me, something he rarely did. "Well now, William," he says, clearing his throat and out of habit looking around for a glass. "Now, William, I have something important to say to you. Pay careful attention, for these words may be the most important in your young life. The terrible tragedy of your brother's death has altered our family situation considerably. Things are no longer as they once were and again we are brutally reminded of what the poets and sages have proclaimed down through the ages, *sic transit gloria mundi*. Now that your sister has undertaken the grave responsibilities of marriage I can at least rest easy so far as she is concerned. She has chosen a young man of probity and prosperity. And speaking of the latter, you might be well advised to strengthen your relationship with your sister in the event that you need material assistance at some future date. As for your older brothers, both are now well situated in the business world, and while I have no great expectations for their success, I would venture to suppose they are reasonably capable of coping with the rough and tumble of life, particularly if they heed Miss Boswell's sound advice. Now as you are doubtless aware, son, your poor father is no longer the man he once was. My attempts to wrest a living from the land have not been conspicuously successful, though I have learned much and suffered much and that can only lead us to wisdom. Still, it has been a lonely and difficult passage since your poor mother's death. And so Miss Boswell and I have now decided to fight the battle of life together. In a word, we are to be married. Now what do you say to all this, William?"

Well, the truth is I didn't have anything to say to it because I was too busy trying to figure out where I fit in. But I didn't have long to wait, for my father said after a minute, "Well, I can understand your silence. There's an element of surprise in all this. It's perfectly natural to receive such news with mixed feelings. But it's all for the best, my boy, believe you me. Now, on the practical side. Miss Boswell has found a buyer for her shop and I have given over this acreage to young Rufus as Ann's dowry. Miss Boswell and I will shortly be starting life anew in a community where the cultural opportunities are perhaps more plentiful. The fact is, my boy, that we're catching tomorrow's 5:07 for Toronto and points west. And so we arrive at the important question of your future. If I thought for one minute that you had artistic leanings or a tendency to scholarship, I wouldn't hesitate to send you to a fine school, even if I had to remain here and work my fingers to the bone. However, I'm afraid that I have seen scant evidence for supposing that an artistic or scholarly life awaits you.

"Therefore, after careful and lengthy consultation with Mr. and Mrs. Fletcher, it's been decided that you will live under their roof for the next few years and apprentice yourself to the office of funeral furnisher. I can assure you that it's an honest trade and, I might add, a necessary one, particularly in these rude climes where a good undertaker can provide the lower orders with an example of civilized behavior during obsequies. You'll find this a particular challenge when you enter an Irishman's shanty. As for your future guardians, Mrs. Fletcher is a woman of the world. A trifle coarse perhaps, but possessed of a kind heart and with an obviously powerful maternal instinct. You'll be the son that's always been denied her, poor woman. Fletcher himself is a decent skin. He has some irritating mannerisms but we must look at the whole cloth and ignore the loose threads. The important thing to remember is that you'll be working for a good Canadian yeoman, a hard worker and honest as your hat. Admirable qualities worthy of imitation in the young."

My father then cleared his throat again and made a lump in one cheek with his tongue. I could tell he was fairly cracking for a drink, and if I'd had a dollar I'd have bet the whole thing that this dry spell was coming to an end and fast. Miss Boswell would have her work cut out for her all right. Still, that would be her problem, not mine. All I could think about was Mrs. Fletcher and sleeping in the same house with her. I was only half listening to my father, who was promising to write faithfully each week and reminding me that Annie would have me to Sunday dinner once a month. And that at Christmas and other festive occasions I would be provided with train fare to visit the city and savor the delights of metropolitan life, etc., etc. Or words to that effect. I'm only giving you an approximation of what my father said in his long-winded way. Anyhow, I recall him finishing up by saying, "And how does all this strike you, William?" So I told him that it sounded all right to me, though secretly I was tickled to be going to the Fletchers'. I wasn't all that fussy about old Fletcher or learning the funeral business. But I'd take all that as it came. The important thing was that I'd be close by Mrs. Fletcher. Of course I didn't realize it at the time but I was crazy in love with her.

Well, the next afternoon my father and I arrived at the Fletchers' front door. I was dressed in my one suit and Miss Boswell had dampened and combed my hair. When Mrs. Fletcher came to the door, she stood back with one hand on her hip and fixed me with a grin. "Well now, Bill. Aren't you the proper little gentleman?" I didn't much like being called little, for I was nearly as tall as her, and so I just looked down at my boots. My father offered his greetings, inquired into the whereabouts of Mr. Fletcher, who, it seems, was over in Phippsville for the day, and handed her the cardboard suitcase which contained all my worldly possessions. As I recall, they included my everyday pants and a couple of shirts, two pairs of woolen stockings, half a dozen romances and a suit of winter underwear. Mrs. Fletcher smiled. "Would you like to come in for a small refreshment before your long journey, Mr. Farthing?"

My father again stuck his tongue in his cheek and then looked back to the buggy, where Miss Boswell sat watching us like a brood hen. And weighing things in his head, my father decided not to cross Mrs. Fletcher's doorstep. He just bowed slightly and said, "I think not, Mrs. Fletcher, but thank you all the same." Then he turned to me. "Well, William. I leave you now in good hands. We'll be together again ere long. Meantime, mind your manners. Always be gracious to a lady and suffer no insulting behavior from the bully boys hereabouts. Remember, you're a Farthing." Then he shook my hand, bade farewell to Mrs. Fletcher, and walked to the carriage.

That first day I was so nervous about being alone in the house with Mrs. Fletcher that I didn't say maybe twenty-five words all afternoon. But that didn't matter, for Mrs. Fletcher was a person who was never at a loss for something to say and she kept telling me how glad she was to have someone to talk to because living with her husband was like living with a bloody ghost. I remember she went down to the cellar and came back with this big piece of watermelon. She cut it up and put it on a plate and we both sat down on the sofa and started in on this nice cool watermelon, which I'd never tasted before. We just sat there eating and slurping this watermelon when all of a sudden Mrs. Fletcher begins to spit the seeds into this little brass spittoon under a chair. We both looked at each other and laughed and after a while I joined her and it became a game to see who could hit this little spittoon the most times. Every time a seed would strike the brass, it would make a little pinging sound and we'd both laugh to beat the devil. Well, we just sat there for the longest time, carrying on like a couple of kids, and when Mrs. Fletcher laughed a little bit of watermelon juice ran down her chin and, reader, if I live another ninety-five years I'll never live through another afternoon when my life seemed so full of happiness and the promise of good things.

Around suppertime Fletcher came home. He took his place at the table, said grace and not much else except to tell me that in the morning he'd explain my duties. After supper he retired to the rolltop desk in his office and spent the rest of the evening reading and writing in his accounting books and looking over some religious material that

4. *The Man in the Boat*

arrived in the mail. Fletcher belonged to a group of people who called themselves Russellites after their founder, Charles Taze Russell. These people now call themselves Jehovah's Witnesses.

Mrs. Fletcher showed me up to my bedroom, which was at the back of the house. It was a nice little room with real wallpaper and a good iron bed. There was a dresser with a mirror too and a chair and my own crockery washbasin, jug and chamber pot. It was palatial after what I'd been used to. Mrs. Fletcher stood watching me as I admired the room. Then she said, "It's going to be nice to have a young man around the house, Bill." Then she held my elbows and gave me a kiss on the forehead. "Nighty-night, luv," she says, and lets go with that braying laugh. Later I heard a screen door bang and, hiking up on one elbow, I saw Fletcher in his shirtsleeves, on his way to the outhouse. I feel asleep and dreamed of his wife and me, bare-naked on a rug spitting watermelon seeds. Tom with his bloody head sat on the sofa and watched us.

The next morning Fletcher showed me around the funeral parlor. First there was this big room at the front, a rich-looking place with heavy purple curtains that reached right down to the floor and a lot of polished woodwork which he said would be my responsibility to keep clean. The room was filled with coffins and Fletcher told me these would take a good bit of dusting and hard work. Then off this room was a little chapel with a colored glass window of the Last Supper and a lectern with a big Bible resting on it. There was also maybe a dozen folding wooden chairs. Behind this chapel was Fletcher's laboratory, and this was where he worked on the dead bodies. I wasn't keen on that place or the big table in the middle of it. This table had a marble top and a big iron wheel which you cranked up or down to get the desired level. Fletcher called this his workbench. Along three of the walls were shelves of bottles and jars containing acids and creams and potions for ministering to the dead. The fourth wall was really a big door which opened onto the back yard and stable. After showing me around the premises that first morning Fletcher handed me a feather duster and told me to get busy.

For the next few weeks things went along much the same and we all settled into getting used to one another. Fletcher wasn't such a bad fellow once you got familiar with his ways. So far as I was concerned the only problem with him was his quiet manner of getting around. In the house he wore these carpet slippers and he could glide around the rooms in these slippers just as quiet and stealthy as a cat. Say I'd be standing in the little chapel, maybe lost in thought and admiring one of the twelve apostles in the colored glass window. Well, there I'd be when suddenly out of the blue and not ten inches from my right ear would come Fletcher's voice. "Have you finished all the brass, boy?" Until you got used to this it could startle you.

Fletcher and his wife never said much to one another and when she did say something it was usually so insulting that I felt sorry for him. For that matter she wasn't all that sociable to me on occasion, especially during the first half of the day. Usually she stayed in bed until noon and Fletcher and I would eat breakfast together. Then along about lunch time she'd come downstairs smelling of orange blossom toilet water, all fluffed up in a pink dressing gown with what looked like rabbit fur around her neck. She wasn't fit to talk to or even look at sideways until she'd had her cup of tea. Then by and by as the day progressed, she'd cheer up and by the middle of the afternoon when she'd put three or four belts of whiskey into herself she'd be in rare spirits and would talk about how she wouldn't mind having someone take the man in the boat for a little sail. At first I didn't know what in hell she was talking about. And old Fletcher, he just ignored that kind of talk.

In late September the weather cooled off and the leaves turned and fell dead to the ground. Sometimes when I was bored with dusting coffins I envied the kids as they passed by the front window on their way to school. But then I'd never liked school very much and I didn't really miss it. And then there were compensations to my job that no school classroom could allow for. Now and then, for example, in the middle of the afternoon and if her husband was away, Mrs. Fletcher would ask me to join her for a drink and a smoke in the parlor. On these occasions she used to say that she was feeling particularly wicked and she'd pour me a glass of watered whiskey and offer me a cigarette, a vice I wasn't used to but soon took up. I'm still smoking them.

"I'm a fallen woman, Bill," Mrs. Fletcher would say, leaning back with her elbows out and one leg hiked over the other. "There just isn't anything I can do about it. I was brought up on the streets of old London town and I just never had a chance to be good. My maidenhead was taken in my sixteenth year." Then she'd snort and laugh and pinch my leg and tell me that the man in the boat would like a little sail. Her hand would sometimes stray across my knee while she told me about some of the gents she'd known in London and the grand clothes they wore and of how they all smelled of tweed and rich tobacco. Those sessions were damned hard on my glands and just about the time I didn't think I could stand it any longer and would have to leap at her, why we'd hear old Fletcher coming up the front steps and I'd jump back to dusting, crimped over the furniture and coffins with the damnedest ache in my parts.

All this time Fletcher hadn't had any funerals to arrange. No one around Craven Falls seemed to be dying that fall unless they were Catholics. The Catholics favored a man over in Phippsville named McCabe. I was just as glad, for I wasn't particular about learning the trade, but as business got slower and slower Fletcher just sat at his rolltop desk studying the bills from the casket company and muttering, "I don't wish harm on man nor woman, but if only someone would pass away." Fletcher, as I've said, was a Russellite and one night a week he went to their meetings. On his meeting night Mrs. Fletcher and I would sit in the parlor and I'd read to her. I'd become quite good at reading aloud and Mrs. Fletcher was keen on those romances I'd brought along in my grip. I had to keep them out of Fletcher's sight, for he considered that all literature except the Bible was the handiwork of the devil. But I enjoyed reading those trashy novels, for it gave me a chance to put all my true feelings into the reading and it was a pleasure to see Mrs. Fletcher sitting on the horsehair sofa all caught up in the story and at the mercy of my telling.

One night as I was reading to her she complained of feeling sleepy. She'd drunk a good bit that day and I figured maybe she was tight. But no, she stood up straight enough and gave my hair a little tug. "I think I'll go on up to bed now, Billy, if it's all the same to you." Well, it wasn't all the same to me and I was really disappointed, for this big love scene was coming up and I had wanted to expound on that. However, a few minutes later she called down and asked me to bring her up a glass of water. Which I did.

Now, I realize that nowadays when you pay your money for a book, you feel entitled to a fairly detailed account of the act of fornication. What you probably want to know is whether people are getting more out of it than you are. Well, let me just say that in my time I've perused a good many of these episodes, including some pretty hot stuff that I found in a crypt in a ruined church in France during the Great War. But after having read a good many descriptions of the act of love, I have to maintain that none of them is half as good as the real event. So while I'm not particularly chivalrous or delicate, as many old blisters in here will testify, neither am I the dirty old man they consider me to be. So I am not about to go into any details of an event in my life that took place over seventy-five years ago. I think it is sufficient to say that a bashful and frightened fifteen-year-old boy had a dream come true when he entered the room of the woman he loved. I might perhaps add that he was invited to sit down on the side of the bed and hold the hand of that woman who claimed to be lonely and frightened in a strange land. And that within the hour he discovered the man in the boat. And took him for a sail.

5

DEATH AND DANGER

ONE EVENING, just after supper, the telephone rang and Fletcher answered it in his office. The door was open and I could hear him talking to the local doctor. This was a week or so after the loss of my virginity and I was in the kitchen helping Mrs. Fletcher with the dishes. She kept asking me to put my arm around her and give her a little kiss but I was leery of being so open about everything on account of arousing Fletcher's suspicions. Mrs. Fletcher, however, was growing bolder by the day and it put me in a bad bind because like any normal boy that age who is exposed to it, I'd acquired an awful appetite for screwing. I just couldn't get enough of it and neither, it seems, could Mrs. Fletcher. So it was a genuine torment to keep our hands off one another. Yet I knew that Fletcher had to be taken into careful consideration, especially with those damn creeping carpet slippers. Already we'd screwed half a dozen times or so, mostly when Fletcher was out to the stable and we could keep a half an eye on him out the back window. But once she came to my room in the middle of the night when Fletcher's snores filled the house. But I didn't care for that arrangement and it showed soon enough, for I couldn't keep my mind on what I was doing. At any time I half expected old Fletcher to suddenly whisper in my ear, "What do you think you're doing there, boy?" Then God knows what might take place!

You have to understand that in spite of her drunkenness and insults and laziness, Fletcher was crazy about his wife. I don't believe I've ever known a man so in love with the wrong woman. If he was to discover me on top of her indulging myself, he might lose his head and put those big hands around my neck. I explained my fears to Mrs. Fletcher. But she just laughed at the notion of her husband turning violent. However, I wasn't convinced. You can't tell what people

34

will do in such circumstances. About the only thing you can depend on is that they won't be reasonable. So I made her promise not to come into my room while Fletcher was in the house. Well, this night I'm telling you about, we were in the kitchen when Fletcher came through from his office, plunging a fist through the armhole of his black coat and clamping on his hat. "Come along, boy," he says. "We've got work to do."

It was a cool October night with the smell of wood smoke in the air and a fine blue haze lying over the town. It was pleasant enough riding along through this, although I was a bit nervous, not only about meeting the dead, but about sitting next to Fletcher. It's damn strange to sit next to a man and try to act normal when all the time you're screwing his wife. It takes a man considerably skilled in deceit to pull that kind of thing off. And I was only a green boy! It was hard to tell whether Fletcher was suspicious or not, for he carried the same dead-pan expression with him all the time. So neither of us said a word all the way across town.

We drove on past the railway sheds for maybe a mile until we came to this tarpaper shack with a coal oil lamp burning in one window. As soon as the horse drew near, a yard dog started barking. From inside the shack somebody yelled, "Shut your hole, you bastard." Fletcher stopped the wagon and we sat there listening to his big mare snort and snuffle and blow, for she'd trotted all the way. Then the front door squeaked open and a big man stood there in his bare feet, wearing only underwear and pants and holding what looked to me like a shotgun. In the yard it was so black you couldn't see your hand. Then this man shouts at us, "Who the —— is that? By God, state your business or I'll blow you halfway up the ——ing tracks. You're on Jake Snipes's property and that's trouble right there." Then the dog started to bark again but he yelled it down.

Fletcher called out, "It's only me, Mr. Snipes. Phineas Fletcher." We stepped down and walked towards the door. "My condolences over the departure of your dear mother, Mr. Snipes," says Fletcher at the doorway. "The Lord giveth and the Lord taketh away. Blessed be the name of the Lord."

At this Snipes puts up his gun, leans against the doorjamb, and begins to cry like a baby. "By Jesus, Mr. Fletcher," he says, gulping down the tears, "my poor old Mum has gone."

As we passed, Fletcher patted him on the shoulder, raising a cloud of dust, and a couple of bugs hopped out of his underwear tops. "Now, Mr. Snipes," says Fletcher, "it's probably all for the best. She lived a good, full life. How old was she? Ninety-one?"

"She was ninety-two, Reverend," says Snipes, blowing his nose into his hand. "As near as any of us can figure."

Snipes was a mean-looking son of a bitch with narrow eyes and what I thought was a full beard. But when he turned into the dim light I could see it was just dirt. I could also see that he was drunk as a fart. He went across the room walking unnaturally straight. Just like a man with a corset or binding material around his middle. He took Fletcher by the arm. "You'll fix her up, won't you, Reverend? You'll fix up my dear old Mum?" Fletcher was paying him little heed but was rummaging in some trash behind the wood stove. All this time I was looking over the kitchen. God Almighty, I'd thought us Farthings were poor. But at least Annie had kept the old homestead clean and she'd seen to it that we had patches on our pants. The Snipes's shack was plain filthy and smelled worse than a hog's hind end. There was this old wood stove with the bottom loaded down with ashes and clinkers. It didn't look to have been cleaned in a hundred years. And there was a table and some rickety chairs. Along one wall next to the stove was a skinny, whipped-looking woman and about eight scrawny kids of all sizes. I recognized some of them from school, especially Everett Snipes. He was two or three years older than me but he'd been in the same class, sitting on the back bench breaking wind or pulling out his tool to show the girls.

These Snipeses were all bad apples, but Everett was one of the worst. Skinning a cat alive or crapping down somebody's well was an ordinary night's entertainment to him. He and his brothers and sisters were always running loose through the town and getting into trouble. In the summer their faces were covered with impetigo sores and in the winter they came to school early to get warm. They'd stand around the stove drying out while their clothes steamed and smelled of piss and wet wool. I also recognized their yapping dog as one of the sons of bitches that took a chunk from my backside on the day of Tom's death. Now he was under the stove with only his snout and eyes showing, but he was watching me and growling deep in his throat. A dog never forgets an enemy and neither do I.

Now Snipes had more or less collapsed on one of the rickety chairs and he sat there bent over with his head in his hands, groaning on about what a saint his dear old mum had been. No one else moved or said anything. In fact, the rest of the Snipeses just looked like a cageful of scared animals. Then Snipes raised his mangy head and began to croak out a song about his mother. I can still remember a few lines of that song, believe it or not. I think it went like this.

> *She was dearer to me*
> *Than a rich man's estate*
> *She was nearer to me*
> *Than a fork to a plate*
> *She was kindness and sweetness*
> *A joy from above*
> *I'll cherish her memory*
> *My old Mum.*

There must have been at least twenty verses to it and he reeled them off with the tears rolling down his dirty cheeks while Fletcher continued to poke amongst this rubble behind the stove, finally coming up with an oil lamp, which he blew the dust from and lit. I followed him into this little room off the kitchen where it smelled twelve times as bad and was empty except for a dresser and a bed. Fletcher put the lamp on the dresser and it was then that I saw this bundle of old gray rags on the bed. Fletcher was leaning over it. When I came closer, however, I saw that it wasn't a bundle of rags at all but a dead woman. Fletcher looked her over for a moment and then said, "We better get her into the box, boy. She's turning fast."

Well, for the next ten minutes or so we worked hard. Fletcher called for Snipes's wife, who came into the room and did as she was told, never saying a word all the time. I can't recall ever seeing a more frightened human being. It wasn't much to load the old woman into the rough box because Fletcher just covered her up with some special sheets and we dumped her in like a sack of grain. She hardly weighed anything at all. Then Fletcher went to work with Snipes's wife, instructing her on what he'd need for burial clothes, and they both pulled open dresser drawers trying to find something presentable.

Then I witnessed what I thought at first was some kind of phenomenon. I know it frightened the hell out of me at the time. I was standing in this bedroom doorway looking into the kitchen and trying to appear casual, as though I did this sort of work every night. Snipes had finished his song about his mother and was now doing some serious drinking from a crock. The kids remained up against the wall just watching him. Now where the Snipes kids were all lined up, there appeared this bar of light and it was growing bigger by the minute. I couldn't figure it out but it was filling up the room and had soon reached over and covered Snipes with blazing daylight. Damnedest thing you've ever seen. I could see now that it was coming through the one window in the shack and was reaching out to touch everything.

After a few more pulls from the crock Snipes started in on a song about some iron miner up near Marmora who liked to screw porcupines. Then in the middle of it he jumps up and I can see he's got a pair of spoons for beating out the rhythm. So he starts to step-dance, and he's pretty good too, plus hollering wild cries. I thought sure he was taken by a fit or something. At the same time there comes into the shack this terrible rushing sound and everything starts to tremble and shake, including the floorboards. An old coffee pot dances on top of the stove and in the light it seems to me that everybody's hair is standing on end. Now I thought for certain that this was an earthquake or some similar disaster, a judgment sent down from God that Tom said would happen like in Bible times. And I began to think that maybe I was singled out for punishment because I'd been screwing another man's wife. That was the very nub of adultery and one of the Ten Commandments. So I started to shake and pray to God to forgive me for my wickedness.

The funny thing was that nobody else in the shack took any notice whatsoever of this noise and light, which was now at its peak and was nearly deafening and blinding. Snipes was step-dancing away, looking like some weird savage, with the kids just staring at him. Old Fletcher was folding up a dress on the bed and muttering to himself. Then the light passed right through the house and damn me for a liar if a train didn't thunder by in the night, not a dozen yards from the front door. Old Fletcher straightened up and took out his watch and said something about the through freight being right on time. Then he told me to grab one end of the rough box and we carried it through the kitchen past Snipes, who just kept on dancing and took no notice of us.

Outside I could see the red light of the caboose disappearing in the darkness. Even after we were a good distance from the shack we could still hear Snipes singing and yelling. Then we heard a terrible whoop and a shotgun blast followed by the sound of shattered glass. Fletcher never said a word until we were nearly home and then he muttered, "He must have finished off the only window they had."

Back at the funeral parlor I pulled open the big door and after Fletcher backed the wagon into the laboratory we unloaded. Next he told me to stable the horse and I took my time, hanging up the harness carefully and rubbing down the big mare. I was poking at the job when Fletcher startled me from behind. "Don't you want to work for me, boy?" he says softly. Then he walked away in the darkness and I followed him across the cold wet grass. As I walked along I looked up and saw Mrs. Fletcher at the bedroom window. She was blowing me a kiss.

Inside the laboratory Fletcher was all business and he moved with the economy of motion that you get from people who know what they're doing. On his marble-topped table was this little old human female, gray and stark naked. Fletcher was already washing her up when he saw me staring. So he says, "I'm going to tell you three things about this profession, boy, and I want you to remember them. The first is this. What you have here is no longer a human being but a cadaver. The good Lord has taken out the human being and transported her to her judgment. The second is this. Banish forever from your mind all the ignorant and ugly superstition surrounding the dead. The dead are entitled to the dignity of a decent burial. And it is our duty to provide them with that. The third is this. Walk the streets with your head held high, because you perform a valuable service to the community."

I'd never heard him use so many words at one time. But then he fell silent and went to work. After we cleaned her up and gave her a few shots of primer or formalin, we got out the burial clothes and brushed them down, stamping on a few bugs that flew out. Then we dressed her and dabbed some color on her cheeks and brushed up her hair and packed her in sawdust. After we'd washed ourselves, Fletcher made a pot of cocoa and we sat in the kitchen drinking it and not saying a word. Some people you can sit with and be quiet and feel comfortable. Fletcher was like that. The truth is I was growing fond of old Fletcher. And a normal person doesn't generally cheat someone he likes.

Business seemed to pick up after that. As I recall, November was cold and rainy and the bad weather and the coming winter just took it out of some older folks and they gave up and died of pneumonia and consumption. There were a fair number of childbirth deaths too. During all this I learned a lot from Fletcher on how to behave in people's homes. I admired that in him. He had good manners, which he displayed wherever we went, whether the homes were rich or lowly. I never once remember Fletcher raising his voice or letting anything get him down, which was remarkable when you consider that his home life was no joke. I figure his religion saved him. He was always scanning those pamphlets that came through the mails from somewhere in the States. And he just went his own way, ignoring strife as though there was some kind of invisible bell jar around his head that shut out confusion. I'm told those old Indian gents who squat on the ground and look away into the distance have come up with the same approach to life. It's admirable but hard to imitate, for you have to have the temperament for that attitude.

Every fourth Sunday I visited my sister Annie. The Talbots came into town every Sunday for church and Annie came with them, carrying herself proudly. After church she and Rufus called by for me. Annie and Rufus lived for the time being in a wing of Lazarus Talbot's farmhouse and, to give her credit, she'd fixed things up nice. There was chintz curtains and good-looking dishes and crockery. They even had a piano. Annie was now giving herself airs, flouncing around in her big-hipped way, already heavy with the coming child. I could see she was trying to smooth out her rough ways and act civilized, getting on me, for instance, about not going to church—which, by the way, Fletcher did not insist upon. Annie was awfully bossy with Rufus and me, ordering us to wipe our shoes and use our napkins at the dinner table. After a big noon meal Rufus and I always played checkers, with me winning ninety-eight times out of a hundred. He was always good-natured about it though, and in the late winter afternoon he'd hitch up the cutter and drive me back to the Fletchers', both of us under the big bearskin and not saying anything, just watching the wind stir the snow across the fields and maybe staring up at the evening star as it appeared above the tops of the pines. When we passed the old homestead the windows were all boarded up.

My life with the Fletchers was growing more complicated by the day. If you'd have told me three or four months before that I'd soon be welcoming a day *away* from Mrs. Fletcher, I'd have called you crazy. But the fact is that's the way things was turning out since I'd become her paramour. She was now visiting me three or four nights a week and I was worried sick that Fletcher would find out. But Mrs. Fletcher wasn't worried. She told me that if her husband got curious, she'd just tell him she'd gone for a smoke in one of the lumber rooms on the third floor. And then sometimes she claimed not to care anyway. She said she was tired of being cooped up in a gloomy old house in a backwoods town. She missed the city with its shops and its well-dressed, good-looking men. So she often talked about running away and when she was in that humor she didn't seem to care whether Fletcher found out about us or not.

It never did occur to her that this sort of thinking didn't take my position into account. When she talked about not caring it made me nervous but by and by the talk would give way to hugging and kissing and before long one of us had mounted the other and there was nobody doing any thinking or worrying. I won't say I didn't like it but I could see, even as a youth, that it was a dangerous situation and sooner or later was going to get us into trouble. For instance, sometimes after we'd screwed, Mrs. Fletcher would get sleepy as a stuffed cat and before long she'd nod off. The fact is we'd both nod off. One morning I woke just before daylight and there was Mrs. Fletcher, her stomach gurgling and the snores working their way through her open mouth. And what a time I had to awaken her! Fortunately, Fletcher wasn't up yet. But I was concerned, especially since Fletcher sometimes got a call in the middle of the night and then he'd come looking for me.

Another worrying thing had to do with Mrs. Fletcher's attitude. She was growing more and more bold and defiant. Often she didn't seem to care what anybody thought. For days she'd never get out of her dressing gown but just sit around drinking and reading those romances. Other times she'd flaunt herself in front of the both of us, sometimes surprising Fletcher by being especially sweet to him. But more often making it plain that she preferred me. It was as if she wanted to make us both jealous so maybe we'd fight a duel over her. I put it down to the childishness of those romances she was always reading. The fact is I was beginning to see just how childish she really was and what a bad bargain old Fletcher had struck.

But she was good to me and there's no denying that. Whenever she cooked a meal, which wasn't often, she'd give me the best slice off the roast. And she was forever buying me things. At Christmas it was embarrassing. Fletcher only gave me twenty-five cents now and then and so I couldn't come up with anything special. But Mrs. Fletcher sent away to Toronto for any number of things. I can't remember them all now but I recall a pair of velvet bedroom slippers and some fancy shirts with real pearl studs. And there was a couple of boys' books which didn't interest me because they were too juvenile and sissy and here I was screwing a married woman and handling dead bodies. It made me mad that she couldn't figure that out. And there was a pound of rock candy and, I believe, a harmonica. The whole thing must have set her back ten or fifteen bucks, which was a good deal of money in those days. At the same time she presented old Fletcher with a cheap-looking hair brush and comb set which maybe cost her a dollar and a half at the local general store. And this, after he'd given her a new silk dressing gown and an expensive toilet set, all inlaid with mother of pearl. Prettiest thing you've ever seen. It was pitiful but Fletcher just took this tacky comb and brush set and the ten-cent tin of shoe polish I'd given him and bowed and thanked the both of us, even going so far as to kiss his wife on the cheek and shake my hand. The man was turning out to be a saint and I was sinking lower and lower into self-disgust.

It got me thinking of escape. Maybe I could catch a freight down to Toronto or out to the Northwest Territories. I didn't let on about this to Mrs. Fletcher, for she was too busy outlining *her* plans to get away. And now she was drawing me into them as well. Her idea was that once winter passed we might take off together. We could go down to Toronto, fob ourselves off as mother and son, take lodgings and look for work. In no time at all we'd be in decent clothes visiting the theaters and museums. I could see how it might work but I wasn't all that keen. One night she showed me forty or fifty dollars she'd been putting away for the trip. She didn't say whether it was housekeeping money or not but I personally think she was going through Fletcher's pockets.

Well, it was a dilemma for me. There was no point in going to live with Rufus and Annie. They had more than their hands filled now with twin boys. Anyway, Annie's superior tone provoked me. As for Ned and Fred, I never once gave them a thought. I had a notion I might visit my father, however, even though I hadn't been invited. The problem would lie in locating him. About the middle of March I got a Christmas card from him. The card was posted in Halifax, Nova Scotia, and had traveled over most of North America before reaching me. The address on the envelope was so smudged that it must have given trouble to the postal people in two countries, for it had gone to a Craven Falls in Ohio and then out to a similarly named place in Oregon before finally turning up in Fletcher's mail box. The writing on the card was pretty nearly impossible to make out but it looked to me like your loving father. However, the envelope was addressed to Thomas Farthing, Esq. I figure my father was well off the wagon when he sent that out. So, I didn't know how to get in touch with him. And anyway, if he was drinking and Miss Boswell was working on him with her temperance tracts, I didn't really want to be around.

So there I was with two alternatives. On the one hand, I could set out by myself. That way I had the freedom to come and go as it suited me. But I risked a fairly hard time because I didn't have more than a dollar to my name. I'd have to travel by freight car, and I'd seen some of the rough customers who hung around the railway yards. They looked like they'd cut your throat for about a dollar. And there'd probably be plenty of nights out in the rain and the cold. Yet if I went with Mrs. Fletcher, what then? Well, the beds would be softer and the food easier to come by, but my life would be more complicated. There'd be just no end to the deceit I'd have to practice. Sometimes, to tell you the truth, I just wished she'd go away by herself and leave

Fletcher and me to live normal lives. The entire dilemma was wearing me out. Between Mrs. Fletcher's visits and my fears of being discovered, I was down below a hundred pounds and wasting fast. One day Fletcher told me he was burying better-looking people than me. He didn't say this as a joke either, for he never cracked a joke in all the time I knew him. No, he just said it as you might comment on the weather. As a matter of fact, Fletcher had been taking a particular interest in my appearance for some time now, or so I surmised. Now and again I would catch him looking at me in a funny way. It wasn't a look of suspicion or threat or anything like that. It was more a look of *concern*. It was as though he was worrying over me. The whole business was making me jumpy.

One afternoon in early April we were called out to a farm a few miles east of town along the Snake River road. A couple of half-crazy brothers tried to make a living out there on a few acres of land. The story had it that they spent most of their time hating one another's guts. The day before we were called out, one of them had gone to the woods to clear some brush and he'd put the ax blade through his shin bone. Somehow he managed to hobble back to the cabin, where the sight of him made his brother just double up with laughter. A neighbor happened along a few hours later and he found the crazy old bastard still in his rocking chair and still laughing. His brother was on the floor, stone dead from loss of blood. That sort of thing used to happen in the Ontario backwoods, particularly in the late winter after two people had been living alongside one another for months. So there was to be an inquest and we were called out to bring back the body.

The weather was dirty. It had been sleeting and raining off and on for a week and the woods were boggy with standing pools of water in places. The Snake River road itself was really no more than a path through the bush with some cedar planking in places, but most of it rotted away since the old logging camps had shut down. When we reached the bridge spanning the river I was amazed at the height of the water. Now the river wasn't big, maybe thirty feet across and normally only a foot or so deep. But with all the rain and the spring runoff, she was fast and high, perhaps five feet and boiling away just a few inches under the bridge. I mentioned this to Fletcher, who took no notice of it whatsoever but urged the big mare on. The horse wasn't all that keen about crossing but Fletcher gave him a few smart licks with the whip and we passed over.

When we got to the cabin the rain let up and a weak lemon-colored sun came out and cast a dismal light over everything. The trees dripped and the ground was soggy under your boots. Inside the cabin we got some help from the doctor and from a neighbor. The surviving brother, a wizened, bald-headed old devil in a red plaid shirt, just sat in one corner trimming a lamp. He was over his laughing spell and was just looking sullen and mean. I was glad to get the hell out of there. The neighbor was a nice fellow and he suggested we stay the night at his place. He didn't trust that river bridge and feared that with more rain she might go. And just as he said it, didn't it start to sprinkle and gradually pick up until it was pelting down fast once more! We all stood around for a couple of minutes while Fletcher secured the rough box. The doctor then decided to take this fellow up on his offer and stay the night at his place. But Fletcher just shook his head and we climbed aboard the dead wagon and started for home.

Before long it was dark, a cold, clammy darkness that closed in around your throat. Fletcher lit a storm lantern and told me to get down and lead the horse. I did this, stumbling through the puddles and tripping over the roots of trees. It was miserable. Then as I groped along, I heard the river. There was no seeing it in the darkness but I could hear it all right. So I stopped and held up the lantern for a better look. Mostly I was trying to gauge the distance between me and the river. Just then Fletcher called down to me to move along. "The bridge is right ahead of you," he shouts. "Thirty to forty steps."

And he was dead right, for I counted thirty-two steps and then felt the bridge railing. There was water swirling around my ankles. The river was now making so much noise that I had to shout. "She's already under water, Mr. Fletcher," I yells. "We'll have to go back." At this Fletcher climbs down slowly and, taking the lantern, walks past me until he's standing in the middle of the bridge bending over for a look with the water thrashing around his pant legs. He stands there, holding the lantern and surveying the situation as though this is nothing more than a temporary nuisance. Then he walks back and tells me to climb aboard. "Say," I asks. "We're not going to cross that bridge, are we, Mr. Fletcher?"

"She'll hold," says Fletcher, taking the reins and tapping the horse's arse with his whip. "Move along, horse," he says.

The horse was anything but eager but a few more flicks with the whip and we got under way. I could swear the bridge was swaying when we got aboard but it was hard to tell because of the noise and the general confusion of mind that occurs in these situations. And then Fletcher did a damn peculiar thing. About halfway across this rickety bridge he stops the wagon cold, pulling up hard on the reins. Yes, stops it cold and the whole thing on the verge of collapse. Then he puts a big paw on my knee and, leaning down, shouts above the noise of the river, "Do you know your Scripture, boy?"

"Yes, sir," I shouts back, wondering if I can make a run for it, because it seemed to me that Fletcher had gone insane on the spot.

Then he shouts, "Marriage is honorable in all, and the bed undefiled; but whoremongers and adulterers God will judge. Hebrews 13:4."

Then he flicks the reins and the horse jumps ahead. Just in time too, for as we crossed over, the whole damn thing went down the river with a terrible groaning sound of splintering wood and rushing water.

6

FLIGHT

———————

FLETCHER never said another word about it but I got the message clear enough. It was time to be on my way. What helped make up my mind even faster was a conversation I had with Mrs. Fletcher a week or so after that episode on the Snake River bridge. As usual she came calling about ten o'clock, but being alert to the dangers involved, I wasn't in a particularly amorous humor and so she contented herself with a long talk. She began to speak again about her dream of getting away from Fletcher and Craven Falls, only this time she introduced a new twist. Now she began to talk about us eventually getting married in some exotic place like Niagara Falls and living as man and wife in fancy hotel suites all around the country. Perhaps we might even cross the ocean and visit her hometown of London, where we'd ride around Hyde Park in an open carriage.

It was the craziest thing I'd ever heard, but I was just curious enough to ask her where she got the idea that a woman could have two husbands at the same time. That's when she told me that men sometimes have fatal accidents or die in mysterious ways, leaving widows with insurance policies behind. Then she began to ask me about the jars and bottles in Fletcher's laboratory, what was in them and which compounds were dangerous, etc., etc. Now I could see what she was thinking of and it made me mad, though I didn't let on. Screwing a man's wife is one thing but participating in his murder, that's something altogether different. Besides, Fletcher was my friend. He wasn't the warmest or friendliest human being you'd ever meet but he'd always treated me fairly. So when his wife asked me if maybe each week I'd bring her a little of the most dangerous chemical, I said I'd think about it. "You mustn't think about it, my little sweet," she whispers in my ear. "You must do it . . . now." Well, after she left I lay in bed thinking about that line and then I realized I'd heard it before. It came to me that I'd read it in one of those romances where a woman and her paramour plot the death of the woman's husband. Mrs. Fletcher, it seems, was turning into a storybook character before my eyes. The only thing for it was flight.

There was some luck going my way here, for Mrs. Fletcher kept her escape money in my room under a loosened floorboard. She claimed that Fletcher sometimes got nosy and poked about the rest of the house. But she'd never known him to enter my room. I'd gone along with that, though looking back now I can see that she put it there in case Fletcher ever found out. Then it would look like I stole it. She was crafty, all right. But I got the money out and I counted fifty-eight dollars. What I thought I'd do was kill two birds with one stone. That is, I'd get away all right, but by myself, thus guaranteeing my freedom. At the same time I'd help myself to half the money, thus putting the face on a little security as well. I felt I was entitled to half the money since I'd been a part of Mrs. Fletcher's plans for so long. Then I didn't feel too guilty either because by taking the money I'd avoid getting involved in murder. Why, I'd be saving Fletcher's life! That's the kind of thinking that goes through your mind when you're making excuses for stealing.

The next day while Mrs. Fletcher was shopping and Fletcher himself was busy in his office, I hid a bundle of clothes out behind the stable. My plan was to catch the 8:25 for Belleville. That train had a connection for Toronto. I knew this, for I'd studied the timetables and schedules in Fletcher's office. After hiding the bundle I went into the parlor and had a big shot of whiskey to steady my nerves. Just before supper Mrs. Fletcher came home with some new gowns. After a few belts from the decanter she was feeling playful and before we sat down she caught me by the wrist and pulled me into the pantry. "How's your little groin muscle, Billy boy?" she whispers. I told her it was just fine. "That's good," she says, "because you haven't had much pepper lately, ducky. I'll be looking for better things tonight. And I been thinking up some new plans for us too." Then she added, "Have you been thinking about what I asked you?" I told her I had and this seemed to please her. We got out of that pantry just as Fletcher came into the kitchen and sat down at the table. He was his usual self and during the meal I didn't do much more than just sit there and watch him as he worked his way through the food with his head down. To tell you the truth I felt sorry for him, especially since I was betraying him in a way. So I only picked at my food and half listened to Mrs. Fletcher go on about the snobbish ladies on the main street.

After supper Fletcher retired to his office with a new batch of pamphlets and Mrs. Fletcher asked me to read to her from a new romance which she had picked up at the library. There was no way of getting out of it, so we went into the parlor and I read that foolish story to Mrs. Fletcher, who sat there hanging on every word. All this time I was thinking about how just a few months can change a person's attitude and also about how desiring something or somebody is at least twice as good as actually possessing them. Well, after I'd read a couple of chapters the hall clock started to strike off eight and I knew I had to make my move. So I whispered to Mrs. Fletcher that I had to go out and water my donkey. She enjoyed colorful talk like that. As I was passing she grabbed my hand and told me to hurry up. The door to Fletcher's office was ajar and he was sitting straight-backed at his desk in vest and shirtsleeves, poring over his pamphlets and looking up passages in his big black Bible. I would like to have said goodbye to him but of course I couldn't.

Outside I slipped into a little grove of lilac trees behind the stable and there I changed into my suit and good boots. Then I stuffed my old clothes into some bushes and checked my money. This I kept in a purse which Miss Boswell once gave Tom for reciting verses from the Gospels. I put a dollar in one of my boots in case of emergency and ran a piece of broken comb through my hair. Then I was off along a back street towards the station. I recall it was a mild damp night with a thin drizzle in the air and patches of ground fog lying in hollows. But it was spring and I was on my own at last and that felt good, though I also remember being a little uneasy in the stomach because of nerves. You have to remember that I'd never been more than ten miles from Craven Falls in my life and there I was setting out to see the world.

At the station the ticket agent recognized me because I'd been down there a number of times picking up bodies with Fletcher. People in small towns are always nosy about your private business, so I told him I was off to visit some relatives in Toronto. The 8:25 was a local and never in much of a hurry but by and by she came along, blowing steam and covering everybody with soot. After we got under way it felt good to be sitting inside listening to the rain slash against the windows and hear the long mournful cry of the steam whistle as we crossed the wooden trestle near Samson Corners. The coach was mostly empty and after a few miles the conductor put his feet up on the seat and went right to sleep. I was too excited to sleep and kept thinking of Mrs. Fletcher back in bed trying to figure out where in hell I'd gotten to. But I was also thinking about what I'd do with myself once I arrived in Toronto. I didn't have any clear-cut plan, and that worried me.

At Belleville I had to wait an hour before catching the train that was coming through from Montreal. It was twenty cars long. I'd never seen anything like it. For nearly an hour I wandered through various coaches trying to find my way. Once I found myself in one of the sleeping cars where a man was trying to undress himself for bed, I suppose, because his bare behind was outside the curtains of his berth. And as the train rocked back and forth his backside would bob out and then disappear. I figure he wasn't used to undressing in such cramped quarters, but God Almighty, I didn't even know up till then that people slept on trains. And then I got a helluva fright when I walked right into this kitchen and met the first black man in my entire life. He was

6. Flight

dressed all in white and was wearing this chef's hat while he scrubbed a big kettle. But I had thought the only black people was in Africa wearing skins. Anyway, I backed out of there and finally got into the passenger coaches and they were all full except the last one, where I met the conductor, a small red-faced man with a miserable disposition. He gave me hell and threatened to throw me off the train, for he figured I'd been hiding until all the tickets were collected. So I showed him my ticket and he grumbled about certain people not knowing when to stay home.

After he left I took the only seat available, which was next to this drummer in a striped suit and derby hat. I could tell he was a drummer from the sample cases which occupied the seat in front of him. I'd seen plenty of traveling men coming up from the station in the livery to Plumb's Hotel. This fellow was about forty and built on the plump side, with the soft pink skin of a scalded pig. He smelt just like a woman who's doused herself with toilet water. His hat was tipped down over his brow and he moved over to make room for me. I wanted the seat opposite him but I didn't have the nerve to ask him to move his sample cases. I could sense he was peering at me, though I sat there looking straight ahead and not moving a muscle. I guess he took me for a hick because of my wet wool suit and shy manner, for after a minute he says from under the hat, "Where are you bound, Dudley?" I decided not to give anything away, so I told him I'd come from Storm Hill, which was a little hole in the woods back of Craven Falls. I said I was on my way to Chicago to visit my father who was a famous poet out there.

Don't ask me why I made all that up. I didn't even know where Chicago was. It was just a name in a geography book so far as I was concerned. But when you take a country kid and put him in with strangers he'll either say nothing at all and sit there like a piece of furniture or he'll open his mouth and say too much. What he'll never do is answer yes and no and leave it at that. So when I told him all this the drummer says, "Is that a fact? Bless my soul. All the way to Chicago! What was the name again, Morley? I don't believe I caught it first time around."

"Tom Fletcher," I says, and right away I regretted that. I shouldn't have drawn Fletcher's name into it but his sly way of asking questions was making me nervous.

Then he pulls out a bag of hard candy and offers me a humbug. "I read a little poetry now and again," he says. "But I don't think I've come across your dear father's name. Of course maybe he doesn't compose the kind of poetry I'm familiar with." Then he nudges me in the side with his elbow and gives me a wink. "Some of the ladies like a little poetry in the wooing. If you know what I mean, Jim." Then he whispers in my ear:

> *Down by the mill where the grass is long and green*
> *I lifted up her petticoats and this is what I seen*

At this he's taken with such a fit of laughing that several people woke up and looked around at us before settling back in their seats.

The drummer's face looked ready to explode with heat and then he started to cough and had to sit up straight with his little pink hands on his thighs. He held his head down and wiped his face with a handkerchief until the coughing fit passed, at which time he looked at me and smiled. "It's a great life if you don't weaken, Bob, but tell me something," he says, reaching over to stuff the handkerchief into his hind pocket and pressing his fat leg against mine. "You look like a young man of the world to me. You'll find Chicago a great place too. I've not been there myself, mind you, but a friend of mine used to go in there. He says it's a terrible town for good-looking women." Then he leaned over and whispered to me, "What about up Storm Hill way? I've never traveled those parts. Are the women friendly?"

Or words to that effect. I can't remember the exact conversation after all these years. All I know is that he couldn't keep his mind off the female sex and he told me how much he was getting from the clerks in the general stores he called upon. Then he took out a pack of playing cards which had pictures of women standing around in their corsets or leaning against pianos with one leg up on the bench. Hot stuff, but nothing sensational after you've experienced the real McCoy. However, he seemed to think they were worth looking at and that's when I made my mistake. He'd been needling me a little about being innocent of the pleasures of the flesh, so I told him outright that all winter I'd been enjoying the favors of a married woman. That's what comes from being young and male and a braggart too. Of course it was just what this salesman had been waiting to hear. He wanted to know all about it, every last detail. And he wanted me to talk dirty when I was telling it. Now, I'm no puritan but I've never enjoyed dirty talk. Anyway, by this time I was fed up with him and the whole subject, so I said I was going to sleep because it was a long way to Chicago. He just laughed and said, "You better do that, Clayton. It's at least forty miles to Chicago. And you'll need all your energy when the married women catch sight of you stepping off the train." He laughed himself into another coughing spell while I turned my back to him.

In a little while the swaying of the train and the rain drumming on the roof and the snores made me sleepy and I dozed off. All that damn talk about fornication must have heated up my brain, for the next thing I know I'm back in my own bed and Mrs. Fletcher is running her hand up my leg. Well, I woke up and damn me for a liar if this salesman's hand isn't crawling up my thigh like a big pink spider, and him stretched out pretending to sleep. Now, I didn't want to raise too much fuss, so I just swept the hand away and told him to keep his fingers to himself. At this he opens his eyes and winks. "No offense intended, Morton," he says. "I must have been dreaming of my dear little wife." Then he turned to the window chuckling away to himself and soon he was snoring away while I sat there watching him all the way to Toronto.

When we arrived the station was crowded with people. Out on the platform the drummer stood next to a porter who was loading his cases onto a trundle cart. He waved. "Good luck in Chicago, Bert," he calls, and waddles off behind the porter. I didn't know what to do or where to go, so I stood there for some time just watching the people come and go and the porters pushing their trundle carts along the platform. It had stopped raining but it was foggy and damp and somewhere a church bell tolled the hours. I guessed the best thing to do was find myself a cheap place to sleep and I was thinking about this when someone plucked my sleeve and asked me if I wanted a cab. He was just a kid about my own age, though he was smaller and skinnier, which is saying something. He was wearing patched britches, an old coat and a peaked cap pulled down over a pair of the worst crossed eyes I'd ever seen. His nose seemed permanently stopped up with phlegm, so he pointed towards a line of cabs parked near the back of the station.

I figured I'd need some help even if I had to pay for it, so I followed him to the last cab, a tattered-looking affair with an old white horse standing like a ghost in the fog. Up on the box the driver sat all hunched over in a greatcoat. He appeared to be asleep. "Hey, Papa!" the kid yells up, "I got you a fare here!" Then he ran a coat sleeve under his nose and hawked up a tremendous gob of phlegm, spitting it a good fifteen feet.

The man pulled his nose out of his coat and looked down at me with crossed eyes. He was skinny too, with a bit of a moustache struggling around his upper lip, though I couldn't make out his features too well in the fog and the dim light from the old arc lamps they used to have. He grunted at me a little and finally says, "He's only a kid. Why didn't you bring me a decent fare?"

"But he's wearing a fine suit," says the boy. "Look at this suit, Papa!"

"I ain't gettin' down to look at no suit," the driver grumbles, and then says to me, "And where might you be goin', sir?"

To tell you the truth I didn't care for the sarcasm in his voice but I called up, "Can you take me to a hotel?"

"Can I take you to a hotel?" he repeats, and shakes his head. "Well, I suppose I can. Yes, sir. I can do that. Only it would be a great help to me personally if I knew which hotel you had in mind. You see, sir, there are at least two hundred such establishments in this city, sir. Not to mention rooming houses, boarding houses, charity houses and church basements."

Thinking of my funds I says, "I don't necessarily want the best."

"Oh, he don't necessarily want the best," says the driver, who now appeared to be talking to his horse. "Did you hear the young gentleman, Silver? He don't necessarily want the best. Then I guess we'll just not bother visiting the Rossin House or the Queen's tonight." Then he looks down at me again and says, "How much was you thinking of paying for your accommodation, sir?"

Well, I had no idea how big-city prices ran, so I told him I was thinking of something in the neighborhood of twenty-five cents.

"Oh, my," says he. "Twenty-five cents. The prodigal son returns. Well, if I'd knowed you was talking that kind of money . . ." Then he took off his hat and scratched a bald head. "Better get in," he says.

But I remembered how Fletcher told me of being skinned for his change once in Toronto. He told me that cab drivers liked to catch you late at night after you'd endured a long train ride and were a little tired and confused in the head. Then they short-changed you. So I asked him how much he'd be charging me and he looked at his horse again and says, "How much will we charge the gentleman, Silver? I wonder if ten cents would be stretching his purse? Have you got ten cents, Midas?" he asks. Well, I had ten cents all right, along with two coppers, and that meant I wouldn't have to fetch out any folding money, so I gave him ten cents and climbed in. The snot-nosed boy got in too and sat on the seat, not saying a word but just looking at me. It made me feel damned uneasy.

Well, we drove through these foggy streets, and God Almighty, they could have been taking me anywhere, I suppose. The only thing I could see out of this little oval window was the dim outline of what looked like a lot of warehouses and abandoned buildings. The air smelled of cold fish. Now and then I'd see a figure moving around or slouching in a doorway. Once a cat arched its back under a lamppost. After a while the cab stopped in front of a seedy-looking two-story house with an outside staircase. There was a sign with ROOMS printed on it over the front door. As soon as I got out, the cab moved off smartly with neither father nor son saying a word. So there I was, left on this deserted street listening to the horse's hoofs fade away on the cobblestone and the creaking of the cab's hinges and springs as it disappeared in the fog. And it made me wonder why in hell I'd given up a warm bed with a ripe woman in it to stand around in the fog of a strange city. But a man never knows when he's well off. Still, I had to make the best of it, so I went over and rapped on the door of this rooming house. Through a dirty curtain I could see a lamp burning inside and then this lanky young fellow comes to the door. He stood there with his arms folded across his chest looking at me and says, "Oh, my withered parts! What have we here?"

"I'd like a room for the night," I says.

Well, he opened the door wide and, bending at the waist, sweeps his hand before him. "Be my guest, sir!" he says.

It made me wonder if everybody in Toronto was crazy or was this just normal behavior for city people. But I went into the lobby. Seated in one corner at a table were a couple of bozos playing cards and passing a bottle back and forth. The tall young fellow went behind a counter and stood there drumming his fingers on the top of it. "One room for the night," he says. "That's seventy-five cents, sport. In advance." It seemed like a lot of money just for a place to sleep but I was stuck with it. I couldn't see the point of going out and wandering around the city in the middle of the night, so I fished into my suit coat and damn the luck if my purse wasn't there! Either I'd dropped it or that salesman had pinched it while I was sleeping. Or that kid in the cab had taken it. Anyway I fumbled around, searching every pocket in my coat and pants while this clerk watches me as if this is the biggest joke in the world. "What's the matter there, bub?" he asks. "You got ants in your pants or something?"

"I've lost my money," I says. "I believe I've been robbed!"

"Is that right?" says this fellow. "Robbed? Did you hear that, boys?" he calls out to the card players. "The young gent here believes he's been robbed. Isn't that a shame?"

One joker throws up his hand and cries, "Oh, mother! Why did I ever leave home and hearth?"

Everybody laughed except me. The fact is I was getting a little sore. The city appeared to be full of smart alecks who derived particular amusement from another fellow's predicament. So I continued to fidget around, looking for my money, getting madder and madder while this long drink of water in front of me raises a number of laughs with the card players. Now I can take a joke along with the next man in line but nobody likes to be ridiculed, particularly if he's tired and fed up and in strange surroundings. And I've got a touch of my mother's bad temper. Still, I tried to keep my head when this clerk says, "Now why don't you just stop fingering yourself and move along?"

"Look," I says. "I'm in a bind here. I don't know my way around town. How about a night's lodgings if I clean up for you tomorrow morning?"

"Nope," he answers. "We run this here establishment like the Chinese laundry down the street. Do you know what I mean, bub?"

I was still looking through my pants and coat but to humor him I says, "No, what do you mean?"

"The Chinaman says no tickee, no laundry. Same deal here, bub. No money, no roomee!"

"Well," I says, "it looks like I was just put on this earth to amuse you."

"Whoa, now," the fellow says. "Take it easy, killer."

So I says to him, "Is everybody in Toronto a son of a bitch or am I just in the hind end of town?" You can see how I was already turning into a big-city joker.

But the clerk just smiled and said, "Well now, you'd better watch your language there, bub, because you're talking like a Yankee now. And for about two and a half cents I'd come around this desk and kick your damned Yankee arse."

"I'm no Yankee," I says.

"We've ways of dealing with Yankee trash that comes across the border. What boat you come off of? I'll bet you're not in this country legal, are you?"

At this the two card players got up and I was old enough to realize it was time to leave. So I backed slowly towards the door and then I was gone, racing through those back streets, though where I was headed I couldn't have told you. One of the card players came along after me for a few blocks and then got winded and quit. I crouched down for a while behind an old barrel. I nearly fainted when a rat ran across my foot. The streets of Toronto were dirty and rough in those days. At least they were in the east end.

After a bit I straightened up and stood on this street corner wondering what in hell to do. I was feeling pretty miserable, though after a while I remembered the dollar in my shoe and that cheered me up. At least I'd eat breakfast in the morning. I began to think about sleeping on some old papers in this doorway when I heard the clop-clop of a horse's hoofs on the cobblestones. And then coming out of the fog like a ghost is a white horse. And sure enough, the same figure is sitting hunched over up on the box. And next to him is the kid. And then I heard somebody clearing his throat and spitting. It was them all right, and I stepped out in front of the cab. They stopped when they saw me. "Well, well," says the driver, looking down at me. "What have we here? Wasn't that hotel to your liking, your majesty?" So I told him what had happened, determined in my mind that if I heard one more bit of sarcasm that night I was going to brain someone with my valise. But when I'd finished, the driver took off his hat and scratched his head and said, "Better come along home with us then. You'll love the decor, and the eats is the talk of the town." Well, I couldn't make head nor tail of his way of talking but I climbed in anyway and the kid jumped down and got in beside me too. Then he cleared his throat and told me his name was Jack Gillies.

The Gillies lived in a four-room shack near the Gooderham and Worts distillery. It was down a sort of back alley called, I believe, Rush Street. Their dwelling, if such you could call it, was squeezed in cheek by jowl with a lot of other tarpaper and wooden shacks, lived in by folks who were all in the same boat. And the boat was called poverty. And none of that was poverty such as you hear about today in this country. There were people on Rush Street in those days who *died* from not getting enough to eat. Every time I hear some old fart in this place bragging about the good old days I remember the Gillies and Rush Street in east Toronto in '96. I'm not denying that some things was better, because they were. But if you were on the bottom of the pile like the Gillies, then you had your work cut out for you. And although I was too young to know much about it at the time, the nineties was also a period of economic depression. They weren't just the gay times you read about in some books.

When we got to the Gillies's that night I was so tired I just followed Jack through a couple of rooms, stumbling over sleeping bodies until we came to a corner where I collapsed on a mattress.

7

ONE SIDE OF THE TRACKS

————————

WHEN I WOKE UP next morning I was in a large room. There were several mattresses on the floor and a wardrobe along one wall with a dirty curtain pulled across it. The room had a door and one small window but the glass was gone. Someone had stuffed some butcher's paper through the hole and by lifting this a little I could see it was a beautiful day with the sun shining down on a mud yard. About ten feet from my nose a young pig rooted in some slops. I could hear talking and laughter on the other side of this door, so I opened it for a look.

Gillies sat in his underwear at the head of this long wooden bench surrounded by a dozen ragged kids, including Jack. His wife stood by the stove stirring something in a pot. She was still a pretty woman but faded and thin as a tent peg. Most of the family was reasonably good-looking as well, except for the badly crossed eyes on some of them and the scrawniness. And all of them was pale enough to have spent their lives under rocks. Gillies invited me to sit down and share what he called "this regal repast." They were eating canned peaches and you'd have thought it was prime ribs of beef the way they were spooning the stuff down.

"You've brought us a measure of good fortune," says Gillies to me. "One of these little toadstools went out this morning and what do you suppose he found on the grassy sward outside our little castle but a five-dollar bank note? So Fortune smiles on the Gillies this day and you are invited to partake." So I had some canned peaches and bread and tea and got introduced to the rest of the family. Gillies asked me where my home was and I told him that I'd come in from the country and was on my way to visit my father in Halifax, Nova Scotia. Again I said too much and mentioned that he was a famous poet down that way.

53

"A poet," says Gillies wryly. "Does he have any money? He must have means. The suit you're wearing is not often seen in these parts." Now, this suit I was wearing was no more than small-town general store issue. Fletcher picked it off a rack a week after I moved in. I mention it to give you an idea of how hard up these people were. I'm afraid I bragged a little and told them my father sold his poems all over the world and I was on my way now to visit him, as we were going around the world by steamer. To which Gillies replies, "Why not tarry a few days here? You could write your dear father a letter and tell him how well you're being looked after by John Gillies and family. You might also tell him of the delightful view and the cosmopolitan charms of this part of the Queen City." Gillies then snorted in disgust and got up and left the room.

As I was to discover over the next few weeks, Gillies was just about the most sarcastic man you could find in Ontario at the time. He was just incapable of uttering a sentence without putting a certain spin on it so that the gist sounded opposite to what he really meant. For example, you might say to him after he'd spent all morning hammering some boards over a crack in the kitchen wall, "That's certainly an improvement, Mr. Gillies." At which he'd throw up his hands and reply, "Oh say, Bill, yes. If I keep it up I wager we'll soon have a residence just like Mr. Massey up on Jarvis Street." Do you see what I mean? The man was totally afflicted with bitterness at life's outrages. Mind you, he had a tough time of it with all those kids and his asthma. And he had a problem finding work. Jack told me that before his father got married he'd been a valet in one of the big fancy homes on upper Sherbourne Street. But he lost that job. Jack didn't know why, and his father wouldn't talk about it. After that Gillies just drifted from one thing to another. He had no trade and even the cab he drove was rented from a man who got a percentage of the fares.

So the family had trouble making ends meet, particularly when Gillies had one of his asthma attacks. Then he'd cough and hack and you'd swear he was about to expire. Mrs. Gillies or Jack and me would help him into a bedroom and there he'd lie with his chest rattling away so bad you could hear it through the walls. Mrs. Gillies was careful with what little money they had and she also went out two or three times a week as a charlady in a rich man's home. Most of the time, however, the Gillies were just one step ahead of the rent collector who came around every Friday. But I'll deal with him in a minute. First I want to tell you a few other things about my life with the Gillies.

Now you might wonder why I decided to stay with this family when it was plain they had trouble feeding themselves without taking on another mouth. Well, my first reason was selfish. The way I saw it, Rush Street might be a good place to hole up in case the Fletchers called the authorities, which seemed likely. The second reason was this. I thought maybe I could help the Gillies by taking on work of some kind. I was taller than Jack or his father and fairly strong for my age despite the wear and tear to my nervous system suffered during my amours with Mrs. Fletcher. So I told them I was taking a little holiday before going on to see my father and at this news Gillies just smiled and didn't say a word. All the kids seemed to think it was a great idea and Mrs. Gillies had no objection. But then she never said much. She was always just cooking or mending clothes or counting the pennies in a tin can near the stove. The kids were of all ages, from the baby in Mrs. Gillies's arms and the two or three toddlers always clinging to her dress right up to Jack, who was just my age but only looked about twelve.

The kids hardly ever went to school and the truant officer was always at the door. Jack was old enough not to bother but he told me that he'd never gotten much out of it anyway because he was always fighting with kids who made fun of his eyes. So he warned me that if I got mad at him for any reason whatsoever, I wasn't to make any jokes about his appearance because then he'd have to give me a licking and sometimes during a fight he didn't remember what he was doing. At first I put all that down to normal bragging, because I felt I could handle him with ease. I discovered how wrong I was one day when we were fishing down off Leak's Wharf. A big kid maybe sixteen or seventeen came along and told us to move off because we were fishing in his spot. Well, Jack wasn't moving anywhere and he told this kid as much. The upshot of it was a fist fight that lasted no longer than a minute. Now Jack gave away at least fifty pounds, but let me tell you he gave that boy an awful hiding. God Almighty but Jack Gillies had the worst temper I've ever encountered in a human being.

Once I got used to the general squalor of the Gillies's household and their living style I actually began to enjoy the idea of not being at anybody's beck and call. The Gillies were a remarkably free family, with nobody telling anybody else what to do. That was the center post of Gillies's philosophy. He was always reading to us from a book by some European and the nub of this book was that no man has the right to rule over another and we can all do without governments and bosses. I myself could never see it working on a grand scale because it seemed to me that somebody had to take charge of things. But Gillies put this theory into practice in his own household and the amazing thing was that it seemed to work. All the older kids had jobs to do, either sweeping or cleaning something, and you never heard anybody giving orders.

My own good intentions about finding work were thwarted for two reasons. In the first place there wasn't much work, especially once the summer came along and there were more kids than jobs. The second reason was that Jack and me took to stealing and it turned out to be more congenial to our natures than work. We didn't steal money or break into stores or things like that. No, what we stole was food, and the main target of our thieving was the delivery wagons. We had a number of methods, which we changed almost daily. There was one, for instance, whereby I might come along a street to a bread wagon. Just as the driver was climbing down from his box I'd clutch my chest and stumble and make a moaning sound before falling to my knees. Well, the breadman would have to satisfy his curiosity, so he'd wander over with maybe a couple of housewives and they'd bend over me inquiring about my health. Maybe the heat's got him or it's something he's eaten for breakfast, they'd say, while I moaned and rolled around. Meantime, Jack would sneak up to the wagon and lift three or four loaves of bread and perhaps a pie and some tarts. When someone spotted him I was nearly always forgotten as the breadman chased Jack. Then I'd leap up and take off in the opposite direction. Sometimes I'd stick a burdock under the horse's harness and he'd go off down the street on his own, thus further confounding the situation and leaving the breadman wondering who to chase.

Jack and I were fast on our feet and we'd use that system until the deliverymen started to look for us. Then we'd just try maybe a straight grab and run, whereby it was just a footrace between you and the driver. Whatever we stole we took home. Gillies always said that what we were doing was perfectly within the limits of his philosophy because the bakeries and the dairies were all run by a bunch of thieves and bosses who didn't deserve to be holding such power over common people. I figure that Gillies was even better than me at making up excuses to justify theft. Sometimes we had things left over, say a couple of pounds of sausage meat, in which case we flogged it to the neighbors, who were only too glad to get it at half the store price. We never worried about anybody talking to the police, because down there in those days the police were generally disliked. They probably still are.

We weren't always stealing. Sometimes we fished off the wharfs or swam out along Cherry Street. On fine evenings we watched the steamers prepare for moonlight cruises, with the finely dressed ladies and gents walking up the gangplank while a band played in the fantail. It was all right. Sometimes we roamed over to King Street and put the bite on some couple strolling in front of the quality shops. Couples were always best, because the fellow didn't like to appear cheap in front of his girl. But you had to be careful, because begging wasn't allowed on the streets of Toronto in those days. Sometimes when I'd see those pretty girls I'd think about Mrs. Fletcher and the female sex in general. There were one or two girls my age on Rush Street who were only too willing to play games but I wasn't interested in kids. At the risk of boasting I might say here that I was turning into a fair-looking young fellow and all I really needed was some decent clothes. My one good suit was now done for, and like the Gillies I dressed most of the time in torn britches and shirt with scuffed ankle boots and a peaked cap pulled down over my eyes. Even so, I sometimes got a smile or a lingering look from the young ladies when they came out of swank places like the Rossin House. However, the doormen always told us to move along. Some nights I'd go with Jack to the old Union Station and hustle fares for Gillies.

About the middle of that summer we had a spell of wet weather. It rained for days and when it wasn't raining it stayed overcast. At nights a thick fog settled over the streets and in the warm damp air it was hard to catch your breath. This weather provoked Gillies's asthma and he just lay in bed hacking and coughing. The truth is, I believe the man had lung consumption, though nobody down there seemed to know. With Gillies not working at all, the money got scarcer and scarcer. Neither Jack nor me could find any work to speak of and it was hard pulling for one and all. Mrs. Gillies just sat in the kitchen fanning herself with an old newspaper and listening to Gillies cough. When he wasn't coughing he was ranting about the system of government under which we lived. The result of all this was that the Gillies fell behind in their rent and the rent collector began to talk about eviction.

Now this rent collector was a case. Instead of seeing himself as an employee doing his job, he always came into the house like he owned it himself. I can still see him making his rounds, pulling out his black book to make his entries. He was a wormy-looking character, in his late thirties, I judged. He had slicked-down black hair and pale skin and he always wore flashy but cheap clothes. I think he considered himself something of a dandy but he could never put it all together, which led me to suspect that he was an ignorant man at heart. For instance, he'd wear a brocade waistcoat but there'd be gravy stains on it or maybe a button missing. Or he'd have this expensive-looking watch which he'd pull out to pretend he was in a hurry, but if you looked close you could see the gold plate was chipping away. And his fingernails was always dirty. Later in my life I was to encounter people similar in style to this man. They were often pimps or shyster lawyers, dressed to the nines but lacking what you might call good taste.

One Friday morning in late August the rain stopped and the sun shone. Gillies said he felt well enough to work again and after breakfast left to hack for the day. Jack and I spent the morning poking about the back alleys around the waterfront and then stole some ice and carried it home in a piece of burlap, figuring to treat the kids, for the day was turning hot. When we got to the head of Rush Street we saw the rent man's buggy, with the horse acting nervous because of so many kids out on the street. Then one of Jack's little brothers told us not to go near the house because Mrs. Gillies had to talk over some business with the rent man and had given instructions not to be disturbed. It sounded funny to Jack and he asked how long the rent man had been in the house. His sister Lucy, who was about twelve, was standing there with the baby in her arms. She said perhaps twenty minutes. Jack then left the ice for the kids and we went on down towards the house, taking our time and not saying anything.

Jack looked grim and paler than usual. I didn't like to ask questions when he looked like that. We went through this broken gate and around to the back near the pig pen. Both of us were quiet as burglars. Soon we heard voices coming from one of the bedrooms, so we sneaked to the window and looked in. I can tell you that it was no sight for boy nor man. Mrs. Gillies sat on the edge of the bed in a gray chemise. She was so skinny and pale in this ragged underwear that she didn't look more than fourteen. Standing over her, buttoning up his pants and smirking, was the rent man. Jack's face was like chalk and the knuckles was also bled of any color. He didn't say a word but just turned from me and walked quickly around to the front door, with me trying to keep up to him. At the front he raised a leg and booted open the door. In the kitchen the rent man was now smoothing down his vest with the flat of his hand and his mouth opened in surprise at the sight of us. Still, he didn't appear overly worried. We were just two skinny little kids to him. Then Mrs. Gillies walked into the room, her neck and face suddenly flushing. She looked long and hard at Jack, who stood there trembling with his fists clenched. And she said in this low voice, "Get out of the house this minute, Jack! Do you hear me? I'll talk to you later. Now get!"

Meantime the rent man collects his coat from the back of the chair and, putting it on, says, "Better do what your mother tells you, Sunny Jim."

It was then Jack sprang. God Almighty, he leaped across the room and, grabbing the rent man by the throat, fires him against the wall. Mrs. Gillies screamed and a queer, sick look came over the rent man's face. Now Jack took the man's measure all right and he dropped him swiftly with an awesome kick in the parts. The man just slumped against the wall on his knees and Jack went to work with those bony little fists tripping back and forth like pistons. It was something to marvel at, even though watching a man receive a beating like that isn't exactly edifying. Jack's mother reached out to grab him and he just back-handed her halfway across the room without hardly interrupting the rhythm of his blows. Then she screamed at me to do something, so I grabbed Jack from behind, because it was plain he was going to kill the son of a bitch right then and there. I finally pulled him away and succeeded in getting him down on the floor, where I sat on him until he cooled out and stopped calling me dirty names. Then I got off him and he just bolted for the door and was gone.

I wanted to follow him but I thought I'd better check out the rent man first. He looked in poor shape, curled up on the floor and moaning. Blood was leaking from his pant cuffs. Mrs. Gillies was hysterical, crying and beating her fists against her head. Fortunately, a couple of neighbors rushed in and tried to shake some sense into her and find out what happened. I didn't envy her the job of explaining matters.

I myself was shaking to beat hell, and the funny thing is you start thinking of yourself in these situations too. The cops would be along to investigate this and they'd want to know who I was and where did

7.   One Side of the Tracks

I come from, etc., etc. Likely as not they'd link up Jack and me with all the recent stealing in the neighborhood. It was a terrible mess and I could see a stretch of prison life lying ahead of me. Thus I figured that the best thing was to get the hell out of there and find Jack. Maybe we could catch a freight train and be out of town before anyone was on to us. So I went into our bedroom for a couple of dollars I'd been saving and a spare shirt. Since Jack was splattered with blood I figured he'd need another shirt as well, so I rooted around in this old dresser. That's where I discovered my purse, empty of course. It was wedged down behind some clothes. Now I didn't necessarily begrudge Jack the purse, because he'd turned the money over to his family. Still and all, it's a disappointment to learn that a friend has stolen from you. Yet I couldn't stand there pondering that, so I grabbed the shirts and climbed out a window at the back of the house. Then I was gone, running and leaping through those back lanes and alleys.

I knew where Jack would go in this kind of emergency. We'd often talked about where we'd hide if the police were after us, so we'd found a spot down near the freight yards. It was in a little hawthorn grove, just a few trees, on the top of a grassy embankment which overlooked the railway tracks. There you could sit undetected and watch the shunting engines working away below or the outbound freights and passenger trains gathering speed on the express lines. Sometimes we'd see tramps reaching out for the climbing rail of a passing boxcar. It was a good little place to spend a hot smoky afternoon. Or hide from the cops, which was on my mind as I hoofed it through those back lanes and over the cinder pathways behind the warehouses and loading sheds. Below me yard engines chuffed along the tracks, sending up big puffs of black smoke. Over to the southwest, off the lake, big thunderheads were piling up for an afternoon storm. Already there were flashes of lightning in a sky the color of gun metal.

When I reached our hideaway the first big warm drops were falling. Inside we were fairly well protected by the leaves and an old chunk of rusty tin which we'd rigged up as a sort of roof. Jack was there, just as I thought he would be, sitting on the ground, hugging his knees and coughing into his hands. He didn't take any notice of me when I sat down beside him. His face was solemn and streaked with dirt and I could tell he'd been crying. I thought I'd cheer him up, so I said, "Look, Jack, you gave that bastard a real licking. He won't pull that kind of stuff again in a hurry."

At this Jack turns to me and says, "What kind of stuff are you talking about?"

"Well," I says. "You know what I mean."

"You just forget what you saw, Bill," he says. "You just forget it. It never happened and I don't want to hear nothing more about it."

"Well, that's all right by me," I says, and I handed him this shirt. "I brought you along something different to wear," I says.

He took the shirt and looked at it for a minute before pitching it into the corner. He studied my face for a few minutes, frowning all the time. Looking, to tell you the truth, as though he'd like to throttle me. Then it came to me. He now knew that I'd seen the empty purse and he was ashamed. But he didn't say anything. Instead he handed me a pint bottle half full. "Here," he says. "You want a drink of this?"

I was thirsty after running, so I took a big swallow. The next thing I know my gullet is afire and I'm choking and spluttering. "Jesus, Jack," I says. "This isn't water!"

This brings a little smile to Jack's face. "You *are* a donkey's arse," he says. "Holy Christ! Do you think I'd be sitting in here hiding from the law and drinking *water?* That's gin you're holding in your hand, chum. Now give it back here if you're going to spit it all over the ground." And he takes a big swallow of the stuff and says after a minute, "I hope I killed that bastard. Maiming would be too good for him." I didn't say anything and he adds, "I don't want you to get any ideas that my mother is some kind of whore."

"Nobody's saying anything like that, Jack," I says.

"I don't want you even *thinking* that. You understand?"

"Sure thing," I says.

It grew dark and a great bolt of lightning forked across the sky. We listened to the thunder and the rain on the roof and the leaves. By and by Jack says, "It ain't the first time she's done that." I couldn't judge his humor, so I didn't say a word. "Once," he says, "maybe five years ago, she done it with some bill collector over on Power Street where we was living. I was too young to know what was going on." I still didn't say a word, though I had the feeling Jack wanted me to comment so he could tell me to shut up. I figured that inside he was just boiling with rage and was looking for some outlet. Then after a bit he says, "Well, what difference does it make anyways? It's all a pile of shit."

"What is, Jack?" I asks.

"Life, for Christ's sakes," he says, and takes another drink before handing me the bottle. So we sat there drinking gin and watching the storm roll out across the lake. Jack took off his shoe and around one foot he'd wrapped a dirty rag. When I asked him what happened he told me he'd stepped on a nail. "Wasn't looking where I was going," he says, getting up to test it. "Oh, this is just fine," he says, hobbling around on one foot. "This is just what I need now. Why, I'll bet I could walk a hundred miles with this foot." He sounded just like his father.

"Well, what *are* you going to do, Jack?" I asks.

He limped around some more and drank the last of the gin. The tin roof was leaking and puddles were forming everywhere. "Ain't life just wonderful?" he says, throwing the gin bottle through the entrance and sitting down in a corner. "I got some baloney and bread here," he says. "Do you want some?"

"Sure," I says. So we eat some baloney and bread and with the gin inside me I got sleepy. There was still light in the sky but the rain was coming down hard. "I got a couple of dollars, Jack," I says, yawning. "If we could catch one of those freights later on, why we could be well gone from here by morning."

To this Jack says, "Oh, I'm in great shape to be running after freights with this foot of mine. Why, I'm as nimble as a goddam alley cat."

"Well, it's worth a try," I says. "We can't stay here forever, that's for certain."

"Oh, I thought you liked it here," he says in that damn sarcastic tone. So I didn't say anything more because there was no talking to a Gillies when they were feeling sorry for themselves like that.

After a while I fell asleep. When I woke up it was dark and still and wet. I didn't know where in hell I was for a minute. When I got my senses together I looked around for Jack. He was gone. I went outside and stretched my muscles, which had cramped up from lying on the damp ground. I was also suffering from my first hangover, with a dry, foul-tasting mouth and an aching head. In the course of stretching I checked out my pockets and found my two dollars was missing. In place of the money was a piece of butcher's paper with a note scribbled on it in pencil. I found a match in one of my pockets and read these words.

Billy
Theres no use yur getteng mixed in with my qwarrl. Im catchin the next train out frum here. I am boroweng thes two dollars from you.

yur frend
Jack Gillies

8

THE OTHER SIDE

THIS PUT ME in a quandary. I could take my chances by grabbing a freight train, though to tell you the truth I wasn't all that fussy about traveling rough by myself. Or I could stay in Toronto and hope to find some kind of work and avoid discovery by the law. So I remained in the hideaway until the middle of the morning thinking over my choices and then decided to spend my last copper on a newspaper and see what happened to that rent man. For all I knew there was murder hanging over our heads. By ten o'clock or so the downtown streets were crowded enough for me to appear inconspicuous and I bought a paper. Sure enough, it was there on the front page. *Man Severely Beaten in Rush Street.* I folded up that paper and hurried away, walking westerly until I came to a wooded area up near where the Ontario legislature now sits. It was parkland then.

There I sat under a tree and read that this Thomas Heywood or Hayman, I can't exactly recall, was the victim of an apparently unprovoked assault which occurred during the course of his duties as rent collector at the home of John B. Gillies, unemployed cab driver. Mr. Gillies was not home at the time of the incident but the police are seeking his eldest son, John B. Gillies Jr., and a friend, William Fletcher, both about sixteen years of age. The paper went on to say that the victim was resting comfortably at the General Hospital. Mind you, that's only an idea of what was written. If you want dead accuracy you'll have to look it up for yourself in the Toronto papers for August of that year. Well, I was glad the rent man hadn't died, but still it wasn't exactly comforting news that I was being sought by the police. So I was sitting there puzzling out what to do when an incident occurred which changed my luck. Here's what happened.

Down the street in front of this huge house was parked a smart-looking two-in-hand drawn by the prettiest little coal-black horse you've ever seen. Now, I don't know what suddenly got into that horse. It could have been naturally skittish or perhaps a bee stung her. Anyway, it started acting up, dancing sideways and throwing back her head. It was raising such a commotion that I forgot my troubles and ran towards her. The little horse was all for dragging her iron halfway up the street but I grabbed the bridle and started talking to her. My experience with Fletcher's horse was valuable here, because a horse can always tell when you're not afraid of her and she'll have confidence in you. So by and by the little mare settled down and I kept patting her and letting her get the smell and the feel of me.

All this time I'm being observed by the buggy's passenger, a girl whom I judge to be about fourteen. A pretty little female, though frail-looking, with a head of blond sausage curls and a colorless little face which is even paler from fright, though she didn't cry out once. She just smiled weakly and looked embarrassed to be sitting there helpless. Just then a man comes running out of this house towards us. He's a big handsome fellow with a smooth face and thick blond hair. He's wearing an expensive suit with a gold watch fob across his vest front. He ignores me at first and says to the girl, "Are you all right, Esther?"

"Yes, Papa," she says in this thin sweet voice. "I'm all right. Thanks to this young man."

"Yes," says her father. "I saw the whole thing through the window. I'm grateful to you, young man. What's your name?"

He held out a big soft hand, which I shook. I figured it was time I went by my own handle, so I told him my name was Billy Farthing.

"James Easterbrook," he says, "and this is my daughter Esther. We're pleased to make your acquaintance, Bill. What line of work are you in?"

"At the moment," I says, "I'm not in any particular line."

Then little Esther Easterbrook says, "Wilson is always complaining that he needs another pair of hands, Papa. Perhaps Mr. Farthing." She stopped and blushed and looked away.

"By George, Essie, you could be right," says Easterbrook, looking at me shrewdly. "What do you say, Bill Farthing? Would you like to come and work for me? We could start you off at . . . what?" Easterbrook closed one eye and looked up at a tree. "Oh, let's say seven dollars a month and your board. Every other Saturday free. You do your own laundry and you get a pair of new boots once a year."

He sounded to me like a man who did a lot of hiring and firing. Well, I accepted his offer on the spot. It was a chance for me to stay off the streets until that business on Rush Street blew over.

Just as we were about to climb into the buggy Easterbrook suddenly clamped a hand on my shoulder and spun me around. "Just one thing, Bill," he says. "What church do you go to?" Well, I'd never gone to church in my life. I couldn't see there was much to it. So I just pulled a name out of the hat and told him I was a Presbyterian. He shrugged and said, "Well, I suppose you can't help that. For a minute there I thought you might be a papist." So we got in, and with Easterbrook at the reins and me sitting behind his daughter in a kind of jump seat, we drove across town. Easterbrook asked me all sorts of questions about my family. I satisfied him by saying that they were all dead and I was a homeless orphan, an answer which made Esther sigh for the sadness of life.

The Easterbrooks lived in this big brick house on upper Jarvis Street. It looked like a castle to me with its turrets and balconies. The last time I saw it was in 1947 when it was a flophouse for drunks, but in the days I'm talking about that house was a wonder to gaze upon. You went through these big iron gates and up this winding driveway to the front door. When we got there that morning the door opened and out hustled a couple of maids and an old butler pushing a wheelchair. In the manner of hired help they all gave me the once-over and right away dismissed me as being lower in the order of things than themselves. Of course, I didn't look too prosperous sitting there in clothes I'd slept in. When they heard the story of the horse acting up there was a good deal of fussing as the three of them huddled around the girl. Then the butler picked her up and I could see the iron braces on her poor thin legs, which looked just like broom handles. They put her in the wheelchair and tucked a shawl around her. She looked up at me and smiled. "Perhaps you'll come up to the house and see me sometime, Mr. Farthing."

"You bet," I says, feeling older than my years. But then nobody had ever called me Mister Farthing before.

By now Easterbrook had climbed down and was standing there with his palms on his hips stretching his back muscles and remarking on the fine weather. It was fine too, bright and clear with the first whiff of autumn in the air. "It's a good day to make money, young man," says Easterbrook, pulling out a real gold watch. "I'm already late. Let's get you over to Wilson and see what he thinks."

I followed him around the house to a stable where a little bald-headed, red-faced man was tinkering with the driving shaft of a phaeton. He was wearing stiff cord breeches, a white shirt and highly polished boots. When he saw us approaching he snapped to attention and barked out, "Mornin', guv'nor."

"Good morning, Wilson," says Easterbrook, standing there with his thumbs in his vest pockets. "This is young Bill Farthing. He came to Esther's aid this morning when that little mare acted up. He's a sturdy and reliable lad in my judgment and he's going to join us. I'm sure you can find plenty for him to do."

"Oh indeed, sir," says this Wilson, looking me over critically.

"Then I'll leave you to it," says Easterbrook, and walks away.

"Come along, lad," says Wilson. "I'll show you the barracks."

So he showed me where I would sleep. It was a clean, orderly little room over the stable. Everything about the place was neat as a pin and it didn't take me long to learn that Wilson was an old soldier. He'd served in the British cavalry in India during the Big Mutiny thirty years before, so he was heavy on the spit-and-polish routine. We soon sized each other up, and it came to this. He wasn't overly fussy about my appearance but seemed glad to have someone around to boss. As for me, I didn't take kindly to being pushed around but I was grateful all the same for a place to hang my hat while a fugitive from the law. In fact, Wilson wasn't bad company, particularly if you got him talking about his adventures out in India. You can generally soften up the worst-tempered man in the world if you can find out what he's interested in and then let him jabber away at it, sticking in the odd question now and again.

When we went up to the kitchen for dinner I wasn't made to feel exactly welcome. One of the reasons for this cold-shoulder treatment by the domestics in those days was this. Jobs in good households were hard to come by and some of the servants resented a stranger taking a job that might have gone to a brother or a nephew. Then Wilson told me the other reason that afternoon. It seems that for most of the summer Mrs. Easterbrook was away at their summer home up on Lake Simcoe. But she was coming home in another week or so and it was putting the hired help on edge. Sitting in the harness room, Wilson dropped his voice when he told me this.

"Now don't get any ideas," he says, "that I'm not true-blue loyal to this here household. Everybody likes workin' for the Easterbrooks. It's one of the best households in the city. Mr. Easterbrook himself is a pure jewel to work for. He leaves you alone to work things out for yourself. And little Esther, bless her heart, is a joy and a treasure forever. And there's nothin' particular wrong with Mrs. Easterbrook either, exceptin' she runs a very fastidious household. She likes things done right and who's to say she shouldn't demand it. My only advice is to stay out of her way. The mercy for us is she never sets foot out here." Wilson then dabbed his fingers on his tongue and brushed an imaginary spot off one of his boots. "Mind you, she'd find things razor-sharp out here. It's just that I don't take easily to criticism and Mrs. Easterbrook has a criticizing tongue." He got up and began to lay out strips of leather for a harness he was mending. "I expect she's got the most criticizing tongue of any mortal I've ever heard. And that includes a sergeant-major named Bates I once knew. Now give me a hand here, Bill."

A few hours later I saw Wilson and I hardly recognized him. He was all decked out in livery and was backing a pair of bays into the phaeton's drive shafts. You see, he also acted as chauffeur when Easterbrook was going out to some special party or meeting.

That night I stood by my window wondering where Jack Gillies was by now and hoping maybe his luck had turned around. A big full moon washed the stableyard and lawn in pale light. In front of me the house was just a huge silhouette. And then I saw young Esther sitting by her window. She saw me too, for doesn't she look down and *wave?*

I waved back, of course, and we sat there for the longest time, just looking at one another and not saying a word.

The next morning Easterbrook came down to the stable pushing Esther's wheelchair while Wilson hitched up the little mare. Every morning in fair weather Easterbrook took his daughter for a ride before going down to his office. He was a manufacturer of business furniture, by the way, and loaded with money, as you've probably already gathered. I can still see them. It's a late-summer morning with the sunlight streaming through the leaves of the trees and the smell of horses and petunias in the air. They made a handsome couple too, with Easterbrook tall and beefy in a fine-cut suit. And his daughter beside him, frail and delicate. After they left Wilson went up to the kitchen for his second cup of tea, leaving me to do assorted chores around the stable. It was then that I noticed the morning paper, which Easterbrook always dropped off to Wilson after he'd finished with it.

God Almighty, I can still recall that headline. *An Unfortunate Mishap. Boy Dies Under Train Wheels.* With trembling hands I read of how the railway authorities had discovered Jack's body lying on the tracks in the terminal freight yards. According to the newspaper the police speculated that Jack, who was wanted for questioning in connection with an assault, must have lost his footing while trying to board a boxcar. And that must have been the way it happened. With that sore foot and those bad eyes he was in no condition to be reaching for boxcar handrails. He knew it too, and that's probably why he didn't want me along. He was such a proud devil that he didn't want to be thought of as a liability. That's how I figured it at the time and I still believe it. The story went on to say that the cops were looking for me under the name of William Fletcher but that it was generally believed I'd made good my getaway. And here the paper opined that I must be a sorry specimen of humanity to leave my partner under the wheels of a freight train.

I was just glad that Wilson wasn't around to see my face, because he would surely have suspected something. I felt bad, not only over Jack's death, but also wondering what the Gillies must be thinking of me. Still and all, there wasn't much I could do except lie low for a few weeks until I'd earned a little stake. Then I guessed I might head out for Halifax and try to track down my father.

Wilson kept me busy and I was glad of that, for it took my mind off things. Fortunately, nobody connected me with this William Fletcher and after a few days the papers dropped the subject. All day I painted and scrubbed and sometimes rubbed down the horses, though Wilson usually liked to do that himself. At nights I'd stand by my window and look up towards the house. And there'd be Esther Easterbrook sitting at her bedroom window looking down at me. We'd wave to each other and then retire. On warm days a maid would wheel Esther out under one of the big elms and there she'd sit for most of the afternoon, reading and sipping lemonade or watching me cut the grass. She didn't go to regular school but had this private tutor, a pinch-faced old maid who came by two or three mornings a week.

One day I was walking back from dinner when I noticed that Esther had fallen asleep in her wheelchair. She was just sitting there with her head down to one side like a little plaster statue. I figured to tiptoe past her and was doing just that when the book in her hand falls to the grass. It wakened her and she opened her eyes to see me standing there and gawking. I suppose she was embarrassed about falling asleep in her chair like an old woman, because she blushed to the roots of her hair. I bent down and picked up the book. And wasn't it the damnedest thing, for it's a book of Longfellow's poetry!

"Thank you, Mr. Farthing," says Esther as I handed it to her.

Then, being naturally boastful and not wanting this girl to think that I was just another ignorant stable hand, I says, "My father enjoys Mr. Longfellow's poetry."

At this she turns these pale blue eyes on me. "But I thought your poor father had passed away, Mr. Farthing."

"Well, yes," I says. "What I meant was, he used to enjoy Mr. Longfellow's poetry. It's a way of speaking."

"I see," she says.

"That's right," I says, stuffing my hands into my pockets. "I think my father was just about the greatest admirer of Longfellow you could find in this country. As a matter of fact," I says, "he was a poet himself. My father, I mean."

"How lovely," she says, but right away I can tell she doesn't believe it. This irks me because I can't stand to be thought of as a liar.

"You don't believe that, do you, Miss Easterbrook?" I says, and maybe my voice is a shade too sharp, because she blushes again and looks down to the ground. Well, I knew I'd spoken out of turn, so I apologized, something I've never been much good at. "I'm sorry, Miss Easterbrook," I says. "You don't have to believe that if you don't want to, though it's true."

And then she smiled again and listen, you'd go a long way to see a prettier face when that girl smiled. If she'd not been crippled I'm sure she could have had her pick of boy friends. I know she looked beautiful to me as she sat there with the sun streaming through the leaves and falling over her long pale hair. Her skin was so light and fine that it had a blue tinge to it. I could even see her pulse beating away at the temple. Then she says to me, "I'll believe you, Bill. If you'll promise to call me Esther."

"Sure thing," I says, feeling stupid. That girl had a way of making me feel like an awkward schoolboy again, though she herself wasn't a day over fifteen. It was just that she had a kind of natural grace, and it didn't surprise me at all to discover years later that she was considered one of the truly fine ladies in the city of Toronto and was known all over the province for her work in charities.

"It must have been wonderful," she says.

"What's that?"

"Why, to have had a poet for a father!"

"Well," I says, "not so wonderful if he drank as much as mine."

This remark produces a sharp little intake of breath and then I remembered Wilson telling me that the mention of alcohol was absolutely forbidden in the household. Mrs. E. was a big wheel in the temperance movement and according to Wilson she'd rather have suffered a thief than a drinker. So I stood there for the longest time listening to the birds. We were both a bit embarrassed but finally she asked me what it was like growing up in the house of a poet. So I told some reasonable lies about life with a genius and how we used to sit around reading books to one another while the neighbors sorely envied us our cultivation. At this she says, "Perhaps you could read to me now and then. My eyes get so tired. And I do love being read to!"

"Well," I says, "I don't know about that. Wilson might have other ideas regarding my duties."

"Oh, bother Wilson," says Esther. "I shall speak to Papa and he'll talk to Wilson, and that will be the end of that."

And that's exactly what happened. Two or three afternoons a week I'd go up to the house, where Esther would receive me in the library. That was some room, believe you me. Three walls of books and a half dozen big comfortable chairs with a log fire blazing in the hearth if the weather was cool or damp. Esther would sit in her wheelchair by the fire wearing maybe a navy skirt with a little white middy blouse all trimmed with blue. Her hair would be pulled back and tied with a ribbon. She always looked so peaceful and proper sitting there while a maid poured tea into china cups and set out little cakes and biscuits. This, I says to myself, is a helluva long way from Rush Street, though in actual fact it wasn't more than a dozen city blocks.

We started with some poetry by Lord Byron, who was a great favorite with Esther. She liked this Don Juan, who seemed to have his pick of women. Then for a change of style we moved on to Sir Walter Scott and I read a few chapters from a book called, I believe, *The Black Prince.* * All in all, we had ourselves some fine times and I'd fill up on tea and currant buns while the rain lashed the tall windows and the fire crackled and the carriages and traps went hissing past on the wet streets. Esther had stacks of books she was anxious to get through, books by Charles Dickens and Rudyard Kipling and one called *Tess of the D'Urbervilles,* which her father had been reading and which she wasn't supposed to have access to because it was considered racy. But she'd sneaked a few looks at it on the sly and remarked on it being a wonderful story. All this stuff seemed several degrees better than the trashy romances I'd read to Mrs. Fletcher, but the funny thing was that the effect was remarkably the same. As soon as I'd get into one of these stories Esther would sit there trapped and dazed just like Mrs. Fletcher.

* The author's remarkable memory would appear here to err. He surely means *The Black Dwarf.* ED.

8. *The Other Side*

Sometimes if the room got a little warm and stuffy Esther would nod off, her little head drooping down to her chest. Then as quickly she'd wake up, sputtering an apology. I didn't mind because one of the maids told me how poorly Esther slept most nights.

One Saturday afternoon a couple of weeks into September I was in the library with her when the servants started bustling about and before long a carriage pulled up to the front door. Esther didn't seem to take any notice of the commotion but urged me to continue reading. She seemed unusually fretful to me. I did as I was told but had to stop shortly after, for Mrs. Easterbrook came into the room. She was a tall, shapely woman who carried herself very erect in this mauve silk dress with a bustle at the back. On her head was a little flowered hat and she was carrying this big box. She ignored me and rushed to embrace Esther. "My dearest darling," she says, bending down to kiss the girl's cheeks. "How is my precious one? I've missed you so."

"Quite well, thank you, Mother," says Esther coolly.

I could tell she was slightly embarrassed for my sake, because her mother had almost walked right through me. Esther then introduced me, at which Mrs. Easterbrook gives me a cold hard stare. "Ah, yes, the new stableboy," she says. "Your father has told me." Then she turned and wanted to know how Esther had been feeling.

This seemed to vex Esther, for she said quite huffily, "Bill is more than just a stableboy, Mother. He's extremely interested in literature. His father was a poet."

Now that wasn't exactly true, that part about me being interested in literature. Esther was the one interested in literature, not me. But like most people who have a grand passion for something, she just naturally assumed that I shared it with her. The truth of the matter was this: I wasn't overly interested in poetry, which so far as I could tell mostly concerned itself with the pain and misery and shortness of life. Any poet I'd ever heard about was either a drunk or couldn't make any sense out of why he was living. They were all bellyachers. Look at my father for an example. Still and all, I found myself defending them when Mrs. Easterbrook draws herself up and says, "A poet, indeed! And what has he written?"

"A book called *Pine Smoke at Evensong*," I croaks. I might as well have had a mouthful of sawdust.

"How interesting for you," she says, looking past me to the servants in the hallway. "Do be careful with those bags."

I was glad to get out of the house, because the atmosphere seemed to have turned around. The maids were more than usually bitchy and even the head housekeeper, Miss Pringle, who had taken to greeting me with a smile at the front door, told me on the way out to wipe my feet the next time I came up to the house.

With Mrs. Easterbrook's return a routine was soon established. In the fall of the year the society nabobs start their season of visiting and entertaining and the Easterbrooks were right up there with the best of them. There'd be people coming to dinner a couple of times a week, so Wilson and me were busy tending the horses and swapping stories with the carriage drivers, who'd stand around the stableyard smoking and bragging about how much their bosses were worth. The big house would be all lit up, nearly every window, and you could stand there with cigarettes and pipes glowing in the dark watching the maids hurry back and forth from the kitchen with dishes of food. By and by there'd probably be piano music coming from the front of the house, for Mrs. Easterbrook was very accomplished on that instrument. Even on nights when they had no company she liked to play after dinner while her husband read his paper and Esther took her usual spot by her bedroom window. Of course, the Easterbrooks did a lot of visiting themselves and then Wilson would have to dress up and chauffeur them. Same thing on Sunday mornings, when they all stepped out in their best for the ride down to St. James's Cathedral. Every Wednesday night Mr. Easterbrook went out by himself. Wilson told me he went to his club to play billiards and make business deals.

Now I didn't find Mrs. Easterbrook too bad, though, mind you, I didn't have to deal directly with her. She was a hard, cold woman and the servants had to be on their toes at all times. As a matter of fact, she let a young girl go that fall because she spilled a little soup on the carpet. That was the story, anyway. There could have been more to it. But a tough woman just the same, and beautiful too when she dressed up and sat there straight-backed playing the piano. But she wouldn't hardly acknowledge your presence. She'd look right through you as though you were an open door. I know she wasn't fussy about me coming up to the house to read to Esther. But Esther had a pretty strong will of her own and there were a number of rows between them. Then Mr. Easterbrook, who was always in the middle, worked out this arrangement whereby instead of coming up to the house, I would spend a couple of afternoons pushing Esther's chair around the block.

While I did this Esther read poetry aloud, which sometimes embarrassed me, for she put a lot of feeling into the words and people would often stare and smile behind their hands. It was an ignorant thing to do, but then the sight of someone reciting poetry from a wheelchair on a city street might be considered amusing. When Esther wasn't reciting verses she'd remark on things that most people would ignore. For instance, she'd see a little sparrow hopping about on the road pecking at a horsebun. And she'd say, "I wonder if that poor little creature will survive the winter? Where will he sleep when the snow comes? Oh, Billy! Life is so cruel, isn't it!" That's what poetry and fine thoughts did to her. Made her imagination morbid and colored everything gray. I'd try to cheer her up by asking what lay ahead for dinner, but she was never very interested in food.

Now I don't want to suggest that Esther Easterbrook was all sad sweetness. She had a good Scotch temper as well and sometimes when she argued with her mother she could screech with the best of them.

8. *The Other Side*

Usually after those fights I'd be asked to hitch up the little mare and take Esther for a drive up in the country north of Bloor Street. She'd sit there fanning herself and not saying a word until we got nearly home and then she'd brighten and be good-natured again. Her health seemed to improve with these outings. She'd get more color in her face. Mr. Easterbrook was so happy that he raised my wages by a dollar a month. He was devoted to that girl and would have done anything to please her.

Easterbrook was considered one of Toronto's most respectable citizens and so it came as a surprise to me when I discovered that he led a double life. About a week before Christmas Wilson gave me the afternoon off to shop for presents. It was a Wednesday and towards evening as I walked along King Street west, enjoying the sight of people shopping and listening to the harness bells of the horses, I spotted Mr. Easterbrook. I could tell his big, broad-shouldered walk anywhere, and there he was ahead of me, walking briskly through this light snowfall. Knowing it was his club night, I found myself curious to find out just what sort of place he shot billiards in and closed business deals. The truth is that Easterbrook had become something of an idol to me. I strongly admired the way he carried himself and wore his fine clothes and seemed so certain of everything. He appeared to be a good person to model myself on, for I was beginning to entertain ideas of becoming a businessman myself. I didn't exactly know what sort of business I was going to get into but I was damn certain that I wasn't going to spend the rest of my life rubbing down horses and shoveling snow. So I followed Mr. Easterbrook, keeping a safe distance behind.

After a few blocks he turned into a side street and went down this little lane to a row of houses. They weren't down-at-the-heels by any means, but neither were they the sort of dwellings you'd expect a man like Easterbrook to frequent. Still, he went up the steps of one of them and knocked softly at the door with a gloved hand. By now I was across the street in an alleyway. When the door opened Easterbrook doffed his hat and walked in. The door closed and a blind was pulled down. It struck me as peculiar, for I'd expected his club to have a fancy entrance with a doorman. So I nipped across the street and up the steps for a better look. There was a little crack where the blind didn't cover and it was just enough for me to see. And what I saw was Mr. Easterbrook being helped out of his overcoat and pecked on the cheek by Mrs. Fletcher.

9

SALLY BUTTERS

THERE'S NO USE saying I wasn't startled. In fact, at the sight of Mrs. Fletcher I nearly fell over the iron railings on those steps. It was all I could do to get back across the street to the alleyway, where I stood hunched against a building trying to keep warm and make sense of life. And here's a strange thing! All the time I'd been living with the Gillies and the Easterbrooks I'd been as chaste as a hairshirt monk, with only a thought now and then for the pleasures of the flesh. My feelings towards Esther Easterbrook, for example, were pure and brotherly. But just a glimpse of Mrs. Fletcher reaching up to peck Mr. Easterbrook's cheek and I was aflame with desire, as they used to say in those trashy romances. And from what I could see before she disappeared behind a door with Easterbrook, Mrs. Fletcher was taking care of herself. She looked a bit slimmer but she was still a fine figure of a woman in her long poplin skirt and white blouse. Her dark red hair was pinned up behind, in the style of the day.

Well, I waited in the alley beating my hands against my sides to keep warm. Then I noticed an upstairs light come on and just as quickly go out. It stopped snowing and the coldness just leaked right into your bones. A couple of minutes standing in one position and you stiffened up like a board. I nearly went to sleep and might have froze to death except I heard a church bell tolling off the hours. Finally the upstairs light came on again and maybe ten minutes later the front door opened and Easterbrook came out. He didn't waste time but moved down the steps quickly, turning just once to nod to Mrs. Fletcher, who was standing in the doorway wearing a kimono. Her hair was down around her shoulders, just as she wore it when she visited my bed back in Craven Falls.

God Almighty, I was jealous! Even recognizing what a fine gentleman Easterbrook was, I hated him at that moment. Mrs. Fletcher too. Oh, I had a great store of ill will for her. Yet I think I would probably have committed a score of crimes for one kiss from her. And this was the woman I'd turned my back on months before! All you can say is that the human male acts crazy ninety percent of the time and I'm no exception. At the same time I was sorely tempted to walk across the street and knock on that door. I had visions of giving Mrs. Fletcher a couple of jolts on the jaw while reminding her that I didn't want any more fooling around with other men. Fortunately I came to my senses and realized that this wasn't the right time for an appearance by me. Standing in her doorway, frozen-arsed and half swallowed up in an oversized, out-of-fashion overcoat would only make me look ridiculous. Instead, I followed Easterbrook. He was a cagy adulterer, and waited until he got to King Street before he hailed a cab. I went on home by foot and nearly perished with the cold.

Since I only spent money on tobacco I had managed to save a few dollars by then, so next day I went downtown to a haberdasher's and got myself outfitted in a new three-button cutaway black worsted suit with a Venetian finish, the latest thing in those days. I also bought a soft-collar shirt with cravat and stick pin, a new pair of boots, an overcoat and a derby. It cleaned me out but it was worth it, for dressed in those clothes I didn't look like any stable hand. Like my father, I had an awful lot of pride and vanity in those times. When Wilson saw me he just shook his head. "Spending all your hard-earned money on clothes. It's a mistake, Billy. Next thing you'll start giving yourself airs and forget your position in life."

I laughed at that and said, "You don't call this a position, do you? Cleaning horseshit out of stalls? You don't think I'm going to settle for this, do you?" And right off I was sorry I put it that way, for maybe I wouldn't be cleaning stalls for the rest of my life but it was certain that Wilson would be, and he knew it too. He didn't say anything but just turned and walked away. And I wasn't big enough to apologize.

The fact is that I was turning bad-tempered and hard to get along with. Even Esther remarked on this during one of our walks. I was growing crabby and short with her and this in turn soured her humor. And that was a shame, because aside from the conflicts she had with her mother, Esther had a pretty reasonable disposition. But this afternoon, the day before Christmas, there were tears in her eyes when she said to me, "I don't know what's got into you lately but you're being perfectly horrid. Please take me home at once."

"All right, I will," I says like a spoiled brat.

I can see now, of course, that the poisons of lust and jealousy were eating at me. It was even a chore to work up the decency to wish people a Merry Christmas.

On Christmas Day the Easterbrooks had this tradition whereby after morning church service the servants and hired help went to the house as guests. While the family had their Christmas meal in the dining room with silver cutlery and china plates, etc., etc., we sat at this big board table in a room near the kitchen. It had been decorated with a Christmas tree, upon which were perched several lighted candles. And there were red paper bells and banners strung across the ceiling. It's a wonder houses like the Easterbrooks' weren't burned to the ground around Christmas. The cook roasted two geese in the big wood range and in general prepared two servings of everything. We got exactly the same feed as the Easterbrooks, right down to the pickles and relish, the only difference being that we ate it off cheaper dishes and in more humble surroundings. There must have been twelve of us, with one or two of the girls leaving now and then to serve in the dining room. There was an awful lot of chatter, of course, because the room was loaded with females except for Wilson and me and the butler Harrison, who was about eighty and deaf in one ear. I was decked out in my new clothes and a couple of the maids were giving me the eye but I was too sulky and miserable to respond.

After dinner we went into the drawing room, where a big fire crackled in the hearth. There we received our presents. I believe I got a comb. We were then served a piece of cake and a glass of punch, non-alcoholic of course. The Easterbrooks themselves did the serving, the idea being that for one hour of the year they would wait upon the help. So we all stood around feeling awkward and eating this cake and drinking this fruit punch which might have been a decent drink if you'd added a half-gallon of whiskey. It was comical, though, to watch Mrs. Easterbrook attending to the servants. It was plain that if she had her way this part of Christmas would be forgotten. She just looked uncomfortable mingling with us lesser mortals. Easterbrook, however, seemed to enjoy it, or at least if he didn't, he wasn't letting on. He walked around the room, straight and handsome, taking empty glasses from the blushing maids and trying to make people feel at ease. I read once where a fellow defined a gentleman as the man who makes the least number of people in a room uncomfortable. Well, by that definition, Easterbrook was a true gentleman. And watching him, I got over my anger. As I looked at Mrs. Easterbrook I could understand why her husband would find Mrs. Fletcher relaxing. There were two or three relatives there helping with the cake and punch. There was one old geezer, Esther's great-uncle. I don't think he had all his buttons, for he went around embarrassing the maids by whispering in their ears and pinching their backsides. All this time he had his dinner napkin tucked in around his throat.

By and by I found myself standing next to Esther's chair. I could tell she was admiring me in my new clothes and finally she reached out and took my hand. "Billy," she says, "I've got a present for you but don't open it here because Mother doesn't know." And she gave me this little package. Then I reached inside my suit coat and withdrew my present for her. "It's a book, isn't it?" she says, looking up at me with tears in her eyes. She looked so attractive sitting there in her starched white blouse and new skirt with this red ribbon in her hair that I just squeezed her hand and felt all the meanness in me depart. Mr. Easterbrook then read the Christmas story from the Bible and his wife sat down on the piano bench and began to play carols. Everybody joined in the sing-along but me, for I'm no singer. But Esther had a sweet little voice and I can still hear her warbling "Good King Wenceslas." We'd positioned ourselves near the heavy curtains at the rear of the room behind everyone else. After a bit Esther tugged my arm and drew me down towards her. Her hot breath smelled like cinnamon toast.

"You're in a better humor today!" she says.

"Yes, I'm all right."

"Then kiss me," she says.

"Right here?" I whispers. "Are you crazy, Esther?"

"Yes," she says. "And happy too!" And she closed her eyes and puckered up in the strangest fashion. I don't believe she'd ever been kissed in a romantic way before. So I kissed her right there in the drawing room and I suppose if Mrs. Easterbrook had turned around at that moment I'd have found myself out on the street, Christmas or no Christmas.

The party was over by late afternoon and we all returned to our quarters, where I opened my present. It was a gold-plated penknife with my initials on it, a handsome little thing which became a valued keepsake until I lost it one night during a scuffle in a boxcar in the state of Missouri. But that was over thirty years later. Now after that party I was so restless that I just couldn't sit still. So after a while I put on my overcoat and went out, telling myself that I was just going for a stroll. But knowing full well that I was following my feet to that house off King Street.

A half-hour later I was standing in the alleyway looking across at this house which was all ablaze with light. At least she's home, I says to myself, brushing away these big lazy snowflakes that had started to drift down and dampen my hat. I stood there for about ten minutes wondering what to do, when the front door opened and *two men, total strangers,* stepped out. It was growing dark and I couldn't see too well but they both looked middle-aged and very smartly dressed. One was a little the worse for drink and he was propped up by the other fellow as they walked along the street. Well, damn me, I says to myself, she's even entertaining them on Christmas Day! So I started to work up this terrible rage. For maybe ten minutes I stood there making imaginary statements such as "How dare you carry on like this?" Or "I've a good mind to skin your hide. Now get in that bedroom and get your clothes off, because I'm going to give you a good ——ing. Then we'll talk about these other men friends of yours." After giving her proper hell in my head I knocked the snow off my hat and walked across the street.

Through the curtains I could see her pouring a drink. She was still wearing the poplin skirt and lace blouse and she had her hair up too. The place didn't look badly furnished, though it seemed bare in spots as though the premises had not been lived in long. I hesitated and then knocked. It was so weak that I could see she hadn't heard it, so I hammered a little harder. She was about to leave the room when she heard my knock. Then she turned and came towards the door frowning. Watching her, I softened up a little. Perhaps I won't be too hard on her, I says to myself. She's had a hard life, when you take everything into consideration. She's entitled to a little weakness. Actually over the past week I'd puzzled a good deal over which approach I should take when we finally met. I favored the tough talk because it seemed more like justice to me. On the other hand a casual, off-hand greeting might impress her as more civilized and grown-up. I could say something like "My, my, what a coincidence!" or perhaps "Fancy meeting you here!"

Well, I was thinking over these matters when she opened the door. I snatched the hat from my head and said not a word. Mrs. Fletcher stood there with her hands on her hips looking at me before saying, "And who the hell are you?"

"Why," I says, "it's me. Bill Farthing!"

She leaned forward for a closer look. "Well, for Christ's sakes," she says. "If it isn't the little runaway himself. What are you doing here, anyway? And close that door, you're letting in a draft."

So I went through the doorway and stood in the middle of this little sitting room fingering my derby and trying to think of something to say. Mrs. F. poured herself another drink and belted it back. I was wishing she'd offer me one, because my nerves weren't all they might be.

Mrs. Fletcher shook her head. "Well, this is something! Sit down and take a load off, kid!" She herself sat down and hiked one leg over the other like a man. "So you flew the coop, eh! Well, you don't look like you done too bad for yourself. Course a good-looking young fellow like you ought to be able to make his own way. What line are you in, anyways?"

"How's Mr. Fletcher?" I croaked.

She only laughed at that. "Same as ever, I guess. Who knows? I haven't seen him since last spring. I left right after you. And don't get any ideas that I was heartbroken and chasing you. Mary Jane Hinks doesn't chase any man, let alone a peach fuzz kid." That comment smarted, for I had been trying without success to cultivate a moustache for the past few weeks. Then Mrs. Fletcher said, "You owe me twenty-nine dollars, by the way. That sneak-thief stuff doesn't sit too well with me. I got friends in this town and I can make it tough for you. So you'd best consider paying your debts."

Now, I've never liked threats and I recovered enough of my tongue to tell her so. I also helped myself to a good slug of her whiskey and experienced a general loosening up. "These friends of yours," I says. "Are you sure they're your friends, or might they just be customers?"

At this she let go another bark of laughter. "Say! Ain't you grown into the saucy little bugger? Well, never mind then. I was bloody cross with you there for a few weeks for leaving me. You hurt my pride, kid.

76

9. Sally Butters

But I'm willing to let bygones be bygones. Do you ever hear from your father? By God, he was a sweet-looking man! And so mannerly!"

I poured myself another drink and listened while Mrs. Fletcher told me of how she arrived in the city and looked up one of her old business associates. She worked there for a while until she acquired some of her own customers. And these customers were respectable gents too. None of your general riffraff got past her door. Still, she confessed to being tired of this life and she longed for a change. Some peace and quiet. You have to understand that the woman was what they call a compulsive talker. She just wouldn't shut up once she got on the subject of herself. All this time, of course, I was desiring her in a carnal manner but she just wasn't interested. She complained about not being the woman she used to be. "Too many gents, Bill. And too much of this stuff," she said, holding up her glass. "God, I'd like to settle into something respectable. If only Fletcher hadn't been such a creepy old devil. Nattering all day about the wages of sin. And that damn town was so far away from everything. Well, never mind," she says, squeezing my knee. "It's good to see you again, kid. Mary Jane never holds a grudge for long." She yawned in my face. "I'm tired right now. But come on Thursday after nine and you can have one on the house. For old times' sake." And before I could retrieve my hat from the chair she had settled back her head and was sound asleep and snoring.

Thus began a period in my life when, like Mr. Easterbrook, I led a double existence, working in a respectable Christian household six days a week and visiting Mrs. Fletcher every Thursday night without fail. I never told her about working for Easterbrook or even knowing him. As far as she was concerned, I was private secretary to a wealthy brewer. I didn't tell her the truth for two reasons. In the first place, since I'd read a few books and was always dressed up when I called on her, she had it in her head that I was getting on in the world. I didn't want her to know that I was just a stable hand. Secondly, I was afraid that if she did know, she might decide to blackmail Easterbrook. Mrs. Fletcher was awful greedy for money and I could imagine her proposing something dangerous. Besides, I liked Easterbrook. He was always a fair man to deal with. And I liked him because he was so fond of Esther and took such pains with her.

And Esther wasn't faring too well either. Being frail to begin with, the cold and the damp just sank into her frame and stayed there all winter. A good part of the time she was in bed with bad colds. That winter the doctor's carriage was parked in the Easterbrooks' driveway two or three times a week. Of course, taking her for walks was out of the question, so it was decided, against Mrs. Easterbrook's judgment, that I'd come up to the house and spend an hour with Esther every day. I was glad of this, because the winter was a slow time and there wasn't much to do except shovel snow now and again and feed and water the horses. So I was glad to go up and read and talk to Esther. I can still picture her, sitting up in bed with that pale hair spread across the pillow and her face a bit waxen from being indoors so much. The air in that room was stale with liniment and mustard plasters. Sometimes if she was feeling a little perky, Esther would ask me to stop reading and, giving me a sly look, ask, "When are you going to kiss me again, Billy?" So I'd fool around a little bit, telling her she was much too dainty a flower to be plucked. Or I might imitate that Heathcliff in the novel *Wuthering Heights* and pretend that I might ravish her at any moment. She loved that sort of nonsense.

Yet as much as I enjoyed those hours with Esther, I was growing more and more restless. There wasn't any future in the stable, and while Thursday nights were a nice break from Wilson's stories about army life, I was looking for something else. I was itching to be doing something, though just what I couldn't have told you. However, I knew this much. Once spring arrived I intended to travel, though just exactly where I couldn't decide. Then, one Thursday night in early March, my whole life changed. I saw exactly what I wanted to do. And what I wanted to do was get down on my knees and worship at the feet of the most beautiful woman who ever breathed air on this godforsaken planet. I'm referring, of course, to Sally Butters, and this is how she entered my life.

On this particular Thursday evening I called on Mrs. Fletcher as usual and I found her showing off a new mutton-sleeved satin dress. She looked so pleased with herself as she paced about the sitting room that at first I thought she'd come into some money. She was always talking about the promises made to her by some of her gentlemen friends. Then she told me we were going out. An old friend, Clara Bishop, was in town with this vaudeville show and had dropped by that afternoon leaving two complimentary tickets. Mrs. Fletcher felt like a night out and suggested I go as her nephew. At first I wasn't keen, because it was a dirty night with sleet and rain in the air. Then too I was eager for my weekly screw, for which Mrs. Fletcher was charging me fifty cents, this payment applied against the twenty-nine dollars I owed her. But to humor her I went along to this vaudeville show, which was performed at the old Bijou Theater.

We had pretty good seats up near the front and we watched a variety of acts and performers, some of which got wildly cheered and others of which got lambasted by an audience made up mostly of men, though there was a sprinkling of women too. One of the most interesting things was the Edison Motograph, and I remember it showed the knockout round of the Corbett-Courtney fight. It flickered a good deal and pained the eyes but you got the general idea. Then there was a fellow who spun a bunch of dishes on the end of a wooden rod which he stuck on his nose. I thought that was a pretty good trick. Then a pair of jokers with charcoal on their faces came on the stage with a sawhorse and stood around telling jokes about how lazy black people are supposed to be. Nearly everybody got a hoot out of that. Following them was this tall fellow and he got nowhere with his speeches from the plays of William Shakespeare. I thought he cut a good figure too, standing there with his hands on his lapels and this big rich voice booming through the hall. However, Mrs. Fletcher and me were about the only persons paying any attention to him. There were soon hisses and catcalls and I believe he cut his performance, for he left in quite a huff and was immediately followed by a couple of dwarfs beating on a bass drum. They set up a series of hoops and chased some yapping dogs through them, blowing horns and firing blanks from a revolver. After this there were some chorus girls who kicked up their legs and showed off their bloomers and got a good hand from the crowd.

Then the acetylene footlights were dimmed and the star of the show appeared. She was written up in the advertising handbill as "Sally Butters, the Belle of the Boards" and she stepped out on stage in this long white dress with this beautiful red hair tucked under a broad-brimmed hat. She twirled a little parasol as she walked. And when she started to sing "Beautiful Dreamer," you could have heard a pin drop in that theater. As for me, you might as well have dropped a hundred-pound bag of wet sand on my head and kicked me downstairs, for looking up at Sally Butters, I went so weak in the knees that I thought I'd pass out. Not being a professional author and at the distance of over seventy years, I can't be expected to do justice to the beauty of that woman as she walked about on the stage of the Bijou Theater in March of '97. I'll only say that looking at her and listening to her sent shivers down my neck and up the backs of my legs. She seemed to have not only the natural sweet innocence of Esther Easterbrook but at the same time a kind of lurking sexiness that I would normally associate with the likes of Mrs. Fletcher.

After she finished her song the audience went crazy. That's the only word for it. Men jumped up on seats and stamped their feet and cheered. One poor fellow in the row next to me just stood straight up and crowed like a rooster with his head thrown back and only the whites of his eyes showing. Then he fell to the floor and foamed at the mouth. Of course he could have been an epileptic overcome by the excitement of the hour, because some friends hustled him away in a hurry. But it's not beyond believing that he was just bewitched by the beauty of Sally Butters. As for me I just sat there, pole-axed by natural beauty. Mrs. Fletcher couldn't see why everybody was making such a fuss, because to her the Shakespearean had put on twice the act. So while the crowd was settling back for Sally's next number Mrs. Fletcher leaned across and told me we were going. Naturally I was distressed to learn this, but she insisted. She told me this Clara Bishop had invited us backstage and didn't I want to see how show folks lived? She said we'd better get there before all the admirers and hangers-on arrived.

I thought it was ignorant to leave in the middle of a singer's act but that's what we did, going backstage along some narrow corridors where all sorts of people were standing about or sitting in their underwear on upturned nail kegs. There were several men in clown costumes and some half-naked women strolling about. The Shakesperean scholar was arguing with one of the dwarfs and the dogs were barking, until somebody threw a shoe at them. It was a regular bear garden back there, and by the fire door there were stacks of flowers and boxes of candy, all destined for Sally Butters. Mrs. Fletcher showed our pass to a skinny little guy in shirtsleeves and he took us down this hallway and knocked on the door. It was opened by a hefty blonde in her middle years. She greeted Mrs. Fletcher like a long lost friend and in we went to this room which smelled of face powder and sweat. There was a couple of seats and a dresser with a mirror and this Chinese screen which had various ladies' undergarments hanging over the top.

Mrs. Fletcher introduced me as her nephew and on hearing this Clara Bishop just threw back her head and laughed. "Oh my God, Mary Jane," she says, wiping her eyes. "You have all the luck when it comes to relatives. This afternoon an uncle and this evening a nephew. Would they be on your mother's side of the family or your father's? By God, I think I'm gonna wet my drawers." And she started to laugh so hard that Mrs. Fletcher soon joined in and I had to smile too. Then Clara Bishop opened a bottle of gin and we each had a few good pulls to keep the dampness out of our bones. Mrs. F. and Clara Bishop sat down and began to jaw about old times; the same stuff about how great things used to be. I sat in an armchair with my feet up, helping myself to the gin and trying to appear sophisticated with my hat pulled down over my eyes. I made it clear that I wasn't interested in any old ladies' reminiscences.

After a few minutes the door flew open and Sally Butters herself breezed in, stopping in the doorway to blow a kiss to some joker who was trying to press flowers on her. She took the flowers and pushed his hand out and closed the door. Naturally I jumped to my feet and plucked off my derby. I suddenly felt like a country hick. My fancy clothes seemed to be just general-store issue and appeared to be shrinking on my frame. Sally Butters was even more beautiful at close hand, and these big blue eyes were smiling at me. When Clara Bishop made the introductions Sally just ignored Mrs. F. and said in this soft musical voice, "I'm greatly pleased to make your acquaintance, Billy Farthing." And all I could do was stand there like a school kid, gawking and trying to get my voice out of my Adam's apple. I'd always thought of Mrs. Fletcher as a good-looking woman but alongside Sally Butters she seemed plain drab. Mrs. Fletcher was listening to Clara Bishop with only one ear. Mostly she was trying to catch what Sally was saying to me and in her eyes was a look which seemed to say "And you just wait. Twenty years from now and you'll have had your day too."

But Sally just ignored her and flounced off behind this Chinese screen, where I soon heard these rustling sounds and then some undergarments were flung across the top. Clara Bishop passed over a peach-colored dressing gown and a second or two later Sally emerged tying

9. Sally Butters

this robe. She came straight over and sat down on this bench next to me. Now all the time she had been in the room, I hadn't mumbled more than two words. However, after a half-dozen more swallows of gin I recovered some heart, so when Sally asked me how I liked her performance I found the words to tell her that it was far and away the finest singing I'd yet encountered in my lifetime. Overhearing this, Mrs. Fletcher snorted but I just went on to praise Sally's act. Having inherited the gift of the gab from my father, I found it easy to tell the girl what a wonderful singer she was. Sally just sat there, canted over with her elbows on her knees and the front of her dressing gown partially open so I caught a middling view of her bosom, and she didn't seem to mind me looking either, though she wasn't in the least brazen. I judged her to be about my age, though she seemed a good deal more worldly. This was understandable, since she told me that she had been singing professionally since the age of six and had traveled all over the United States and Canada. She was eager to know about my life too. What did I do for a living? Did I have a girlfriend? Did I enjoy going out in the evenings with my aunt?

We must have talked for half an hour and then it got too much for Mrs. Fletcher. She didn't even try to conceal her bad humor when she suggested we be on our way. Sally got up and went to this bouquet of roses on the dresser. She took one of the flowers and came back and handed it to me. "We'll be in town till Saturday night, Billy," she says. "Then we go on to New York City. Maybe you'd like to take me to an ice cream parlor tomorrow afternoon. That is, if your auntie doesn't mind." My face was aflame and I didn't even glance at Mrs. Fletcher before saying that I'd look forward to taking her to the Palm Room of McConkey's Restaurant for tea. McConkey's was the smartest restaurant in Toronto at the time and it was where all the sophisticated young lovers had their assignations. So Sally told me to ask for her at the front desk of the hotel the next day at four o'clock, and I walked out of that room on air. I simply couldn't believe my good fortune. This was a girl probably desired by hundreds of men all over North America! And she wanted me to spend an afternoon with her!

In the carriage Mrs. Fletcher was in a terrible temper and I wasn't feeling any too sociable either. Outside her door we stood in the slush and argued. "How dare you humiliate me like that?" she asks. "Making calf eyes at that little tart."

"Mind your tongue now. Miss Butters is no tart."

"My royal arse she isn't. I'll bet she's had more of it than I have."

"That's hard to believe."

"It's all over her face."

"Takes one to know one."

"Don't you be saucing me, young Mr. Farthing. You've become quite the little swell since you've been in Toronto. Quite the little fancy gent about town. Well, maybe you'd like to start paying the regular fare like the other gentlemen. From now on it's two dollars and I'd like the balance of your debt in advance. By next Thursday." I just turned and walked away. When I got to the corner I looked back. Mrs. Fletcher was still standing in the doorway. "Clara's told me all about that little buttered bun," she shouted. "You'll learn the hard way." I walked on, too excited even to think about the rain that was soaking me through to the skin.

It was late when I got back to the stable but I heard Wilson up and about in his room, so I knocked on his door and walked in. He was in his nightshirt preparing for bed and I suppose I startled him, for he looked at me sharply. "Well, you're keeping fine hours these nights," he says.

"Wilson," I says, crossing the room and sitting on the edge of his bed. "Listen to my news. Tomorrow I'm having tea at McConkey's with the most beautiful girl you've ever laid eyes on." And I proceeded to tell him about my evening at the theater.

When I got to the part about meeting Sally at four o'clock the next afternoon, Wilson held up his hand and said, "Wait now. Hold on a minute. Let's just hold our horses here. In case you've forgotten, you've got a job here, Bill. Now you may not think it's much of a job, because lately you've had some bloody fancy ideas about who you are and what you're here for. But this here job is what keeps you off the street. It keeps food in your guts and it keeps those fancy clothes on your backside. Now you can come into my room in the middle of the night and sit on my bed and tell me what a great ladies' man you've become. You can do all that if you like, Billy boy! But don't tell me that you're going to meet any lady at four o'clock tomorrow afternoon, because you've got a job around here, hard as that may be to live with. And tomorrow, I'm planning to get the summer rigs ready for the fine weather. So I'd be very surprised if you didn't have a paintbrush in your hand come four o'clock."

"Now look, Wilson," I says. "Try to be reasonable. This girl is beautiful beyond your wildest dreams. Men go crazy over her. They line up at the stage door to give her presents. And now she's invited me to spend the afternoon with her. And you want me to paint buggies?"

"I do," says Wilson firmly. "Not only want you to paint buggies but bloody well insist that you paint buggies."

"You're being unreasonable," I says, getting hot under the collar.

"I don't think so," says Wilson, agitated himself now and striding around the room in this striped nightshirt. "And since the subject's come up," he says, "we might as well talk about it. Something's happened to you in the last few months, Bill. I don't know what it is but I don't like it. In a few words, you've become too big for your britches. Even little Esther, bless her heart, notices it and wonders what's got into you. And she thinks the world of you too. You used to show her a little kindness now and again. But it seems you've become too busy, dressing up in your fancy clothes and playing the dandy."

9. Sally Butters

"I don't want to hear any more of this," I says. "I'm going to bed. And I'm taking tomorrow afternoon off too."

"Well, you do that, mister," says Wilson. "Just do it. And maybe there won't be a job waiting for you when you get home."

"Maybe," says I, "this isn't exactly what I call home." And I slammed the door and went to my room and lay on the bed for the longest time before falling into a restless sleep.

The next morning Wilson didn't say a word to me while we fed the horses and cleaned out the stalls. God Almighty, I hate working alongside someone who gives me the deep freeze. But that's the way it went all morning. Along about noon I skipped dinner and instead heated two buckets of water and unwrapped a bar of perfumed soap I'd been saving. I gave myself a good scrubbing, for I wanted to make sure there wasn't a trace of horse smell on my person. By the time Wilson returned from his meal I was dressed and practicing how to stroll about casually with a walking stick, an instrument I'd lately acquired but hadn't been game enough to use. However, I thought it would make a good impression on Sally, so I was giving it a few twirls in front of the horses.

"My, my," says Wilson, standing in the doorway and holding a couple of paintbrushes. "Aren't we grand today?" I said nothing to that but flicked a speck of dust from my boot. "And are you still going to defy my orders and spend the afternoon with that tramp then?" he asks.

"Watch your language, old man," I says. "I'm seeing a lady."

"I'll have to speak to the guv'nor about this."

"Well, speak to him then," I says. And I stepped past him and walked briskly across the grass.

It was a fine spring day, with the sunlight pouring down through the bare branches of the trees and only patches of snow here and there against the fences. By the front drive I saw Esther. She'd just been wheeled out by Harrison and when she saw me she waved in an excited fashion. I couldn't pretend I didn't see her.

"Billy!" she cried as I walked over. "What a wonderful day! And now we can have our walks again! I'm feeling fine." Then she noticed how smartly attired I was and she remarked, "Why, Billy! What's the occasion? And you're carrying a stick? Are you going to court me, then? Oh, I do hope so. It will be great fun. But your intentions must be honorable."

She wanted to play our old games, you see, but all I said was, "I'm afraid I can't take you for a walk today, Esther."

She pouted at this and said, "Why ever not, may I ask?"

"Because, Miss Esther," says Wilson, charging across the grass towards us. "Because his little lordship here is spending the afternoon with a burlesque queen. That's why."

Esther turned pale at the news and then looked down at the book in her lap, my Christmas present to her. "I didn't know," she says meekly.

"Oh, yes indeed," says Wilson. "Our friend here has got himself a little dish of trifle downtown. And now he don't want to work for a living."

"I think I've heard quite enough, Wilson," says Esther, still looking down at her lap. "Please take me inside at once."

"Right away, Miss Esther," says Wilson, glaring at me and turning the wheelchair around.

I didn't say anything, for there wasn't much I could say. Wilson had said it all, though it came out in a crude way that was bound to be misunderstood. I figure Wilson just didn't understand the depth of Esther's feelings towards me. But I remember saying to myself, Well, the hell with all this, anyway. Nobody's going to ruin this day on me. I'm going to have the time of my life. But there's no denying the incident had put a crimp in my good humor, such as it was.

I took my time, because I didn't want to appear *gauche* by showing up too early. But it was a warm day for March and my suit was just too heavy for the weather. I'd taken off my winter underwear but I was still perspiring when I arrived at the theater. I didn't go directly to the hotel, because I was still an hour early and I thought I'd spend a few minutes looking over the posters, which had large photographic reproductions of Sally. Then I thought I'd buy a ticket for that night's performance. When I arrived in front of the theater, however, a workman with a long brush and a bucket was sticking up a new poster. Sally's picture was gone and in its place was this advertisement for a temperance meeting to be held that night. Standing on the sidewalk admiring this was a tall fellow in black and two middle-aged women, one stout and one thin and both dressed for a funeral. When the man turned and smiled at me I could see by his collar that he was a preacher. The women had the same pickle faces and thin mouths that I remembered on Miss Boswell.

"Where's the vaudeville show?" I asks, putting on an innocent face. "I've just arrived in town and I've been told it's a first-rate piece of entertainment."

The preacher closed his eyes and looked to the sky. "Thank the Lord," he says. "You've been saved from a degrading experience, my boy. The sinful exhibition to which you refer has been closed down by a special meeting of the city council."

"They were sent packing," says the stout woman, thrusting out a jaw that looked like a stone ax.

The preacher touched my coat sleeve. "I implore you, my boy, not to let the evils of the city corrupt you. Come to the meeting tonight. Hear me speak on the evils of drink."

"For the drunkard and the glutton shall come to poverty," says the other woman, a scarecrow.

Well, you might as well have hit me in the chest with a mallet. "Has the troupe left town, then?" I asks, mopping my brow with my tie.

"We are not acquainted with the comings and goings of low characters," says ax jaw.

9. Sally Butters

"I beseech you, my boy," says the preacher, thrusting a pamphlet into my hand. "The doors open at seven. It's only a silver collection."

Well, I hurried away of course, almost running to the hotel. I went right to the room clerk, a breed of men I've never been overly fond of because of their tendency to rudeness and spite. This joker was no exception. He was a skinny little blond fellow with a brocade vest and a lot of pomade on his hair. He was chewing a toothpick and reading the paper, looking bored like they all do. I asked him politely if he wouldn't mind ringing up Miss Butters' room and telling her that Mr. Farthing was waiting in the lobby. He didn't seem to hear me, so I asked him again. Then, without bothering to look up, he muttered, "Not here anymore."

"But she asked me to come around at four o'clock," I says.

"You and every other stage rat in town," he replies, working that toothpick around and still not looking up.

"Well, I wonder," I asks, "whether you'd be kind enough to tell me where Miss Butters and her friends have gone?"

He looked at me for a moment and I could see a mouthful of rotten teeth. His breath was bad enough to warp a door. "This ain't no information center," he says, and goes back to his paper.

By now I was fairly wrought up. Everything had gone sour for me. I had Mrs. Fletcher, Wilson, and Esther Easterbrook all mad at me and for nothing. So this insolent bastard appeared to be just the right sort of person to take out my feelings on. Besides, I was bigger and healthier-looking than him. So I grabbed him by the shirt collar. That surprised him, and a bunch of buttons came off in my hand.

"Listen, you wormy little bastard," I says. "When you talk to me, you look at me, though personally I could do without your ugly face. But right now I'm asking a question. And I'll repeat it once more. Where did Miss Butters and her friends go?"

I was choking him pretty hard and he was turning a little green at the side whiskers. Which could have been because he'd swallowed the toothpick. But he croaked out, "They took the train for New York City."

I let him go and turned and walked out. On the sidewalk by the entrance I bent over and puked up some green poison. Then I bought a bottle of whiskey and looked for a hole to hide in.

10

AMERICA

LIKE MY FATHER, I had a pretty good appetite for alcohol and I could see the attractions of hiding behind a bottle of whiskey after meeting with disappointment. And nobody was more disappointed than me after hearing that Sally Butters had left town. I wasn't fit to do anything constructive, and so for the next few days I just sat up in my room rolling cigarettes and drinking whiskey. And you have to remember that I still hadn't seen my seventeenth birthday. Through the window I watched Esther sitting in her wheelchair in the sunlight or when it rained or was cold she'd be by her window, glancing up from her book now and again to look over my way. We hadn't said a word to one another since that terrible afternoon. I felt sorry for her. I felt sorry for myself. I felt sorry for the whole damn world and when the air smelled softly of rain and damp earth I felt like crying. Of course, you must understand that I was in love and about all I could do was sit in a chair or lie in my bed trying to conjure up every detail of Sally's face. Now in spite of his talk Wilson didn't inform Mr. Easterbrook of my eccentric behavior. Maybe Esther warned him against making trouble. Or maybe he just sensed I had some grievance against the world and wanted to be left alone for a while.

I spent about a week in this dissipated state before I decided to do something about it. Now maybe I did the wrong thing in running away that Sunday afternoon. But it doesn't do a particle of good to look back and say I should have done this or I should have done that. You're just stuck with what you make up your mind to do. And I made up my mind on this particular Sunday to catch the next train for New York City and find Sally Butters and tell her I loved her. At the time it seemed the only sensible course to take. It came to me about the middle of the afternoon. Wilson had driven the Easterbrooks over to some family's for a Sunday visit. I threw some underwear and stuff into a small black bag and then sat down and wrote a letter to Esther. Or I should say, I tried to write a letter to Esther, for I made several stabs at it, tearing them up one after the other. I finally got something down, the gist of which was that I had greatly enjoyed knowing a lady and that I wished her luck but I had to move on because I was looking for my father. That was a lie, of course, though not a full lie, for in the back of my head I still thought my father and me might cross paths. I put this letter in an envelope and sealed it and left it in Wilson's room with instructions to pass it on.

As I wandered about Wilson's room I envied him his life more or less. There were his polished boots all standing in a row. And in his dresser drawers were his shirts, all starched and waiting to be worn. He had a little desk and everything on it, pen, inkwell, Bible, a book of Kipling's poetry, a tin of leather polish, it was all lined up like a parade square. Wilson knew where the hell his place in the general line-up was! While me, I was like a fellow running up and down the line, not knowing whether to jump in at the front, the middle, or the end. As Wilson put it, I didn't know my place, and he was right.

Well, I took my time poking around his room and I suppose I was hoping someone would come along and talk me out of leaving. But nobody did and I wandered around opening cupboard doors and desk drawers. In one drawer I noticed some money. In Wilson's orderly way there were bundles of bills in various denominations, all secured by rubber bands. There were stacks of coins as well. It looked exactly like a bank teller's drawer. I was somewhat low in funds, so I withdrew ten dollars, figuring to send Wilson back the money with maybe a buck for interest after I got a job in New York City. I never did, by the way, and I mention it here only to illustrate another kind of morality mustered up by people when they're stealing. Then I picked up my valise and headed downtown for the train station.

The New York train left at eight o'clock, and after I'd paid for my ticket I only had a buck or two left over for eats. I was now a good deal more worldly, even though this was only my second train ride. So when the gates opened I was there first in line and got myself a good seat facing the head of the train. And like an experienced traveler I sat there with my legs crossed and my hands sunk in my pockets and my hat tilted down over my eyes. And sitting there I thought what a good idea it would be to send Mrs. Fletcher a postcard from New York City. That would fix her for thinking of me as a kid. You can figure for yourself the sort of cocky young smart aleck I was turning out to be.

What I remember most about that trip is hunger. I didn't want to arrive in New York without any money, so I was being careful. It wasn't so bad at night but in the morning the steward came through the coaches ringing his triangle for breakfast and people started stretching and heading for the dining car. Those that had berths came through looking all fresh and powdered while those of us who had slept sitting up headed for the washrooms to wash our faces. Now and then the door to the dining car would open and I'd get a whiff of frying bacon and toast. It nearly made me faint.

Along about the middle of the morning a woman got on at this little town. I can't remember the name of it now but it was situated on the Hudson River and the water sparkled away in the sunlight. Well, this woman was having her problems. To begin with, she had her hands full with luggage and hat boxes and cartons of this and that. Don't ask me why she didn't check it all on her ticket, but there she was with all this stuff, a sickly-looking woman too, about thirty or so, pale and thin and about ready to collapse. She also had a squawling baby in her arms and a little brat about five, all decked out in a sailor suit, was clinging to her skirts. That is, until he sized up the place, and then you couldn't keep him still. After the conductor pushed all her junk up into the luggage rack she sat down opposite me. But the kids were too much for her, what with the baby yelling and the one in the sailor suit wanting to escape now and bother people. Every so often she'd get up and haul him back and I was hoping she'd give him a good licking to tone him down but it was plain she couldn't accomplish much with that baby in her arms. So like a fool I volunteered to hold it for her. She smiled sweetly and handed over the infant and then set out after the brat. He was bothering a fat man across the way who was trying to read a newspaper.

Well now, I thought, as I jiggled this baby on my knees, she'll settle that other one down. But no, she just took him by the hand and led him back to the seat. In no time at all he was up again and troubling people. So this woman just kept getting up and fetching him back without a word. After a while the kid got tired of that routine and decided to vex me. Sitting down next to me, he began a series of annoyances that little kids are good at. Things like peering in your ear or marching fingers through your hair and over your face. All the time, mind you, I'm holding this baby and the woman has made no move to relieve me. Instead, what she did was get out this trashy novel and start to read the damn thing, taking no more notice of me than if I'd been invisible. By now the baby had gone to sleep. It was just a dead weight in my arms but every time I shifted a little it would open its eyes and look ready to bawl. The older kid kept tugging at my pockets and asking for candy. I didn't like to act ignorant and ask this woman to take back her family, so I just sat there hoping maybe she wasn't going too far and listening to my guts rumble with emptiness.

A couple of miserable hours passed and along towards noon the steward again came through ringing his triangle for lunch. At this the woman closed her book and, reaching up to the luggage rack, brings down this big parcel wrapped in rough brown paper. By now the baby had awakened and she took him from me without a word. So the baby sat on the seat next to her, wide awake and perky as hell, watching her unwrap this parcel and lay out the damnedest lunch you've ever seen. There was a ham and a chicken, potato salad and three or four different kinds of pickles, bread and biscuits and a whole raisin pie, which the kid in the sailor suit stuck a finger into, scooping out the filling. Meantime the woman had tucked into this spread, and I don't believe I've ever seen a woman eat with such speed and determination. I had her figured for someone who might have trouble spooning down a little lukewarm gruel. Instead of which she gnawed away at a drumstick in one hand while scooping up a spoonful of potato salad with the other. Now and then she poked little bits of bread and meat into the baby's mouth. In no time at all the three of them had reduced that lunch to a pile of bones and a crust. There's no use telling you that I wasn't invited to partake.

Half an hour later the train stopped at this town just outside New York and the woman got up. She could have started when the conductor came through five minutes earlier hollering out the name of the town. However, this woman waited until the train had stopped and nearly everyone was off. Then she started gathering up this paraphernalia she carried around with her and the first and only words she ever spoke to me were "I wonder if you'd mind assisting me, young man." That along with this smile which seemed a little icy to me, maybe because I didn't jump quick enough to suit her. Between me and the trainman and another fellow we got this woman's stuff out to the platform. But she must have held the train up at least ten minutes, for the conductor kept walking back and forth with his watch in his hand. He was just fuming. The last I saw of that woman she was being helped into this carriage by a chauffeur who was bowing and scraping and having his shins kicked by the kid in the sailor suit.

When I got into New York City on that afternoon in March of 1897 I was flabbergasted. I'd always thought Toronto was a busy place but New York made it seem like a country village. For a start, the streets were nearly always crowded with people on foot as well as carriages, hacks, delivery vans, bicycles, and horse-drawn streetcars. It was bewildering. I couldn't get over the number of people on the streets. As I was to learn later, however, the streets were always filled with people even before daylight because in those days it wasn't unusual for a man to start work at five o'clock in the morning and finish at nine that night. And even when the shops and factories were operating, there were still lots of people out on the streets, and most of them were looking for your job. If you had one. You see, everybody was on the hustle and the reason for this was that ninety percent of those people were immigrants who'd been kicked out of their own country or had escaped some European war or famine. The truth is, you were hard pressed to find anyone who could speak two words of English and so you had to take your directions from the big Irish cops who stood on the corners fingering their handlebar moustaches and twirling their two-foot-long skull-crackers.

It was an exciting place to be, and as I wandered among these

Italians and Russians, Frenchmen and Jews, Greeks and Lebanese, I said to myself, God Almighty, this is America! Where anybody can make a bundle. If you put your nose to the grindstone and know a politician or two. I'd read that somewhere and the funny thing is, the same sentiment was expressed to me on my first day in New York by a one-armed man named Frank Sullivan. He ran a saloon on East Eighth Street and I'd stopped there after walking over half the city. For the price of a nickel stein of beer I was enjoying the free lunch, taking more than my share of the salami and bread, pickled herring and hard-boiled eggs. The saloon was empty and Sullivan was tired of polishing glasses and talking to himself. When I think of it, I've never met an Irishman yet who could stand to be by himself thinking things over for longer than five minutes.

When Sullivan learned that I'd just arrived from Toronto he astonished me with the news that he'd been in Upper Canada, as he called it, thirty years before, fighting with the Fenians at a place called Ridgeway. I nearly choked on my beer, though of course I didn't say anything about my father but just listened. After a while Sullivan began to talk about life in New York and of how he hoped to retire in another few years and return to the "oulde sod," as he called it. "Sure, you used to be able to make a good dollar in this town," he said to me. "Until that damn Dutchman showed up and started poking into things. Still and all," said Sullivan, drawing himself a beer and raising it high, "praise the Holy Mother, the bastard's left town. I think he's down in Washington now." After a few polite inquiries I discovered that this Dutchman was none other than Theodore Roosevelt, who later became the President of the United States. According to Sullivan, Roosevelt had just resigned as head of New York's police commission and Sullivan saw this as a great thing, for Roosevelt had cleaned up a lot of graft and corruption around town. Now saloon keepers like Sullivan were looking for a return to the old days when, as he put it, "you had a cop in one hand and an alderman in the other."

So we jawed on about that, with Sullivan bragging about the money he'd made a few years before when things was wide open. He was amusing to listen to, a big, lantern-jawed fellow with a head of shiny black hair parted down the middle and combed over his ears. He had a big, tobacco-stained moustache and, as I've mentioned, only one wing, having lost the other in a brewery accident twenty years before. But he was remarkably nimble with that one mitt, which for sheer size and strength was hard to match. From the thumb to the tip of the little finger it could span fifteen nickels, and over the years Sullivan had devised novel ways of doing things with it. Like drawing off a beer or opening half a dozen oysters for a customer. Like most Irishmen he talked too much, but the talk was usually diverting and he seemed to enjoy my company, for I've always had the gift of nodding my head in the right places when stories are told.

The upshot of this conversation was the offer of a job. Sullivan claimed he needed someone around the place to help him, and he wanted somebody who could speak English. I accepted on the spot, after assuring him that I was a Roman Catholic with Irish blood on my mother's side. I can't remember now what he paid me, probably no more than a couple of dollars a week, but my room and board came with it and that's the most important thing when you're homeless and low on funds. He gave me this little room in a loft over the tavern. It wasn't much of a place but it was dry, and after I'd cleaned it up and got rid of the rats I settled down pretty well.

A typical day at Sullivan's Saloon went something like this. I'd get up around eight and go down and draw the air out of the beer spigots. Then I'd have a couple of glasses of beer and maybe a pickled egg for breakfast. After a smoke I'd set about airing the place, opening up the shutters and the front door if the weather was fine. I'd also make sure the trap door from the sidewalk down to the basement was open so the brewery boys could roll their kegs in there. It was then usually time to sprinkle some fresh sawdust on the floor and serve a customer or two. It might be some scrawny little kid wanting a pail of beer for his old man who was in bed dying of thirst. Or it might be just some fellow who needed a shot of whiskey to get him started. About this time Sullivan would arrive with a couple of buckets of sandwiches made fresh that morning by his wife and kids. Sullivan had about a dozen kids and his wife had promised them all to the Church. So he'd show up with these sandwiches and then the deliverymen would start arriving with barrels of oysters and sides of beef and hams and pails of pigs' knuckles and jars of dill pickles. It would take till about eleven to sort all that out and by then we were into lunch time and I'd wait on tables and wash glasses and plates. We'd be hopping until the middle of the afternoon, when business would tail off. Then I'd sweep out the place and Sullivan would allow me a couple of free hours.

As soon as I was done I'd rush out and buy a copy of every paper available in the hope of seeing Sally's picture advertised in the entertainment sections. Sometimes I'd go for a walk hoping to come across a vaudeville theater where she was performing. But after a couple of hours I'd head back to Sullivan's to get ready for the evening rush. That usually started in the late afternoon when the Irish navvies came in after work. Then Sullivan and me would be hard at it for several hours and sometimes there'd be a squabble or two, though none of that rough stuff ever bothered Sullivan. He was what they called an able man, despite his one arm, and at the sight of trouble he'd be over the marble to sort things out. And then because he was Irish and not afraid to lay on a buck in the right places, he had plenty of friends at the local precinct and the beat cops were always dropping in for a free drink. They kept an eye on the place. We'd close at one o'clock and by the time we'd cleaned up it was getting on to three and I'd go to bed listening to the Jewish peddlers trundling their empty carts through the streets to the Third Avenue Market.

I suppose I was drinking and smoking too much for a young fellow but it was an interesting life, though at times when I wasn't busy I'd fall into a grim humor. I believe that came out of my discouragement over not finding the whereabouts of Sally Butters. There was nothing in the papers about her and when I telephoned a number of booking agents I was puzzled to learn that they had never heard of her.

One day I decided to tell Sullivan about my problem. I half expected him to laugh but in fact he listened and was generally sympathetic. He told me a story about a girl he'd loved when he was my age. But she rejected him and entered a nunnery. Sullivan married her sister and hadn't had a moment's peace since the day before his wedding. The story brought tears to his eyes and a bottle of whiskey to his hand. And since business was slow, we just leaned across the bar for a couple of hours, sipping malt while Sullivan talked about life and how it was more or less a cheating experience. I wasn't particularly interested in his personal philosophy, but that's usually the way of it. You ask somebody for advice and he starts to ruminate on life and what a terrible bargain it all is. The only fellow worse than that is the one who's always optimistic and is forever uttering fresh statements such as "Don't worry. It'll all come out in the wash." Or "Every cloud has a silver lining."

Anyway, I finally got Sullivan off the tragedy of his own life and back to my problem, which was how to find a beautiful red-headed girl in a city the size of New York. Sullivan finally suggested I ask Findlater. He was the man who knew what was going on in the city. In fact, he was supposed to know what was going on everywhere. As the saloon keeper put it, "That Findlater! He's the divil of a man. He's got the world in a jug and the stopper in his hand! Of course I can't say that he'll help you, Bill. But there can be no harm in asking."

11

FINDLATER

I WASN'T SO SURE about asking Findlater. Nor did I share Sullivan's witless admiration for the man. I believe Sullivan's high opinion was based mostly on the fact that Findlater was a grown man and still unmarried. He was a free enough spirit, all right, popping into the saloon once or twice a week and then disappearing for several days. He had an opinion on everything and laughed a lot, though he also had a mean side to him. I'd watched Findlater beat a man half to death for accidentally spilling a drink down his vest. In fact, I saw him as a loud-mouthed character, just the kind of man you generally try to avoid in a bar. The sort of man whose behavior isn't easy to predict. For instance, one morning when business was slow I was reading the newspaper when Findlater came in and ordered his shot of whiskey and beer chaser. I served him and went on reading, knowing full well that he was studying me. After five minutes he says, "Hey there, sonny! You read pretty good. Where did you learn to read like that?"

"What do you mean?" I says.

"What I mean is, you don't move your lips like most folks. How do you manage it?" At the time I thought he was pulling my leg. It was only later that I found out he was dead serious.

Now, I have to try to describe Findlater, because he's a fairly important character in my narrative and in fact he was to come in and out of my life over the next fifty years. And say what you like, blemishes and all, he was a remarkable man. Even now, I can't make up my mind about him.

To start with, it was hard to determine his age. He could have been twenty-five or he could have been fifty-five. He was a good-sized man, maybe six feet tall and broad through the chest and shoulders, tapering down to a pair of bandy legs. He put you in mind of an aging prizefighter, bulky on top but still springy in the hams. He had a big head of brown thick hair and a set of handlebar moustaches. Beneath big bushy eyebrows were a pair of eyes filled with shrewdness and cunning but also laughter. In those days he favored checked suits, which always struck me as a bit loud in taste but expensively cut. He also liked patterned shirts, with a Windsor knot in his tie. He wore yellow shoes and a round pot hat, which he traded in warm weather for a straw katy. There was always a couple of stone rings on the little fingers of both hands and a gold watch fob across his vest front. I suppose on first notice you'd take him for a sharp character and you'd not be too far wrong, for he never disguised the opinion that the world was easy pickings for the man with his head screwed on right. How he earned his living was something of a mystery though it was generally believed he was a minor racketeer.

Despite my misgivings about him I decided to take Sullivan's advice. A few days later I was sweeping the floor preparing for the evening rush when Findlater walked in and stood at his usual spot. There were only a couple of customers in the place at the time, so Sullivan hustled over and served Findlater. Out of the corner of my eye I watched him sipping his drink. I was trying to gauge his humor before I approached him.

It was hard not to stare at Findlater, because he was very fussy when it came to personal habits, especially the consumption of eats and drinks. So he stood there sipping whiskey with these huge fingers all splayed out in what might appear to another man to be an almost ladylike style of drinking. Not that I ever saw anybody offer such a comment, but it did look comical. Take eating for another example. Findlater tried his damnedest to be careful and delicate with a knife and fork and for a while he'd succeed. But then he'd forget and start to wolf down his food or maybe stop to pick a piece of meat from his teeth. If there was a napkin or a clean handkerchief handy he'd start off patting his lips. But by the end of the meal he'd be blowing his nose on that napkin. The truth is, he was greatly attracted to good manners and admired anyone who appeared to have an ounce of breeding in him. I've seen him stand in awe before the worst scoundrel because this man didn't chew the lemon in a finger bowl or could recite a sentence without grammar mistakes. A man like my father, for instance, would have impressed Findlater to a ridiculous extreme.

Well, there he stood, looking dead ahead into the bar mirror and frowning at himself. I judged he was in a foul temper and decided to postpone asking him any questions about Sally. Thus I continued to sweep and had almost forgotten about him when he turned around and, leaning back with his elbows on the bar, surveyed my work. Then he says, "What do they call you, pal?"

"Bill Farthing," I says, leaning on the broom.

Then Findlater says,

"How many beans make five, Bill Farthing?"

11. Findlater

I wasn't going to be made a fool of by no sharp-dressed racketeer, so I answers right back, "Two in each hand and one in your mouth."

Findlater chuckled to himself and flipped a half dollar toward me. I figured that he wanted me to catch it but I just let it sail right past and bury itself in the sawdust. Now a half a buck was nothing to sneeze at in those days, especially if you lived on my wages. But I wasn't going to dig in any sawdust for anybody's money and Findlater watched me for a while and then he says, "Nobody's ever traveled very far on the end of one of those things, pal." I looked at him and he was smiling. "The broom, Bill, the broom," he says. "It's a poor device for getting anywhere in this great land of ours. Come along with me." And he grabbed my arm and, spinning me around like a cop, straight-arms me through the doorway and out onto Eighth Street.

It was a warm, sunny day and the street was filled with traffic. There were people hurrying by on the sidewalk, peddlers hawking their wares and the clatter of cabs and carts and streetcars. Findlater stood there watching all this with his arm around my shoulder. He took a big deep breath, filling his lungs with the smell of rotten fruit, horse manure, and human sweat. Then he said to me, "You see all this, Bill? This is the future you're looking at, boy. This country is going to make those funny talking monkeys on the other side of the ocean sit up and take notice. Why, look at all these people! There's guineas and chinks and kikes. They all used to be Europeans. Now they're Americans. They've all come over for the big foot race, Bill. And the ones who run the fastest get the prizes. Unless, of course, you know a few short cuts." Then he shook my shoulder. "They tell me you've come down from the British provinces. Now that was your first smart move, because from what I've heard there's bugger-all up there but fish and fur-bearing animals. I don't know why you fellows didn't throw in your lot with us when we thumbed our noses at King Georgie." He took another deep breath. "Just imagine, Bill. In another couple of years we'll be into a brand-new century. Oh, there's going to be some great things taking place as we move along there. I read the other day about a horseless carriage. There's supposed to be one or two in town, though I ain't seen them yet. But this damn thing moves without benefit of the animal. Some smart bugger has invented this engine that pushes it along. Damnedest thing you've ever heard of. Come on, I'll buy you a drink."

So we went back into the saloon and Findlater insisted on buying me a drink while he talked about his plans. One minute he talked about owning a string of whorehouses because, as he put it, "There's always a market for the pleasures of the flesh, Bill." The next minute he was talking about Africa and of how one day he planned to travel there and fight savages while looking for diamonds. He said he'd had his eye on me for the past few weeks and liked my style. "I liked the way you read that paper, Bill. Nice and quiet and all to yourself. And you've got good manners too, even when you're working in a shithole like this. A man can't talk to most of the people in a neighborhood like this. They're all too ignorant. But I'm betting you've been to school and have read a few books. And so do you know what's truly painful to a man like me?"

"No," I says. "What?"

"What's painful, Bill," he says, "is to see a young man from a good background stoking the lime to the shitholes of a saloon outhouse. It ain't right somehow."

"It's honest work," I says.

To which he laughed. "A fellow like you. Why, you should be a young stockbroker or a lawyer. With a diamond stickpin in your tie and a pretty little gal on your arm. You're going through the spring-time of your life and you should be stopping to smell the daisies, not cleaning up beer and chawed-on pigs' knuckles."

When he mentioned pretty girl I was set to ask his help in locating Sally. But just then Sullivan came over and he didn't look too pleased either, which was understandable since the place was getting busy and I hadn't done a tap of work in half an hour. But I could also see that this was a delicate situation for the saloon keeper, for he didn't want to offend Findlater, who was suddenly looking moody and withdrawn. So Sullivan finally says, "Excuse me now, Mr. Findlater, but I wonder if I might borrow my helper here. Young Bill. Sure the place is startin' to fill up and I've got my hands full."

"What's that, Frank?" says Findlater, not moving an inch but staring across the saloon. "What's that you said?"

"Why, I said I need Bill here, Mr. Findlater."

"No, no, no," says Findlater, turning towards us. "That's not what you said."

Sullivan looked puzzled and then says, "Sure now, I've forgotten the exact words but . . ."

"What you said, Frank," continues Findlater, "is, and I quote you, I got my hands full. Now what you should have said, of course, was I got my hand full. Right?"

Sullivan didn't know what in hell to say to that. You could never tell whether Findlater was joking or not. Well, Sullivan, his face growing dark and stormy, mumbles, "I guess that's what I meant, all right."

"Of course it is," says Findlater. "It ain't right for a man with only one hand to say I got my hands full. It don't make sense. Ain't that right, Bill?"

Sullivan shot me a murderous look and I could only shrug. By now everyone was yelling for more drinks, while Sullivan stood there fidgeting, trying to work out his next move.

Then Findlater surprised the both of us by saying, "Anyways, Bill ain't workin' for you anymore. He's throwin' in his lot with me."

To which Sullivan says, "Mr. Findlater. If you could give me a day or two notice . . ."

Findlater ignored this. "I know a young man who's lookin' to study

11. Findlater

barkeepin'. He'll be around tomorrow mornin', so don't take on like it's the end of the world, Frank. Bill here is destined for greater things than servin' beer to these monkeys. No offense intended." Then he lifted up his glass and says with mock surprise, "Will you look at that? Unless my hat's on wrong, that there's a twenty-dollar bill." And he picked it up and stuffed it in Sullivan's shirt pocket. "It must be the house's money, because it ain't mine. You should be more careful with your change, Frank."

Then Findlater took my arm and steered me through the doorway once more. I glanced back and the last I saw of Frank Sullivan he was back pumping beer and uncorking bottles, reaching up now and again to touch his shirt pocket, that one arm just a white blur of motion.

Outside Findlater hailed a hansom cab and we drove over to Third Avenue and stopped at a haberdashery, where he stood me to a new summer outfit, linen suit, yellow shoes, straw hat, the works. All this time I'm trying to figure out just what sort of a game Findlater is playing. Maybe, I says to myself, he's one of those rich queers who's looking for a playmate. But nothing of that nature ever took place and in fact as the evening wore away the notion of Findlater not liking women appeared more and more comical. Well, we walked around for a while, dodging into a saloon now and then for a beer. It was a nice way to spend the afternoon and I felt sophisticated and grown-up walking around the streets of New York City in my new clothes. We ate dinner at the Astor Hotel at Times Square and Findlater told me something about himself. I didn't know whether to believe it or not. Some of it sounded all right, but there were chunks of it that didn't fit together.

He told me his father was one of the original forty-niners out in California. After years of looking all over the country, he'd finally struck it rich. Findlater's mother, like my own, had died giving birth to him in a tent in the mountains. The birth was difficult and his mother needed help. But at the very moment she was about to give birth, Findlater's old man struck a rich yield and was busy staking it. It took him until the last light of day to get his claim staked. By the time he got back to the tent, his wife was dead. Though not before she'd delivered Findlater, who weighed fifteen pounds. Findlater's old man told him the story later on. According to him the whole thing was a piece of unfortunate timing. The mountains were swarming with prospectors and you couldn't expect a man who'd spent thirty years looking for his fortune to walk away after finding it and run the risk of somebody laying claims to it.

All that sounded reasonable to Findlater's old man, and the funny thing is that Findlater felt exactly the same about it. Anyway, his old man made millions out of it, though this was never enough and he was always looking for more. So instead of hauling up at a nice hotel and learning to refine himself or maybe take a trip around the world and see how other people lived, the old man kept strapping a satchel to his

back and walking through the bush and mountains of Oregon and
Washington clear up to the Fraser River in British Columbia. And
Findlater walked right along with him too from about the age of six,
after having lived with relatives in St. Louis. So all his childhood was
spent in cabins and tents far from civilization, which might have accounted for his rude ways. He finally came down with lung consumption and spent a number of years in a lung hospital out West somewhere. It probably saved his life too, for it kept him from accompanying his father, who set out after silver in Peru and never came back.
One story had it that he died of fever and another suggested that he
was devoured by the native peoples. After he got out of the hospital
Findlater discovered that his father had been swindled out of all his
money by the banks, so he had to fend for himself for a number of
years.

"It was tough for a while, Bill," he said to me, wiping his mouth
on the edge of the tablecloth. "But I'm a natural-born businessman
and I soon got myself into various enterprises. Ran a bank once in
Springfield, Illinois. Had some dealings in the oil business with Mr.
John D. Rocketfeller. Now there's a cute one, by Jesus. You have to
get up pretty early in the morning to get the handle on Mr. John D.
And you'd better count your fingers when the deal's over too." Findlater went on like this for some time while we worked our way through
a mixed grill and a couple of bottles of French wine. How much of it
was lies and how much of it was truth I can't say. Of course, he wanted
to know about me as well, and so I told him that I was the son of a
poet. Like any son I bragged a little extra about my father's achieve-
ments, so that he came out being fairly famous over in England. At this
Findlater slammed his fist on the table. "I knew it, Bill. I'm seldom
wrong about people and I knew the minute I saw you read that paper
that you had class. You and me could make a great team. It's all out
there just waitin' to be plucked." And so saying, he stuck a forefinger
in his mouth and pulled out a good-sized piece of pork chop.

Then a little incident occurred which will give you an idea of how
much importance Findlater attached to proper behavior. What happened was this little old lady came into the dining room. She looked
rich and had an important air about her and was weighted down with
brooches and jewels. But she was feeble as hell and had to be guided
along by the headwaiter. They sat her down at the table next to ours
and fussed around her and left. Then I noticed she'd dropped a little
lace handkerchief and it was lying on the carpet next to her chair. So
I excused myself to Findlater and, getting up, walked over and retrieved this little handkerchief. Handing it to this little old lady, I says,
"Excuse me, madam, but I believe you dropped this a minute ago."

"Why, thank you, young man," she says, and reaches for her purse.
"May I give you a coin for your trouble?"

"No, thank you," I says, holding up my hands. "It was my pleasure."

Well, nothing to that, you might say. It was just something you'd normally do. But Findlater couldn't get over it. "God, Bill," he says to me in what passed for a whisper, though everybody could hear him. "The way you handled that was real style." Then he looked at the dead end of his cigar and I thought I detected a sigh. "I wish," says he, "that I could have done that."

"Done what?" I asks.

"What you just done," he says, tilting his head towards the old lady, who was now sawing her way through a two-pound porterhouse steak.

"Well, I didn't do anything special," I says. "I just handed her back her handkerchief."

"It don't matter. I couldn't have done it."

"Why not?" I asks.

"I'd have taken the money when she offered," says Findlater with a straight face.

I had to laugh at that. "Why, you appear to have enough money," I says. "I don't believe you."

"Having money ain't got nothin' to do with it," says Findlater, lighting his cigar. He appeared to be getting grumpy. "I just know," he says, "that I couldn't have done what you done. Not in a million years. Let's get the hell out of here."

Out on the street we hired an open cab and drove up Broadway smoking cigars and admiring the fine evening. People strolled about the entrances to hotels and band music drifted across the town from various parks. Findlater's good humor returned and he began to talk again about what a great country America was and what a helluva future it had. Which I had to admit made sense to me, for all around you in those days was this air of buoyancy and confidence. Looking at the beautifully dressed ladies walking arm in arm with their beaus made me think of Sally, and so I turned to Findlater and said, "I've come to New York to look for a girl. Will you help me find her?"

It was dark and I couldn't see Findlater's face to tell whether he was smiling or not, but after a moment he says, "Is she a relative of yours, Bill?"

"No," I says, and spent ten minutes telling him about Sally and how we were supposed to rendezvous.

To me Findlater was a man of the world, and so I expected him to be intrigued and pleased by this story of love and adventure. When I finished, however, he said, "A word of advice, Bill. Don't lose your marbles over these show-business characters. Take it from a man who's had a little experience along those lines. They're penny stock, Bill." He waved his cigar at the lights and the crowds on the streets.

"Why, there must be at least a dozen heiresses walking around the city tonight. Just dying to make the acquaintance of a handsome young fellow like you."

"I don't want any heiresses," I said. "The one I'm looking for is the most beautiful girl in the world. And I know she likes me."

"That's what they all say, Bill. Tell you what let's do." And he laid a big hand on my shoulder. "If it's girls you have on your mind, I know a place."

"Not girls," I said. "Girl."

Findlater's cigar glowed in the darkness. "You're talking like a Quaker, pal. Taste the grapes before you buy." I suppose I was sulking, for Findlater started to laugh. "All right," he says. "I'll tell you what. If you're so desperate to find this little singer of yours, I'll ask around. Right now I want you to forget about her for a few hours, because we're going to a party. And mind, I don't want any hangdog looks." And he instructed the driver to take us to a place somewhere in the lower twenties off Fifth Avenue. It was my first visit to a whorehouse.

12

RECREATION

Now I EXPECT some of you may have been in a whorehouse once or twice, though it's unlikely there are many of you still around who ever visited a first-class establishment of seventy-five years ago. I'll do my best to describe it and also tell you about the damnedest contest I ever witnessed in my life.

The house itself was a very respectable brownstone dwelling with a wrought-iron fence around the front and a little gate. We were met at the door by a maid in a short black skirt and white apron. She recognized Findlater right away and curtsied and invited us to come in, calling us messieurs. She was French, you see. The place, to use Findlater's words, was "very classy." This maid left us standing in a vestibule, from where we could hear piano music and voices. It sounded just like a neighbor's party down the street. The place was expensively furnished, though in what I can only call heavy taste. That is, the window curtains were thick purple velvet and the carpet had an Oriental design. Everything was dark and a bit grim-looking except for a number of statues of little naked babies shooting arrows or holding goblets. The cuspidors were solid brass and all the pictures had gilt frames. The whole effect may have been tasteful but, as I say, somber and heavy. I remember thinking that if you took away the statues, Phineas Fletcher could have worked out of this part of the house.

We stood there for a few minutes holding our hats. Findlater hummed a tune and inspected a picture on the wall, which showed a half-dozen devils chasing a blond-haired nude woman down a road. Moments later the maid returned and, making another little curtsy, stepped aside for the biggest woman I've ever seen in my life. She must have weighed three hundred pounds and she was dressed in this purple gown with three strands of pearls falling across this enormous bosom. Her snow-white hair was all tricked out and fastened with brooches and pins. She was what you might call an imperial sight, and when she saw Findlater she opened her arms. "My stars," she cried. "Is it really you, Cass? Where the hell have you been hiding yourself these past few weeks?"

"Business, Mary," says Findlater, hugging this huge woman.

"Business, my eye," says our hostess. "You haven't found yourself another sweetheart, have you?" She stepped back and looked at Findlater severely.

"No fear, Mary," says Findlater. "But look. Here's a young friend of mine I'd like you to meet. This here's Bill Farthing. He's come down from Canada to make his fortune. He's a gentleman, Mary, and his father is a famous poet over in England. Now, Bill, you say hello to an old and dear friend of mine. This here's Mary Kettle."

"Welcome to my place, Billy," she says. "You enjoy yourself. Any friend of Findlater's is welcome at Mary Kettle's. Now come on, you two. You know, Cass, you just missed half the police commission. Things are loosening up again now that that ——ing Dutchman's gone."

"True, Mary, true," laughed Findlater as we went down this hallway.

Before we got to the door Mary Kettle stopped and put her hand on Findlater's chest. "How are you feeling tonight, Cass?" she asks.

"Fit as a fiddle with all the strings in place," says Findlater.

"Good," says Mary. "Now I'll tell you something. What we got in here tonight, among other things, is a couple of braggarts. Well, one of them is doing all the talking. They're officers off a merchant ship. They came highly recommended but I've never heard anybody talk like that little one. If he can —— as well as he can talk, I'll retire tomorrow. But listen. Do you feel up to making them look a little foolish? I know you can do it if you set your mind and your other end to it."

"Why not, Mary?" says Findlater. "Lead the way."

So she squeezed his arm and in we went to this drawing room. It was large and done up in maroon wallpaper with a number of love seats and chairs. There was a dozen or so women, mostly young and good-looking, and they were sitting around in satin gowns, with plenty of bosom showing. The air was thick with tobacco smoke and perfumed powder. In one corner an old bald-headed black man played a piano and one of the girls sat next to him on a bench humming a song. These were six men in the room, including two who wore dark blue uniforms. We stood there for a minute and then Mary Kettle clapped her hands and yelled, "Look at what the dog dragged in, girls!" Well, when the girls turned and saw Findlater, each of them shrieked and came running over to kiss and hug him. They were just like a bunch of schoolgirls and I could see that the two sailor boys didn't like it very much. Before this they'd had the girls pretty well to themselves and now they sat there abandoned. One of them was a young blond giant with the face of a perfect simpleton. His partner was smaller and darker and yapped like a terrier.

12. Recreation

After things settled down, Findlater and me walked across the room and this girl brought us each a shot of whiskey. She winked at me, though I wasn't interested for she wasn't my type, being too bony and muscular, with a square jaw and somewhat angular in feature. Also, she used too much powder and stuff on her eyes and face. However, she seemed keen on me and kept winking. Findlater encouraged me to be friendly with her but I had my eye on a pretty little redhead who put me somewhat in mind of Sally Butters, though of course she wasn't anywhere near as beautiful. Well, after a few minutes this bony girl invited me to a picture show. I shook my head but Findlater said, "Go on, Bill. Be a sport. It's only a few little pictures. The latest stuff from Paris. I'll come along with you." This girl then took my arm and we went into a little room where they'd set up a stereoptican. Somebody turned out the lights and a few pictures came flickering across the wall, showing a man and a woman undressing. To tell you the truth, I found it boring and I said as much to Findlater, who didn't answer. All I heard in the dark was a giggle and then somebody took my hand and put it between their legs, and God Almighty, it was that bony whore. And she wasn't a woman at all but a man! I yelled and the lights came on and everybody clapped and laughed, especially Findlater and Mary Kettle.

I thought it was a dirty joke to play on a fellow and I was going to clear out, though just where I would go I had no idea. But Findlater put his arm around my shoulder and says, "Now, don't be a poor sport, Bill. Everybody gets that little routine when they come to Mary's for the first time. Alec didn't mean any harm. It's just a little joke between friends. Now what do you say we enjoy ourselves? Play us a tune there, Uncle," he yells to the piano player, who begins to pound out a lively number. Findlater then grabbed a skinny blonde and, twisting her around, danced across the drawing-room floor. By now the place was filled with men, all well dressed and prosperous-looking. Every few minutes a couple would get up and leave the room. As I say, I had my eye on this little redhead, who by now was sitting on this big blond sailor's knee. They were listening to the other sailor brag about the big fellow's prowess. According to this little sailor named Jack the girls had a real treat in store when this big fellow called Swede got into an amorous humor.

Even though he was a smart aleck little son of a bitch, I have to say that this Jack told a good story and he had a number of the girls plainly intrigued. Even those dancing stopped and listened while Jack told about the time in Marseilles when this Swede subdued a huge Amazon woman in a heroic three-hour tussle. The girls' eyes were growing bigger by the minute. Then he told about another time when the big fellow had fixed up a whole houseful of hungry females in Boston. By now, of course, this dumb-looking Swedish ox is the most popular man in the house. The girls were crowding around him and pinching his leg. I may have been jealous. I know I was still mad about that joke played on me in the dark room. Now the best thing to do when you're mad in a whorehouse is get yourself laid. It'll take all the meanness out of you, and that's why I think screwing is one of the most beneficial pastimes for humans. So with this in mind I walked over to the little redhead still perched on the Swede's knee and I says, "Come on now, sweetie, you got a customer here."

I don't believe I was acting particularly rude but the fact is that she was so wrapped up in another of Jack's stories that she just shrugged me off. All of which created a diversion for Jack, who says to me, "Why don't you leave the girl alone, Short-arm? The boys' room is down the hall."

Now that got a good laugh from the girls. I got a little warm in the blood and replies, "I was just beginning to wonder whether this is a whorehouse or a public library, because all I've heard around here is some old woman telling dirty stories."

That got a laugh from Findlater across the room and the piano player chorded out the first few bars of the Wedding March. This Jack then jumps to his feet and says, "You remind me of a kid I shipped out with once. On an English scow by the name of *Brittania Rose*. The kid was a cabin boy and a cute little bugger too. We used to call him the all-day sucker. Maybe he was a relative of yours?"

That got another laugh. Even the big Swede got that one and chuckled. Then I says, "I don't believe you've got a blessed thing in your pants or you wouldn't sit here all night yapping about your tall friend here."

For a change I got a snicker from the girls, but Jack put the grab on my shirt front. "You better watch your mouth now, sonny. You're stepping out of line."

But quick as lightning Findlater had pushed his way through the girls and grabs Jack's arm. "Better keep your hands to yourself, admiral," he says. "This here's the son of a famous poet you're talking to."

And then damn me if he doesn't do a cute thing! What he does is take Jack's nose between two big fingers and he gives it a helluva twist. Jack yells in pain and the big Swede jumps to his feet. Now it looked like an ugly situation developing but just then Mary Kettle appears with a couple of new customers. Sizing things up quickly, she claps her hands and says, "Now, boys. This is a house of pleasure, not strife. If you're all so anxious to prove what big lads you are, I got a better idea." She gave us all a big wink. "Now listen," she says. "What say to a little peaceful rivalry here between the two biggest buffaloes on the range?"

Jack had cooled down a bit, so he asks, "What are you talking about?"

"Well now, sailor," says Mary. "You've been entertaining my girls all night with nice stories about your friend there. Let's see if your stories hold water." Then she brought out a big silver watch from inside her bosom. "It's nearly eleven o'clock. I propose a little contest here between your friend and Findlater. The one who tops the most of my girls between now and six o'clock tomorrow morning is the winner. The loser pays the house for all favors incurred."

12. Recreation

The girls cheered while Jack rubbed his reddening nose and says, "All right, mother. You got yourself a game. That is, if fancy pants here thinks he's up to it."

Findlater was busy on a big cigar but he was smiling through the smoke. "Well, Findlater?" says Mary. "What do you say?"

Findlater took a drag on his stogie. "What I say is, it sounds like fun. And just to make the competition sporting, let's put some real green on the line here." And he takes out this billfold and peels off a hundred bucks. "You got that kind of money, captain?" he says to Jack.

Jack and the Swede went into a huddle and by and by they came up with a hundred between them. The money was then thrown into somebody's hat and a number of the customers, mostly businessmen, began laying side bets. Before long the hat was filled with paper money. Then Mary Kettle spelled out the rules. Each man was assigned a room and the girls were bound on their word to deliver a fair and honest verdict on whether the screwing was successful. Their judgment was to be based not necessarily on tricky performance but sheer simple accomplishment. The point of it was whether the contestant could perform the act of copulation.

After Mary Kettle finished, Findlater tucked a bottle of whiskey under his arm, winked at me and, grabbing that skinny blonde, he climbed the stairs amid general applause. The Swede followed right behind, accompanied by a short, heavy girl in an orange dress. The rest of us sat around smoking or bought drinks from Alec, who sashayed around the room with a tray of glasses. Nobody felt like dancing, though the piano player kept tinkling away. Mary tried to interest a few of the customers in her girls but nobody seemed eager, which was not surprising, for if there's one sure thing that will take a man's mind off sex, it's a sporting competition where there's money on the line. Jack didn't say much, for a change. He just sat there stroking his beak and looking fairly satisfied with events.

Not more than ten minutes had passed when down comes the girl in the orange dress and she announces that the Swede is ready for the next one. Now maybe fifteen minutes later this second girl comes down, blowing us all a kiss. I remember she was a witty little thing and she drew a laugh by suggesting that the Swede was long in the leg but short on imagination.

"Never mind his imagination," says Jack, "that's two for us, and to my way of thinking, your man's in trouble, Short-arm. Are you keeping score, mother?" he says to Mary.

"Don't you worry about the score, sailor," says Mary. "I'm keeping it, all right. Up you go, Alma." And up goes number three to the Swede.

Just after that the skinny blonde comes down the stairs and tells us that Findlater is in top form. "He told me there's no use a girl not having some fun out of this arrangement too," she says. "And ladies and gents, that man knows what he's talking about." Everybody cheered and up went the little redhead, holding her skirts and taking the stairs two at a time. I felt a flicker of lust watching her go.

Meantime the Swede had progressed to number four, though he was beginning to slow down. I figured Findlater for an old hand at this game and guessed he must be pacing himself. Then from his chair Jack starts to feel sprightly again. "It looks," he says, "like Swede is gonna do the same thing he done once down in the Caribee Islands." And he launched into another tale about the Swede's amazing powers. Now he was good, mind you. No doubt about that, and after the fifth girl climbed the stairs I began to think maybe Findlater had more than his work cut out for him. The atmosphere in the house was growing suspenseful. Nobody was leaving and the betting customers were now watching those stairs for signs of life. The piano player had long gone to bed. Then about three o'clock Findlater showed signs of gaining. He was clearly the popular choice, and a boozy cheer went up when the Swede asked for time before number six. By now Findlater's fourth girl had come down and she told us he wanted some eggs and a quart of buttermilk.

"No fair," yells Jack, jumping out of his chair. "We didn't mention anything about food."

"Now keep your pants on," says Mary Kettle. "Your man can eat too, if he's got a stomach for it." At which Jack bounded up those stairs.

Before long both contestants came down for breakfast. Findlater was barefoot and wearing only long underwear and his pants, which were held up by brilliant red suspenders. The Swede wore his tunic, jumper and trousers, and he moved with painful slowness. Findlater sat down with the skinny blonde on his knee and began to eat. "How are things holding up there, Dutchie?" he says with a mouthful of egg. The Swede didn't say a word but just ate slowly while Jack stood behind him and rubbed his neck like a trainer at a prize fight. After Findlater had drained the last of his buttermilk he says, "Now I feel like a little female company. Who's lookin' for a treat?"

It was now getting on to four o'clock and through the window curtains you could see a little gray daylight. But nobody was falling asleep, because the action picked up for a while. The Swede seemed to gain energy from the eats and his performance was described by a well-spoken girl as "merely adequate." But the little redhead was number eight and she came down after a few minutes looking disgusted. "The Swede can't haul coal anymore," she says. "He's just tuckered."

"It's a lie," says Jack, and he's up those stairs in no time. Soon we heard him yelling and pounding at the Swede's door. "Wake up in there, you son of a bitch," he hollers. "Our money's on the line here."

Yet Findlater was still taking his own sweet time and at a quarter past five he still had two to go to beat the Swede. I recall Mary Kettle taking out her watch and saying, "Well, that big hound had better get on with the job and stop those monkeyshines." She said that because all the time Jack was yelling at the Swede there were such squeals and laughter coming from Findlater's room that you'd have thought there was an orgy going on. And maybe there was.

106

12. Recreation

Now with fifteen minutes to go they were tied after seven women each. The eighth were standing by each door awaiting admittance. By now everybody in the house had forgotten what you might call propriety and we'd all climbed the stairs and were in the hallway outside the rooms. Jack managed to awaken the Swede for a final effort and the two number eights entered the rooms. Before long Findlater called out, "Hey, Dutchie. How are you doing in there? Can you rise to the occasion?"

That was a cute remark and got a laugh from all of us. But Jack then came to the doorway where we were all crowding around. "All right, all right, get back," he yells. "He can't do nothin' with a crowd gawking at him."

"He can't do nothin' anyway," says the girl. "You might as well all come in." She was sitting on a chair with her feet up and she was smoking a cigarette. The Swede lay on the bed looking dazed.

Then Jack says, "I got a notion we're being bamboozled here. How do I know your friend ain't fakin' it?"

"Why don't you go in and see for yourself, dearie?" says Mary Kettle.

"Well, by God, maybe I will," says Jack, and he barges through the doorway to Findlater's room. There's a shout and a hoot of laughter and then Jack comes storming out looking like he wants to eat the world. Into the Swede's room he goes, where he's soon yelling, "Get up out of there, you blockhead. You've cost me a pile of money tonight."

Everybody crowded into Findlater's room. He was sitting up in bed in his underwear and Mary Kettle opened a bottle of champagne and sat down on the bed beside him. The business gents slapped Findlater on the back and the girls hugged him. And damn me for a liar if that isn't a true story.

13

GOLD FEVER

AFTER THIS I shared lodgings with Findlater. The first thing I discovered was this. Findlater was neither a rich nor a successful racketeer. He just appeared that way to people like Frank Sullivan. No, Findlater was just what you might call a petty crook, always looking for a way to make a buck. Still and all, it wasn't a bad place to live and you could meet lots worse roommates than Findlater. The room itself was large and clean, for Findlater was particular when it came to personal hygiene. We lived in a white frame house which needed a coat of paint but which was otherwise in fair condition. Our room was on the top floor overlooking Washington Square. In those days that part of New York was known as Frenchtown because of the amazing number of Frenchmen who'd settled there. Not that there weren't lots of other foreigners too. Findlater and me, for instance, ate our meals in a German restaurant where the food was tasty and cheap. I found life pretty good under these circumstances. Findlater knew everybody in the neighborhood and appeared to be well liked. Some of his popularity rubbed off on me, though I was generally quiet and withdrawn, which Findlater took for good manners. When we walked down the street, for instance, he'd always be talking to people, giving away a spare cigar or a nickel to some bum, while I remained aloof.

Now you might wonder how we came by our money. Or I should say, how Findlater came by the money, since our income was due entirely to his enterprise. He enjoyed a hand of poker and made a fair bit of money at cards. Did he cheat? Of course he did. Any gambler who is serious about earning his living cheats. You can't just depend on the laws of chance, because they favor no one in particular. Findlater also turned a pretty good fist with a pool cue and then he seemed to have his nose in a racket or two, though it was always small-time stuff.

I remember one occasion when he brought home a valise loaded with gentlemen's dress stockings. A few hours later some fellow who looked like an Arab came along to the room and took away the valise, leaving Findlater at the door counting a roll of bills. He seemed to make enough at this sort of endeavor to keep body and soul together. I know his clothes were always brushed and pressed and he always had good colognes and shaving creams. Nor did we ever have complaints about the rent from the landlord.

Now, you also might wonder why he kept me around the premises, feeding and clothing me and giving me a couple of dollars now and then for spending money. Well, you'll remember how I told you that Findlater felt himself in real need of an education. He not only wanted to be a rich man but he wanted to be a well-educated rich man. And he had it in his head that I came from quality people and was educated, which I didn't exactly deny. So he wanted me to answer questions now and again on such subjects as etiquette, which he was eager to learn. So he'd steal a book from the public library and he'd sit all afternoon in the big armchair by the window puzzling over some problem in good manners. When I'd come in he'd be ready with the questions.

"Now blame it all, Bill, listen to this," he'd say. "Here's a situation that needs workin' out. It says this. Suppose Mr. and Mrs. White are havin' this tea party. And they invite Mr. and Mrs. Black. Then who happens to be walkin' by on the street but Mr. and Mrs. Green. And they decide to drop in for a visit. Now at the same time, staying with the Whites is her maiden aunt Miss Brown. Now supposin' you're Mr. White and the job of sortin' out all the introductions falls on you, what's the polite way of doin' it? I know there's a way, though it looks goddam complicated to me. You see, this maiden aunt throws a wrench into the works by being an old lady, who's got to be treated different. That's the trick part of the question as I see it."

Now that kind of problem was never exactly a part of my everyday childhood experience back on the farm. At the same time, however, my father had always insisted when sober that we pay attention to such things. I don't believe it did much good with Ned and Fred, who were always abnormally uncouth, but it rubbed off on the rest of us more or less, Tom being the natural suave gentleman and Annie turning into a fussy farm wife and me being perhaps a cut above average. So I could answer such questions with reasonable accuracy.

The other thing Findlater paid attention to were the stories and theories of successful men in business. He spent a lot of time painfully working his way through twenty-five-cent books with titles like "Ten Steps to Successful Living" or "How I Made My First Million." Some of these books would inspire him to change his personal habits for a day or two. And thus he'd swear off cigars and whiskey and women and he'd take up some form of physical exercise following the instructions in Chapter Three, which might be called "Your Body Is a Vessel and You Are the Captain." I'd wake up and see him in the middle of the room in his underwear, waving a pair of Indian clubs and shivering his arms up and down in some loosening exercise. To my way of thinking that was the worst kind of foolishness, for it didn't suit his nature. So after a few days he'd get bored and go out and buy himself a cigar and a bottle of whiskey, coming home at three o'clock in the morning to tell me what a sorry specimen of humankind he was.

When Findlater wasn't gambling or reading his books on self-improvement he was poring over the classified advertisements in the daily newspapers. He was fascinated by items such as "Tea planter wishes partner for lucrative operation in Ceylon. Capital required." He'd ask me to write letters to these people and now and again the promoters of these ventures came around to interview Findlater. I remember one Englishman who turned up in a shooting suit and deerstalker hat. I believe he was organizing an expedition to the Belgian Congo. Even a kid like me could have told you after five minutes that this guy was a crackpot. But Findlater was so impressed that his only regret was he didn't have the money to go along. Another fellow tried to sell him a velocipede franchise in Palestine, claiming that all the camels there had fallen prey to a variation of glanders. According to him there wasn't a live camel left in the Holy Land and the people had no way to get around. A few days later we read that this fellow was a confidence man and had been arrested by the police.

From time to time I'd ask Findlater about Sally Butters and he'd say that he was asking around but it was a big city and there were at least two hundred vaudeville and minstrel shows. I got the feeling that he wasn't trying very hard to locate her.

It must have been towards the middle of July when Findlater came down with gold fever. I'd been out walking on this warm night and when I came back to the room I found Findlater pacing back and forth. Now and then he'd stop his march to pour some whiskey into a moustache cup. At first I thought he was in some kind of trouble. But he soon put me straight as to what was bothering him. "Damn it all to hell, Bill," he says. "We need some money, and we need it fast."

"What's the trouble?" I asked. "What's going on?"

He looked at me like I was crazy. "There's no trouble, boy," he says. "But where in hell have you been all day? Under a rock? Ain't you seen the papers? You're never going to amount to anything unless you keep up with what's goin' on in the world. Just look at this now!" And he waved the front page of the paper in front of my eyes. All I could see was the word *gold* before he snatched it away again. "Listen here. A ship loaded with gold nuggets landed at San Francisco yesterday and there's another one due at Seattle any day. Why, it's probably there now. And it says here that people on that boat in San Francisco have come bearing gold nuggets as big as hickory nuts. They got them in the Klondike. That's up in the northwest part of your country, Bill. In the Yukon territories. I remember my old man talking about the Yukon when I was just a kid. He was always convinced there was gold up there. Christ Almighty, it's just a stone's throw from Russia. We've got to get in on this." He was pacing up and down again. He'd rolled the newspaper into a cylinder and was whacking himself on the back of the head with it. "Just think of it. A bunch of fellows stepped off that boat with sacks of gold. Trunkloads of it. Goddam millionaires now! And six months ago they didn't own more than the clothes on their backsides."

The whole thing seemed too much for him to fathom and he sat down exhausted with his legs spread out, fanning himself with the paper. After a minute he says, almost to himself, "They started with nothing and now those boys are holed up in fancy hotels taking baths in champagne wine. Bill, we've got to get out there and get ourselves some of that gold. Why, the railroads are already announcing excursion trains. Do you know that a couple of fellows I play pool with have already left? We got to get ourselves some financing and get the hell out there."

Now when a fellow is pursuing a subject like that and generating his own enthusiasm along the way, the last thing he wants to hear is discouragement. He doesn't want anybody throwing cold water on his dreams, which is what I did, in a manner of speaking, when I suggested to him that most of what he read about this gold strike was probably just paper talk that a person couldn't half believe. Now, at the time what I was trying to do was preserve what some Roman once called in Latin the *status quo*. That means the state of things as they are. And as far as I was concerned, the state of things was pretty good. I had a clean bed, good eats, and change in my pocket. What more could a young fellow want? It never seemed to occur to me that all this came by Findlater's pocket. I wasn't doing a shred of work and in fact was growing as lazy as Ludlam's dog. I spent a good part of my time dreaming. I saw myself wearing a fine new bowler hat and wing collar with a diamond stickpin up front. Spending my afternoons at the vaudeville matinees and my evenings with the chorus girls at smart cafés. And one day Sally Butters would spot me and inquire from a friend who the handsome young gentleman was. Then we'd marry and live on the top floor of the Ritz Hotel, which was then the fanciest in New York City. So things were pretty good just the way they were and I couldn't see any point in traipsing right across the continent for gold that probably wasn't there to begin with.

Findlater was so disappointed at my general lack of enthusiasm that he got into a regular huff, gathering up bits of clothing and opening drawers, trying to appear busy while holding in his rage. Then he says to me, "You have it your own way, Billy boy. Just stay around this town and look for stage singers, which by the way are a dime a dozen. You just stay here and amount to exactly nothin'. But there's an opportunity of a lifetime waitin' out there in those Yukon territories and I ain't gonna let it slip by."

"Well, go right ahead," I says. "Go on out and make your fortune.

I wish you all the luck in the world, though I don't know where you're going to get the money to transport yourself out there. Maybe you're going to get it by playing pool for five cents a game or passing off dollar watches to tourists."

Of course I had no right to say that and I had it coming to me when he jumped across the room and, grabbing my tie, put me back none too gently against the wall. Then he pushed a big fist under my nose and said, "Now you just listen a minute to me, pal. It seems to me you might just be growing a little too big for your britches." That remark sounded familiar enough. "Now I like you, Bill," continues Findlater, "and I hope I ain't holdin' the wrong opinion of you. But that don't mean I'm gonna take any sass from you. So you just better watch your mouth when you talk about me and how I make my money. There's no need for you to make fun of an ambitious man. No need at all." Then he let me go and we both fell into this terrible sulk whereby we walked about the room avoiding each other and not talking.

The next morning when I woke up Findlater was sitting at the table writing things down in a little black notebook. In front of him was a small pile of bills and a stack of coins. He appeared to be working out sums, an occupation he was very diligent at. By now our tempers had cooled but there was a definite edginess in the air. Now, most times when that happens to two people who are living at close quarters you get a helluva lot of exaggerated politeness. Nobody ever says "Good morning" or "How are you feeling?" What's more apt to happen is that one or the other will say something like "Excuse me, but I believe that's my boot under your chair." Or "If it's all the same to you, I think I'll open this window." And the other party always replies, "Why, sure. Go right ahead. Am I in your way? I beg your pardon." Well, that's the sort of nonsense that went on all morning between Findlater and me. The truth is, neither of us was man enough to apologize to the other.

That afternoon I decided to look for work so I would be independent. Now, things were pretty good in the way of jobs. That is, if you wanted to bend your back and work up a sweat. There was a lot of new buildings going up in New York in those days and they were always looking for hod carriers and the like. However, I wasn't going to get anything like that walking about in my fancy clothes, and in any case I wasn't sure it would suit my temperament. I thought instead that I might look for something in the line of shop assistant in one of the big department stores. So I sifted all these thoughts through my head as I walked along Fourteenth Street on this particular day. By and by a thunderstorm built up and the lightning and thunder crackled and there was a helluva downpour. I stepped under the awning of Huber's Museum, which wasn't a museum at all but a vaudeville theater. And, as was my custom, I scanned the advertising material next to the ticket office. And God Almighty, there it was! Down near the end of the program! *Sally Butters. Romantic Song Stylist.* Naturally

13. Gold Fever

I forgot about work and bought a ticket for the matinee, which was just beginning.

I had a seat near the front and I was so excited that I suppose I fidgeted, for a couple of rough-looking birds behind me told me to sit still. They'd brought a bag of ripe vegetables and fruit to throw at the performers. The show was just about the same as all the others I'd seen and so I suffered through the tumbling acts and the black-faced comedians. When it came time for Sally to appear, I sat there figuring out how to kill the first joker who threw a tomato at her. Maybe I'd tear loose a seat and slam him over the head. Or carve out his heart with my little penknife. What would Esther Easterbrook think of her gift then, I wondered. But it never happened, for instead of Sally, out comes this old swag-bellied fool in a clawhammer coat and proceeds to imitate a steamboat race on the Mississippi River while dodging various cabbages and oranges. After him there was a bunch of girls kicking up their heels, but Sally wasn't among them. Then they rang down the curtain and played the "Stars and Stripes" and the house lights came on.

Well, I was determined not to leave that theater until I'd seen Sally and told her how I was willing to devote the rest of my life to her happiness. Thus I made my way backstage. Surprisingly enough, it was almost deserted back there, with performers already dressed in street clothes hurrying by me for the exit. At first I thought of fire and sniffed for smoke as I explored the various empty dressing rooms. Some people had even left clothes behind. Finally I heard a noise behind this door and I pushed it open. A short, bald-headed man in his shirtsleeves was stuffing clothes into a suitcase and talking to himself. Every now and then he stopped to swallow some whiskey from a pint flask. He noticed me as he plucked two neckties off a dresser mirror. "Don't ever go into this business, son," he says to me. "You'll die of a broken heart."

"I'm looking for a girl named Sally Butters," I says, pointing to her name on the program.

"Yes, sir," he says, without paying the least attention to me. "They'll break your heart in this racket. If you want my advice, son, you'd be better off in a sound trade. Something that's got a future. Like maybe a blacksmith. I got a brother-in-law who's a blacksmith and he's always done well, though he's as thick in the head as shit in a bottle." He picked up the flask. "Care for a drink?"

I shook my head. "Now listen. I've been looking for this girl. She was supposed to sing this afternoon. It says right here." He bent down and squinted at the program. And he laughed. "What's so damn funny?" I asks. "It happens that I've been looking for this girl now for months."

"Well, I'll tell you something, son," he says, taking out his watch. "I'm not inquiring into your business, because it ain't none of mine. But I'll tell you this. About four hours ago I was looking for the same lady myself for the simple reason that she was hired on to sing five numbers for us. But she's gone. And what did I have to do? Put Hooter McPhee on, and he's got to be the world's worst imitator of steamboats. The audience didn't like it. You heard them. I don't blame them. I wouldn't pay money to listen to that man either. But what the hell could I do? I had to fill a spot. Oh, this business isn't worth it! It isn't worth the pain. I'm giving you fair warning. Have a drink?"

I waved away the bottle. "Where did she go?" I asks.

"Where did she go?" he says, shaking his head. "Where have they all been going for the past couple of days? Out to the Klondike gold diggin's, that's where! Why, somebody told me that dance hall girls can make a hundred dollars a night out there. Those fool miners are probably just dying to throw their money away. I was at Leadville, Colorado, twenty years ago when they discovered silver. Talk about throwing money away!" He snapped shut the buckles on his valise and pulled on a suit coat. "If you want a job, son, you're welcome to this one, though personally I ain't recommending it. I go through a bottle of Hood's Sarsaparilla every week and that'll give you an idea of the state of my nerves."

"Where are you going?" I asks.

"To the Klondike," he says. "Where else? If I can't relieve those miners of some of that gold my name ain't Freddy Huggins. You can finish that whiskey if you like." And he was gone, slamming the door behind him.

The only thing I could do now was to hurry back to the room and tell Findlater that he'd been right all along. And that if he was still looking for a partner to go west with him, I'd be only too glad to be chosen.

14

HO FOR THE KLONDIKE

You'd have to go a long way to meet a happier man than Findlater when I told him that I wanted to go to the Yukon Territory with him. I didn't mention anything about Sally but merely said I'd changed my mind and felt that the trip might be educational, for it's generally known that traveling broadens the mind. Well, I couldn't have said anything that would have pleased him more, for Findlater always stood in awe of the word *education*. "I'd not thought of it that way, Bill, but damn it all, you're dead right. Of course travelin' broadens the mind." Then he grabbed me by the shoulders and hugged me. "I knew you'd come to your senses, Billy. God, what a team we'll make! And in no time at all we'll be pickin' up those gold nuggets. But first we got to get ourselves some financin'."

"And how do you propose to do that?" I asks.

"Well," he says, getting up and going to his dresser. "While you was out I purchased a few little items from a friend of mine. With the proper merchandising they should pay for our fare to Seattle. After that we can think about something else. Now what do you make of these?" And on this handkerchief he laid out about two dozen diamond rings. On first glance it looked like a fortune but of course they were only made of paste and glass and chicken wire.

The next day I performed my first act of larceny with Findlater. What we did was go to the city hall and stand outside the office where they peddled marriage licenses. In those days immigrants by the hundreds lined up for these licenses, so the place was crowded with marriage brokers hanging around waiting for their commissions and a number of gents like us selling everything from life insurance to funeral plots. I would say that without exception these salesmen were all shysters. Now, what Findlater would do was corner a couple just as they left this office and were happily babbling away to themselves in a foreign tongue. He'd congratulate them and then give them *free* this cheap scroll upon which was written the words to "The Stars and Stripes Forever." You never saw such grateful people! Then, as they stood there pumping his hand, he'd take out this velvet case and there would be three or four of these fake diamonds sparkling and glittering on the cloth. After he'd laid out the rings he'd start his sales pitch, which was mostly in sign language. Usually he'd put the ring on the girl's finger and let her admire it. When her fiancé saw how happy this made her, he'd usually fork over the ten bucks, convinced he'd made a bargain. Now some were outright suspicious but most stopped and politely listened. Nearly all of them were afraid to offend anyone who spoke English. I tried my hand too, and after a few refusals made a sale. When I took the fellow's money I felt the briefest touch of conscience knowing that his bride would have a green finger within a day or two. I imagine Findlater and me got a number of marriages off to a rocky start that summer.

By the middle of the afternoon we'd flogged the rings and had about a hundred bucks, so we cleared out. That night we left our premises for good, conveniently forgetting two weeks' rent that was owing. By raw daylight we were eating ham and eggs in the dining saloon of the *Pacific Flyer* and while I gazed out the window at my first stretch of countryside in months, Findlater was deep into conversation with two businessmen. Most of the talk centered on the long journey ahead and the possibility of diverting the boredom by a game of chance involving fifty-two cards.

What do I remember about that first trip across the United States of America? I suppose I should have looked more at the scenery, but people have always interested me more than rivers and forests and flatland and mountains. Mostly I was alone, for Findlater spent the entire journey looking at a poker hand. Thus I amused myself by studying the passengers. Now, not everybody aboard was stampeding for gold. There were plenty of regular travelers, entire families and the like. But there was also a goodly number bound for the gold fields, and you could always pick them out from the others. As I saw it, they fell into two distinct types. The first type were rowdies, loud-mouthed fellows who drank a lot and would pick a fight for two cents. The long train trip bored them silly, so after a while they'd look around for some childish pastime to amuse themselves with. They might take the scissors to a fellow's whiskers or snip his suspenders while he slept in his seat. Sometimes they'd fart and then look around, blaming it on some little old lady. They ruined the conductor's health and made eating in the dining room a regular endurance test. And, by the way, most of those jokers never made it up to the Klondike. Either they ran out of money or ended up in jail or just didn't have the gumption to last.

Now the man who succeeded almost always belonged to the second type of stampeder. This man was generally a loner and you could tell by the way he carried himself, rigid and withdrawn, that he had the fever. Usually he didn't stir too much from his seat but just sat there day after day, affecting to look relaxed with his cheek in his fist as he stared out the window. But inside he was boiling away with ambition to be a rich man. He might be just an underpaid bank clerk or a schoolteacher. Or he might be an older man leaving behind a family and a prosperous business. Whatever—he was now transformed into a new person with a fanatic's eye in his head. The only thing a fellow like that could see as he crossed America was gold. And you knew looking at him that he wouldn't rest until he'd done his damnedest to find some.

By the time we reached Chicago I began to think I was destined to be hungry while traveling by train. The fact is that we were eating only once a day, skipping breakfast and supper and making do with the midday meal. The bread and rolls were plentiful and free and we filled our pockets after every meal but your stomach still growled. The reason for this was that we were running out of money because Findlater was losing at cards. He played all day and about midnight he'd return to our seat, his clothes reeking of cigar smoke and his eyes rimmed with red. He'd sit there for a while, not saying much and sometimes shaking his head and laughing. To look at him you wouldn't guess he was losing. Then he'd say, "By God, I've got myself into a game with a real operator, Bill. A former police captain from Philadelphia. I don't believe I've ever seen a slicker devil with the cards. He's got a number of tricks I haven't seen before, though I will say I'm learning fast. The man is an educational experience. Did I mention that he's carrying a sidearm?"

"No," I says. "You didn't. What about the other fellow?"

"A boozer! And rich too. But I'm afraid he's lost his shirt and buttons. I just left him. He's as stiff as the pecker in your pants. Now if I'd just had a couple more like him. But that Captain Spraat! By Jesus, he's clever."

"How much have you lost?" I asks.

"Game's not over yet, Bill. Not by a long shot. We resume competition tomorrow at nine. There's another couple of fellows wants in."

"But," I says, "if you can't win against this guy, why not quit and cut your losses?"

"Can't do that, Bill."

"Why not?"

"The captain has my I.O.U. for five big ones."

"God Almighty," I says. "Not five hundred dollars!"

"I'm afraid so, Bill. And by the way, I'd appreciate it if you kept your voice down so as not to spread alarm."

"How did you ever get hooked like that?" I whispered.

Findlater scratched at the stubble on his jaw. "I thought I might be able to outfox that son of a whore if I kept at it long enough. But he's been too sharp for me. He knows I'm cheating but the fact is that he's out-cheating me. And he looks like a sore loser too."

"Well, what are you going to do now?" I asks.

Findlater dropped his cigar to the floor and stepped on it. "I've told these jaspers that I'm a big-shot jam manufacturer from Albany, New York, and that I'm on a selling trip. My company is wiring me extra expense money at Seattle. Now I've told the captain that if by the time we reach Seattle I'm still in arrears, I'll settle things there. Of course, what I'm hopin' to do by then is figure out how in hell he's doin' it. Either he's palmin' the cards or he's got some kind of mirror system but I'm ——ed if I can figure it." Findlater then stretched out his legs and tipped his hat over his eyes. "Well, tomorrow's another day, Bill, and we'll just see." And with that he goes right to sleep and is soon snoring with everybody else. He was never a man to let anything get him down.

At dinner the next day Findlater reported that he was just holding his own but the former policeman was raising the stakes. Already a stockbroker had left the game to be replaced by a drunken stampeder who'd been cleaned out in fifteen minutes. They were now playing three-handed stud at five bucks a chip. "I also believe," says Findlater, sneaking a few dinner rolls into his coat pocket, "that our friend the captain is a fugitive from justice. That's just a guess, mind you, but he's dropped a hint now and then, and that should make it a little more comfortable for us, Bill." So I asked him how he figured that out and he said, "Well now, look. Think about it. If the captain is tryin' to avoid detection, he's not going to press too hard with the authorities if things don't go his own way."

"Maybe so," I says. "But suppose he decides to take the law into his own hands. You did say he was carrying a gun, didn't you?"

"Yes, I did," says Findlater. "But damn it all, Bill, I'm trying to look at this situation on the positive side. You know something? For a young fellow, you're awful damn gloomy."

Later I strolled through the club car to get a look at this police captain and he was a tough-looking customer, all right. A big, beefy fellow with thick black moustaches and his mouth set in a grim line. I watched them play for a while and though Findlater was getting off some good jokes the captain didn't smile once.

That afternoon I saw my first Indian. We were crossing a patch of desert and boulders. There were mountains off to the west and as we sailed through this little town about a half-dozen Indians stood on the platform and waved to us. They wore flannel shirts and work pants, and except for the long braided hair and ten-gallon hats, I'd have taken them for Italians standing around after church on Sunday. Those Indians put me in mind of my father and his dream of living on berries and moose meat among tribes of natural people. It made me wonder what had become of him and Miss Boswell, and I spent the rest of that day feeling sad about everything.

A couple of days later we arrived in Seattle, Washington. I was damn glad to get off that train, suffering as I did from back cramps and bunged-up intestines. Findlater owed this Barney Spraat eight hundred and fifty dollars and naturally Spraat accompanied us off the train. He was a sullen man of few words and he trudged along beside us carrying a cheap-looking pebbled black valise. I didn't like him and he didn't appear overly fond of me either. If Findlater was worried, he wasn't letting on. He kept babbling away about what a great morning it was and how good it felt to be alive. At one point he bent down and scooped up a handful of dirt. The street was so jammed with people that you could hardly move but Findlater elbowed himself some room and he shoved this handful of dirt under the captain's nose and says, "Do you see that, Barney? What do you think this is in my hand?"

A number of people stopped to listen. The captain gave Findlater a queer, suspicious look and says, "Dirt."

"Well, of course it's dirt!" says Findlater. "But Barney, my friend, it's more than just dirt. This here is the soil of America. And we should thank God on our bended knee that we live in a country where the opportunities are so great."

"Amen to that, brother!" said a bearded character from the crowd.

"Why, look at all these people, Barney!" says Findlater, spreading out his arms. "They come from every walk of life to try their hand at wooing old Dame Fortune. What a great thing it is to be alive and enjoying all this! Don't you think so, Barney?" Spraat looked baffled and then says, "Where's this telegraph office?" He wanted his money and you couldn't really fault him for that. After five days on a train the last thing he needed was a sermon on America delivered on a dusty street.

So we moved on through this crowd. Findlater was right about one thing. Seattle was packed with the damnedest collection of people and animals you ever saw. It was like a big street carnival with everybody trying to sell you something or inquiring as to when the next steamer left for the Klondike. Little kids stood on street corners peddling rotten apples or holding up signs telling you where to buy boots or underwear. A man would pluck you by the sleeve and say, "Goin' to the Klondike, mister? Come around to McDougall's on Canal Street. He's just got in a brand-new shipment of canvas pants. Ten percent below anyone else. They won't last. Now I'm doin' you a favor." Of course you knew that they were probably two hundred percent above what they would have been a month before.

There were people in that town of all sizes and descriptions. You'd see maybe a gang of Chinamen pulling a wagonload of work shirts and pickaxes. Or there'd be fellows strolling about in brand-new mackinaws and big hats and boots that creaked as they walked. These jokers pretended to be real miners. In fact a week before they'd been selling shoes in Kansas City or calling home the cows in some godforsaken farm in upper Michigan. The streets were filled with animals too. On one corner you'd see perhaps a half-dozen yapping dogs whose owner was trying to peddle them to somebody. Across the street there might be burros or ponies or a pair of old oxen standing at a hitching post like statues.

After making a few inquiries we found ourselves opposite Western Union and Findlater says, "Now we're in business, boys! We'll step across to the telegraph office and then we'll find ourselves some breakfast and settle with our friend Barney here. Boys, I don't know about you but I'm so hungry I could eat the arse out of a dead skunk and whistle through the hole for more. Now mind, I'm buying."

We were standing in this crowd when suddenly Findlater reached out and lunged after this little fellow in a herringbone suit who was hurrying to catch a streetcar. Findlater missed him and then seized Barney Spraat's arm. "Your wallet, Barney!" he says. "I saw him take it. That little fellow in the herringbone. Look, he's gonna board that tram!" Another puzzled look crossed the police captain's blunt features and he slapped his pockets. "Come on, Bill," says Findlater. "We'll get that sneaky little bugger." And before I knew it he was pulling me through the crowd. Over my shoulder I saw the captain making his way too, though he was not a nimble man on his feet. We just managed to squeeze through the streetcar door before the conductor closed it. We could see Barney Spraat running along behind the tram for a few yards and Findlater was shouting at him, "Don't worry about a thing, Barney. We've got him cornered. We'll meet you at the Western Union in a half-hour." Spraat finally stopped and stood on the tracks with no change of expression on his face. I have to say he was a good man at hiding his true feelings.

We ate breakfast in a hotel dining room and Findlater said, "I'm disappointed in Captain Spraat. I thought he would have carried more than three hundred dollars in his purse. He must have kept some in his shoe or maybe in that damn valise." But three hundred dollars was better than nothing, for Seattle was a poor place to be without money, prices being ten times higher than anywhere else. Now Findlater had it in his head that we'd get up to the Yukon for a couple of hundred dollars, pick up a bushel of nuggets, and be back before winter. Innocent as I was, I didn't think it would be that easy and it made me consider that maybe his story about prospecting for gold with his father was a load of cod wallop. But he wasn't alone in thinking it would be easy. A lot of people felt the same way.

Not that we weren't warned. That first night in Seattle we talked to an old-timer who was sitting on some timber in a lumberyard peeling an apple. He told us to forget about the whole thing. The steamship companies were charging several hundred dollars over what it was worth and anyway they were booked for weeks ahead. And a fellow would need at least three or four hundred dollars' worth of gear if he was serious about gold digging in the North Country. He was a sober-faced old fellow and he waved his arm at the clumps of men who stood around in the hot night smoking and talking. "I know what digging for gold is like," he says, "and half these yaps will curse the day they ever set foot in the north."

14. Ho for the Klondike

But Findlater couldn't abide a pessimist, so after this old fellow enumerated about ten perfectly sensible reasons for not bothering with the Klondike, Findlater says, "Goddamit to hell, Gramps. Can't you look on the bright side of anything?"

The old stampeder didn't stir but just finished his apple, wiping his knife on his shirtsleeve. "I'm just tellin' you what I learned in forty years of diggin' gold, mister," he says.

"Well, why are you goin' then?" asks Findlater.

"Cause I'm a damn fool," says the old fellow. "That's why. And so are you. And so is the lad here travelin' with you. So are all these men here on the streets and sleepin' in barns and alleyways awaitin' those boats!"

"Well," says Findlater, "I ain't buyin' your song and dance, old-timer. Bill here and me are goin' up to those Yukon territories and we're gonna get ourselves a trunkful of those nuggets. Then we're comin' back and we're gonna buy ten suits each and stop up at every fancy hotel in this great country. Then when we get tired of livin' like that, we're gonna sail around the world in a first-class accommodation. Meet up with some of those nabobs in Arabia and places like that."

The old fellow just greeted all that with a cracked laugh. He was still chuckling when we wandered over to a crowd that was listening to a preacher thunder away on the sin of greed. He had a good subject there, for you'd have to go a long way to find more naked greed than was on display in that town. The preacher, a lean, handsome man in a frock coat, was steaming right through the Scriptures from Genesis to Revelations noting passages that dealt with accumulating money. *It is easier for a camel to go through the eye of a needle than for a rich man to enter the Kingdom of God.* Sections like that! A friend of his circulated in the crowd peddling New Testaments for twenty-five cents apiece.

Standing right next to us were a couple of strong-smelling drovers. They were dressed in sheepskin jackets and gave off the pungent fragrance of a cattle train. They were drinking and having a time mocking this preacher. "You tell 'em, Reverend," one yelled, and his partner, a tall toothless drink of water with a bad eye, cupped these dirty hands to his mouth and shouts, "Give us that part again about the meek inheritin' the earth."

Then Findlater stepped out in front of both of them and he grabbed a handful of the tall one's flannel shirt and he says, "You smell ten times worse than a sheep's arse and your manners ain't all they might be either. Now there's two things I don't want ——ers like you makin' fun of. One is the flag of this great country. And the other is the Holy Christian religion. Now get the hell out of here before I kick your dirty backsides all the way to the sheep pen where you come from." And the drovers didn't wait to be persuaded either but took right off.

"God bless you, friend!" yelled the preacher, and his partner came through the crowd and shook Findlater's hand.

"Brother," he says, "the good Lord smiles on what you just done. I hope you'll accept a Testament with our compliments. The word of God is a friend in the night."

"I thank you," says Findlater, taking the Testament, which was nicely wrapped up in white tissue paper and bound by gold-colored string.

We left shortly after and Findlater was in a good humor when he said, "I guess we'd better find ourselves a place for the night, Bill. We'll just have to part with a few more of the good captain's dollars." With that he reaches for his wallet and damn me for a liar if the purse isn't gone! "Well, goddamit to hell," says Findlater, stopping in the middle of the street and slapping his clothes, looking much the same as Captain Spraat had looked earlier in the day. "Why, I've been robbed," Findlater roared to everyone passing by. It seemed like the worst insult ever handed to him and at one point he buttonholed a stranger and said, "Do you know what's just happened to me in this goddam town? Some thieving no-good son of a whore has stolen my purse." The stranger broke loose and hurried away, for which I didn't blame him.

Well, Findlater carried on like that for some time, complaining about Seattle being a den of thieves and where were the goddam police when you needed them, etc., etc. I finally managed to calm him down and at the same time come across a place advertising sleeping quarters for a dollar a head. It was an outrageous price to pay for sleeping in a stable but it was the best we could find. The place was filled with snoring men and smelled worse than those two drovers but we found ourselves a spot up in the loft and sat there leaning against the wall. After five minutes Findlater says, "You know, Bill, that's the first time anybody's done that to me. The very first time."

"Well, maybe," I says, "it's just the way things even out. After all, the captain probably isn't sleeping any too well tonight either. I read a book once where this fellow used philosophy to argue that it's six of one and a half dozen of the other."

Findlater thought for a moment and then he laughed. "You know, you're right, Bill. That fellow with the philosophy is right too. A fellow is a fool to get upset by life's little misfortunes. Why, who knows what tomorrow will bring if you keep a sharp eye in your head. Sometime maybe I'll look up that book. It sounds instructional." He'd fetched out the Testament and was working on the gold string, trying to pry it loose. But it was tighter than wire and Findlater says, "Well, it was nice of that little feller to give me one of these Bibles but he don't exactly encourage people to read it by hiding it behind this string." He finally broke it with his teeth and then he unwrapped the tissue paper and found himself staring at a neat little triangle of chopped newspaper. He must have looked at it for ten seconds before saying to me, "Will you look at that now, Bill? That little skunk put one over on me. And I'll bet he picked my pocket into the bargain. By God, that

122

took nerve!" And the humor of it struck him so hard that he started to laugh. He laughed until men woke up cursing and shouting for us to pipe down. But Findlater was still chuckling to himself when I dozed off.

Now, losing that money put us in a fairly desperate situation. And next morning, after washing up at a fire hydrant, we walked around the streets of Seattle, keeping a weather eye in our heads for Captain Spraat and figuring out how to get some money. All the time I kept thinking how crazy I was to be running all over the continent chasing a girl I'd only talked to for an hour of my life. But such is the strong and magical power of love! Then something happened that changed our fortune. First, we noticed this fight outside a saloon. It wasn't much of a fight, because the contestants were so unevenly matched. This big, rough-looking joker in a mackinaw had collared a skinny little fellow in a suit and straw hat and he was holding him out at arm's length, just shaking him like a cat with a mouse. It was getting a laugh from the loafers who can always be found loitering outside a tavern door. We never did find out how it started but it was plain that the little fellow was in for a thrashing because his opponent was drunk enough not to know his own strength. Findlater never cared for an uneven fight and I figure he wasn't in the best humor anyway owing to his empty stomach. So what he did was step between them and say to this big fellow, "Here now, you half-arsed excuse for a man. Why don't you pick on someone more your size?" And a few seconds later Findlater left him lying in the dirt with a swollen nose and a few gaps in his teeth.

The little fellow was so grateful that he insisted on treating us, and over flapjacks and bacon he told us his name was Sam Dowd. He'd come up from California the minute he'd heard about the gold rush. He could have gone to San Francisco but he said he wasn't too welcome in that town. He'd been in Seattle for two weeks but was clearing out that afternoon. Now this statement was genuinely intriguing, because everybody else was flocking to the city, not planning to leave.

"What line are you in anyways, Sam?" asked Findlater. We'd both taken an instant liking to this courteous little dandy.

"I've been in a number of lines, neighbor. And not all of them too straight," says Sam, smiling and cleaning his teeth with his own gold toothpick. "I've been down to Leadville, Colorado. I've followed all the big strikes over the past thirty years. Trying to make a dollar here and there." Here he leaned forward on his elbows and whispered, "Fact is, boys, the law and me ain't exactly bosom friends. Now you take I've been in this selling business for the past couple of weeks. But it seems the police aren't exactly overwhelmed with what I'm selling."

"And what would that be?" I asks.

"Evaporated food, son," says Sam, leaning back in his chair.

"Well, what's wrong with selling evaporated food?" asks Findlater.

"Nothing much," says Sam. "Unless you happen to sell evaporated food that really evaporates. In say about two weeks."

"Well now, by God," says Findlater, smiling. "That's something, ain't it?"

"Yes, sir," says Sam. "And business has been brisk. I really hate to leave this place but I'm going with about five thousand dollars. Which isn't bad money for a couple of weeks' work."

"Five thousand dollars!" cries Findlater, and Sam calmly put a finger to his lips.

"Neighbor, the walls have ears."

Findlater leaned forward. "Sam, you're manna from Heaven. The fact is that Bill here and me need a stake to get us up to the gold fields."

"I'll be honest with you, Mr. Findlater," Sam says. "I advise against getting into this business. For the past couple of days I've been followed by a detective. I just shook him off this morning. You see, the trouble with my line is that I'm competing with the merchants. They're all as crooked as a dog's hind leg but they get away with it because they're respectable businessmen. They go to church on Sunday morning after counting up the week's receipts. But the truth is they're gouging every poor devil who passes through this town. Some of them have marked up goods by a thousand percent. And they get away with it because the greenhorns will pay anything to get outfitted. So when a fellow like me comes along and tries to make a dollar out on the street they cry no fair and go running to the police. I'm unfair competition, you see. So I got this detective looking for me and I'm clearing out this afternoon. Heading down to New Orleans. Now that is a civilized town."

Findlater just shook his head in admiration. "By God, Sam, you sure got your hat on straight. But look here! Bill and me are in bad shape. We could use an angle or two."

"Well, look," says Sam. "If you're down on your luck I'll be glad to advance you a hundred dollars. If we meet again and you're in better financial shape, you can repay me. If we don't cross paths again, I'll write it off as a thank-you note for helping me out back there."

"That's white of you, Sam," says Findlater. "But the truth is, you were talking about five thousand dollars a minute ago. That's the kind of money I had in mind."

Sam finished his coffee and frowned at us. "I'm not denying the money is there to be made. And it can come fast if you know who to work. But what I want you to appreciate is the risk involved. They are looking for people in the evaporated food business, Mr. Findlater."

"Hell's fire," says Findlater. "What's a little risk? You have to take a risk every day of your life. Even legitimate businessmen take risks. I'll bet John D. Rocketfeller takes risks every day."

"Well," says Sam, smiling, "with due respect, neither of you is any John D. Rockefeller. But look, you did me a favor back there and Sam

14. Ho for the Klondike

Dowd never forgets a favor. If you're that anxious to try your luck on the street, you better come back to my place and I'll show you a few things."

Sam rented several rooms on the third floor of this brick house. There were flowerpots on the window sills and a brushed rug mat at the doorstep. Everything was clean as a whistle and you could tell that you were in a respectable part of town. In his sitting room Sam spoke quickly and quietly and as I listened to him I couldn't help thinking what a wonderful teacher he would make. "All right," he says, "I want you both to give me your undivided attention, because I haven't much time. Rule one. No matter what line of business you get into, and no matter if you conduct that business down on the waterfront among the worst riffraff in this country, a good confidence man always lives in a good area of town. Not necessarily the most expensive, because rich surroundings call attention to themselves. You don't make your headquarters in any fancy place, but on a street like this. People here take pride in their homes. They are respectable solid citizens. Lawyers, schoolteachers, merchants and so on. You never see a policeman in this neighborhood, because there is no need of one. These people do all their stealing down on the main street and then come home to water their lawns and play with their children.

"Rule two. You keep regular hours. You leave in the morning and you come back in the evening and you don't arouse suspicion. You smile at your neighbors, lift your hat to the ladies, and pat the heads of their children.

"Rule three. You don't offer too much information about yourself but you do invent a nice little family of wife and three children back in St. Paul or Spokane. And you tell them you can't wait to get your business cleared away in Seattle because you miss your family so much. My landlady Mrs. Parker reckons, for instance, that I'm a drummer working for a food company out of Portland. And that's what she should think. Now, I'm sure you noticed that before we left the restaurant I telephoned someone. Now, who was that someone? It was Mrs. Parker. Why?

"That brings us to rule four. Never depart from convention unless that departure is adequately explained. People are creatures of habit and they get easily upset or suspicious when habits change. I called Mrs. Parker, for instance, to tell her that I would be having two gentlemen back for a business discussion. If I hadn't, the sight of two strangers entering this house would get the neighbors talking. Now Mrs. Parker has done it all for us. The word has got around that I'm having business associates in for tea and there wasn't a single person behind their curtain when we walked up the front steps fifteen minutes ago.

"Rule five. When you're living in these kind of lodgings, avoid tobacco and alcohol. That way you'll always be in favor with people like Mrs. Parker and her neighbors. It's been my observation that a man in this country can be a bank robber, rapist, or swindler. None of these pastimes will hurt his reputation with women like Mrs. Parker half so much as if he takes a drink of gin or smokes an after-dinner cigar. So never miss the opportunity to condemn them as evils. Now, I asked Mrs. Parker over the telephone to bring us up some tea. That way she'll be able to look you over out of the corner of her eye and feel more comfortable about having you in her house. So I wonder, Mr. Findlater, if you'd mind removing your hat. That's in the interests of authenticity, because you're supposed to be a successful business-man from Spokane and young Bill here is your partner."

Findlater snatched the hat from his head as though it was afire. Then a few minutes later Sam opened the door and admitted a stout, gray-haired lady who carried a tray of cakes and teacups. Sam Dowd treated her like a queen and she was so flustered she could only blush like a schoolgirl. "Thank you, Mrs. Parker," he says, stuffing a dollar bill into her apron pocket. "You're a wonderful reminder of my own dear mother." After she'd gone and Sam had checked at the door for departing footsteps he turned to us and said, "Rule six. Don't be afraid to grease the palms of these good citizens. They'll never admit it but they love a dollar bill more than God or their children."

Then he made a washing motion with his hands and said, "Now let's get down to particulars. What you're both going to do is sell this handsome little valise and its contents for the sum of one hundred and fifty dollars. You're going to sell it to some greenhorn with gold in his eyes who's just blown in from Buffalo, New York, or Winnipeg, Manitoba. With a little practice you'll soon recognize the sort of man who'll be interested. He'll be traveling light and he'll want to stay that way. He won't even be particularly interested in mining gold himself but living off them who do. In other words, he'll have a scheme or two of his own. The town's full of them. First you take a look at his hands and make sure they're soft even if they're not clean. That'll mean he's an indoor man and probably hasn't been farther north than Puget Sound. So your customer for this little item is a man who figures to buy this valise for one hundred and fifty dollars and then sell it up in the Klondike for fifteen hundred. All right now! What's in this little bag, you ask?"

Sam had now removed his coat and was walking back and forth like those fellows who demonstrate six-bladed paring knives at county fairs. "I'll tell you what's in this bag, gentlemen," he says. "Food and drink enough to keep a grown man alive and healthy in the far north for a full year. Yes, a grown man, gentlemen. And giving him at the same time a menu as varied and nourishing as the Palmer House Hotel in Chicago, Illinois. Thanks to the modern miracles of scientific pack-aging, you can carry enough food in this little satchel to feed yourself three meals a day for fifty-two weeks or one full year." Sam snapped open the buckle on the valise and began to lay out little tins and bottles on the table. "Milk tablets," he says, holding up a bottle. "Scientifically dehydrated from the finest Jersey milk. Eighteen percent butterfat content. Coffee lozenges which dissolve instantly in water for a delicious hot drink in the middle of your busy day. Desiccated olives to dress up your Sunday dinner." He then held up what looked to me like a roll of sausage. "This, friends," he says, "happens to be split-pea soup. All you do is slice a piece off the roll, submerge in hot water, and in seconds you have a piping-hot bowlful of nourishing soup. Thirty-five bowlfuls to the roll. Do you like scrambled eggs first thing in the morning? Well, who doesn't, is what I ask. Look now!" And he held up a bag of yellow powder and poured some into a skillet. We followed him to the kitchen, where he cooked this powder on a little vapor stove. In a few seconds he had a panful of scrambled eggs simmering away.

Findlater and me both tasted those eggs and declared them delicious. Sam then took this bag of yellow powder and says, "Smell that!" We both sniffed it. "Well?" says Sam, looking at us in triumph.

"I can't make it out," says Findlater.

I took a pinch of the stuff and tasted it. "There's no egg taste to that," I says.

"Course not," says Sam. "Because what you're tasting there is plain old corn meal at ten cents a peck."

"Goddam," says Findlater in amazement.

"A little sleight of hand and you switch for the egg powder. Best thing is to merchandise all this at night. Look for a barrel fire on cool nights. You've seen crowds of men standing around them. It makes everything easier if they can't see you too closely. It should be easier with the two of you working this. I always had to do everything by myself."

Well, Sam showed us a number of other clever things and then he told us we could buy these evaporated food valises from a friend of his for twenty-five bucks, giving us a clear profit of a hundred and twenty-five on each sale. He wrote down the address of this fellow and added a special note to the effect that we were friends. And to show you what a good fellow Sam was, he gave us his one remaining sample valise and advanced us a hundred dollars. "And now, boys," he says, "if you'll excuse me I have to get cleaned up and packed, for I've got a train to catch. I wish you both the best of luck." So we shook hands and I was sorry to leave, for Sam Dowd was one of the nicest fellows I've ever come across. I never saw him again but I'll tell you that by chance I read a few years later in the *Police Gazette* how he was shot to death by a rich man's son down in Louisville, Kentucky, in some dispute over a horse race. I was sorry to read that, for he certainly treated us fair and square.

That very night Findlater and me decided to try our hand at selling this valise. We figured that if we were successful, we'd buy another three or four the next morning. It was a rainy night and before long we found one of these barrel fires in a vacant lot and there were ten or fifteen men huddled around it telling lies to one another. The sort of patter Sam suggested was right up Findlater's alley, and though he wasn't anywhere near as smooth as Sam Dowd, he had a fat man from Salt Lake City pretty nearly convinced when a couple of detectives stepped out of the darkness and arrested us both. In a matter of hours we were standing in front of a judge, who gave us a terrible calling down, claiming people like us were besmirching the good name of Seattle. Then he sentenced us to three months in jail.

15

THE DIRTIEST HOLE ON THE
FACE OF THE EARTH

THE DIRTIEST HOLE on the face of the earth! That's what I called Skagway, Alaska, when I first set eyes upon it on a gray, freezing day near
the end of February of 1898. But first I'll tell you how Findlater and
me got up there. The authorities in Seattle released us from jail sometime in November, I believe it was. They gave us twenty-four hours to
get out of town. That was Seattle for you; a town of hypocrites and
crooks. I never met an honest man all the time I was there and even the
mayor himself had run off to the Klondike and got into some kind of
trouble. And they thought we were besmirching their good name!

Well, what we did was ride the lumber trains north through the
state of Washington and right across the Canadian border into Vancouver, British Columbia. It was a cold and miserable journey that I
wouldn't wish on my worst enemy. We stayed in Vancouver a few
days, mostly bumming money, and then took the ferry over to Victoria
on Vancouver Island. That was a busy little port at the time, for a lot
of people were shipping out of there for the Yukon. And Findlater was
still determined to get up there come hell or high water. And now so
was I. That was a funny thing about the Klondike and anybody who
was up there in '98 will tell you the same thing, though I don't expect
there's too many of us left. But the thing was this. Once a person set
his mind on getting there, it took an awful lot of misfortune to discourage him. So a fellow might suffer the worst kind of calamities—
storms at sea, scurvy and near-starvation, frostbite, broken bones, snow
blindness, damn near anything you could throw at him—just to get
there. Then, as often as not having reached Dawson, the first thing this
person would do was find a steamship office and book passage home.
It was hard to figure.

At Victoria Findlater and me worked as stevedores. Our nights was spent in a little room, where Findlater showed me card tricks or read from his books on self-improvement. We passed a good bit of the winter that way, saving our money in the hopes of getting a stake by spring. I won't say I didn't get discouraged and sometimes I even thought of returning east, but Findlater wouldn't hear of it. "We're just being tested, Bill," he used to say. "It's only a question of time before Dame Fortune smiles upon us and we'll see those gold fields shinin' in the sunlight." And him with the arse in his pants patched fifty different ways.

But one morning our luck changed. If you can call what happened to us luck. We were down on the wharfs when a commotion broke out on the deck of a lame-bottomed old sternwheeler called the *Southern Franchise*. A fellow told me that this old tub had done duty on the Mississippi River during the American Civil War. But here she was going into the north Pacific in the month of February. But that was hardly surprising, for anything that floated was pressed into service, the demand for transportation being so great. So the *Franchise* had come up from San Francisco and was taking on a load of cordwood at Victoria. This commotion was a fight between two deckhands and Findlater and me watched it until the first mate threw both the combatants down the gangboard and told them to find their own way home. That's when Findlater shouted up, "Tell me, skipper. Do you need two good men to replace those fellers?"

The mate smoked a clay pipe and scowled at us. "You ever worked on a steamboat before?"

"Have we ever worked on a steamboat before?" says Findlater as though that was the most foolish question ever devised by a human. "Why, we've worked the Bay of Fundy," says Findlater. "Up the Rascal River to Saskatchewan and Fort St. Whoop. We've gone the length of Manitoba from Ball's Falls to Crippled Hip Creek."

The first mate was as ignorant of geography as Findlater but like most people he didn't want to let on, so he just pointed his pipe at me. "He don't look too hale. Can he do a man's work?"

"Who?" says Findlater. "This young feller? Why, goodness sakes alive. Listen. This lad's father was a pilot on the St. Larry River, working out of Halifax, Ontario. Livin' on water is more natural to him than God's green earth."

The first mate sucked his pipe and then says, "You'll have to make a round trip. We ain't givin' no free rides up to Skagway."

"That's fine by us," says Findlater. "We ain't interested in grubbin' around in the earth for useless minerals. What we're both lookin' to do is ply our old trade. Out on the water with the salt spray in our faces and the feel of the ship yawin' in the wind."

"I hope you work as well as you gab," says the mate. "Get your gear and come aboard."

"Unfortunately," says Findlater, "our gear was stolen last night by some Canadian sneak thief. The town's full of them, you know."

15. The Dirtiest Hole on the Face of the Earth

"Well, get the hell on here anyway," says the mate. "We're behind schedule already and the old man don't like it."

And that's how Findlater talked us aboard the *Southern Franchise,* though needless to say, neither of us had ever set foot on a regular boat before. Findlater confided to me with a wink that he was a veteran of half a dozen ferry rides around Manhattan Island. Considering all that, we managed to get by. We observed how others handled ropes and pulleys, and anyway there was so much confusion that hardly anybody noticed mistakes. The boat was so badly overloaded that a number of passengers expressed fears to the captain, a giant black-bearded man who stood in the wheelhouse drinking from a huge mug. He never said a word or even appeared to be listening to what people told him.

Besides people and horses there were a number of goats and several dozen crates of chickens, and all these creatures were parked next to our sleeping quarters. It was a regular stink hole and it got worse as the days passed. The only sight on that boat worth looking at was a couple of dozen dance hall girls who were bound for a Skagway saloon.

The only word I can think of to describe that journey is nightmare. Our troubles began the very next day when we ran smack into a stiff northwest wind howling down from the wastes of Siberia. By the following morning it was a full-strength gale and the *Franchise* was tossed about like a matchstick in a gutter full of spring rain. I was down with a fearful case of seasickness, holding on to the sides of my bunk with a billy goat's arse not ten feet from my nose and about six inches of water sloshing around the floor. The horses were crazy with fear and I figured it was only a question of time before they broke loose and stamped me to death. Findlater tried to force a little whiskey between my teeth but I couldn't swallow anything. Findlater seemed to be living just on whiskey. He'd won a jug in a card game on the first day out and he carried it with him wherever he went. On the third day I staggered out on deck for some air. The wind had dropped, though the seas were still foaming and awesome to look upon. The old *Franchise* was almost totally covered with ice, so she looked like some prehistoric monster paddling her way through the water.

The day before we reached Skagway one of the boilers exploded, scalding the engineer and one of his helpers to death and causing panic among the passengers and crew. Everybody was running this way and that. Except, of course, the captain, who stood up in the wheelhouse looking as becalmed as though he was out on the Mississippi on an August afternoon. By then I was over my seasickness, so I could help herd the passengers into the main state room, where the first mate hoped to calm them down while the boiler was fixed. This meant that I had to move along various passageways, knocking on doors and escorting people. The air was filled with steam and from below came this terrific hissing sound. A number of people thought we were going down, including me. Then I opened this door in the first-class cabins and there was Findlater sitting on a bunk. And damn me if he didn't have this pretty little dance hall girl sitting on his knee. He had one hand around her waist and the other was clutching his whiskey jug. "Close the door, Bill" was all he said. He never mentioned the incident again but then Findlater wasn't the sort of man to boast about his *amours*.

The boiler was eventually repaired and we limped into Skagway Bay on a raw afternoon in which snow flurries dusted your hair. We had to anchor a mile or so from the town and then everything was transferred to barges and scows. That was a job, with the horses kicking like fury as they were winched over the side. Then there was all that cargo to move by hand and the passengers kept getting in the way because they were dying to set their feet on firm ground again. The first mate nearly went out of his head trying to get things organized. He stood up on the Texas deck with a big bullhorn shouting orders. In the wheelhouse the captain drank from his mug and looked like a stone statue.

Now you might not believe what Findlater and me did next, but it's the truth. Our problem was how to get the hell off that old tub and get ourselves lost in Skagway. That's where Findlater's little girl friend came to the rescue. She fixed us up with some rouge and face paint, outfitted us in ladies' fur hats and big coats, and we got in the middle of the dance hall girls, who all thought it was a good joke. Being first-class travelers, they were the first to be winched over the side in a lifeboat and so Findlater and me were laid down in the water so gently and rowed ashore by a gap-toothed sailor who kept grinning at me and winking, the damn fool. Once ashore we shucked off the clothes, thanked the girls, and started walking along the beach. The girls were met by a fishy-looking character in a fur coat who loaded them aboard a wagon and drove them into town. Tramping along that stony beach was just like walking through a big army camp. There were hundreds of tents with men cooking meals over campfires or shivering in their underwear as they washed in pans of ice water. There were piles of lumber and stacks of hay and bundles of cartage goods as high as a house. There were horses and donkeys and everywhere you looked teamsters cursing their animals.

Skagway was at one end of the bay and another town called Dyea was at the other end three miles away. Both of these settlements were terminal points for the so-called American routes to the gold fields. If you started at Dyea you had to cross over the Chilkoot Pass. If you began at Skagway, you had to tramp over the White Pass, better known as Dead Horse Gulch. That's the way Findlater and me went that spring. Now Skagway was considerably bigger and more popular than Dyea. Being an entranceway to the gold fields, it had attracted some of the worst characters on the North American continent and probably Europe as well. One of the first things you noticed in Skagway was the uncommon number of handguns and the fact that people weren't averse to using them whenever things didn't go their way. I myself saw a fellow shot down in an alleyway after a trifling argument over a woman. When we got up to Dawson later on, I noticed a real contrast, because there the Mounties were in charge and they wouldn't allow anybody to carry a gun without a license. That way a difference of opinion ended in a bloody nose or a broken jaw but nobody was shot. But in Skagway there was no such control and every man appeared to see himself as sheriff, judge, and executioner.

The town itself was mostly shacks and tents, though there were a few makeshift wooden warehouses and packing sheds and saloons. The streets were crowded with knots of men standing around, and every second word was *gold*. There was always somebody spinning a yarn in which some fellow lost his outfit on the trail and went crazy. So the streets were never empty day or night and as you walked along you'd hear a lot of laughter and piano music from the bars, which were always overheated and stuffy and had a bad smell. But bad smell or not, that's where Findlater and me headed for on our first day in Skagway. It was a place called the Pack Train and we stood at the bar rail and spent the last of our money on bad whiskey. It just seemed the natural thing to do. A half-hour later we were shivering out on the street in our city clothes when Findlater put his hand into his breast pocket and withdrew a long brown billfold. "Now, Bill," he says, "I think we'd better get ourselves some winter underwear 'cause there's a draft up my pant legs that's freezin' my parts." That man had nimble fingers! I figure we'd have starved to death without those fingers.

The first thing we did was find a boardinghouse, where we laid down money for a week's keep in advance. Then we visited a dry goods store and got fitted out for northern weather. We were behind a screen at the back of the store, standing in our underwear, when this joker pulled the screen aside and poked a long-barreled revolver at Findlater's chest. Now Findlater never liked guns and he put his hands right up. "Now, easy does it, brother," he says. "You wouldn't shoot a man with his pants down, would you?"

"Who says I wouldn't?" replies the fellow, and cocks his gun. Then he just walks around us for a minute or two, not saying a word but now and again kicking at our heap of old clothes on the floor. He was short and dressed in a fur coat and cap. Well, he bent down and pulled out this brown billfold from Findlater's jacket. "Well, lookee here now," he cries. "Say! Are you boys enjoyin' yourselves in Skagway?"

"You bet we are, sir," says Findlater. "This here is the greatest little town we've seen in a coon's age. We was thinkin' of settlin'."

"Is that a fact?" says the gunman, tapping the billfold against his jaw. "What line of work would you boys be in, anyways?"

"We're just lookin' right now," says Findlater.

"Seems to me," the gunman replies, "that your line of work might

just be takin' things what don't belong to you." We never said anything
to that. "Course," continues this gunman, "I ain't got nothin' personal
against stealin'. Long as a man's got sense enough to know who he's
stealin' from. The fact is that a couple of cheechakos like youse could
get your heads blowed off real fast in a town like this. Yes, sir. Real
fast. Now, you take this here billfold. The fact is that it belongs to a
gentleman name of Black Jack Yates. And Mr. Yates is a good friend
and business partner of Mr. J. Randolph Smith. And Mr. Smith runs
this here town. So you see what kind of a pickle you got yourself into.
Now you get dressed directly and come along and meet your betters."
And he marched us across the street and into a saloon, where we were
escorted through the crowd to a back room.

It was a smoke-filled, dimly lighted place with eight or nine men
standing around a pot-bellied stove. They stopped talking when we
came into the room. Behind this big desk was a trim-looking character
with a black spade beard, dressed in a Prince Albert coat, white shirt,
and string tie. He looked up at us for a minute and then resumed
scanning a stack of ledgers on his desk. The gunslinger pushed Findlater and me forward until we were standing in the middle of the
room. I couldn't make out the others too well, because although it was
only the middle of the afternoon it was already dark outside and the
only light came from a coal oil lamp on the desk and the occasional
flicker from the stove door when someone opened it to spit tobacco
juice.

After a minute a tall fellow stepped out in front of us and says to
Findlater, "By God, you're the cute one, ain't you?" And he took
Findlater's suspenders in both hands and gave them a helluva snapping. "You bought those duds on my money, you big thieving son of
a bitch. I've a good mind to cut off your ears and mail them home to
your dear old mum." That got a laugh from the assembly and even the
gent behind the desk smiled faintly and shook his head with a look
that suggested that these lower orders can sometimes be amusing.
That gent behind the desk, by the way, was none other than the famous
Soapy Smith. Then this tall fellow, whose name was Black Jack Yates,
says, "I just don't know what we ought to do, boys. Here's a couple of
fellers come into town. And on the very first day they pinch a
respectable citizen's purse. Seems to me that takes an uncommon
amount of gall."

The tone of Black Jack's reprimand was not without an element
of good-natured admiration and this seemed to loosen up Findlater a
bit, for he said, "Now, wait a minute, gents. Bill and me are real sorry
about that purse and we'll pay back every nickel with compound
interest. But put yourselves in our shoes this morning. There we was,
a couple of strangers come north to better ourselves. Anxious as the
next fellow to get ahead in this great land of ours. But the fact is, we
were a bit down on our luck and in need of a stake. We've been told
there are all kinds of business opportunities up in these parts. And I'll

never forget what a friend of mine used to say. He used to say, 'This country can always use another businessman like me.' "

Soapy Smith looked up from his ledgers and in the smoky light of the oil lamp his face looked yellow above the neat black beard. "Who said that to you?" he asked Findlater in a soft voice. Smith was a southerner and had this drawling voice that was easy on the ears. Unless he lost his temper, which I saw a couple of times and then he sounded like a screeching woman.

Findlater, seeing the opportunity to deal directly with the boss, says, "I beg your pardon, sir."

"That sayin' you just mentioned," replies Smith. "The only man I ever heard say that was a good friend of mine named Sam Dowd. I worked with him in Leadville, Colorado. He taught me an awful lot. Sam was a square shooter all the way."

"I can only add Amen to that, sir," says Findlater. "Sam is a great personal friend of ours. Matter of fact, we was workin' with him only last summer in Seattle."

Smith looked interested. "And how is he, by the way?"

Now that was all Findlater needed. Before long, nobody was talking about any wallet and Findlater was deep into conversation with Soapy Smith, who had to admit that Findlater had pulled a good one in lifting Black Jack's purse. "Even out of ignorance that was bold, very bold," he kept saying from time to time until even Black Jack laughed and slapped Findlater on the shoulder and told him he had more nerve than a canal horse. Then somebody brought out a bottle of whiskey and Smith introduced us to a number of his associates. There was Old Man Tripp and Blue Jay Brown and a number of others whose names I've now forgotten. Smith practically owned Skagway at the time and he'd surrounded himself with some of the best bunco artists and confidence men on the North American continent. Naturally Soapy Smith was the sort of man Findlater admired and Smith liked to be flattered, so they got along well right from the start. As far as I could see, there wasn't much choice, given our circumstances. In that town either you were for Smith or dead set against him. And he did have some enemies too.

The upshot of all this was that we went to work for Soapy Smith. I don't suppose there's any harm in revealing this now, because I can't believe the authorities are going to come looking for an old man who engaged in unlawful practices while a callow youth over seventy-five years ago. Having a natural gift for deceit, Findlater was put to work at one of the oldest and simplest games in the world. I'm referring to the trade of thimblerigging, whereby a rubber pea is supposedly hidden beneath one of three walnut shells and the customer is invited to guess for a fee. Findlater received his instructions from one of the best in the business, a man named Blue Jay Brown. What hands that man had, and a nice fellow too! But he could move those shells so fast over a table that it would nearly burn the eyeballs out of your head trying to keep track of them. All the time he was maneuvering those shells he'd chatter away about everything under the sun. Findlater never acquired that degree of skill but he was damn good and he cleaned out a number of cheechakos, which was an Indian word for newcomer or green hand.

As for me, I was put to work in this fake telegraph office that Soapy Smith had set up just off the main street. He had a number of these phony business establishments scattered around the town. This telegraph office was just a shack with a business counter and a fellow sitting in his shirtsleeves tapping away at the Morse code looking like he knew exactly what he was doing. Nobody seemed to be bothered by the fact that there weren't any wires leading from the shack to the telegraph poles. For that matter there weren't any telegraph poles, for the north wasn't then connected to the outside world by telegraph. Yet people flocked in to wire home for money or pass along greetings to sweethearts and relatives.

I worked in that office for a number of weeks as a clerk and we had some interesting routines. One of them went like this. As soon as somebody who looked fairly prosperous arrived in town, one of Soapy's men would seek him out and welcome him to Skagway, passing himself off as a local merchant. He'd buy this newcomer some drinks and find out all he could about the fellow's hometown, family, church, business associates, and fraternal organizations. If he belonged to one of the latter, Soapy's man would lean across the table and whisper, "I knew you were one of us as soon as I laid eyes on you. Put it there, brother." Then he'd give him the secret handshake of the Loyal Muskrats of America or whatever. That sealed the friendship right there and this Muskrat from Vinegar County, Iowa, or Hamilton, Ontario, would thank his lucky stars that he'd come across such a friend so far from home. As soon as he'd found the newcomer lodgings and tucked him in for the night, Soapy's man would come across to the telegraph office and he'd sit down with me and we'd figure out where this Muskrat seemed to be the most vulnerable. Was he the sort who'd send five hundred dollars home for his mother's funeral? Would he bail out a younger brother who got into trouble in a strange city and didn't want to alarm the rest of the family? One of the sure-fire messages went something like this:

UNCLE REUBEN PASSED AWAY YESTERDAY STOP LEFT
HOUSE TO ME BUT ALL OTHER ASSETS TO YOU STOP MONEY
TIED UP UNTIL YOUR RETURN STOP MUST HAVE FIVE HUNDRED
DOLLARS FOR IMMEDIATE LIVING EXPENSES AND FUNERAL
ARRANGEMENTS STOP PLEASE REMIT AND RETURN HOME AT
ONCE STOP YOUR LOVING SISTER AGNES

After typing this message on a piece of telegraph paper, I'd put on my Western Union uniform and rush over to the fellow's hotel. Within fifteen minutes he'd be forking five hundred dollars over the business counter in the telegraph office and trying to figure out how to get home.

When it came to extracting money from people, Soapy Smith had a simple philosophy. I remember him saying to me one day as we stood by the window in his office looking out at the street, where crowds of men stood around gawking and talking. Soapy stood there rocking on his heels and jingling some coins in his pocket. "Son," he said, "to get ahead up here you don't have to find a gold mine. All you got to do is find the man with the gold mine."

So that's how most of the winter passed for Findlater and me. Soapy wanted us to stay on with him but we were both anxious to get on up to the Yukon. Findlater was still convinced that by summer we'd be picking up bushel hampers full of gold nuggets. As for me, I still believed that I'd find Sally. Of course I was a frequent visitor to the saloons and dance halls and I made a number of inquiries. But nobody had ever heard of Sally Butters. One little girl did tell me between dances that perhaps Sally had taken the all-water route to the Klondike. This girl claimed to have nearly gone that way herself but had changed her mind at the last minute. Going by the all-water route meant you took a steamboat all the way up the coast to Norton Sound and then went up the Yukon River in behind the mountains. If Sally had gotten away early enough the previous summer she just might have made it that way before the freeze-up.

The other reason why Findlater was anxious to be going was simply this. Findlater was shrewd enough to see the handwriting on the wall for Soapy Smith. "Bill," he said, "if I read this town right, it's time you and me was movin' on, because these good times ain't gonna last. Now Soapy's a smart feller and nobody's disputin' that. But he ain't as smart as he thinks. He's fleecin' too many respectable folks and the word's got around. This town's got a bad name all the way down to California and the law-abidin' citizens don't like it. It's bad for business. It's like what Sam Dowd told us down in Seattle. What Soapy is doin' is scarin' away customers. And there's no worse sin in America. So you and me would do well to clear out before things really turn sour." Now just how right Findlater was can be illustrated by true history, because a few months later this vigilante committee was formed to clean up the town and Soapy Smith himself was shot dead in a gunfight with a fellow named Frank Reid.

Towards the end of March that year I came down with a bad case of grippe. I couldn't do anything but lie in bed and cough and sweat. Findlater was concerned for my health and now and again he'd bring one of his girl friends from the dance hall to look me over. Findlater had this notion that a female was especially helpful around a sick man's bed. But the females he brought around knew about as much as a five-year-old when it came to tending the sick. Often as not they'd turn up with a bottle of gin and a mandolin and before long there'd be a party in progress with Findlater and the girl singing while I lay there about five coughs away from pneumonia.

By and by, though, I recovered and one evening in April it turned uncommonly mild, with the fresh sweet smell of evergreens perfuming the air. I decided to get out and see what was going on, so I dressed and went down to Jimmy Ryan's Nugget Saloon, where Findlater sometimes worked his shell game or played cards in the evening. I was weak on my pins and as soon as I got to the saloon I knew I'd made a mistake, for the smoke and the heat and the noise set my head spinning. One of the bartenders put a glass of whiskey in front of me and said, "Haven't seen you around lately, Bill. You look like hell. I believe I've seen better complexions on a custard pie." Just then a squabble erupted a few feet away, involving two of the dirtiest, meanest-looking scoundrels you've ever laid eyes on. These characters wore long rabbit-skin coats and slouch hats and their faces were just dirt and hair, so you couldn't really tell whether they were white men or not. Well, the fracas got straightened away and one of the waiters put the run to them. Just as they were going by me, one of them crashed into my shoulder and sent me spinning. "Get out of my way, you little pissmire," he says to me, "or I'll squash you like a bug." I was too dizzy to answer.

A few minutes later I left and was glad to get out in the fresh air again. Taking my time, I walked along the street and soon I was away from the main section, in this little alleyway between some warehouses. I always took it because it was a shortcut to the boardinghouse. Then I heard footsteps behind me crunching in the snow. When I glanced over my shoulder I saw these two characters in the rabbit coats. I had a notion to run but my legs just wouldn't carry me along with any dispatch. After a few more steps I heard this voice say, "Don't be in such a hurry, little feller. We ain't gonna hurt you much."

"No," says the other. "We'll just knock out a few teeth and maybe break a leg and an arm. You'll be right as rain in a year or two."

Well, —— you, I says to myself. You're not getting off that easy.

So when they caught up to me I threw a punch at this big mound of rabbit fur. But I was merely stroking the air, for there was no power in my arms, and it didn't take them long to pin me against the wall. Still, I worked loose an arm and flailed one of these jokers in the parts. He grunted and then swore a blue streak. Down we went after this other fellow struck me a blow behind the ear. We wrestled around in the slush, eyeball to eyeball, while the other one jumped around trying to aim kicks at me. Just as often he'd hit his partner, who'd yell out, "Blame you anyways, that's me you're kickin'." They were just about the most incompetent pair of assailants you'd be likely to meet, but being in a weakened state I was no match for them. Then, just as this fellow was getting the better of me, with his long dirty fingers around my throat, I recognized him. And I threw back my head and bawled out, "Hold on for Christ's sakes if your name's Ned Farthing, because you're choking your own brother to death."

16

ON TO DAWSON

HE LET GO OF ME, and breathing hard, says, "I ain't Ned. I'm Fred. That's Ned up there kickin' your backside. Now what in hell are you talkin' about?"

"Christ Almighty, Fred," I says. "I'm your brother. Your own flesh and blood. Don't you recognize your younger brother Bill?"

Fred grabbed my chin and pulled my face to within inches of his. He smelled worse than a dead polecat. "Well, goddam these eyes of mine," he says. "Lookit here, Ned. This is young Bill for sure. What in hell's name are you doin' up here, little brother?"

We got to our feet and I says, "Well, I was just about to ask you the same question. I thought you two were still at the pickle factory in Belleville."

"Hell, no," says Ned. "We haven't worked at that in over two years. We been around. We got down to Toronto once but they throwed us in jail for vacancy."

"Vagrancy, you dumb bugger," Fred says. He was always just a touch sharper than Ned, which isn't to say he was any genius.

"We come up lookin' for gold," says Ned, wiping his nose on his coat sleeve just as he used to do back on the farm. "But we ain't seen none yet. Course, we just been in town a few hours."

"If you're talking about gold in the ground," I says, "that's farther on. Up in the Yukon behind the mountains. As a matter of fact we're going up through the White Pass in a couple of weeks ourselves."

"Is that so?" says Fred. "And who's we, little brother?"

So I told them about Findlater and I couldn't resist a little bragging. It's always been a weakness with me and so Findlater emerged as a fairly successful businessman with me as his junior partner.

139

After I'd finished Fred felt the cloth in my overcoat and says, "Well, you seem to have done all right for yourself and we're real proud of you, ain't we, Ned?"

"Why, yes we are, Billy," says Ned. "You've done good and I'm sorry if I jumped you back there."

"That's right," says Fred, suddenly hugging me. "Why, you're our little brother. Our own kith and kin. I always said that after poor Tom passed away in that terrible tragedy we should have took care of Billy here, Ned. You remember me sayin' that? Billy here is all we got left now that Annie's married and Daddy's gone with Miss Boswell." I was anxious to hear about my father but they weren't too helpful. "Ain't heard hide nor hair of him in some time, Bill," says Fred. "The last we heard was a letter addressed to Annie over a year ago. From someplace out west. He and Miss Boswell was holed up in the mountains doing something religious. They've joined some kind of church out there. We couldn't make nothin' out of it. And then Annie kicked us out of her house just because we'd had a couple of snorts. Oh, she's a holy terror now, Bill. Not fit to live with. I don't know how Rufus puts up with her. Course, he never had much gumption, that man. But say, Annie is just a ripper for respectable livin' these days. She's got these two brats now and they're always spoutin' Bible verses at you. Annie's a big number in the Methodist church too. She thinks she's too good for her own flesh and blood."

"That's right, Bill," says Ned. "She ain't the same girl at all. I've always said she should have stayed with Snake Skinner. Snake was a good egg. Course, last time I heard he was in the county jug."

"Shut up now, Ned," says Fred. "Young Bill here ain't interested in Snake Skinner. He's interested in his own flesh and blood." Fred put his arm around me. "You appear to have growed into a real handsome young buck, Bill. I'll bet the women are crazy wild for you. And look at us! Just a little down on our luck, as you can see. Why, we ain't eat a bite of food in three days. That's why that blow I struck you back there didn't kill you. You was lucky, little brother."

Then he talked about the various hardships they'd endured over the past couple of years. I didn't believe half of what he told me and I could see that they were just about the worst pair of wharf rats you'd be likely to encounter in a town not exactly endowed with high-class people. But they were my brothers, and against my better judgment I took them back to the boardinghouse and persuaded the landlady to warm up some beans and make a kettle of tea. We took all this up to our room and Ned and Fred soon made themselves comfortable, sitting back in the only two armchairs and scooping the beans into their mouths. I opened both windows and smoked like hell. After they'd cleaned up the beans Fred said, "You wouldn't have a little whiskey to put in this here tea, would you, Billy? I've had this cold in my chest for the longest time. And whiskey seems to be the only thing that'll loosen her up." So I got him some whiskey and he sat back and

140

smoked one of Findlater's dollar cigars. Between puffs he says to me, "You look a little pale around the gills. I hope you're takin' good care of yourself, because if you ain't, I'm gonna have to give you a lickin' like when you was a little fellow."

Well, all the time we were sitting there I was thinking about Findlater and what he would imagine when he saw Ned and Fred. Of course, Findlater had the notion that I came from high-quality people, and these backwoods Ontario oafs weren't going to do much for his opinion of me. I was thinking about that when I fell asleep. The next thing I knew Findlater was standing over me with the lamp in one hand. "Wake up there, Bill," he whispers. "Are you all right?"

"Yes," I says, coming out of sleep. "What's wrong?" For a minute I'd forgotten about Ned and Fred.

Findlater raised his lamp and peered into the darkness of the room. "What in the name of righteous is lying over there on the floor? At first I thought they were some breed of animal come in out of the cold and I was going to fetch a chunk of firewood. But the sound of them is human."

"They're my brothers," I whispered.

At this Findlater brought the lamp to my face. "You're playin' a joke on your old pal, Bill?"

"Well, actually they're half-brothers," I lied. "Twin sons of my dead mother by her first husband. I ran into them tonight. They just arrived in town and they're a bit up against it. I couldn't see them sleeping in the snow."

"I'd say they been sleepin' in worse than that from the smell of them," says Findlater, putting down the lamp.

Neither of us said a word for several minutes but just sat there listening to Ned and Fred's snoring and snuffling. At one point Fred barked out in his sleep, "Don't hit me, mister. I'd fight you fair and square if it wasn't for this bum arm of mine." Then he snuffled and snorted again.

"Well, I guess there's nothin' for it but to go to bed," says Findlater. It was the first time I'd ever heard him sound even mildly discouraged over anything.

Now, Findlater and I planned to leave Skagway in a couple of weeks. The trail through the mountains was still packed hard but once spring arrived it would be just a rutted mud road. Now, however, we seemed stuck with Ned and Fred. I certainly didn't want them tagging along and I figured maybe the best thing to do was give them a few bucks and send them on their way. But getting rid of my brothers proved to be a lot tougher than that. I suggested next morning that there might be work down at the sawmill or packing freight over the Pass. But they weren't having any of it. The truth is that the atmosphere of a saloon was more congenial to their natures, and before long Findlater and me had a couple of star boarders. They treated Findlater with a good deal of respect, jumping out of their chairs whenever he entered the room and it was Mister Findlater this and Mister Find-later that. Findlater was flattered by all this attention even though it came from such lowly quarters. But the other roomers complained of the smell, and it was hard to choke down a bite at supper when Ned and Fred sat there wolfing their food. The landlady was soaking us hard for having two extra people in the room and even at that she wasn't satisfied. She warned us that they'd have to go. "I think you'll have to tell them, Bill," said Findlater to me one morning. He was on his way to the barber's and had tried without success to have my brothers accompany him. They were still wrapped up in their rabbit coats on the floor.

When Fred woke up I explained to him that neither Findlater nor I had anything against them but we didn't see them staying with us as a permanent arrangement. In fact, we planned to push on in another week and so maybe it would be a good idea if they thought about what they were going to do. Now, when a situation like this arises, it's peculiar how everything gets reversed. The party that's been causing the trouble takes on this injured air, while the innocent side starts feeling all guilty and mean.

As soon as I'd finished Fred jumped to his feet. "You're dead right, Bill," he says. "And you don't have to say one more word. Neddy and me will be goin' right along and you and Mr. Findlater will be free and easy."

"Well," I says, "I didn't mean you had to go this very minute. I was thinking more along the lines of you making some plans."

"Don't say another word," cries Fred, holding up his hand. "We understand the situation, little brother. And we're gonna get out of your hair right this moment." He kicked at Ned, who was still sleeping. "Wake up, Neddy. I'm talkin' at you. We're travelin'."

Ned rolled over and grunted. "Where we goin', Fred?"

"Never mind," says Fred. "Just get up and shake a leg." Then Fred put both hands on my shoulders. "Listen, Bill," he says. "Would you do me one more little favor? I ain't askin' much."

"Sure," I says, reaching for my wallet.

"No, no, no," says Fred, wagging his head. "You and Mr. Findlater have been real good to us and when I make my first million dollars in gold bunion I ain't gonna forget it. But listen here. I don't like to have to tell you this, but poor Ned there, what with bad eats and rough livin' over the past few months, well, it's affected his health poorly and the poor boy's now got a crop of boils on his backside that would break your heart. I gave them a good lancin' yesterday but they want a little of that Dr. Gold's Yellow Salve to help them along. Now, I'm still not right on the geography of this town. Do you suppose you could direct me to the store that sells that brand of medication?"

"Why, I'll go myself!" I says.

"Would you, Bill? Would you do that for your old brother Fred?"

"Sure," I says. The truth is, I was so glad they were moving I'd have walked halfway across Alaska if I thought it would have sped them along.

I was away perhaps fifteen minutes and when I returned the door to our room was wide open and they were gone. And if you imagine they cleaned me out, you're absolutely right. Some seven or eight hundred dollars, the sons of bitches! I'd hidden it in the clothes cupboard under some loose floorboards, just as Mrs. Fletcher had done back in Craven Falls. And I'd always considered Findlater unwise because he carried his money right on his person in a money belt! Well, after discovering the theft, I believe I went insane for five minutes or so. I remember bounding down the stairs and running smack into Findlater, who was freshly shaved and smelled of bay rum. When he heard my story he howled with laughter. "Oh, Bill," he said, "that's a corker. That's just about the best of the day. Your own brothers. Oh God, I can't stand it!" And he had to sit down on the stairs to compose himself.

I spent the next couple of days looking for them. I suppose if they weren't my own brothers I'd have gone to Soapy for advice, but his boys played rough and I didn't necessarily want Ned and Fred killed. But either they were holed up somewhere in Skagway or they'd slipped down to Dyea. I never did discover their whereabouts or recover my money. A week later we left town ourselves, with Findlater staking me to half his money. He was always good that way. I was glad to be leaving Skagway, and though Soapy was sorry to see us go, he wished us all the best.

Now there was another problem about getting into the Yukon in those days. In the fall of '97 a number of early-bird stampeders had slipped into Dawson. By traveling with just the clothes on their back they managed to get there before freeze-up. But once there, of course, they had no supplies and there was none to buy, because things was scarce up that way over the winter months. So, as the winter wore on, a good many of these people nearly starved or froze to death. Because of that the Mounties passed a law forbidding anyone to set foot on Yukon Territory without having a year's supply of food and tackle. Now, all the Mounties were doing was trying to protect people from their own stupidity, but it meant that a fellow had to have several hundred dollars' worth of supplies if he aimed to prospect for gold. And all these supplies—beans and blankets and cooking pots and all the rest of it—they all had to be trucked through the mountains, then loaded on a scow and sailed down the Yukon River. A helluva job, and I'll tell you the truth, neither Findlater nor me was exactly devoted to manual labor, which as far as Findlater was concerned was the name of a Spaniard. To get past the Mounties Findlater came up with a clever ruse. We dressed as preachers and put a half-dozen suitcases filled with Bibles on a horse belonging to a fellow Christian. He only charged us seventy-five dollars because, as he put it, "I wouldn't want to high-roll a couple of the Lord's servants."

So that spring of 1898 Findlater and me and thousands of other knotheads walked over Dead Horse Trail. It was called that because of the fearful toll it took on horses, who just fell down dead from exhaustion or were beaten to death by frustrated men after the animal couldn't go any farther. The trail was just one long line of men and animals snaking through the mountains, with nearly everybody staggering along under the weight of their loads. I heard about a man and a woman who lugged an entire steamboat piecemeal over the Pass that winter. I don't necessarily believe it, but it could have happened. I know I talked to a fellow who was carrying the various parts of a grand piano. And he assembled it on the other side too and shipped it down to Dawson, where I heard he sold it to a saloon keeper for three thousand dollars. So nearly everybody had something on their backs except Findlater and me.

But even without a load that was a brutal march, and one of the greatest sights these eyes have ever seen was Lake Bennett on the other side of the mountains. From there it was all downriver, five hundred miles to Dawson City. Of course, when we arrived the river was still frozen, and everybody was busy building some sort of barge or scow that would carry them downstream come the break-up. The air was filled with the sound of saws and the smell of wood dust. We called that place Canvas City, because it was just thousands of tents set up on the snow and strung around the shores of the lake. The first thing Findlater and I did now that we were in Canadian territory was get rid of our preacher outfits. Findlater didn't mind employing that disguise to get past the Mounties at the border, but he had too much respect for the Christian religion to set himself up as a false preacher. We sold our Bibles to a man with a barge in exchange for passage to Dawson. He later made a handsome profit out of those Bibles.

We spent the next few weeks at some of the most pleasant and natural pastimes of man, namely drinking, smoking, and playing cards. Now and again we visited one of the canvas whorehouses and enjoyed some fornication. Other times we sat in the spring sunshine and watched fist fights between two fellows who'd been partners all the way from someplace like Boston or Berlin. They had got their supplies together and helped one another over the Pass and lived in one another's pockets for months. But they often snapped under the strain of the sawpit. The sawpit was where you planed your logs down to build your barge. And it took a good bit of patience to stay friends with your partner, because one fellow stood up on this platform and sawed down while his partner underneath bucked the big six-foot saw upwards. That took a good deal of coordination and level-mindedness and Findlater and me used to lay bets on how long it would take before the joker on the bottom would come out of the pit rubbing his eyes and clearing the sawdust out of his throat while he called his partner a worthless good-for-nothing son of a bitch.

Towards late May, or it might have been early June, the ice broke up. Overnight the tents were struck and the whole damn city just dissolved before your eyes. Everybody piled aboard various craft, and that trip downriver was no picnic either, for there was plenty of white water and we had a rough ride at times. But late on a Saturday afternoon we arrived in Dawson, nearly a year after starting out from New York City. It was a raw-looking place, just slashed out of the forest, with the usual makeshift buildings—saloons, dancing pavilions, trading tents, and brothels. Everywhere was the screech of sawmills and the banging of hammers. Like in Skagway, there were roaming bands of men wandering up and down the dirt roads. Findlater clutched one fellow by the arm just after we set foot in town. "Where's the gold, brother," he asked. "Where's the nuggets?" The fellow just smiled vacantly and walked away. He acted like we were all in on the biggest joke in the world. And in a sense that was true, for by the time we got there all the best claims had been staked and there probably wasn't one stampeder in a hundred who even made his expenses.

We went to a saloon, which was generally the best place to get information on where to eat and sleep and find out who was telling the biggest lie. We stood at the bar having a drink and after a while I had to take a leak, so I made my way to the rear. Usually there was a little hall leading to the outhouses in the alleyway behind. Now just as I was passing down this hall, I heard a number of female voices laughing behind this door. It sounded like a party, for I also heard corks being popped. Then just as I got abreast of the door, it flew open and several dance hall girls came running out. One little trick, still holding a bottle of champagne, kissed me right on the mouth and said, "Hello, sweetheart. Welcome to Dawson." It was a nice greeting, all right. After they'd filed past, damn me for a liar if I didn't find myself staring at Sally Butters! She was sitting on a table, dolled up in a dress of black velvet with high boots. There were actual gold nuggets sparkling in her hair. When she saw me her beautiful blue eyes opened wide in alarm and she uttered this little cry. "Billy Farthing! Is that really you?"

"Hello, Sal," I said, my voice a bare croak and my knees trembling.

"Oh, Billy!" And she jumped down and ran across the room and flung her arms around my neck. "Billy, Billy, Billy," she cried. "Have you followed me all the way up here?"

"I believe I once said I'd follow you to the ends of the world."

At this her big eyes filled with tears. "But I thought you were just kiddin' me. I thought you were just talkin' the way young spooners do when they're courtin'. Oh, Billy!" And she hugged me again.

"What's the matter, Sal?" I asked. "Aren't you glad to see me?"

"Oh, Billy, that ain't it," she says. "It's just that you came too late."

"Why is that?" says I.

"I was married ten minutes ago," says she.

"Oh!" says I. And then I think I congratulated her before I passed out.

17

ROUGH JUSTICE

———

WHEN I AWAKENED I was lying on a divan and Sally was leaning over me, applying damp cloths to my brow. Next to her, looking amused, was this short, blond-haired, rabbity-looking character. He was dressed like the tinhorn gambler he was in a long dark coat, fancy vest, and string tie. Sally brought me a glass of brandy, which I took without a word. Then she said shyly, "Bill? I'd like you to meet my husband, Johnny Madill. Johnny, this is Billy Farthing."

"How doody, son," said the gambler, offering a long soft hand which I found repulsive and refused to shake. "Sally's told me a lot about you," says Madill. "No hard feelings, I hope. I'm throwing a little party to celebrate our nuptials and announce the beginning of our honeymoon. We're taking a boat out tomorrow for San Francisco. Then we're going on to Europe. Too bad you couldn't come along. But you can come to the party."

"Please, Billy," says Sally. "Won't you come? We can still be friends, can't we? Say you'll come for my sake."

"Sure he'll come," says Madill. "Let's go, girl." And he turned and stumped stiff-legged towards the door.

Madill had a cork leg and, as I found out later, he used to hide cards in it. He was a bit of a character around Dawson and people called him Corky Madill. That cheating limb got him into trouble in Fairbanks a few years later after the gold discovery there. The story I heard was that a tough miner caught Madill cheating and tore that cork leg right off the stump and beat Madill to death with it. You've probably heard of men dying by their own hand but Madill represents one of the rare cases of a man dying by his own leg.

But that was all in the future, and to watch Madill stumping around the saloon floor that evening you'd never have guessed that any harm could come his way. That party remains mostly a blur in my memory. There were bright colors and swirling lights and fiddle music with champagne poured down my throat and the sweet powdered skin of dance hall girls. Madill spread the news that I was a jilted lover and I soon became a figure of pity and amusement. All the girls felt sorry for me and they'd sit on my knee or ask me to dance. Findlater came over to sit at my table and I remember him saying as he watched Sally and Madill dance, "By God, Bill, you can pick them. That little girl's a hummer. It's just too bad you lost out to that wooden-legged character, but unless I miss my guess, you wouldn't have stood a chance anyway. That little girl looks like she's used to money and that's something you ain't got. But cheer up, pal. There's plenty more in the stable."

Then Madill made a little speech in which he said he was turning over the next dance "to that game little Canadian who came all the way up to the Klondike and arrived ten minutes late." Everybody cheered and somebody pushed me to my feet and into Sally's arms and we danced a waltz. There were tears in Sally's eyes and when it was finished she ran from the room holding a handkerchief to her face. Madill didn't even notice but just ordered more champagne. The party got louder and Madill started playing little jokes on me. He'd come up and say something like "Why, you lucky little so-and-so! Just look at this now." And he'd pluck a gold nugget out of my ear and lay it on the table. Everybody whistled and cheered. By and by Madill grew tired of that game and started to dance by himself. He moved around with amazing agility on his game leg, but then he took a swirl too many and fell crashing into a bunch of chairs. He sat there on the floor laughing while somebody poured a bottle of champagne over his head.

It was all too much for me and I stood up and, holding on to the table for support, pointed my finger at Sally, who was now standing in a corner. "You married a fool," I shouted. That didn't sit too well with Madill's friends and the atmosphere turned ugly. In no time at all I punched a man who I fancied was laughing at me. Then somebody crocked me from behind with a bottle and after that things are fairly vague in my memory. I know that next day Findlater told me how he carried me out like a bag of feed over his shoulders and the thing he remembered most was the stricken look in Sally's eyes as we left.

The next day, after drinking about a pailful of water, I wandered down to the wharf. Most of the town was there to watch the steamer depart for the outside world. Corky Madill and Sally stood on the deck. Corky carried on like a fool, throwing kisses to his friends and yelling, "What a night, boys! She was every bit as sweet as she looks!" He was disgusting and a liar too, for Madill was impotent, as I found out later. Beside him Sally blushed fiercely and gave me a little wave. It struck me that she was already ashamed of her hus-

band, who was now holding his nose and pulling an imaginary chain
as the boat whistle blew. The man had no dignity at all. Then the
deckhands cast away the lines and everybody cheered as the boat
backed into the current and got her heading. Then she blew again
and, with the foam churning around her stern, slipped downriver
and disappeared around a bend. Soon there was only wisps of smoke
curling into the clear summer sky, and with them my dreams of
contentment and joy.

Sally's marriage to that card shark left me in such a sour humor
that it's a wonder Findlater didn't throw me out into the street.
However, I would have been grateful if he had, for then I could have
felt even more sorry for myself.

We weren't in Dawson more than a week before Findlater won
a house in a poker game. It wasn't much of a house, being only a
frame shack on the edge of town along the river. The original owners
were pulling out, disgusted with their failure to find gold. That was a
fairly common feeling in Dawson that summer. But Findlater was not
built that way. It wasn't in his nature to stand around and feel sorry
for himself. He was convinced that we'd strike it rich and he was
soon involved in a variety of schemes. He became a good friend of
Sam Bonnifield's, the owner of the Bank Saloon and Gambling House,
and he dealt faro three or four nights a week at that establishment.
He also did a little actual gold mining, having won a share of a claim
in a card game. He visited it once and returned shaking his head.
Maybe the gold beds weren't all they were supposed to be, but that
was all right too, for Findlater was convinced his future lay in the
business world. "That's where the money is, Bill," he'd say. "I can see
now that I was just a jackass to think there'd be gold nuggets lyin'
around waitin' to be picked up. But you live and learn. And there's
still money to be made in these parts. You mark my words."

Findlater couldn't fathom my lassitude and he'd fidget and puzzle over me. "Blame it all, Bill," he'd say. "I wish you'd come out
and have some fun. And lay off drinkin' that rotbelly by yourself.
You'll get cramps in the head sittin' here drinkin' that. You've got
plenty of youth and juice. You should be out enjoyin' yourself."

He was right, of course, but I was just too damn miserable and
contrary to admit it. On the other hand, it seemed to me that Findlater was incapable of imagining how anyone could have deep feelings for a woman. They were always just dance hall girls to him.
Probably he was just too busy figuring out ways to become a successful businessman. He was fascinated by people who had novel ideas
for getting ahead in this world. I recall one fellow talking about
going down to Cuba and getting into the sugar business now that
the Americans had kicked the Spanish out of that country. For a
week Findlater could only talk about fields of sugar cane. Another
character was an electrical engineer named Henry Smithers. He
spent several evenings telling us about the magical properties of

17. Rough Justice

electricity and what a future it had. He was working on an electric massage belt which he claimed would ease the suffering of ten million rheumatism victims. He told us Thomas Alva Edison was interested. Findlater considered this Smithers a genius. I thought he was a fraud, though likable enough and no worse than some of the other characters who turned up at our shack for a hand of poker every Sunday evening. Sunday was a closed day in Dawson, the Christian Mounties maintaining a strick observance of the Sabbath even in that frontier atmosphere. This meant that people looked for places to drink and play cards, and so a number of private dwellings entertained guests.

It was at one of those Sunday evening parties that I ruined Findlater's best business venture in the Klondike. It had to do with onions. One day in late August Findlater bought a whole wagonload of onions from a riverboat man. Then he tore up the floorboards of our shack and made a root cellar for them. I thought he was crazy, for there must have been a ton of onions under our kitchen floor. But Findlater just laughed. "Listen, Bill," he said. "In a few weeks these little darlings will be scarcer than a dance-hall singer's maidenhead. A fellow told me that last winter they were fetching five dollars apiece." He tapped a thick finger to the side of his head. "This is what's called speculatin' and it's the secret of successful men like Gould and Rocketfeller. They're always ten steps ahead of the ordinary human."

Around the middle of September the weather turned cold and the river froze. In the mornings there was a dusting of snow on the ground. Tree stumps wore little snow hats and the air was so crisp it seemed to ring like frozen iron. With the cold weather, I changed too. I resigned myself to living without the woman I loved and decided instead to become a saint. I gave up booze and tobacco and Findlater couldn't persuade me to visit the dance halls or whorehouses of Dawson. I figured that in the old days monasteries were filled with people who carried around the same attitude. If you're disappointed in love, you put on a hair shirt and look down your nose at other sinners. I didn't wear a hair shirt but I punished myself with hard work. All day I sawed and split firewood, stacking it in neat rows by the side of the shack. I cooked and washed and when I wasn't reading the Bible, I'd take a bar of soap and scrub the walls. Findlater was tickled to see me so busy but I think he found my pious manner a hardship.

Now that was a winter for you! Fifty below zero was a common temperature and if it was bone still you didn't dare go out of doors. All you could do was sit by the stove and listen to the trees cracking with frost. It sounded just like gunfire. In the morning you could see the smoke from Dawson's stove pipes rise straight into the air and hang there, suspended like strands of rope.

And Findlater was right about his onions. By early December we were getting a dollar each for them. I say "we" because he always included me as his partner. Our Sunday evenings became popular in that part of the world because in place of hard cash Findlater used onions. Before anyone arrived, he'd prise open a few boards and fill a little satchel with onions. I can still picture those Sunday evenings. There'd be four or five playing, with another half-dozen looking on and waiting to get in the game. The air was so thick with tobacco smoke that the oil lamp sometimes sputtered from lack of oxygen. The sheet-iron stove would glow red and smoke your pants if you stood too close. Outside the stars looked as big as jewels and probably you'd hear a sled dog howling. I'd sit in the corner watching the players or maybe reading the Bible, listening to Findlater say, "I'll see that and raise you two onions." And there on the table would be a pile of nuggets and some crumpled bank notes and three or four onions.

On one such evening in January the game was progressing as usual when there came a loud rapping on the door. As was the custom of the north, someone yelled, "Come on in and be quick about it." The door opened and three half-frozen figures staggered into the cabin. They stood there swaying and blinking at us, their eyebrows rimed with frost. One of them kicked shut the door, to which Findlater only said, "Easy on the timber, boys," but I could tell he wasn't impressed with their manners. The first fellow was tall and wore a long greasy coat with bone buttons. On his head was a round pot hat tied down by a scarf which was wrapped around his chin. The other two were just as tall but skinny as sticks. As a matter of fact, that's what they were, a couple of Stick Indians from upriver. One of them was dressed in an old faded mackinaw and the other was a mean-looking cuss in a long coat and a plug hat. All three of them had scurvy sores on their necks and behind their ears. "Step up to the fire there and warm yourselves," says Findlater, and the three of them shuffled over to the stove and stood there rubbing their hands.

Then this mackinaw Indian began a long, high-pitched keening sound that raised the hair on the back of my neck. He looked to be in some kind of trance, but it didn't seem to bother his partner in the greasy coat. He pulled a bottle of whiskey from one of his pockets and took a long pull. "Don't worry about him, boys," he says in a twangy voice. "That's his medicine stuff." He handed the bottle to Plug Hat, who took an uncommonly long swallow and shuddered a little before wiping his mouth.

"The name's Jack Wade," says Greasy Coat. "Originally from Arkansas. Now workin' a claim upriver a spell. These here Injuns are my two partners." He pointed to the chanting Indian. "That there is Barking Dog."

"He sounds more like whining dog to me," says one of the players, and everybody laughed, including Jack Wade, who thought it was a very witty remark and said so.

"The other fellah here," he says, "is a chief's son. He's got a real pretty name in the Stick lingo. They call him On-weh-weh-weh-po-po-po-weh. In English he goes by Slam-the-door-in-your-face!"

17. Rough Justice

"Mighty fancy handles," says Findlater, studying his cards. "Now maybe you boys wouldn't mind stepping back from the stove and sharing the heat?"

"Why, surely not," says Wade, stepping to one side.

The swirl of conversation resumed whilst these three stood around the stove passing their bottle back and forth. Then Wade says to no one in particular, "We come to town for a little fun. We got ourselves a poke here!" And he held up a little leather bag. But lots of people had pokes. It was nothing unusual, so someone said, "Just wait your turn and youse can set in."

"That's neighborly of ya," says Wade.

Then this Barking Dog stopped his song long enough to stick a finger into this pot of stew that I had simmering on top of the stove. He licked his finger and said, "Good, good!"

Now I might have let that pass. But there is one thing about being a saint. And that is you build up a good store of ill will towards your fellow humans. All that denial and sacrifice is against nature, and so you become touchy and ready to pounce on another person at the first sign of weakness. So when I saw this Indian poking his fingers in my stew I didn't say, "Excuse me, but would you mind getting your fingers out of my stew." No, what I said was, "Get your dirty fingers out of my stew, you redskin devil!" In accompaniment to that I jumped to my feet.

But this Barking Dog didn't take offense. He just grinned and, coming to attention, snapped off the crispest salute you'd meet on a parade square. I could see now he didn't have all his buttons, but there was plenty of grumbling from the card table. "Did you see that?" said one player. "Why, he stuck his ——ing finger in the stew! Can you beat that?"

"Let the cobbler not go beyond his last," says Findlater.

Then this other Indian, Slam-the-door-in-your-face, steps up in front of me. I suppose he took exception to me yelling at his partner or maybe he was just ashamed that his partner hadn't cut the tongue out of my head, for he seized the Bible out of my hand and began looking through it, though I don't believe reading came easy to him. So I grabbed it right back.

"Easy now, Door," says this Wade. "Let's have no unnecessary hostilities."

But Plug Hat sticks a finger in my chest and leans forward. I believe his breath smelled worse than the bottom of a parrot cage. And he says, "You son of bitch."

"And you're a heathen bound for hell," I says.

At which he pulls out a hunting knife, the blade gleaming in the oily light. "Me cut off your river," he says. But just then Wade yelled something and sprang forward, catching his friend off balance. The knife fell to the floor, or I wouldn't be here to tell you this. I myself fell backwards over a chair trying to avoid serious wounding. But Plug Hat caught me in a headlock that was just like a vise. Those matchstick arms had more strength than you could imagine. Then the whole thing got fuzzy, because Plug Hat very smartly rapped my head against the wall and the stars came right into the room, a whole shower of them. Somebody plucked him off my back and then another body sailed over me. The room was soon in an uproar. I remember being on all fours and somebody stepped on my hand and somebody else booted my arse. When I got to my feet I picked up a chair and broke it over Barking Dog's head. He was standing by the fire eating stew. After I hit him, he snapped off another salute and fell over stone cold. Findlater threw a man clear across the room, where he landed in the corner on his neck. He was one of Findlater's best friends, a French-Canadian strongman named Albert Gagnon. Then somebody knocked Jack Wade right into the stove, and over the stove went, with the pipes coming down around our heads and soot and hot coals spilling onto the floor. In a few seconds flames were shooting up the walls and catching the coats hanging on the pegs. "Let's get the hell out of here," somebody yelled. "She's gonna go." And then we all scrambled for the door.

Fortunately everybody got out, and fast, because it only took about two minutes before what had been a fairly tidy little home was just a pile of ashes and charred timbers. We all stood around watching it, with nobody saying anything and everybody feeling a little ashamed because the whole thing had been started by foolishness. Findlater stood in his pants and underwear stroking his chin and looking pensive. I went over to him and said, "I'm sorry, Findlater. This was my fault."

"Don't worry about it, Bill" he says. "It's just the fortunes of war."

And then, from the smoking ruins came the most delicious smell you could imagine. It filled the clear cold air and almost made you cry out for the sheer savoriness of it. It was Findlater's onions, of course, now roasted below the floorboards. "Well, boys," says Findlater, "we might just as well make the best of it. So let's dig in and have ourselves a feed." So everybody grabbed a stick and, poking among the floorboards, forked out these onions. Then somebody brought forth a jug of rum and before long a sledload of dance hall girls arrived from town, attracted by the fire. Soon we had a party going and there might still be some fellow alive besides me who can remember that onion roast, because it became quite famous in Dawson that winter and was talked about for some time in those parts. I always admired Findlater for the spirit with which he met misfortune.

There must have been upwards of a hundred people partook of that feast and at the end of it Findlater and me had about a dozen places to sleep. We ended up at Sam Bonnifield's, where we both went to work, with me waiting on tables while Findlater continued to deal faro. Then we ran into some bad luck. One Friday night about eleven o'clock Findlater and I were taking our break at a little table near the back when Sam Bonnifield came through the crowd flanked on either side by a Mountie. Sam never did smile much, but this time he looked grimmer than usual. Then this Mountie says to Findlater and me,

17. Rough Justice

"There's a gentleman in this bar who says his pocket was picked on two occasions this evening by each of you."

Now I knew why Sam was frowning. He ran the straightest saloon in town and his reputation was at stake. Findlater and me were no angels but we'd always played it straight with Sam and the accusation annoyed Findlater. "And who is this so-called gentleman?" he asked.

"Just a minute," said the policeman, and walked back through the crowd.

Then Findlater said, "Believe me, Sam, we're being made fools of by somebody. Bill and me have always played straight with you."

Sam said nothing. He just looked down at his shoes and rocked a bit on his heels. Then the Mountie returned, and God Almighty, who was following him but Barney Spraat, the ex-police captain from Philadelphia. There he was with his hard fat and his walrus moustache and heavy hands. "Them's the two," he said. "They cleaned me out right in this saloon. Not more than fifteen minutes ago."

"That's a lie," I said.

"Why don't you search 'em?" says the captain.

Now as soon as he said that, I knew Findlater and me was in trouble. For instance, I suddenly had the uneasy suspicion that the right breast pocket of my smock was a trifle heavier than usual. And I'd not noticed it until the captain opened his mouth. So the Mountie said, "I'd like to look through your pockets, son." They were tough but they were always polite. Well, of course they found the captain's wallet in my pocket. They found another one on Findlater. Sam looked at the both of us and shook his head and walked away.

It's a corker how that Barney Spraat with those thick fingers was so deft as to fool the both of us. Mind you, the saloon was crowded but still and all it was a piece of workmanship that I had to admire. Lifting a man's wallet requires a good bit of craft with the fingers. But putting a wallet *into* a man's pocket is the work of an artist.

We got six months on the woodpile for that, the sentence passed by the legendary Sam Steele who some of you may have read about. He was the local commissioner of the day. On our way to the Stockades we saw Barney Spraat standing on the street in his big fur coat. I suppose he'd just had a meal, for he was standing there picking his teeth.

"Look at that bastard," says Findlater. "Gloating away, but still too miserable to even smile."

"Well," I said, "It's bad enough to be caught when you're really stealing. But to be framed like this is hard to take."

"Don't give it a thought, Bill," says Findlater. "Look at it this way. The old captain there had his troubles down in Seattle after we filched his money. Now it's our turn. There's a kind of rough justice to these things."

18

——ED

THAT MORNING there were three of us new to the woodpile. Besides Findlater and me there was this Englishman named Percy Finchwhistle. He'd been caught cheating at cards. Percy was a slender fellow with a gaunt, delicate face. Although he wasn't much older than me he looked frail as an old woman and suffered with this racking cough which I took as a sign of lung consumption. Percy was in a class by himself. Most of the other prisoners were rough-and-tumble types who blew their noses with their hands and then wiped them on the seat of their pants. But Percy always used handkerchiefs for his coughing spells and he washed them out every night and left them drying on the stove. On that first morning, it wasn't hard to tell that he'd never had an ax in his hands before, let alone split cordwood. On his first swing he nearly put the ax through his boot. Working alongside him, I said, "Here! Let me show you how to use that thing before you cripple yourself for life." So I showed him how to grip the ax and how to put a heft on it but not wear yourself out within an hour.

"I'm most frightfully obliged to you, old man," says Percy, and then Findlater showed him a trick or two and before long we had him reasonably proficient. However, he had no wind for that kind of exertion and after a week the Mounties saw that, and put him to work in the washhouse.

But right from that first day the three of us stayed together. As Percy used to say, "I'm ever so grateful to you chaps. There's such a lot of rough nobs about." Which was funny, because Findlater and me weren't exactly quality. Percy, however, appeared to be. Although he was a little loose in matters of general honesty, he came from high-class people. He told us his oldest brother actually sat in the House of Lords. Like my father, Percy was the youngest son and a remittance man.

His father was dead, having been gored to death by a rhinoceros during a hunting trip in Africa. "Stuck like a pig on a stick and carried away," said Percy one evening. "A shocking experience for a six-year-old child." His mother lived on their two-thousand-acre estate in the west of England. Percy had knocked about a good bit, as he put it. He'd been all over Canada and the United States.

Findlater loved to hear him talk and through those long winter nights the two of them argued the merits of the English and American systems. Findlater might say, "Blame it all, Percy, you're dead wrong. Why, take your country now! All them lords and ladies ridin' around on horses chasin' a pack of hound dogs and not earnin' a cent of wages while all them poor peasants in their little straw huts are grubbin' in the ground. You can't get away with that kind of bullshit in my country. There it's every man for himself and everybody's got a chance to make a dollar bill for himself. Look at all our great men. Boone, Crockett, Abe Lincoln. They hacked a livin' right out of the virgin forest. And made somethin' of themselves. Mind you, I'm not sayin' we couldn't use a little smoothin' over in the manners department. But nobody ever amounted to nothin' sittin' around with their grandmother eatin' crumpets and tea."

Percy always took that sort of thing with a good humor. "But my dear fellow," he'd say, "you can't possibly imagine that that is all we do. Why, look at our responsibilities. Our burdens. There's India, Africa, Australia, Canada. Rude, untamed lands filled with savage peoples who need civilizing. The sun never sets on the British Empire."

Being a Canadian, I was caught in the middle and very seldom asked for an opinion. Or maybe I was and I didn't have any.

So that winter passed in custody and the only excitement was a fire that damn near destroyed the entire town of Dawson. I think it happened sometime towards the end of April. I recall it was a cold night and the Mounties hustled us out of bed to help. Nobody worried about us escaping, because there wasn't any place to go. We worked all night in the freezing cold and managed to save half the town.

In late May our sentences came up for review and the authorities decided we'd learned our lesson. All winter Percy had been saving his regular bank drafts and he had a good bit set aside. To show you the kind of fellow he was, he offered to pay our passage out, and Findlater and me took him up on that because we were stone broke. Percy was going back to England, though from the sounds of his cough I had doubts about him making it. Findlater was headed for Chicago, where he planned to team up with Henry Smithers the electrical wizard. Smithers had sent him a letter hinting at some project that would revolutionize the morals of America and make them five million dollars as well. Findlater asked me to go along but I had no ambitions along those lines. I just wanted to get out of Dawson, for it reminded me too much of Sally and that cork-legged cardsharp.

My spell of Bible reading and meditation had come to an end

with that onion roast. I was now about to enter a dark period of my life during which drunkenness and debauchery were the general rule and sobriety and clean living the exception. Maybe it was my disappointment in love. Or maybe it was just bad blood. There was my father's love of drink and his general irresponsibility. And there was my mother's bad temper. You could see that all mixed together in my two brothers. Whatever the cause, I fell into a period of prolonged degradation which lasted nearly three years.

We booked passage on a river boat to Norton Sound and once there took a steamer third-class to San Francisco. All that trip Percy stayed in his berth with this bone-rattling cough while Findlater and I doctored him as best we could. After the ship docked we got him to a hospital, where this doctor took one look and said, "He'll never make England in that shape, boys. My advice is to leave him for a few weeks until he gets his strength back. Then he should go right into a sanatorium. I know two or three first-class establishments not far from here where the air is sweet and dry and maybe we can heal those lungs. But look! Before we get down to details. And I hate to bring this up. But what about the old mazzoola?" Findlater and I looked at one another, and the doctor, a big, brown-bearded fellow, chuckled. "Well, this isn't exactly a charity ward, eh! Now, at the risk of sounding crass, I'd like to know a little more about the ways and means, I'm speaking of green, the old spondulicks! In a word, who's paying for the sick man's keep?" So I explained to him how Percy had money, and as a matter of fact I wrote his mother Lady Finchwhistle in Oxfordshire, England, and explained the situation. Meantime we pawned Percy's gold watch and personal jewelry and turned over the money to the doctor, who promised to look after him.

So we left Percy there, lying on a bed and looking more like a skeleton than a human. "Take care, little fellow," said Findlater, shaking his bony shoulder. "Someday you'll come back to this country and see I was right about things."

"Goodbye, Percy," I said. "And good luck."

Percy waved weakly to us and smiled. "Thanks for everything, chaps. And keep your peckers up!"

Findlater and me continued eastward to Chicago, where he got off the train to begin what he called "my new life in electricity." There was a half-hour wait, so I went out on the platform to stretch my legs and say goodbye. Findlater shook my hand and I believe there were tears in his eyes. "You are the damnedest young fool," he says. "I just don't know why in hell you're goin' back to that frozen-arsed country of yours when all the opportunities are waitin' for you right down here. Why, I read the other day where a man down in Oklahoma walked out into his backyard to go to the privy and there, gushing up around his cabbages, was oil. Now he's livin' in biscuit city." The conductor yelled "Aboard" and I shook Findlater's hand again. Then he says, "Tell me somethin', Bill, before you go."

"Name it," I says.

Findlater scratched his head. "I've been tryin' to figure out why Percy would say 'Keep your peckers up!' That don't seem like decent language for a nobleman." So I explained to him that it was an English expression for keeping up your courage and that my own father used it. And Findlater said, "I'm gonna miss havin' you around to explain that sort of thing to me, pal." Then he whipped out this booklet. "Here's a little goin'-away present. You take care now." And I jumped aboard as the train started to move. In the carriage I opened the book. It was called *Rags to Riches: Ten Short Profiles of Successful Americans.*

Now I am not going into any particular details about the next three years except to remark that without much difficulty I turned into a dirty, unshaven bum who spent his last copper on drink and was not above stealing to keep body and soul together. I might also add that this was the most relaxing period of my life, inasmuch as I had no standards to live up to. I traveled over most of Canada. From Halifax, where I searched for my father before remembering that he was now supposed to be out west, all the way out to Vancouver, where I worked as a bartender before being fired for drinking on the job. In the fall I followed the harvest trains to Saskatchewan, making just enough to see me through the winter. I lived in cheap rooms where the landladies sometimes felt sorry for me and sent around preachers who lectured on the curse of drink. I usually just laughed at them, and once a big, raw-boned Baptist pulled me out of a chair and rattled the teeth in my head. "Don't mock the Lord's servants, son," he said to me.

In Toronto I walked past the Easterbrooks' home on a fine summer day. They were having a garden party and behind the big wrought-iron fence fancy-dressed people stood laughing and talking and drinking lemonade. In one corner of the lawn children played croquet and from her wheelchair Esther played too. She looked pretty as a picture. Wilson and several other drivers were back near the stables, standing around an automobile, which was a novel sight in those days. I was glad to see Esther happy but I also felt miserable and ashamed standing there in dirty clothes that smelled of gin. And I had been such a dandy with such big ideas when I left! I also visited the house where Mrs. Fletcher lived, and after walking around the block a dozen times rapped on the door. But the occupants had never heard of her and were none too polite in telling me so.

In late March of nineteen and two I reached bottom right in Toronto when I was chased from a grocery store, my pockets filled with bottles of vanilla extract. Like a rat I hid under some wood shavings in a boxcar and after finishing the vanilla went to sleep. Sometime in the middle of the night I was awakened by a kick and there were two figures standing over me in rain slickers holding a lantern. Maybe none of you have known this kind of humiliation, and I don't wish it on you. To be dragged out and kicked and humbled by your fellow man is a grievous loss to your dignity. There wasn't any government agency to look after you in those days, so if you were down on your luck you had to depend on the charity of your fellow man. And I always found that about as thin as boardinghouse soup. So these two railwaymen kicked me out onto the cold gravel and I scrambled through the dark just like an animal. The train was chuffing and steaming and taking on water. I stumbled through a ditch and noticed by the station sign that I was back in Belleville. It was a mild night with a mist in the air and the sound of water running in the wayside brooks. I decided then that the thing to do was return to my home in Craven Falls.

It's a funny thing. I'd never liked the damn place much when I lived there but now I felt like crying just to be so close by. I believe I entertained some wild hope that my father would be there to meet and shelter me. All night I walked the spur line north, with the frogs croaking in the marshes and the dripping night all around me. At dawn the eastern sky blazed a glorious red for about ten minutes and then it clouded over and the rain came down. Once or twice I jumped out of the way of passing trains and by noon I reached the outskirts of Craven Falls. I could see Jake Snipes chasing two or three kids around his shack, waving a piece of cordwood in the air. Because of my miserable appearance I went around the town and took the township road westward. I came upon the old homestead an hour or so later and it looked worse than some of the dives I'd been living in over the previous three years. The roof was still on but the windows were all gone and the crows were flying in and out, and my father certainly wasn't living there. Those crows must have been foraging in the old house, looking for things to build their nests with, for one big fellow flew right overhead and when I nipped him on the tail feathers with a stone he dropped a piece of paper at my feet. The writing on it was blurred by time and the weather but you could still make it out. It was dated July 1895 and must have been composed shortly before Tom's death. Here it is.

> *I am weary of the struggle*
> *I am burdened by my fate*
> *I will take tomorrow's ferry*
> *Across the river Jordan.*

That gives you some idea of the grim cast of his mind.

It was nearly nightfall when I reached Annie's home, and for a few minutes I just stood out on the road and admired the substantial prosperity of the place. To judge by the new barn and stables, Rufus was doing all right for himself. The house was in darkness except for a dim yellow light at the back. I figured that was the kitchen, where they must be sitting down to supper. The mere idea of home-cooked eats nearly made me faint. I started up the lane and of course the usual farm dog got wind of me and came charging towards the gate, barking his foolish head off. I snatched up a piece of a broken limb and waved it at him in a menacing fashion. He continued the racket but kept a respectful distance. I was halfway down the lane when the back door opened and a figure stood out on the stoop holding a lantern. I could see in the dusk that it was Rufus, tall and straight in his flannel shirt and bib overalls. I heard him say, "There's someone out there, Ann. Most likely a tramp. What do I do?" A couple of kids were squalling in the kitchen.

Then Annie came out the door and pushed Rufus to one side. From where I was, she appeared to have grown a good deal stouter but her big rough voice was just the same as it boomed across the gathering darkness. "What in hell's goin' on?"

"I think there's a tramp out there," says Rufus mildly. "Scout's givin' him trouble."

"Well, I'll tramp him, all right," says Annie. And she yells out to me, "Get off this property, you mangy son of a whore." Which struck me as unlikely language for somebody who was supposed to be such a big skirt in the local Methodist church. Of course, that was according to Ned and Fred, and their word wasn't worth the bung stop in a barrel. Meantime the dog had worked his way behind me as dogs are apt to do and he kept me busy circling. I was just about to open my mouth in greeting to Annie when she leveled this long-barreled rifle and fired. The explosion damn near deafened me and a breeze of wind sailed past my right ear. The dog took off and hid somewhere in the bushes. "Get movin' now," my sister yells, "or I'll give you the other barrel where it'll do some good."

Methodist church or not, she was still the big, bad-tempered girl I'd always known, and when I heard her cock the hammer again I couldn't see any point in dying in the mud of their farmyard just to inform them that I was back in the neighborhood. But I hesitated and the damnable woman fired again, knocking the slouch hat from my head. That was definitely good riddance, and so I scooped up my hat and ran. Then somebody shied a stone at me and a squeaky little voice yelled, "You get away from my Ma's house!"

And Annie screeched like an old jay, "Leslie! Get back here before I skin your backside raw!"

So I was left to wander down a country road in the backwoods of Ontario in the middle of the night. I had the notion I might return to Annie's the next day and try my luck in full light. Mercifully the rain stopped and I dragged myself along, thinking I'd return to the town and ask for refuge in the jail. When I reached the outskirts, however, I was so overcome with hunger and fatigue that I couldn't go any further. As it happened, I found myself at the cemetery and so decided to sit for a while and gather my strength. The moon slipped through the clouds and washed the tombstones with light. I saw our family stone, with the names of my mother and poor Tom and little George there inscribed. Almost at once I fell into the deep sleep of exhaustion and dreamed I was down beneath the cold grass, sleeping next to Tom like in the old days.

I was awakened by the sound of carriage wheels and the creaking of harness. It was light, but a thick ground fog lay about clinging to the stones. My joints were stiff with the cold and dampness and when I stood up it took a while to get everything working. Then through the trees I saw a hearse. It was hard to figure, because it was so early and there weren't any mourners. I got down behind a stone and watched as the hearse passed by me and stopped at a freshly dug grave. Phineas Fletcher climbed down slowly and stood for a minute staring at the hole. Old Fletcher! His shoulders were stooped and he moved like a very old man. Just then the cold in my system gave vent and I drilled out the damnedest sneeze you've ever heard. Old Fletcher was never a man to be easily startled, not even in a graveyard in the murky half-light of dawn. So he looked over my way and said calmly, "I don't know who you are, but if you've got two hands on the ends of your arms you can help me put this casket into the ground. There's a dollar bill in it for you."

Now here was a dilemma. I wasn't fussy about making myself known to Fletcher, as I was generally ashamed for my behavior in his household. But a dollar was something I was sorely in need of. Then too, I'd changed a good deal in six years, and with my face covered by dirt and a beard, I figured he might not recognize me. So I stepped out and walked towards him. Fletcher watched me approach through the gloom and then he says, "A man of the road, is it? Well, I suppose it's fitting. Our own dear Lord was a wanderer!"

Now that casket was a beauty. It was varnished oak with silver handles and must have weighed half a ton. It damn near killed me to lift one end. The funny thing is that I remembered that casket from the sales parlor in Fletcher's house. It was never sold because nobody could afford it. After we got it into the grave Fletcher opened his purse and took out a dollar. "I'm grateful for your help," he says, and turning away, began to fill in the grave.

It was very queer. An expensive casket but no mourners! Not even a gravedigger. So to be polite I asks, "And who might the deceased be?"

Fletcher stopped to blow his nose and, pointing at the grave, says, "There lie the mortal remains of my dear wife, Mary Jane Fletcher." It was startling news! "She meant everything to me," says Fletcher, the tears sliding down his long, homely face. "I found her in a place of sin. That was before the Lord touched me. And I brought her home and we were happy. In time she would have mended her ways. I know she would. And then out of Christian charity I took a young fellow into my home. His father was a poet and I should have known better. But I didn't, and this young fellow seduced her. He led her down the paths of wickedness, and him only a boy at the time. Then he ran off with money he stole from me. Poor Mary Jane. She followed him and turned once more to a life of sin. He must have cast a spell over her, for I do believe he was a servant of the devil. Then this winter past, Mary Jane wrote to beg my forgiveness and ask for help. And I went down to that wicked city of Toronto and brought her home big with child. But the good Lord had other plans for her and he saw fit to take her from me. The ways of the righteous are hard, Stranger. The narrow path is no joke."

"True," I says gruffly, to disguise my voice. "And what about the child?"

"At home, thank the Lord," says Fletcher. "Sleeping in her innocent cradle watched over by a friendly neighbor woman. The only person left in town that will speak to me. Craven Falls is narrow-minded. None of them understood what a fine woman my wife really was. But I still prefer my future to that young Bill Farthing's. The Lord will deal with him in time. I understand he's a desperado somewhere in the United States, runnin' with loose women of the stage."

It was the longest speech I'd ever heard Fletcher make, and he was still talking when I slipped away and walked down the road into town, reflecting on the queerness and contrariness of life. There I was, crazy for Sally! Yet she had eyes only for Corky Madill. On the other hand, Mrs. Fletcher had hankered after me and wouldn't give her husband the time of day. Yet he was madly in love with her! It was all very strange. But I figure Mrs. Fletcher must have filled her husband's ears with that cock-and-bull story about me leading her down the paths of wickedness, etc., etc. But even if I had taken the time to tell Fletcher my side of things, it would have been useless. Fletcher believed what he wanted to believe and you can never argue with a man like that. He'd go to his grave not knowing the truth. But what difference does that make when you come right down to it?

And here's another thing I thought about as I walked along that morning. There was a fairly young woman I'd lain beside many a night. And now I'd lowered her casket into the ground! When you bury somebody you've been intimate with, it makes you think about large matters. Such as, how much time have I got and what am I going to do with it? My father was always worrying over these questions and he nearly always settled them with a bottle of Bullseye whiskey and a poem. But there I was, in my twenty-second year, and to tell the truth, looking more like a man in his fifty-second. Attired in filthy clothes and with the teeth in my head loosened from bad diet. Sleeping in ditches and chased from doorsteps by my own family! I was disgusted with myself. So I decided then and there to change my life. I decided to become a good citizen.

19

I BECOME A GOOD CITIZEN

———————

IT CAME TO ME with the clearness of a religious experience. I was
wasting my allotted time on the planet. If I kept up my present style
of living I'd be lucky to see twenty-five. Whiskey and cigarettes and
general irregular habits had undermined my constitution. And for two
years I'd also been engaged in a running battle with the clap, picked
up in a Vancouver frolic. Findlater was right all along. A man doesn't
have all that much time and so the thing to do is to make money,
because you're just a doormat for most people if you don't have money.
I was too incompetent to be altogether crooked, so I decided to get a
regular job with wages and try to climb upward. I never bothered
getting in touch with Annie. I set out for Toronto right away, traveling
on a flatcar of the Grand Trunk Railway. I took any job I could find in
that city. I cleaned chimneys and outhouses, removed people's furnace
ashes. It was low work but it gave me a stake and allowed me to outfit
myself. In a few weeks I was presentable enough to land a job clerking
in the housewares department of the T. Eaton Company.

The pay was terrible but it wasn't a bad job and I worked at that
for several months, during which time I became acquainted with the
salesmen who dropped in to see the department manager. One of these
salesmen was a nice old fellow named John Quill. He took a liking to me
and suggested that I become a salesman out on the road. There was
more money in it, according to him, and a fellow could get ahead
faster. He recommended me to his company and the upshot of it was
that I got a job selling paint. Poor old Quill! About three months after
they hired me I was working his territory because he was considered
too old and therefore let go. I don't know what became of him but I
didn't give it a minute's thought at the time. You can't stop and worry
your head about things like that when you're trying to get on in the
world.

19. I Become a Good Citizen

With regular eats I put some flesh back on my bones. And because of my natural vanity I spent a good bit on clothes, so that when I stepped into a general store in a new pinch-back suit and derby hat, I wasn't the ugliest man in town.

One of those towns I'll call Elmhurst, because of the number of fine elms lining its streets. That's not its real name, by the way, but I prefer not to have its true identity known. It was a nice little village of eight hundred or so with two hotels, four churches, an ice cream parlor, and a box factory, right in the heart of Ontario's most prosperous farm country. I had one of my best accounts in that town, by name of Pickett's General Mercantile and Dry Goods. It was a thriving business owned by a dry, thin widower in his late sixties named Lawford Pickett. His daughter Merle worked in the store with him. She was a spinster lady who wouldn't see thirty again. Not the most comely woman you'd ever meet, being tall and thin like her father with large, prominent teeth and just the suggestion of a moustache creeping along her upper lip. Her hair, tightened into a bun, was already speckled with gray, though I could tell she regularly put stovepipe blacking to it. She didn't help herself in matters of dress either, always choosing to wear the drabbest blacks and grays. Her whole life was centered on the Presbyterian church, where she took part in several activities.

Pickett liked me. He used to say that I reminded him of his son who had died in a drowning accident when he was in his early twenties. Pickett was a slow, melancholy man whose only pleasure lay in pointing out how well his store was doing. I believed him, for it was always crowded when I was in there and there was no competition to speak of in the community.

After a while he began to invite me to his house for supper. We'd have a glass of raspberry cordial, for they were death on drink. Then we'd sit down and the housekeeper, Alma, would serve the food. She was a lame woman and elderly. Pickett would ask Merle to say grace, and this was always a terrible ordeal for her because of her bashfulness. She'd go all blotchy in the face and then mumble some words over the food, which was always plentiful and delicious. After supper we'd go into the parlor, which always smelled of stale lemon oil. Merle would sit down at the piano and play some hymns, making a pretty good fist of it too, though I never cared for those droning tunes like "Yield Not to Temptation" or "Rescue the Perishing." After a few more weeks Merle managed a shy smile over the bolts of cloth while I showed her father my paint samples.

On one of my visits that fall of 1902 Pickett didn't seem interested while I wrote up his order. "Oh, never mind that now, Will," he said. They called me Will because they thought it sounded more dignified. "Come over and see Merle, because she's been waiting for the past two weeks to ask you something." And he took my arm and we went over to where Merle was serving a couple of ladies. Now, with customers she displayed a certain savvy, wasn't a bit backward, and knew how to drive home a bargain like her father. "Now, Merle," says Pickett, "I'll look after these ladies. Will is here now."

Merle blushed and looked away as we walked down to the back of the store and stood by the nail barrels. Now, I was a breezy young fellow in those days, full of beans and sales chatter. I knew how to talk to country people in their stores, so I says, "Well, Merle, it'll soon be time to put the woollies on. The paper says snow any day now."

Merle blushed again and then, staring hard at a barrel of number-nine roofing nails, croaks, "Church fowl supper tonight. Will you be my guest?"

It all came out in a rush like a little kid's recital, and coming from this tall, bony woman, it struck me as damn comical. "I beg your pardon, Merle," I says. She mumbled again and as I leaned forward I could smell her lavender sachet. Thinking to have a bit of fun, I says, "You smell like the green fields of May, Merle." Which just about finished her. Her thin bosom heaved and fell and she turned and fled into this little office where Pickett kept his ledgers.

I stood there smiling and then Pickett came up, rubbing his hands. "Well, Will? What do you say?"

"Why," says I, "I'd consider it a privilege to accompany Merle to the fowl supper tonight."

"Now you're talking turkey," says Pickett, digging me in the ribs. "Listen! Those church women put up a great feed. Turkey, mashed potatoes, punkin pie. All you can eat. You might even meet a few new customers too. It beats sittin' in an old hotel room."

He was right about that. My business life may have been booming but my social life had taken a real downturn. The truth is that after a number of years of fleshly pleasures I was now existing like a monk, except that instead of religion, I was living around the paint business, spending my evenings and Sundays writing up orders and studying my competitors' catalogues. So I willingly accepted the invitation and from that night on and for the next several months I courted Merle Pickett with a view of matrimony.

The way I looked at things was this: selling paint was all right, but progress in those days was slow. I knew fellows who'd been at it for thirty years and were still living in hotel rooms and day coaches. The only people who got ahead quickly were the sons and nephews of the president. And in many ways it was a boring life. Always cracking jokes with the rubes and smiling at their brainless gossip. To relieve the boredom I started carrying a flask, though I hadn't seriously touched liquor since the night I was kicked out of that boxcar. But I found that a nip or two made the evening more tolerable, especially if you had to sit around hotel lobbies listening to soft-handed salesmen lie about the chambermaids they'd screwed. To tell you the truth, I could see myself in twenty years turning into that fat joker who tried that monkey business with me on the train when I was just a runaway kid. Now on the other side of the coin, there was Merle. She was no beauty prize and when I compared her to Sally Butters I could have cried. And indeed did many a night. But it seemed to me that if the store went along with her, it wasn't such a bad deal. Then I also figured that after living with a man she might liven up a bit.

So there it was, as neat as logic. Pickett wanted a son-in-law. Merle wanted a husband. And I wanted to be a successful business-man. It represented an unusual situation in real life, because every-body involved would get what they wanted. So I took the courting of Merle Pickett seriously, sitting in church halls and holding her big dry hand while I listened to some dame screech her way through "The Holy City." Wobbling on my ankles at the skating parties and eating my egg sandwiches at the box socials. Between visits I wrote Merle letters and, like my father, I wasn't shy with words on the page. Pickett was tickled by all this. Sometimes he invited me to speak at his Odd-fellows Lodge and I'd give a little talk which might be entitled some-thing like "God Is the Businessman's Best Friend."

Thus I proposed marriage to Merle Pickett and was accepted. On a warm Saturday in late May of nineteen hundred and three we became husband and wife. The church smelled of lilacs and Merle stood beside me, a full head taller and stiff as a poker in white organdy. Things went along fine until the minister laid out that part about anybody knowing of impediments preventing the two of us from lawfully joining together and then I heard snickers from a few loafers at the back. I remember thinking to myself, You bastards will be laughing out of the other side of your mouths in another few days when you clomp into the Mercantile asking to put your chewing tobacco and lamp wicks on the books. In the afternoon the Women's Institute pre-pared a supper for us and then there was a square dance. I'd thought we might take the evening train to Toronto and go on to Niagara Falls for a day or so. It seemed to be the smart thing to do when you got married. But Merle wasn't having any of that. As she put it, she wasn't going to travel to any strange town with a man. She said the word *man* as if it was some species of bug, perhaps a praying mantis on her neck.

So maybe you've already guessed the problem I had to face over the next five months. Merle didn't mind the externals of marriage, such as having me around the dinner table or walking her to church or working in the store. But she couldn't bring herself to partake in the intimacies of married life. On our wedding night she made it plain as the staves in a barrel that she wanted nothing to do with sex. It didn't help either that on that night those jokers who had given me the business in church showed up outside Pickett's house and gave us what they called a shivaree, banging pots and pans and letting loose a live chicken, which flapped its wings and squawked and settled on the bedroom window sill looking in at us. At the time I was sitting in a wingback chair and Merle was struck rigid on the edge of the bed, still attired in her wedding dress. Then a voice from below said, "You better be careful up there, little city feller, or Miss Merle will just wear you clean to the bone." Pickett got out his shotgun and chased them away.

After they left I said to Merle, "It's customary, Merle, for a husband and wife to sleep together."

She sniffed a little and wrung her hands and said, "I know, Will, I know. But I'm sorry, I just can't. I can't see myself doing *that*. I've watched dogs on the street. It seems so ridiculous."

"Well, dogs is dogs and humans usually go about it in a slightly different fashion," I says. "But even supposing I admit to the general comedy of the position you find yourself in, it can still be a pleasurable experience."

"Oh, I wish I were dead," she says.

I went over and put my arm around her but she only flinched. Oh, you can laugh all you like in this age of loose living. But what you have to remember is that Merle was a small-village Presbyterian. And also the pleasures of the flesh weren't so commonly sought after as they are nowadays.

Well, God Almighty, I'm no beast, so I tried to comfort her. "There, there, now," I says. "Don't carry on so. We'll not bother with anything too exotic tonight. Maybe if we just got undressed here in the dark and just lay down alongside one another. Just to get used to the idea of sleeping together."

"Oh, Will!" she says. "I couldn't! Not undressed. Not in the same bed. With a man!"

"Well, damn it all to hell, Merle," I says. "Excuse my language. But this is our wedding night."

"Oh, Will!" she says. "Just let me get used to the idea. Perhaps if you could sleep on the floor."

"On the floor, for Christ's sakes," I says.

"Please, Will. Just for tonight."

Well, the idea was incredible. To spend your wedding night on the floor while your bride slept in a feather bed not five feet away. But that's what happened to me, and moreover before I fell asleep Merle says, "Will? You won't take advantage of me while I'm asleep?"

"Oh no, Merle," I says. "You're as safe as in a nunnery with me."

"Please don't make fun of me, Will."

"I'm not making fun of you, Merle."

"Promise."

"I promise."

"Thank you, Will."

"That's all right, Merle."

"Goodnight, Will."

"Night, Merle."

Some wedding night that was!

Of course, nobody was any the wiser, and in fact the way Merle fussed over me during our first few weeks of marriage probably led people to believe that she was the most contented bride in the province of Ontario. I know Pickett used to wink at me and whisper, "You're just what the doctor ordered for that little girl, Willy. I haven't seen her this happy in years." And he'd give me another wink and a nudge with his elbow. "You can't beat a little bit of the you-know-what, eh! Probably Merle takes after me. My goodness, I was fond of that when I was a young fellow. But my poor wife. She never put much store by it."

But in fact our marriage remained a marriage in name only and its chaste nature got on my nerves. Maybe Merle wasn't the most attractive woman in the world but she was my wife. To give her credit, she was working up courage and after a couple of months we'd progressed to the point where we'd at least lie abed together in our nightdresses. But there were severe setbacks. I remember lying there wide awake one night while Merle snored beside me. I was thinking of poor Mrs. Fletcher and of how she'd loved her screwing and of the differences in people. Thinking of Mrs. Fletcher put me into an amorous state and, turning over, I slipped a hand between the legs of my sleeping wife. But no sooner was this done than those two shafts locked tight as a vise, sending a sharp pain through my wrist and forearm. At the same time Merle says, "You promised, Will."

"So I did," I says, jumping out of bed. "So I did." And I spent the rest of the night in the wingback chair trying to figure out if it was all worth it.

Once I tried to point out to her that the Scriptures had things to say on the conduct of husbands and wives. "Lookit here, Merle," I said to her one summer night when she didn't look half bad in the moonlight. " 'And unto the married I command, yet not I but the Lord. Let not the wife depart from her husband.' " And licking my fingers, I turned over some more of that thin Bible paper. "And how about this," I says. " 'Wives, submit yourselves unto your own husbands as unto the Lord.' Now what could be clearer than that for a Christian?"

At which she only burst into tears. "Oh, you're just trying to confuse me."

Sometimes I'd get so depressed I'd go down to the store and, walking through the dark aisles, reflect on the fact that it would all be mine one day. Because if everything wasn't going all that smoothly in the marriage bed, business was booming. A couple of years before I was just a common bum, plucking the cap from my head as I asked for nickels on street corners. Now I walked around my own store in a striped shirt with rubber armbands, keeping an eye on the kids who loitered near the candy cases and sultana barrels. And I didn't let anyone get away with too much credit either. A few people grumbled but there wasn't much they could do about it, the next closest store being over in Latchfield, two miles away. I gave the traveling salesmen a hard time too, getting all the free samples I could and making them buy me soft drinks over at the ice cream parlor. I found Pickett too conservative, so I had the place painted up and brought in a lot of new electric fixtures to highlight the merchandise.

Merle and I worked in that store from seven in the morning till six at night serving customers and then we spent another couple of hours going over the books together, with Merle never missing a penny. More and more old Pickett began to spend his time at the barbershop playing checkers with his cronies. Sunday was our only free day and sometimes after church Merle would pack a lunch and I'd hitch up the buggy and we'd drive out to the country for a picnic. On summer evenings we'd stroll through town, watching little kids roll their hoops along and young people on their bicycles heading for the band concert in the park. Whenever I hear a band, I don't think of my army days or parades or concert halls. I think of Elmhurst in the early years of this century. It's a warm evening in August and people are sitting in their shirtsleeves on the grass or wooden benches around the band shell.

What I'm saying is that it was a fairly civilized life if you could ignore the general hypocrisy and dullness of a small Ontario town. And in my particular case, the lack of sex. But what made life really bearable was making money. And I had other plans for getting rich too. Nobody yet owned an automobile in Elmhurst. Country people are apt to be suspicious of anything new, particularly if it smokes a lot and makes a terrible racket, which most of those early cars certainly did. I used to see one now and again when I visited Toronto on a buying trip and I was impressed. Along with Findlater I believed those contraptions had a great future, because it seems to me you can't go wrong when you invent something that eliminates effort, humankind being naturally lazy. The general drift of things from the wheel to the rocketship has been to get us somewhere faster and with less work. So I couldn't see how a machine that would get you around without the bother of feeding, barning, and tending a horse could miss in the long run.

Thus I decided to make inquiries, which I did on our new store letterhead, Pickett & Farthing General Goods & Merchandise. Your Dollar Goes Farther at Farthing's. I invited two or three automobile companies to consider me as a potential franchise holder. Henry Ford himself expressed interest and praised my enterprise in a personal letter. Ford made an excellent motorcar too, a Model A runabout which sold for eight hundred dollars. But I didn't like his terms. I also considered the handsome curved-dash model made by Ransome E. Olds of Lansing, Michigan. But being a good citizen, I eventually chose a Canadian-built machine called the Huffman Wheeler and I became their authorized agent for central Ontario in the spring of 1904. Before that, however, let me tell you what happened one Saturday in the fall of my marriage year.

I was fidgeting in the barbershop, impatient to get back to the store because business was brisk, with the women buying underwear and such. But Merle was going to some damn engagement party at the church next day and I needed a haircut. So I sat there thumbing through an old *Police Gazette*. The *Gazette* was standard reading in those days, with its stories about prizefighters and blood crimes and swindles. It gave you a good general picture of the seedier side of life. So as I sat there reading this magazine, God Almighty, what do I see but a story about Findlater and his partner Henry Smithers.

You'll recall how Smithers wanted Findlater to help him promote some device which would improve the general morals of America and make them a fortune too. Well, according to the *Gazette,* this device was a belt wired to an electrical outlet and worn in bed at night by young unmarried men. The general idea was to prevent your hands from drifting beneath the covers for immoral purposes. The way it worked was this. If a sinful notion entered the wearer's head and his hands sneaked down there, the contact produced a mild electrical shock. Findlater called this thing the "Bachelor's Belt" and he promoted it to church organizations, women's institutes, and men's clubs. It was widely advertised in Sunday-school papers. The only problem was that the damn thing was no good and because of short circuits and loose connections, several young men got badly burned in the privates. There was any number of lawsuits before the courts, and Findlater and Smithers were now in Leavenworth Prison out in Kansas.

Poor old Findlater! That very night I wrote him a letter, telling him in general what had happened to me over the previous three years, though omitting all my rough times and boasting a good deal about my prosperity. It's human nature to do that when your friends are in difficulties. About a month later I received a reply, which I now produce for your interest.

Fort Leavenworth Kansas
October 18, 03.

Dear frend Bill—I was sure glad to receeve yur letter. You are dead rite about evil company and I have learned my leson. Henry Smithers lied to me and I am payin my penalty as all persons ought too. You didn't mention in yur letter about whether you are still studyin fur the ministry. The warden who will be readin this here letter will be tickled to learn that I am now back in good company. They treat us real well in here and I have no complaints. Only if you cud send me a new bible as mine is near worn out from use.

Yur best frend
Cass Findlater

P.S. A year ago in Chicago I dined in company with a former aquaintance of yours. You wil remember Mrs. John Madill. I wonder if you knowed that she is now a widow. Her late husband crossed the bar up in Fairbanks last year. The unfortunate lady asks to be remembered to you and the mention of yur name brung tears to her lovly eyes.

Now that letter had a strange effect on me. Hearing about Findlater and Sally put me in mind of my old life and how different it was to my present circumstances. But it was the news of Sally's widowhood that was the most troubling. She was a free woman now, and judging from Findlater's letter, she still thought about me. I suddenly felt a general restlessness passing through me, with accompanying thoughts about what I was doing with my life. On the day I received Findlater's letter I hardly paid any attention to the customers. I just stood at the store window watching the leaves fall and then went home early, leaving Merle to close up. Pickett was away to an Oddfellows' supper.

Back at the house I retrieved a bottle of whiskey I'd stashed behind the privy. It had been there since my wedding night. Now I brought it into the house and topped up the decanter of raspberry cordial. Old Alma, the housekeeper, was out, so I sat in the parlor with my feet up, sipping raspberry whiskey and thinking of Sally and of how it might have been if we'd got married and settled down. Of course, I couldn't see her in a place like Elmhurst. She'd prefer city life, but that would have been all right with me too. I saw myself walking down a fashionable city street with Sally on my arm and her twirling a little parasol. And people saying, "There goes the former Miss Sally Butters, star of the musical stage. And that handsome young man is her husband, the successful entrepreneur Will Farthing." Then walking right into my dream was Merle, heavy-footed and plain as a penny.

"Well," she says. "What are you doing in here? And get your feet off the piano bench, for goodness sakes. Where have you been anyway? I had to close up the store by myself." You have to understand that Merle Pickett was no longer the big shy sunflower I courted in the spring. With each passing day she was growing bossier. "You don't look so well," she says. "You're all flushed. Are you coming down with something?"

I could tell she was curious about Findlater's letter, which jutted from my suit-coat pocket. Now, when I'm feeling low and miserable I tend towards sarcasm, so I says, "A dear old aunt of mine passed away."

"Oh, Will, I'm sorry," she says.

"It's all right. I'm just trying to compose myself. She raised me from childhood."

"You never told me," she said, sitting on the edge of the sofa with her hands folded in her lap.

"Will you have a glass of raspberry cordial with me, Merle?" I asks. "Just to be sociable."

"Why," she says, and hesitates. Anything to do with pleasure required careful consideration for Merle. "Well, perhaps a small one," she says.

"Good for you," I says, and walked over to the sideboard and poured her a good big glass of cordial and whiskey.

19. *I Become a Good Citizen*

We sat there for a while and after she'd finished the cordial she says, "Has this been up from the cellar long? It seems to have a riper taste. It's much better than Dad's last batch."

"Yes," I says, refilling our glasses. "It's an improvement."

After a minute Merle asks, "Why have you never told me about your family, Will? This aunt, for instance? Was she a woman of means?"

"If you mean did she leave me any money, Merle," says I, "the answer is no. She was poorer than Joe Cunt's dog. Lived in a sod hut with a couple of chickens and a scrawny pig. Did I never tell you about my poor upbringing?"

Merle blushed and sipped some cordial. "I don't know how to take you tonight, Will. I've never seen you like this before." I never said anything to that but just filled our glasses and we sat there for some time before Merle said, "Maybe a hymn would cheer you up, dear?"

It was the first time she'd ever called me dear and I figure it was about as close to a truly passionate outburst as you'd ever get from Merle. So I says, "Well now, that sounds very nice, Merle. Just let me fill your glass up again and help you to the piano stool and we'll get cracking with a bit of music here."

So Merle sat down at the piano and struck off about four bad chords of "Abide with Me." I stood by her side and sang. Worst noise you've ever heard but Merle loved it. "I didn't know you could sing, Will," she says. "We must do this more often." Then the music grew a little boisterous as Merle fetched out a Methodist hymnal which had lain in disgrace for many years in the music cabinet. We finished off the cordial and Merle says to me, "Will? I want to be a good wife to you."

"I believe you, Merle."

She giggled. "I can't seem to make my legs go, Will. Would you help me up the stairs?" So I helped her up the stairs and on the top landing she fell into a heap and started to giggle. When a Presbyterian gets taken with the giggles it is a sight to observe.

By and by I got her undressed and that evening, five months after our wedding day, our marriage was consummated. In fact, our first-born, Ernest, was conceived on that occasion. Later on Merle was deathly sick and I had to hold her head over the night pot. I don't know if she ever realized she'd been drunk. She never mentioned anything about it to me. And she never again invited me to sing.

20

RESPONSIBILITIES

———————

AFTER THAT EPISODE our marriage became more or less normal. Merle had no great taste nor talent for the conjugal act and after a while I myself lost interest in it. Besides, my business activities took up most of my time and energy. Pickett suffered a heart attack that winter and so Merle and I had to manage the store completely by ourselves. In the spring I went into the automobile business, renting an abandoned creamery off the main street as a showroom. The Huffman Wheeler was a sturdy little machine that gave a lot of satisfaction, though there were engineering problems that were never entirely corrected. The 1904 model had a single-cylinder horizontal engine that put out five horsepower with a top speed of fifteen miles an hour. The runabout retailed for eight hundred and fifty dollars and if you wanted a tonneau seat it would cost you another hundred. I sold my demonstrator the first week to a doctor over in Latchfield. The only problem with that car was the reverse gear, which tended to slip, so that backing up became a problem. But it was a remarkably light automobile and, as I used to tell my customers, "Look at the time and trouble you're saving by driving this machine. It's not that big a job to get out and lift up the back and turn it around. You can't expect progress to come at you in one big leap."

My eldest son, Ernest, was born in July of that year and on Sundays Merle and I would get into our motoring dusters and take the baby for a drive around town. Pickett wouldn't go near the car. He feared for his heart because of the noise and convulsions, for the Huffman also tended to buck a good deal, and in fact it took about a year of steady driving before you could operate it with any degree of smoothness. The following year our twins, Emily and Enna, were born and we had a houseful with Merle and me, Pickett, the old housekeeper Alma, and three kids.

20. *Responsibilities*

Merle's life revolved around the store and the church. In many ways I can now see that Merle was ahead of her time. She was really one of these modern feminist women that you hear so much about these days. Merle wasn't all that fussy about men or children and she seemed to be happiest—no, not happiest, because she was too stern-minded for that—let's say the most contented, when she was working on the store ledgers or chairing a meeting of the Ladies Benevolent Society. And to give her her due, she had a good head for business and a flair for organizing things. She was always a president of this and a vice-president of that. But as for the two of us, a coolness developed with the passing years. The conjugal act was never insisted upon and only occasionally indulged. More and more we went our separate ways and the only time we got together and felt a part of anything was when we ciphered the store accounts each night.

To give you an idea of how we drifted apart, I stopped going to church. One summer morning I sat there fanning myself while the preacher droned on about Leviticus. And I just said to myself, Well, the hell with this noise, and got up and walked out. Now, the reason I did that was that it didn't make any sense. The heat and the words just stifled me. Of course I caught hell from Merle, who came home fuming, "You disgraced me in front of the whole town. How could you?" The kids pulled at her skirts and old Alma clomped around on her bum leg getting dinner while Pickett sat wheezing in a chair and looking at us with his unhappy eyes. But no matter how she stormed I wouldn't go back and after a while she gave up, though she never ceased reminding me that I was a heathen.

So on Sunday mornings after they'd all walked out to church I went through my own little ritual. What I did was take a pint flask of whiskey and get into my Huffman Wheeler and, opening up the throttle, drive out to the country. God Almighty, it felt good to be out there on a summer morning, with the whiskey singing in my blood and the air rushing past my face. Sometimes I'd just let out an awful blast of curse words, and I always felt better afterwards. People began to talk. They always do in small towns when they're confronted with eccentric behavior. But I didn't give a damn. There's always been a streak of queerness on my father's side of the family. Probably my mother's too. Well, I'd get back from one of these little outings just as people were returning home from church and sitting down to their mountainous plates of roast beef and potatoes and turnips and pie. Maybe the car backfired more than I thought it did at the time. And maybe I'd be a little mellow while Merle lit into me. "I don't know how you can carry on like this. You're disgracing yourself before the town. You seem to forget we have a reputation to uphold in this community. The business is bound to suffer," etc., etc.

"The hell with it," I'd say. "They'll buy from us because there's nobody else around. What I do on Sunday mornings is my own damn business."

And so it would go, with little Ernest pointing a finger at me and saying, "Papa is a heathen." Ernest and the twins were Picketts through and through. They even looked like their mother, with the same sharp angularity, and there was a flintiness to their nature. No sense of humor either. And they always sided with their mother in a dispute.

Aside from my Sunday mornings, the only thing that cheered me up was the occasional letter from Findlater. You'll recall that he wanted me to send him a Bible, and I did just that. But it was returned nearly a year later. The package was all tattered and you could see it had been to several destinations, with the words "Addressee Unknown" stamped all over it. From that I concluded he was a free man again, and this was confirmed by the arrival of letters over the next several years. They came from different places. Findlater was into various things and he was always vague about the details. One year he might be importing peanut oil from Brazil but the next time he wrote he was speculating in Pennsylvania pig iron. I seldom wrote to him because he never seemed to stay in one place too long and my letters were always returned unopened.

Now all this time I wondered about my father too, and so I wrote my sister to ask if she'd heard anything. Annie wrote back to say that there were two stories about him, either of which could be true. One was that my father jumped off a mountain in Alberta during a religious fit. The other story had it that he was a hopeless lunatic, though nobody knew where he was being kept. I didn't believe either story. Annie also said that Ned and Fred were back in Craven Falls living in a shack next to Jake Snipes and bootlegging and thieving. I could believe that. The entire tone of Annie's letter suggested that she had more or less written off her family as a general disgrace and she considered me no exception, though I had used the store's letterhead when writing her.

My automobile business suffered a grievous blow when a fellow opened a Ford agency over in Latchfield and one day, probably about 1907, the box-company owner returned from Toronto in a new Packard touring car, which I had to admit was a beauty. One morning I looked in the mirror and saw gray in my hair.

Then Merle got pregnant again following one of those haphazard intimacies that occur from time to time in even the worst marriages. Needless to say, she wasn't very happy about it. That was 1908, and on Halloween night of that year an unfortunate accident took place. Some local hooligans pushed over our privy with poor old Pickett inside and the general shock to his heart killed him. It was a terrible way to end your days on earth and we were all outraged, though we never did find out who was responsible. Aside from that, the incident upset Merle so much that it hastened her confinement and one night a couple of weeks later she woke up with terrible labor pains. I ran for old Dr. Spence and he rushed right over and delivered my youngest son. The poor little beggar only weighed four pounds and was frail as a new leaf. Even the doctor didn't expect him to pull through. When

20. *Responsibilities*

I went in to see Merle she lay there pale and exhausted and I felt sorry for her.

"Is it going to live?" she asked.

"You bet he's going to live, Merle," I said. "That's going to be a fine healthy boy soon. What do you want to call him?"

She just turned her face to the wall and said, "Call him what you want. I don't care."

Which pretty well summed up her attitude towards him. Maybe he seemed too much like a Farthing to please her. Or maybe it was just that he'd been conceived when she'd already taken a strong dislike to me and my ways. I know that after he was born I moved into a bedroom down the hall and we never performed the conjugal act again. Merle could live without it and I got my pleasure now and again from a red-headed farm girl named Nellie Lundrigan who was crazy about automobiles.

I gave my youngest son the name of William Thomas and as he grew I was pleased to see him turning out to be more Farthing than Pickett. He may have been the runt of the litter but he had plenty of pepper and could keep up his end against Ernest and the twins. I remember one day when I came home early. Old Alma was out back in the vegetable garden and all the kids were inside. I heard this pounding on the downstairs closet door and when I opened it, there was little Bill. He was about three at the time. But instead of crying he just glared at Ernest as though to say, You can't frighten me. Ernest was seven at the time, and big for his age, a sullen, mean-looking boy in his Buster Brown pants and fruit-bowl haircut. He stood by the kitchen pump with a disagreeable smirk on his face.

"Where the hell are your brains, boy?" I says to him. "Locking up your brother in a closet like that! He could have suffocated to death."

"I don't care," says Ernest. "I don't care what happens to my smelly little brother. And I don't have to listen to you either. Mother says I don't. She says you aren't a proper father. You take the Lord's name in vain and you keep whiskey in your room. Mother says you're a heathen and someday you'll roast in the devil's ovens."

"Well, maybe I will," says I. "But meantime I don't have to stand here and take that kind of sauce from a whelp like you." And I took down his breeches and laid the palm of my hand flat across his arse until they could hear him howling clean down to the railway station.

So there we were, almost two separate families living under the same roof. In a sense I could feel myself slipping away from things altogether. Mind you, I wasn't doing too bad with the automobile franchise, though the competition was getting keener every year and the Huffman engineers couldn't seem to devise a sensible reverse gear. The store was doing fine too, though Merle was moving out more from behind the counter and taking over in the office. I handled the travelers and the ordering and we hired a couple of young girls to wait on customers. But my heart wasn't in any of it. And even now I can't

175

exactly say why. It's not that my home life was all that bad. It was tolerable, and while I was regarded as something of a queer piece in the town, most people let it go at that. It was just that I never laughed at anything anymore except sometimes little Bill or if I got a letter from Findlater. He'd drop me a note to say he was back in New York staying at Mary Kettle's and was doing a land-office business in meat pies or stomach trusses. He never mentioned a word about Sally. She just seemed to have slipped out of my life, though I often dreamed about her singing on the stage of the Bijou Theater.

From the time he was about four I took little Bill along on my Sunday morning excursions into the country. He liked it better than Sunday school and he sat there with me down by the river enjoying a bottle of soda pop while I sipped whiskey. He was sharp as a tack and he'd say, "Why do you drink that whiskey, Dad?"

"It makes me feel good, Bill," I'd say.

To which he might wrinkle his nose and say, "But this soda pop doesn't cheer me that way. I'd like to feel good too."

"Well, you see, whiskey is not good for little boys. It might make you sick."

"Well, why would it make me sick if it don't make you sick?"

"Say doesn't, not don't. And sometimes it does. Make me sick, that is. If I drink too much of it."

"But you just said it made you feel good."

And I'd say, "Now look there! That old chicken hawk is swooping down over the meadow looking for his breakfast."

It was always a relief to divert him because a four- or five-year-old child can corner you with all the most important questions. I'm speaking of those questions you can't answer with a load of facts. Now little Bill, when he wasn't asking questions, was making up poems. I could see that he was headed for the same camp as people like Esther Easterbrook and his poor Uncle Tom. That is, the camp for people who go through life bumping their heads against questions that have no answers and getting perplexed by things that most people can't even see, let alone care about.

Merle gave me an awful time over these Sunday mornings. "You mark my words," she'd say, pointing her finger at me. "You are ruining that boy's moral character. Encouraging him to fill his head with all that foolish poetry. What he should be learning is his Bible lessons."

"Never mind the Bible lessons for now," I'd say. "The boy takes after his grandfather Farthing. That's to say, he has a poetic soul. Something a God-fearing, cheese-paring Presbyterian like you wouldn't understand."

After a session like that Merle always flounced off to the parlor, where she'd play a hymn with unusual vigor. When Merle was vexed she liked to punish the keyboard and that was always a sign for little Bill and me to slip out the back door.

In the second week of November 1913 it rained hard every day

20. *Responsibilities*

until Sunday, which dawned bright and cool with the first whiff of winter in the air. It looked to me like the last good day for a drive before the freeze-up. It was little Bill's fifth birthday and I packed a lunch and the two of us set out just as Elmhurst was parading to church. In honor of Bill's birthday I squeezed the horn five times on our way out of town, thus outraging a number of my fellow citizens, who were convinced I was already drunk. I wasn't, but I'd had a few nips and was feeling all right. I was in my thirty-fourth year and looked every day of it. My temples were now flecked with gray and I'd put on a little weight around the middle. But all things considered, I was contented enough. If you're the least bit sensible you'll reach a time in your life when you stop day-dreaming about what might have been and accept what is and make the best of it. The old-time Greeks had a word for this but I can't recall it.

That morning the roads were badly rutted from the week's rain. It was real washboard, with potholes you could disappear in. The 1913 Wheeler was a pretty fair car but it was the last production model the Samuel Huffman Company made before declaring bankruptcy, owing to the large number of lawsuits from people with back ailments and ruptures. The car now had a twenty-horsepower, four-cylinder engine which could move you along at thirty miles an hour in third gear. Little Bill and I ate our lunch down by the river, sitting on the running board out of the wind. For his birthday I gave him a big thick scribbler and a half-dozen pencils, and he got busy right away on a poem about a car ride. Then we climbed aboard and started home. I remember teaching him a song that was all the fashion that year, a little piece entitled "The Ribbons She Wore in Her Hair Were Blue." Now maybe it was the whiskey, though to this day I'll swear on a stack of Bibles that I wasn't anywhere near drunk. But the truth is I couldn't have been paying proper attention, for as we crested a grade the right front wheel hit a Christly big pothole. The car lurched badly to the right and I heard a loud crack, which must have been the front axle snapping. Then everything went black as my head hit the big wooden steering wheel.

When I recovered my senses I saw that little Bill was gone. I remember the door on his side was jammed and I spent the longest time humping my shoulder against it before doing the sensible thing and climbing right over it. I ran along the roadside splashing through the brown puddles. Then I saw him. He lay face down in long dead grass. One arm was tucked beneath him at a peculiar angle. When I knelt down I knew right away that the life was gone from him, for a big rock near his head was smeared with blood. Some of you may know what it's like to lose a five-year-old child. One minute he's there, full of vitality and curiosity. And the next minute he's finished forever. And I had this burden too. I had to kneel beside my son knowing the clear and certain truth that his death was my fault. If I'd been more mindful, the child might have grown to manhood. As it was, he lay there already graying with death as his blood cooled. And I was filled with such sorrow and self-hatred that I still come up tight in the throat over sixty years later.

A farm family coming home from church discovered me kneeling beside the boy. Probably they were one of the families we'd hooted at on our way out that morning. But if they were, they didn't let on. I remember somebody grasping my arms and guiding me to the buggy. Then the man put little Bill's body into the back and he took off his overcoat and covered him. I thought it was the most decent thing I'd ever seen done in my life but I couldn't find the words to thank him. In fact, no one said anything all the way to town. Even the two children sat beside their mother with faces as solemn as stone.

Maybe little Bill wasn't Merle's favorite but he was still her son and I'm not likely to forget her face when that farmer carried Bill to the door. I remember Merle saying, "Oh Lord! Is he dead? Take him upstairs." And the farmer carried him through the doorway while Alma and Ernest and the twins looked up from their dinner plates and said nothing. "I knew this would happen," Merle kept saying, twisting her dinner napkin in her hand. "I knew it. I could see it coming." She didn't once meet my eyes but looked across my shoulder. Then she went into the parlor and closed the door. It was the first time I ever heard her weep.

I went up the stairs and the farmer, coming down, stepped aside and let me pass. In my room all I could think about was how to kill myself. Neither Merle nor I had any firearms in the house, because we set no store by them. So I just lay on the bed trying to figure out where I could get a revolver or a shotgun. Downstairs the doorbell chimed all afternoon and I could hear voices and the chink and clunk of cups and saucers. In the early evening Alma knocked at my door and said softly, "I brought you a little supper, Mr. Farthing. A little cold ham. You should eat something. I'll leave the tray here by your door." People were being kind, when what I wanted them to do was walk up to me and spit in my face and call me a worthless four-assed mongrel of a man.

I never went to Bill's funeral. I remember it poured a cold rain which later turned to snow. From my window I could see the buggies moving along the street to the cemetery, with their black canvas tops shining with rain and the horses damp and glistening. Most people thought I was too drunk to attend. In fact, I was doing what I would continue to do over the next several months. That is, just sit in my room and stare at the walls and repeat over and over those two famous words "if only." Probably I went down and ate with the rest of the family but I honestly can't remember any particular meal.

Merle plunged right back into the store and the church and, of course, that's the proper way to do it. Work like hell and keep your mind occupied. But I had no heart for it. I couldn't face the salesmen's stories in the store. As for the automobile business, it was dead during the winter anyway. And then the company folded around Christmas and some joker came up from Toronto and slapped a lien on the damaged Wheeler and a few spare parts in the showroom. I didn't care.

So that painful winter passed away and by March I was back in the store, though working only in the stockroom, for I still couldn't face the townspeople. Once my day's work was finished, I was back in my room. I don't suppose I said fifteen words to anybody all winter. And I kept away from the booze too, though I was just cracking for a drink at times. With my return to the store a new relationship developed between Merle and me. It seemed that I was no longer an equal partner but just an employee. I was never again asked to peruse the accounts, nor, for that matter, was my opinion solicited on anything. None of this bothered me in the slightest, by the way.

One beautiful warm Sunday morning in late April I was sitting up in my room doing not very much when Merle called up the stairs. "There's some people here to visit you," she yelled. "They've come up from Toronto." I couldn't imagine who in hell would be visiting me. Who did I know in Toronto except a few drummers? And they'd never give you the time of day unless they wanted you to buy a bolt of muslin or a hundredweight of kerosene. Then Merle hollered again. "They say they're old friends of yours." So I went to the window and parted the curtains and looked down through the fresh green leaves. In the driveway, gleaming in the sunlight, was a big maroon Pierce Arrow touring car. And standing with one foot on the running board and looking things over with a smile was none other than my old traveling companion Cass Findlater. But even more startling was this! Seated in the back of the Pierce Arrow, twirling a parasol and smiling at the spring morning, was the love of my life, Sally Butters!

21

A NEW LIFE

IT WAS HARD TO BELIEVE after all those years, and I had to rub my eyes
to make sure I wasn't dreaming. But there they were, all right! And the
damnable thing was this. Neither one of them looked much different.
Findlater had put on a little weight, but then he'd always been a good-
sized man and his big, loose-jointed frame carried another dozen
pounds with no trouble at all. His moustache was still full and black,
and I can tell you, there were more gray hairs in my own head. He was
well decked out too, though as usual his suit was a bit loud, with a lot
of checks and swirls of bright thread running through it. But it fit him
as snug as a skin and looked to be hand-tailored. As for Sally, damn
me for a liar if she didn't look ten times better than when I last saw
her, on the upper deck of that little boat as it steamed out of Dawson
harbor. Perhaps that was because then she looked a little wistful and
peaked, thinking of her future years with that tinhorn gambler. But in
the back seat of that Pierce automobile she looked, well, *radiant* isn't
too strong a word. She was dressed in this peach-colored gown with
white gloves. All that lovely red hair was piled under a broad-brimmed
hat with flowers on it. And she was laughing at Findlater, who was
performing some tomfoolery with his straw hat, rolling it down his
sleeve like a hoop and catching it with his other hand.

At the time it passed through my head that it would be fitting if I
just expired from heart failure at the sight of Sally. Something like the
old hermit who glimpses perfect beauty before he croaks. And I looked
a bit like a hermit too, leaning against the window ledge in my undershirt and old duck pants, unshaved and smelling of my own salts.

I could see now that Findlater's antics with the hat were meant
to amuse my son Ernest, who stood by the side door solemn as an old
owl. Then I heard Findlater say to the boy, "Do you like that auto-

mobile, pal? That cost four thousand dollars F.O.B. Cleveland, Ohio. What do you make of that?" Ernest said nothing but just went on picking his nose. That boy often irritated me. He never seemed to have any spunk or curiosity about life. Findlater reached into his vest pocket and withdrew a silver dollar. "There you are, chum," he says, handing the coin to Ernest. "That'll start you on your way to becomin' a businessman. Mighty oaks from little acorns grow. You've heard that, ain't you, kid? Say, where's that scamp of a father of yours?"

Merle must have been watching all this, for I heard the door open and her voice say, "Ernest! Come along now. It's time for church. And give the man back his money. You know you're not supposed to accept money from strangers." I felt sorry for the kid. Dull as he was, a buck is a buck and no nine-year-old boy likes to part with a gift like that. But he was always obedient to his mother and he handed the dollar back to Findlater, who just shrugged.

"Didn't mean any harm, Ma'am. There's plenty more where that came from, you know."

"I'm sure there is," says Merle. "Come along now, Ernest."

Meantime I'd climbed into my good pants and scraped some whiskers off my face in the hope of looking halfways presentable. Merle called up again, "We're going to church now. Are you coming down to talk to these people?"

I noticed the way she said "these people." It was like her. It was also like her not to invite them into the parlor. Although she belonged to the best Elmhurst society, that woman was as ignorant as one of those peasants from the Dark Ages. She just didn't know about some things. You see, to her Sally and Findlater had the smell of the big city about them. And wasn't it in the big city that you'd find all the worldliness and sin?

So I yelled down, "Invite those friends of mine into the parlor and be goddam quick about it or there'll be hellery raised under this roof."

A man can only take so much and then he's got to protest. That was my first rebellious cry in months. Merle didn't reply but a few minutes later I heard Sally and Findlater admiring the parlor furniture.

I can tell you, my legs trembled as I descended those stairs in my blue serge suit, which just hung on me owing to the fact that I'd lost about fifteen pounds over the winter. I was so tongue-tied at first that I just stood gawking by the parlor entrance. Findlater was sitting on the piano bench finger-playing "Old Black Joe." When he glanced my way he immediately jumped to his feet. "Why, excuse me, sir," he says. "You must be Bill's father. He's told me a lot about you and your poems."

And I said, "Hello, Findlater. It's me. Bill."

Findlater craned his neck forward and, squinting his eyes, studied me for several seconds. "Well, for cryin' out crawfish, it is you, Bill. Lookit here, Sal. Here's our boy." And he was across the room in a couple of steps and hugging the breath out of me. "Well, Bill, old pal of mine. How in hell are you?" He pushed me back and fixed a critical eye on me. "My stars, you don't look so hot, son. But listen, we heard about your tragedy and you got our sympathies. Ain't that right, Sal? Look at this boy now!"

Sally got up and walked towards me smiling. "Dear Bill," she says in that low musical voice. "It's so nice to see you again." She touched my coat sleeve with her hand and it was like an electric shock going up my arm.

"Let's all sit down and take a load off our pins," says Findlater, flopping into the love seat. "Well, it's a treat to see you, Bill, though you look a bit tuckered. Say, you wouldn't have a few glasses handy, would you? I got a little bourbon here. It'll take the dust out of the pipes."

He took out a silver flask, and I got some glasses. It was my first drink in months, and I won't say it wasn't welcome.

"I guess you're not half surprised to see us, eh Bill?" says Findlater. "And you're probably wonderin' how Sal and me got together. The fact is we met last month in a hotel lobby in New York where Sal was workin' a show. Then she told me that the show was comin' up to play Toronto. So I took a gander at the map and I saw that this little place was only a couple of hours' drive from Toronto, so I says to Sal, How be I go up with you and we'll pay a visit to our old pal Bill Farthing? It's been somethin' I been meanin' to do for years, Bill, but I've never managed it. Been too busy. Been all over the world, you know. South America, Arabia, the valley of the Nile, where our good Lord himself was brought up. But lookit here, have some more of this corn liquor. It's supposed to be twenty-five years old." He drained his glass. "Nice little home and family you got here, Bill. And you've lived here all these years? Well, isn't that a son of a gun? I'd never have figured you for the slippers and pipe. Wild horses couldn't drag me to the hearth."

All this time Sally and I were glancing at one another and then looking away. My heart was pounding so hard I was afraid she could hear it, and her face was burning with a high color that only made her prettier.

Findlater looked down at his big yellow shoes and said, "But holy doodle, there's been a lot of water pass under the old bridge since we shared bunks in the Yukon, pal. By God, those were the days! And those two brothers of yours! Now there was a pair of rascals, if you don't mind me sayin' so. And do you mind, those damned onions and that fire! I thought sure I'd make my fortune with those onions. And the whole shootin' match went up in smoke when you picked a fight with that redskin! Oh, you missed a party there, Sal. Our boy here was a hot-headed young devil in his day."

I ignored Findlater's recollections and said to Sally, "How long will you be in Toronto?" My voice seemed unnaturally high for a grown man.

"The show finished last night, Bill," Sally replied shyly.

21. A New Life

"And where do you go from here?" I had visions of taking a night train to St. Louis or Edmonton.

Sally just looked away and then Findlater said, "Sally's off to England in a couple of days, Bill. She's gonna be married over there."

"Married?" I said.

"That's right," says Findlater. "She met this nice English feller down in Philadelphia. She was in a show down there. What was that called, Sal?"

"'A Maid in Maytime,' Cass," says Sally in a voice so low you had to strain to hear.

"That was it. 'A Maid in Maytime,'" says Findlater. "A helluva nice show too. I saw it three or four times myself. There's a scene where Sally comes out all dressed up like a little schoolgirl with a pinafore and her hair all done up in sausage rolls. And she sits on this long swing and it's pushed by the fellow she's in love with. And all the time she's singin' him this song. Prettiest damn thing you've ever seen. Anyways, this English fellow. Did I mention that he's a duke or an earl or something? He turns up for every performance and is so struck by Sally that he asks her to marry him. You can't blame the girl for acceptin' that kind of an offer. The fellow is rollin' in money and has five or six castles. That show-business life looks glamorous but after you've tramped the boards for as long as Sally here, you're entitled to marry and settle down. Maybe raise a little family." Sally blushed and looked down at her lap. "So we're off to England so Sally can get acquainted with the duke's family and they can have a nice June weddin'."

"Did you say *we*, Findlater?" I asked.

"Correct," he says. "England is one place I've never been, so I'm takin' a holiday. Been workin' too hard lately. I'm into crushed stone these days. Road building, eh! The automobile is changin' everythin', as I predicted it would. I can foresee the day when we'll have roads clean across this continent. And I hope to supply the crushed stone for all of them. But I need a little breather, so I'm gonna slip over there and see how the king and those counts run that country. It never made any sense to me."

"I'd like another drink, Findlater," I says.

"You bet, pal. Help yourself. Then what say to a little lunch? I saw a hotel on the way into town that looked passable. I'm treatin', and I won't take no for an answer."

We had lunch at the local hotel and I wish you could have seen the heads turning when Sally walked into that dining room. The waiters and busboys were bumping into one another and spilling soup, for they couldn't keep their eyes off her. Findlater slipped the head-waiter a twenty-dollar bill and we were served wine even though it was Sunday and against the law in those days. We sat there for three hours, just drinking wine and talking about the old days, and it was the first decent time I'd had since before Bill's death. And I'll tell you something that really made me happy. Maybe Sally was planning to marry this duke but all the time we sat there we held hands under the table, and I began to entertain the wildest dreams of a new life with Sally by my side.

We were the only ones left in the dining room when Findlater pulled out a gold watch the size of a small saucer and said, "Sal, I think we'd better be goin'. It's kind of a shame, Bill, that you couldn't come along with us. We could have a wonderful time. Just like the old days. But don't worry. I'll take care of Sal here and see that she gets delivered up to that duke in first-class condition."

"Oh, Cass! Don't say it like that," said Sally, with tears in her eyes.

Out on the street I helped her into the Pierce Arrow and as she settled herself she leaned forward and kissed my cheek. "Dearest Bill," she says. "If only we could have got together. I don't know what I saw in Johnny. He was such a skunk. The marriage wasn't normal. We never was intimate, if you know what I mean. And now you're married! Life's so unfair, ain't it?"

"Yes, it is," I says, blowing my nose. "Goddam this dust anyway. We need a rain to dampen these streets."

Findlater had walked around the car inspecting the tires by kicking them. Now he put on a pair of driving goggles and a peaked cap and climbed in. You could hardly hear the motor running on those big Arrows. "Well, Bill," says Findlater. "Keep your pants on straight. And Abyssinia. That's a joke for I'll be seein' ya! Get it? Mind you, let go of Sal's hand there now, because unless I'm mistaken, we're movin'." I hadn't even noticed that I was running alongside the car.

"Goodbye, dearest Bill. Take care of yourself," Sally cried.

"You too, Sally," I says, letting go of her hand. "I'll see you again. I swear it."

She waved a white gloved hand at me and the big car disappeared in the dust. I was left standing there with a half-dozen town kids who'd been admiring the Arrow. I walked home not knowing whether to be happy or sad. And I suppose I was both. I was happy because Sally liked me a lot. I could see that. And I was sad because life was suddenly so damn complicated.

Of course I never heard the last of that afternoon. Over the next week Merle kept after me, and though I wouldn't have guessed it before, I believe she was jealous of Sally. All I heard was, "So that's the sort of company you used to keep. Vulgar people! That woman is nothing more than a common strumpet. I've never seen anyone so brazenly dressed."

Now that visit from Findlater and Sally accomplished one good thing. It took me out of my meek stage and reminded me of the kind of man I once was. So I started to fight back, and when she'd begin one of these tirades on Sally I'd say, "Shut your hole. She's twice the woman you'll ever be. The fact is, you're not a woman at all. You're a cross between a cash register and a Presbyterian hymnal." We went at it pretty thick and heavy for a while, though to give Merle her due, she never resorted to tears like some women. She always stood her ground and the only thing she'd do when I'd start insulting her was walk out of the room in a huff.

The fact is, I was ringing inside with excitement. I was so excited I could hardly eat, and the reason for this was a letter from Sally which she sent on the day she sailed for England. Here it is so you can judge for yourself the state of mind I was in.

S.S. *Granatania*
Montreal, May 1, 1914

Dearest Bill:

It was sure nice to see you again. How I wish things was different. I mean you being married and everything because I will tell you the truth. If you wasn't married to that woman I would dearly give you my all because I have ever loved you dearest Bill. If you don't mind me saying so I don't believe your wife understands you. I have done some things in my life that I'm not proud of but I'm not and never have been a home-wrecker. So altho it will always be you who will have my heart, I must say adiue to my dearest Bill.

Your loving friend
Sally

P.S. Cass sens his regards. He is certainly sweet in looking after me and has booked me a nice state room with running water and flush toilet tho I am nervous about crossing the ocean thinking of those poor peolple who drowned a couple of years ago on the Titanic. I hope you will pray for my safety.

Sally loved me! She said so. And if she loved me, what difference could anything make? It was as though I'd been dead, with all my feelings lying dormant for years. Now I was reborn, filled up with passion and juices. And what did I decide to do? Why, I decided to follow her, that's what. I figured that if I could get over to England before Sally married that duke everything might work out fine. Find-later had said something about a June wedding, and so all I could do was keep my fingers crossed and hope that I got there on time. I was sorry I hadn't asked for the name of the duke, but then I couldn't see how there would be all that many dukes marrying American show girls. Once I got over there I'd declare my everlasting love to Sally and we could start to make something of our lives. Maybe we could come back to Canada and go out west, maybe even conduct a search for my father. The papers were full of stories about the thousands of immigrants settling out there. I wasn't about to go busting any sod, but what I thought I might do is open a store. Findlater would probably finance me, for he didn't appear to be short of cash.

Now, I knew that Merle would never divorce me. In those days divorce wasn't respectable like it is today. Most people then would live side by side for fifty years miserable as hell, rather than admit defeat to the neighborhood. Besides which, it was complicated and expensive. In the long run it took an act of Parliament to get free. So as I saw it, the only thing Sally and me could do was go and live somewhere in sin, as they used to say.

Now I'll tell you something that isn't exactly inspiring about most human beings, though I believe it to be the truth, And it's this: There is no more exhilarating feeling in the world than shucking off responsibilities and clearing out of a restricting atmosphere. It's just like whiskey on an empty stomach. Now, I'm not necessarily condoning this kind of behavior but merely describing the feelings that accompany it. What happens is that you get this delicious feeling of being alive. You're in on something that nobody else is, so you turn crafty and secretive. And you tend to look on other people following their ordinary pursuits with a feeling of superiority. All right, Merle, I'll move that barrel of flour just like you say. You bet. But don't think I'm going to spend the rest of my days doing your bidding. That's what happens. Meantime, I got hold of timetables and schedules and studied them in my room. Oh, the sweet happiness I derived from reading those columns of departure times and outbound vessel dates with arrivals in Liverpool and Southampton. They were every bit as much poetry to my soul as maybe the Songs of Solomon are to you.

My plan was simple. One night when Merle was out to a meeting I waited until Alma put the children to bed and was settled down by the kitchen stove with her knitting. Then I went upstairs and packed a small grip and took a last look at my three children. I liked them well enough, though I had the uncomfortable notion that I wouldn't admire them as adults, because I could see them turning into the kind of tight-lipped, life-hating, stony-hearted Protestant storekeepers who end up running things in this country. So I just stood at their bedroom doors and wished them luck. They weren't the kind of kids that went in for kissing. Then I went down the stairs, and taking a key from a desk in the hallway, walked over to the store. In the office I knelt down and opened the safe and helped myself to four hundred dollars. I figured I'd put eleven years of my life into that store and marriage and hadn't drawn anything beyond spending money. At this rate my salary worked out to thirty-six dollars and change a year. That's just about what a Chinese coolie got for helping to build the Canadian Pacific Railroad. As I closed the safe door I thought about the night I left the Fletchers' house. I was fleeing from a woman then too. And stealing her money! But then it isn't so unusual to repeat yourself in life. Most people make the same mistakes over and over again.

Nearly a dozen years before, I'd walked in the front door of that store as a dapper and somewhat brash young salesman, cracking jokes with old Pickett and winking at his shy, gangly daughter. Now I was

21.   A New Life

sneaking out the back door like a thief! At the train station I bought a ticket for the Toronto train and ignored the ticket agent's nosy questions. A couple of hours later I was checked into the Walker House Hotel, standing with a foot on the bar rail and looking up at a picture of two stags drinking in a river. That was the night I listened to that old coot tell me about the Battle of Ridgeway and how my father got wounded in the foot. If you've got any memory at all, you'll remember I told you about that near the start of this book.

22

ENGLAND

I LEFT MONTREAL a couple of days later, traveling steerage on an English vessel which had seen many a better day. That would have been about the first week of June. I've never been a man of the sea, and that trip was an ordeal which I believe surpassed the discomforts I endured aboard the *Southern Franchise* in '98. People told me later that the ocean was as calm as a mud pond all the way across. Perhaps it was. All I know is that when we landed at Liverpool I had to walk around the wharfs for half an hour leaning against buildings. After I got my land legs back I took the next train for London and felt more comfortable with those iron wheels under me, even though I was squeezed into a compartment with six other people. I remember looking out the window at the tiny villages with their stone walls and now and again a big mansion set back behind some trees where maybe a duke or a baron lived. And I couldn't help wondering whether at that very minute Sally wasn't sitting down to tea and muffins with the duke's folks. Or maybe Findlater was sitting in somebody's drawing room telling a marquis about the wonders of the automobile and crushed-stone roads. It made me realize that I had no definite plan for finding either of them. Back in Elmhurst, Ontario, it hadn't seemed like such a big job. But as the train neared London it came to me that it mightn't be as easy as I'd thought.

However, I wasn't about to get discouraged, and this wasn't the first time I'd stepped into a strange city not knowing a soul. London looked dismal enough in the dusk. Under a drizzle the cobblestone streets shone like oil and the sides of buildings were gray as ghosts. But I had a regular routine for these situations. I'd used it many times during my period of moral decay before my marriage. The main thing when you set foot in a strange city is to get yourself cheap, clean lodgings. There's nothing more depressing than tramping the streets with a valise in your hand and no bed for the night. Now, what I'd do was this. Once I got off the train, I'd walk as far away from the station as comfort allowed. Far enough anyway so that you're no longer in the company of traveling strangers but are surrounded by local people. Then I'd look for a tavern which catered to a fairly respectable class. Once in the tavern I'd order a small beer and strike up a conversation with someone who wasn't just a barfly but a regular patron having his evening drink. After a while you get to know who's who in a bar just by watching how fast they drink and whether they slouch or stand and so on.

Once I got my man I'd tell him my predicament, which in a nutshell was this. I was in the city looking for my mother, who I hadn't seen in twenty years. I'd run away as a boy but now I'd managed to make a little home for us and I wanted my aged mother by my side so she could enjoy her remaining years in peace and contentment. Meantime, I needed a cheap, clean room while I conducted my search. It never failed to work.

So on that rainy June night in 1914 I stopped in at a place called the Pied Bull, a nice little public house tucked down a side street, several blocks from Euston Station. As soon as I ordered my beer I could tell that the fellow to my right was sizing me up out of the corner of his eye. He was a tall, stoop-shouldered young man with a long, serious face the color of sealing putty. His teeth were stained brown and he wore these round, wire-rimmed glasses. Even though it was a mild summer evening this character had a big gray scarf wrapped around his throat and a flat cap on his head. His nose was mostly in a mug of black porter and he was the kind of drinker I'd normally ignore, for he had a surly and suspicious face and appeared to be the type who liked to argue about politics or religion. Except for this fellow the place was empty and I was thinking of trying the bartender with my story when my neighbor to the right says, "Then you'd be an American?"

"No," I says. "A Canadian."

"Ah, yes," he says, draining his porter mug. "That would be the place our friend Voltaire mentioned. What was it? Acres and acres of snow."

He sounded like the Irishmen I used to serve in Frank Sullivan's saloon in New York. As for this Voltaire, I'd never heard of him, but he didn't know much about geography, for there are parts of America that have heavier snowfalls than Canada. I passed this information along to the Irishman.

"Is that a fact now?" he says. "Well, the dear knows, I'd never have guessed that." In the manner of bar conversation nothing more was said until our glasses were refilled. Then he sighed aloud and said, "Ah, America! It's me dream to go there someday. I've bags of cousins in New York City." I told him he'd feel at home there because it was full of his fellow countrymen, and I mentioned that I once worked for Frank Sullivan. This seemed to improve his opinion of me and after a minute he invited me to sit at a table. Once seated, he leaned over and whispered that he didn't think much of London or Englishmen. "An uncouth race, my friend," he whispered. "Behind all the polish of their steam engines and brass fittings, you'll find a nation of barbarians. Why, look what they done to the poor boors down in Africa!"

"Well, if you don't like it here, why not leave?" I asked.

"I've got a pretty good position in a counting house," he says. "I've worked there for ten years now. Not that I wouldn't throw it up tomorrow, mind you. Oh, I get by, you know. I do all right. The reason I'm not leaving for America is otherwise." And he left it hanging there for a few seconds, as an Irishman is apt to do with his story. Finally he says, "The reason I can't go to America is simple. But you must promise not to laugh or by the hokies you'll have me to answer to. There's lots worse with their dukes than Martin Rooney when the going gets rough. What did you say your name was?" I told him my name and he stuck out his hand. "Right then, Farthing, now listen. The reason I can't go out to America is because I'm in love."

Well, now that surprised me. I'd never have taken him for a man who was troubled by romantic love. And as I was in love myself, he interested me. It isn't every day you meet a total stranger in another country who is in exactly the same predicament. I didn't know Rooney more than ten minutes before I was dying to tell him about Sally and me. But you can't beat an Irishman at the game of conversation. So I had to listen while he went on about a girl named Alice Fry.

"Sure she's a grand girl, Farthing. The cream of the cream. She's English, mind you, but she can't help that. She's a lovely girl. I've known her for ten years. I'll never forget the first day I laid eyes on her. She was just a bit of a thing then. Wearing a dark green pinafore, with her hair done up in the curls and all. And by the way, Farthing, don't get any filthy ideas into your head." He cleared his throat with a drink of porter and lit one of my cigarettes. "Over the last ten years I've watched that girl grow into a young woman. She's a sight now, I can tell you." He sighed again. "Well, one of these days perhaps! It's not unusual for an Irishman to marry late, you know. It's no disgrace to be a bachelor in your middle years. My mother's brother Uncle Liam, he married at fifty-eight and raised a family of nine. Oh, we Irishmen bide our time, you can depend on that! So do you see now why I can't go out to America? Alice is only sixteen. She's too young to leave home."

"Does she love you?" I asked.

"Of course she loves me. Are you making a joke of this, Farthing? That's a dangerous game, and I'm giving you fair warning." Then he frowned before saying, "I'm going to tell you something else too. And just one word of ridicule or raillery and off comes this suit coat. Are you ready, man?"

22. *England*

"What in hell are you talking about, Rooney?" I asked.

"Maybe you just think I'm nothing more than a counting house clerk at twenty shillings a week, but I'll tell you this for a start. I also happen to be a poet." This made me smile, and right away Rooney plucked off his glasses. "That's the one," he says. "That's the straw that broke his back. I'll not sit here and be laughed at. If you think for a minute that us poets are a lot of soft wood sitting around in velveteen coats like our late friend Mr. Wilde, you're very seriously mistaken. So you can prepare to defend yourself as of this moment." He groped for his porter mug and, not being able to locate it, returned the glasses to his head.

"Just a minute, Rooney," I says. "I was only smiling because I was thinking of my poor father. He was a poet and it never did him any good. He had a bad time of it and some say he's ending his days in a madhouse."

Rooney leaned forward with an elbow on the table. "Oh, you mean we suffer? Oh Jesus, you can say that again. Suffering's our game all right, and no mistake. Oh by Christ, I'll tell the world! What did the great P. B. Shelley say about our lot? An Englishman, but an excellent maker of pomes. 'Our sufferings and our griefs/ Are there for all the world to see!' God in Heaven, but that man could crack out a line too. Oh, don't talk to me about suffering, boyo! We poets know the letters of that word. Just look at this now!" From an old purse he carefully unfolded a page of yellowed newsprint with a poem on it. He sat back with his arms crossed. "Go on, man. Read it. For your soul's sake."

I looked at it and it seemed no better or worse than the usual tripe you read in daily newspapers. "I wrote that pome on me first night in London ten years ago," says Rooney. "Right off the Holyhead train and I was eating chips and bangers in the grill bar of Euston Station. Pushed me plate away and composed it on the spot. There's sufferin' and loneliness in there, by God, and plenty of it. And I've got a trunkful of such pomes in my room. I've never been fortunate enough to see another one in print, but the day will come. All my other pomes are addressed to Alice. Don't you see? The girl's me muse. She inspires me to flights of rapturous versifying."

I wasn't interested in his damn poetry or this Alice Fry. I was interested in lodgings for the night and it seemed to me Rooney was about the last man in London to count on for advice. So I was thinking of clearing out of there when Rooney says, "I'll bet you just stepped off the train at Euston, Farthing. I think I detect the smell of soot on your coat sleeves. Well, you're in luck, man, because if it's a doss you're looking for, I know just the place. There's an empty room at my landlady's."

"Your landlady's?"

"Yes, man. Mrs. Fry's. Alice's mother. Seven bob a week, a fortnight in advance, and you'll have the room next to mine. Robertson moved out last week. His bank transferred him down to Brighton.

And good riddance to bad rubbish is what I say. That man was always hanging around the parlor in the evening. I can't remember him going out more than half a dozen times in the two years he lived in that house. I won't say he wasn't bad-looking, if you like those big square-jawed blond fellows with their teeth all in place. And then because he could play the pianoforte, he thought he was the stuff with Alice. You don't by any chance play that instrument, do you?"

"No," I replied.

"There they'd be," says Rooney, getting up and tapping his flat cap into place, "Robertson playing and Alice singing. He monopolized her. None of the rest of us could get a word in. I'll tell you this. I wasn't sorry to see him go. So let's move along now before Mrs. Fry lets that room. And mind your grip there or somebody will pinch it. You must never trust the natives, for the English are fundamentally a deceitful race."

I followed Rooney out of the Pied Bull and along a number of dimly lighted narrow streets. Now and then we stepped aside for a hansom cab which came clopping by over the stone. In doorways several dark figures huddled with their cigarettes glowing. Once a female voice called out to us, "Like a bit of crumpet, luv?" Rooney walked ahead of me, his shoulders hunched forward and his scarf streaming down his back.

Mrs. Fry's house was one of a row of houses, each with a little stone stoop and wrought-iron gate. To tell you the truth, it was better than I expected. Before we went in Rooney stopped me with his arm. "Now, Farthing," he says, "from the looks of you, I'd say you weren't born yesterday. So you'll be understanding that it's an imperfect world we live in and there's a toad in every garden." He looked up at the house. "Now in this particular garden, the toad happens to be Alice's brother Charley. Six feet high and fifteen stone. Filthy temper and favors Bass ale, of which he drinks a great amount on Saturday evenings. Not a friendly man to drink with either, and my advice is to avoid him. He works as a butcher's helper down at Skelpington's. All day long sawing away at the carcasses of animals. Cutting through the bone and flesh. Destroys the poetry in a man and builds up the arm strength. Charley Fry's not what you'd call a sensitive man, Farthing. Ergo he and I don't see things the same way. So now you can appreciate that my love for Alice has been perforce carried on in a clandestine manner. Do you follow me?"

"Yes, I think so," I says.

"Fine then. Let's get along. We're already late for tea." In the hallway Rooney flicked off his cap and unwrapped his scarf, sniffing the air with a sour look. "Bloody sprouts again. The woman's mad for them." He patted down his sparse brown hair and rubbed his glasses with a piece of rag.

From a room off to the right comes this high-pitched voice. "Is that you, Marty?"

"It is that, Mrs. F.," says Rooney.

"You're late again, Marty," says the voice.

"So I am, Mrs. F. So I am," Rooney says. "And the usual abject apologies are tendered. But listen, I've brought a guest who's interested in the spare room."

Just then a big woman came towards us, wiping her hands on her apron. "Marty, Marty, what's been keepin' you? The sprouts is all cold."

"Now, Mrs. F.," says Rooney, "I'd like you to meet Mr. Farthing here. He's from Canada."

"From Canada!" says Mrs. Fry, looking me over carefully. "Well, well, well. And what brings you to London, Mr. Farthing?" A fat white hand had fluttered up the side of her face like a pigeon. It was now patting her hair into place.

So I told her I was looking for my mother. All this time Mrs. Fry studied me with the usual suspicious landlady's eye. However, I could bear the scrutiny, for I was still living off the capital of respectability and my clothes and manners were in good shape. After I'd finished this cock-and-bull story about my imaginary mother there were tears in Mrs. Fry's eyes and Rooney had taken off his spectacles again and was rubbing them, for they'd fogged over.

"Well, the dear knows, I wasn't aware of that," he muttered.

To which Mrs. Fry says, "Well, God bless you, Mr. Farthing, and you're certainly welcome in this house. Come along now and have a nice cup of tea."

Before we entered the dining room Rooney put his arm around my shoulder. "By Jesus, Farthing," he says, "I'll tell you honest and true. That search for your mother is a grand thing. Listen, it's inspired me. I've already got a pome forming in me head. Half done, it is. Came to me in a bloody great flash while I was standing there listening to you. I'll finish it after tea and let you have a gander."

So we went into the dining room, where Mrs. Fry was standing by the sideboard. Her son Charley was finishing his supper at one end of the table, forking the last Brussels sprout into a mouth the size of a groundhog hole. He was a bruiser, all right, a thick-limbed, bullet-headed member of the species, who only grunted when his mother introduced me. I think the fact that I entered in company with Rooney had something to do with his lukewarm reception, for all the time we were in the room he just glared at the Irishman.

Also seated at the table was the object of Rooney's affections, Alice Fry. She was a plump, pink-cheeked sixteen-year-old in calico, pretty enough but no Venus de Milo, and in fact, at a certain angle, her jawline looked as tough as a stevedore's. She was an early-blooming, overripe peach that was ready to fall from the tree if she wasn't plucked. I could see her within half a dozen years weighing two hundred pounds and making some poor devil and three or four kids miserable. What Rooney saw in her I couldn't imagine, but then how do you ever know about these things? I know that all during that supper she batted her eyes at me in what I can only describe as a flirtatious manner while her brother asked me if I knew a Canadian named Tommy Burns. He'd been heavyweight boxing champion of the world before he was flattened by Jess Willard. Charley followed prize fighting, as I wasn't all that eager to learn. I had to confess that I didn't know Mr. Burns, but then Canada was a fair-sized country and, as I courteously pointed out to him, there were more than half a dozen people in it.

After the meal I was only too glad to be shown to my room, which was small but clean, with a good hard narrow bed, a dresser, a chair, and a small window which opened on a kind of courtyard behind the house. It had been a fatiguing day and I was nearly asleep before my head hit the pillow. But then there came this soft tapping at the door and Rooney's voice through the keyhole. "Are you decent, Farthing? Can I see you for a minute?"

"All right," I said, without much enthusiasm.

So in he came and stood by my bed with his arms crossed. Then he says, "Well, what do you think, man?"

"About what?" I asks.

"Why, about Alice, of course. Isn't she the darling girl?"

"She's very nice," I said.

To which Rooney struck his brow with the flat of his hand and began to pace back and forth. "Very nice?" he says. "Very nice? Good Lord, man, does a person describe the Mona Lisa painting in Paris, France, as very nice? Does he look over the Munster Mountains and say, 'Oh, that's very nice!' Did you not say that your father was a poet, Farthing? And did none of his grand feelings for life rub off on you at all? Very nice indeed." He turned towards me and pointed a finger. "'Very nice' is the words of a matter-of-fact man, Farthing. A man who doesn't know a couplet from a cutlet and couldn't be bothered asking." He walked towards the door and put his hand on the knob. "It pains me to say so, Farthing, but I believe I've misjudged you. So I'll be sayin' goodnight now."

I'd a good mind to let this lanky, thin-skinned jabberbox go to his bed in that frame of mind but then I thought, Well, I did owe him something for bringing me to this place. So I said, "All right! Look, Rooney! You didn't let me finish. Alice is not just very nice. She's a lovely girl. I can see why you like her."

"I can't hear you over here," he says.

"I said she's a lovely girl."

He walked back towards me and sat on the bed. "Didn't I tell you that all along? You bet your knee she's a lovely girl, and don't you forget it." He stopped and thoughtfully picked his nose. "I knew you had an eye for beauty, Farthing. But like so many people in these times, you're ashamed to admit it. Think you'll be taken for a fancy pants. Well, I can tell you that not all of us poets are that way inclined. But that's what people think when they hear a man expounding on the wonders of natural beauty. Of course I'm referring in particular to the native tribes of this island we're sitting on. Their bloody heads are always crammed full with numbers and calculating. How many times is two times the compound interest on a five-pound note calculated fortnightly? They always want to know what the bloody Bank of England is thinking. Well, I say who gives a merry catch-all for what the Bank of England is thinking? Do you see me drift, man? There's no bloody poetry in their souls!"

He finished with his nose and did a neat job of slipping the findings under my bed, though people are never quick enough for me with those maneuvers. "Anyway," says Rooney, "it's nice to know that there'll be somebody in this house who'll be around to converse with me on matters of intellectual and poetical import. Speaking of which, you'll be interested in this." He took a piece of paper from his coat pocket. "You'll remember me saying just before tea that this search for your poor mother lit the fires of inspiration in me soul. Well, just listen to this. It's a lovely bloody thing, if I do say so. And I'm not ashamed to say there's a few marks on the page which are my own eye water, for the composing of it put me in mind of me own poor mother back in County Tipp. Now listen to this—

> *Your hair of silver crowns your head*
> *I remember every blessed thread.*

Now, by Jesus, there is a couplet! And listen to this!"

Rooney began to pace back and forth again while he read his stuff. I can't remember any more of it, though I can tell you this much. The only worse lines I've ever heard were recited by a man named Jake Snipes on the night his mother died. After Rooney finished he said to me, "There now, Farthing. And that's a fitting welcome to you in this strange land. Speaking of which, and tomorrow being Sunday, I'll take you around this city and show you some of the sights. Westminster Abbey, where they crown their bloody kings, the houses of Parliament, where they pass the laws to keep the rest of us poor. And the Tower, where they've lopped off the heads of so many decent skins down through the ages of time. I've heard it said they still have people locked up in there with chains and shackles on their arms and ankles. Sultans from Turkey and black niggers from Africa, mostly chiefs of tribes who wouldn't sit down when me nabs came through to take over the country. Why didn't they shoot them, you might ask. Oh, that would be too simple for the English. So they bring them back here to London and let them rot a bit in the Tower. I'll show you the place tomorrow. It'll turn the stew in your stomach."

He finally left and I got to sleep and it seemed I was only out a few minutes when I woke up to another knocking on my door. But it was morning, sure enough, for the sunlight was pouring through the little window into the room and the air was filled with the sound of church bells. After another knock I heard a voice say, "It's Alice Fry, Mr. Farthing. Mum thought you might like a nice cup of tea in your room this morning."

"Well," I says, hesitating, for I've always liked to wake up by myself and slowly. That was one good thing about Merle. She was the same way and we never got in one another's hair in the mornings.

Anyway, before I could say another word the door opened and in came Alice Fry, wearing a brown muslin dress and with her hair all tied up in ribbons. "Mum and I are just off to church," she says, "so we thought you might like a cup of tea, being as you're not familiar with the Sunday routine around here. If you don't go to church, like that Irish atheist in the room next to you, you have to fend for yourself on Sunday mornings. There's bread and jam and tea on the sideboard in the dining room. But being as it's your first day, we thought you might like a cup of tea in your own room. I'm awfully sorry I found you in your nightshirt." I could tell she wasn't sorry at all. Then she said, "Mum's told me why you've come to England and I think it's the most beautiful thing I've ever heard. So does Charles."

"Thanks for the tea," I says, wondering when the hell this brainless child would leave.

Then she says, "It's none of my business of course, Mr. Farthing, but you'd be well advised not to get too chummy with Martin Rooney. He's a man who doesn't pay his debts, Mr. Farthing. He borrowed a pound from Charles when he first moved in and he still hasn't paid it back. That's nearly ten years ago. And he's always borrowing from Mum. I don't know why she puts up with him, but she does. She says she feels sorry for him. Charles would have thrown him out of the house years ago but Mum won't hear of it. I just thought I'd warn you."

"Fine," I says. "I'm warned."

Poor old Rooney! When it came to love, it seemed he was as blind as the back of his neck. However, he was all eyes when he showed me around London. Such as when we stood outside Buckingham Palace in a downpour, with the water soaking the cigarette he'd just bummed from me. "Look at that place, Farthing, and remember. It was purchased with the blood of subject peoples. They say the floors of the royal bedchambers are paved with pure gold. Can you fathom it, man? And all these poor wretches walking about the streets!"

Well, I didn't know about the royal bedchambers, but he was certainly right about the streets. London was filled with poor people in those days. It wasn't unusual to see an eight-year-old child in knee pants and bare feet standing outside a public house selling newspapers or matches. And old men and women shuffling along the streets with great bundles on their backs looking for a place to sleep. And whores! God Almighty, I'd not seen so many whores since my days in Skagway! I hadn't figured the English for being so horny, and maybe they weren't, but the whores were there in plentiful numbers. They often stood in alleyways or very likely you might see them sipping a mug of tea in a subway station grill; young, skinny, sorrowful-looking girls and older women too, all clapped up no doubt, though I personally never tried them. Of course, there were fancy areas too. In Park Lane and Piccadilly, which overlooked some beautiful parks where according to Rooney the kings and their friends used to perform acts of debasement with their horses on Sunday mornings.

Now, to give you some idea of what life was like at the Frys', I could describe Sunday dinner, which was eaten around the noon hour after church. Sometimes we were served toad-in-the-hole, which is an arrangement of sausage and pastry, but mostly it was the old Ontario village fare of roast beef, potatoes, and a vegetable, usually sprouts, with gooseberry trifle for dessert. At one end of the table would be Mrs. Fry, all done up in her Sunday finery and nattering on about the minister's sermon while directing Charley on how to carve the roast he'd lugged home from Skelpington's the day before. I noticed that Mrs. Fry was partial to Rooney, for she'd always say, "Now, Charles, give a nice piece of the outside to Mr. Rooney. He doesn't eat half enough to keep a bird alive." All this time Rooney would sit there with his chin in his fist blinking at Alice, who, I have to admit, couldn't keep her eyes off me, though don't get any idea that I was encouraging her. Charley, meantime, was busy with the meat, carving away with a furrowed brow, his tongue between his lips and his great bulk tight as your fist in his Sunday tweeds.

After dinner Rooney and I went to the parlor, where Mrs. Fry played the piano and Alice sang in a pleasant, high-pitched voice. The music was lively and entertaining, with Mrs. Fry favoring old standards like "Millie Met Me by the Bridge" and "The Road to Bliss." Sometimes she'd play an Irish ballad for Rooney, prefacing it by saying, "Now here's something special for you, Marty." Charley never attended these sing-alongs, preferring to visit his favorite pub, The Three Balls, though how he could drink beer after eating three pounds of beef and a dozen potatoes was always a mystery to me.

After giving it some thought, I decided that the best way to look for Sally or Findlater was to check out the various hotels, beginning with the most expensive and working my way down. I could only hope that I wouldn't be too late. So that's how I spent my first week in London, tramping the streets and visiting these hotels. I had plenty of rebuffs and humiliations too. Some of the hired help in those fancy places were more snooty than the aristocrats themselves. I remember one long-nosed room clerk in a wing collar and swallow-tailed coat saying to me, "As a rule we do not cater to Americans," and handing some old dame her mail before even finishing his sentence. That was pure ignorance, I thought.

I began to get discouraged after a week or so, for there wasn't a sign of them. I remember one morning sitting in my room pondering the foolishness of a man who leaves his family and a good business to cross the ocean with some far-fetched plan for personal happiness. As if personal happiness ever had anything to do with real life! So I sat there thinking about all this and, I suppose, feeling sorry for myself. Rooney had just left for work, knocking on my door to inform me that he was "off to the horrors of the mercantile world." He said that through the keyhole every morning, and that is one thing that will drive me crazy in short order. I mean somebody coming out with the same line day in and day out at exactly the same hour. Rooney was in perky spirits, for he claimed to be rattling off ten poems a night, all addressed to his mother. He said they'd rival the Alice poems and together they'd make a volume for publication, the idea being to show how two different kinds of love for females reside in the male breast. That's how he put it. He was so grateful to me for inspiring him that he wasn't going to bother me for a loan, even though he needed the money for paper.

Charley had left for the meat market hours before and I sat there and watched Mrs. Fry waddling down the street behind the house with her basket on her arm, off to the butcher's, the baker's, and the candlestick maker's, where she liked to "chew the fat" with other landladies. Downstairs Alice was singing while she went about her various chores, for she helped her mother with the running of the house. After a bit I heard her coming up the stairs. Then she rapped on my door and walked in with fresh bedding. I sat on the chair and didn't pay her much heed, for my mind was otherwise occupied. After Alice had finished making the bed she walked around it, and just then doesn't she pretend to trip over my foot and fall right into my lap. The boldest thing you've ever seen! "Oh, excuse me, Mr. Farthing," she says. "It was my fault. And now you've saved me from a nasty fall. And my, but you're stronger than you look!" She wasn't in any hurry to get up either, and I'll confess to being mildly tempted to rash behavior. You must remember that I'd absented myself from sexual activity for some time. As a matter of fact, I couldn't exactly recall my last piece of tail. And here was this big ripe girl sitting on my lap!

However, I began to think of the consequences. It's the consequences that always spoil the fun of anything. And the particular consequences arising from a tumble with Alice Fry could be a pregnancy. It was enough to freeze the blood in my veins. With Alice pregnant Charley would carve me up like the Sunday roast. Then damn me for a liar if Alice didn't tell me I was the handsomest man she'd ever seen and after I found my Mum, why didn't we both go out to Canada together. She promised to be a good wife. By the way, I'd never told any of these people I was married, and maybe that was a mistake. But imagine! A sixteen-year-old girl proposing to you! And practically begging you to have a little hors d'oeuvre before the feast. But, being wary of trouble and not wishing to complicate my life any more than it was, I unwound her arms from my neck and said I was old enough to be her father.

Now that was exactly the wrong thing to say, because it pleased her, you see, to be spurned in this manner. If I'd come right out and said, "I'm not interested in you, Alice," that would have been the end of it. She'd have gone off in a huff and not spoken to me for a couple of days. And that would have saved me a lot of trouble, as you'll find out in a few minutes. But just mentioning age as I did gives a girl a chance to do some foolish thinking. And what goes through their heads is this. "Well, if it's only age that's keeping us apart, why, we're coming closer together all the time." Do you see what I mean? It gives them a chance to put the whole relationship on a familiar footing and then what happens is you're condescended to by a teenager.

To give you an example. No sooner had I mentioned the great difference in our ages than Alice gave me this look of mock coyness and, trying to be stern with me, says, "You haven't another sweetie, have you, Bill?" No more Mr. Farthing! Now it was Bill! Well, I said I didn't but wondered what her mother would think if she came home and found her daughter sitting on my lap. At which Alice jumped up. "You might be surprised, old man," she says, pinching my cheek. Already the girl had it in her head that the only thing keeping us apart was age. At the door she said, "I'm going to serve you cold soup for dinner, Bill Farthing. That's a punishment for treating me like a child." Then, putting her hand across her mouth, she giggled and left me sitting there with this worry crowding my head. The last thing a grown man needs when he's looking for the woman he loves is a moonstruck young girl pining after him.

So I resolved to be as careful as I possibly could be with Alice Fry. This was not as easy as you might think, for Alice decided to make a nuisance of herself. I tried to discourage her in the friendliest way, but this she only took for shyness. And there's nothing that will make a naturally forward girl more eager than a hint of bashfulness in a man. So she'd catch me in an upstairs hallway and pin my arms against the wall, for she was a strong girl. And she'd say, "In another few days I'll be seventeen, Bill Farthing. Do you still think I'm a child?"

"Now, Alice," I'd say, "you're a very nice girl, but I'm late. And isn't that Charley's footsteps I hear on the stairs below?"

Even Mrs. Fry noticed things and said to me one evening, "Alice isn't half taken with you, Mr. Farthing. I'm so glad you're a serious man and not the type to take advantage of a flighty young girl's nature. She does take on with some of the young gentlemen we have, though it's all quite innocent, you understand."

I wasn't so sure about that, and anyway a mother is always a poor judge of her own daughter's emotions. For example, a mother never thinks her daughter is capable of anything approaching lust. Now how could Rooney miss seeing all this, you might well ask. It's a reasonable question, though the answer isn't simple. The only one I can think of is that you see what you want to see. In this respect Rooney was a lot like old Fletcher, inasmuch as he could never detect the flaws in his loved one.

Now aside from all this monkey business with Alice Fry, I wasn't getting any nearer to Sally or Findlater. One thing was certain. They weren't registered in any of the big-name hotels. I thought of placing an advertisement in the newspapers but I wasn't sure that Findlater ever bothered to read them. Or Sally either, for that matter. Well, I needed help. And the only person in the city of London who might be helpful was Martin Rooney. He knew his way around the city and he read all the newspapers and so was in on the social gossip, forever bellyaching about the wasted lives that the royalty lived. I figured that maybe there was some shortcut he could suggest. Maybe there was some list of dukes and barons and earls telling you which ones were bachelors and where they hung their hats most of the time. So one Saturday night towards the end of June I invited Rooney down to the Pied Bull. After drinking a couple of pints of stout in complete silence he said to me, "Say, I've got a grand title, Farthing. 'Me Heart's in the Hearth.' What do you think of that?"

"It sounds good."

"Do you really think so?"

"Yes."

"So do I. If you could see your way clear to loaning me a quid, Farthing, I'd refill your glass."

"Never mind," I says. "I'm buying."

So after another drink I plunged right in and told him the whole story of how I'd left my wife and family and thrown up everything to come to England to find Sally. Now what I figured was this. As he was a poet, even a half-assed one, he might be sympathetic to the idea of a man sacrificing for beauty. After all, he was harping on beauty most of the time. But as I told my story the expression on his face changed from interest to disapproval and then to glumness.

After I'd finished he said, "Well, as far as stories go, that's the daddy of them all, Farthing. Good God, man, have you no sense of responsibility at all? Leaving your poor wife and kiddies to fend for themselves. It's the most disgraceful thing I've ever heard." He took a long swallow of porter and stared at me. "And all that business about your mother and you lookin' for her. That's just a load of cod wallop then?"

"Yes," I says. "I never knew my mother. She died giving birth to me." At this Rooney took off his glasses and rubbed them with his piece of rag. There were tears in his eyes. "Well, there's no need to carry on like that," says I. "You don't really miss a mother you've never known."

"Oh, who cares about your bloody old mother," he says, blowing his nose. "Don't you see what you've done, man? You've taken the heart out of me pomes."

"What are you talking about, Rooney?"

"Me pomes, me pomes," he shouts, banging his fist on the table. "I suppose it's expectin' too much for you to understand that when a pome comes from a false source, then the pome is false too. Holy Jesus, the whole bloody lot of them will have to go. You've caused me anguish, Farthing. Me pomes go in the Thames tomorrow. And you're coming along too. You'll see how a man can work his fingers to the bone for nothing. Yes! You can stand there and watch me scatter me words on the bloody English water. Jesus, Joseph, and Mary."

He went into a sulk and I fetched another pint of stout for him. "Cheer up, Rooney," I says. "It can't be that bad."

"It can't, eh?" he says. "A lot you know about the workings of the poetic temperament, Farthing!"

"Well anyway, will you help me out?"

"With what, man? With what?"

"Why, to find my girl."

"Find your girl?" he says, his voice just a squeak. "A common chorus girl. And this is your idea of a problem beside a man's life work? Jesus, where's your sense of perspective, Farthing? Now lend me a quid, for I want to buy Alice a present for her birthday. Thank Christ me pomes to her aren't falsely inspired."

The next day, true to his word, Rooney wrapped his latest poems in butcher's paper and we set off for the Thames before noon. I went along to humor him, for I still hoped he would help me find Sally. So we were headed for the Victoria Embankment and about the noon hour we found ourselves on the Strand. It was a warm, sunny day and I thought a drink might not only slake our thirst but cheer up Rooney before his great water ceremony. His long horse face was more than normally gloomy. So I told him it was my treat and we were about to enter this public house when I looked up the street towards Charing Cross Station. And damn me for a liar if coming through the crowd of late-morning churchgoers, standing out like a big canary in a yellow checkered suit, was Findlater himself!

23

TROUBLE

He was coming straight towards us, marching along briskly with his elbows out, tipping his hat to the ladies as he stepped around them. Well, you can imagine how happy I was to see him and when he drew about ten feet abreast of us I said, "Findlater! You're a sight for sore eyes!"

He looked up and stopped in his tracks. Then a broad grin crossed his face. "Well, good God, Bill. Is that really you?"

"It is," says I.

He shook his head as though he couldn't believe his eyes and then walked up to us. "Give me your hand, Bill," he says. "It's mighty good to see a friend, especially one from the New World. But what the Sam Hill are you doing over here anyways?"

"Where's Sally?" I asked. "I've come for Sally. We love each other. She wrote to me. She told me."

Findlater took my arm and fixed me with a grim look. "Sally was married a week ago, Bill. Up in Scotland somewheres. They were up at this fellow's estate shooting wild turkeys. Did I tell you her husband's an earl or a baron or something? I met him over lunch a couple of weeks ago. I can never get these fellows straight. About the only thing I can figure is that none of them does an honest day's work."

"Amen to that," says Rooney, who'd been standing there all this time hugging his parcel of poems.

"Who asked you, bub?" says Findlater. "You mind your beeswax." So I introduced Rooney, and Findlater stepped back and said, "Well, I'm sorry, friend, but I took you for a bum standing there cadging drinks. No offense. Any friend of Bill's is a friend of mine." Then he turned to me. "God, I'm sorry, Bill, but you have to understand how Sal looks at it. There you was back in Canada. All married and settled down. You should have told her you was plannin' to come over here. What happened to your wife, by the way? She looked strong as a bull to me."

"I just left her," I said.

Findlater shook his big head at me. "And that nice little business too, eh! Well, that's a shame, Bill. But you got to look at it from Sally's angle too. There's no security in show business. All that dancing wears down your heels over the years. This old coot she's married is a good egg. He must be pushin' seventy-five, so he won't make too many demands on her, if you get my meaning. He looks fit as a fiddle, though. He's takin' her cruisin' on the Mediterranean for the honeymoon. Well, come on in and have some lunch. God, it's good to see you!"

To say that the bottom fell out of my world at that moment would be just about right. I followed Findlater and Rooney into the public house and sat down. It was all just a swirl of noise and smoke. I recall Findlater making a fuss at the bar because they didn't carry bourbon whiskey. He finally came back to our table with some Scotch and beer and a plate of sausage rolls. "God, I can't figure these Englishmen out to save my soul," he says.

"You could spend a lifetime in vain doing that," says Rooney, dipping his beak into a pint.

"I mean, damn it all," says Findlater, "I'll give you an example. I'm stayin' at this private club, see. It's a high-class joint, with bankers and stockbrokers and the like of that. I was having lunch with some of these people the other day and I was explaining the properties and workin's of the pneumatic tire. How it was gonna change road buildin' and a whole bunch of other things over the next ten years. And you'll never believe this, but you know what? They weren't interested." Findlater shook his head in amazement. "One old fellow says to me that the automobile is a passin' fad, like the velocipede. Everybody laughed at that except this German fellow. A man named Phlug. He's got a brother in Hackensack, New Jersey. This Phlug was all right, though he liked to blow his own whistle too. He says the English have shot their bolt. Claims the Germans are way ahead of everybody in rubber and steel. I just told him to stop right there. Nobody, I says to him, is ahead of the good old U. S. of A. in rubber and steel. This German fellow kept calling me Herr Findlater. Why do these people call you Herr, anyway? What's wrong with good, old-fashioned Mister? But say, listen! I wanted to ask you a question, Bill, because you were generally up on these things in the old days. Or maybe your Irish friend here knows. What's this word *cad* supposed to mean?"

Rooney was only too happy to explain the word, while I sat there thinking of Sally being chased naked around a bed by an old degenerate somewhere off the coast of Italy.

As for Findlater and Rooney, they took to one another right away, with Rooney asking all sorts of questions about the United States, which was right up Findlater's alley. Finally Findlater asked Rooney what line he was in.

"I'm in the world of finance, Mr. Findlater," says Rooney, "but as our mutual friend Farthing will attest, my true vocation is literature. In a word, I'm a poet."

"Is that right?" says Findlater. "Well, poetry is somethin' I never had much time for, though I admire a good pome. Not everybody can write one."

"And some of us," says Rooney, looking at me, "are falsely inspired and therefore work our fingers to the bone for naught." He turned to Findlater. "Do you see this bundle, Mr. Findlater? Within the hour it goes into the Thames."

"You mean the river?" says Findlater. "What in hell for?"

"It's a long story," says Rooney, "but let us just say that I was deceived by someone I thought was my friend." He pulled a sheet from the bundle and looked at it. "Unless you know the anguish and suffering that goes into these efforts, Mr. Findlater, you couldn't possibly appreciate how it hurts me to have to throw away these pomes."

Findlater was now looking at the piece of paper and after a moment he picked it up and began to read, his lips moving slowly. Then an amazing thing happened. A single tear slipped down one cheek. He wiped it away, but it was followed by another. When he finished reading, Findlater wiped his nose on his sleeve and said to Rooney, "You throw that beautiful pome in the Thames River and I'll personally break your nose."

Behind the spectacles Rooney's eyes registered shock and alarm. "Did you say beautiful, Mr. Findlater? You liked it then?"

"Liked it?" said Findlater. "It's the most beautiful thing I've ever read in my life. I don't understand big words and I've never been much for fancy learnin' but I know what I like and I like this. And so will millions of Americans. Why, I can see it now!" He suddenly grasped Rooney's hand. "Do you know what you need? It's Morton, isn't it?"

"Martin," says Rooney, his eyes now blazing with excitement.

"What you need, Martin," says Findlater, "is somebody to promote your pomes." He turned to me. "Have you read this man's work, Bill? Listen here now.

Few things in life are so precious and fine
As the thought of you dear old Mother of mine.

I mean damn it, that's beauty pure and simple."

"May I shake your hand, Mr. Findlater?" says Rooney.

"I may be a rough stone, Martin. Bill here can tell you that. But I can tell you one thing."

"I'm sure you can," says Rooney.

"That pome I just recited has a beautiful thought in it. And do you know something else?"

23. *Trouble*

"I do," says Rooney. "But go on, man."

"Do you know where that pome should be?"

Rooney thought for a moment, taking off his glasses to blow on them. "Yes," he says. "I can see the place for it. Between the covers of a book. Jesus. A gilt-edge calfskin with satin markers, headbands, onion paper, the whole bloody business."

"No, no, Martin," says Findlater, scraping his chair closer. "You've got it wrong. That's not the market for this item." He paused while we all took due notice. "The market for that beautiful sentiment is the kitchen wall of every home in America. These pomes of yours should be treasured by every American who's ever known their dear old mum's kisses. Do you see my point, Martin? Why reserve all that beauty for a few snobs who go to fancy colleges like Harvard and Yale?"

"I do indeed see your point," says Rooney, "and I applaud it."

Findlater began to expand on his idea. He could see nice wooden plaques, highly polished, not too expensive.

"How about divan cushions?" says Rooney. "A nice bit of velvet with brocade stitching. Strong colors. Say purple and gold. For the emphasis."

"I'm writing that down, Martin," says Findlater. "I'm making a note of it."

And he was too, scribbling it down on a piece of paper. Well, they went on like that for a while, while I sat there wondering what in hell I was going to do with my life. With Sally married there was nothing left for me to do but go back to Canada or the States and make a new life for myself. Maybe I could go along with Findlater.

At closing time we stood outside the public house and none of us was feeling any the worse for wear. Findlater looked around and breathed deeply. "Boys, I can tell you this much. I can hardly wait to get back to the fresh air of my own country. Everything's so damn old here. Even the buildings have a bad smell."

"It's English history you're smelling," says Rooney. "The smell of unjust wars and bloodshed and the lives of innocent people. It's graven on the stones of this wicked city."

"Well, I wouldn't know about that, Martin. History's not my subject. What's past is past. It's the future I'm interested in. That's the problem over here. Nobody's interested in tomorrow. Everybody talks about yesterday. It don't make sense to me." He shook our hands again and said, "I've got a few days left, Bill. Why don't you come around to this place I'm staying at tomorrow? We'll have a few drinks. It's kind of snooty and the food's terrible. Always feeding you these little cabbages. About the size of a golf ball. What do you call them?"

"Brussels sprouts," says Rooney, making a sour face.

"That's it," Findlater says. "But we'll have a chance to jaw about the old days."

"What time?" I asks.

"Let's say in the early afternoon, about two. I'll tell you something, boys. I got a little card game going over there this afternoon and these things usually go on until the small hours. These Englishmen think they can play poker, but they're babes in the woods." He had Rooney's poems under his arm. "And don't you worry about these here pomes, Martin. They're in good hands and I've got great plans for them. I'll be in touch with you soon as I can line up some business interests."

"I've got another collection, Mr. Findlater," says Rooney. "Grand things they are. Addressed to a girl named Alice."

"Great," says Findlater.

He was on his way before I remembered to ask where he was staying. He stopped. "It's a place called the Knob's Club, Bill. On Wellington Street. Just around the corner from that market where they sell those little cabbages and flowers and things." And he was gone, elbowing his way through the crowd.

For the rest of the day Rooney never shut up about his meeting with Mr. Findlater and the imminent publication of his pomes in America. At supper that evening Mrs. Fry clasped her hands to her bosom and cried, "Oh, Marty. I'm so pleased for you. And I'm sure if this Mr. Findlater is a friend of Mr. Farthing's, then he's a proper gentleman. But I do hope you won't forget us when you become famous."

" 'Tis a hard thing to say, Mrs. F.," says Rooney. "But I'll tell you this much. There are matters in this life of ours as important as fame."

He was looking straight at Alice, who spoke up with a pinch of sharpness in her voice. "I'm sure Mr. Farthing could write verses too, if he set his mind to it."

To which Mrs. Fry replies, "Mr. Farthing's far too busy looking for his Mum, Ally. I'm sure even Marty would say that's more important. And how, by the way, is your search coming along, Mr. Farthing?"

"Very well, Mrs. Fry," I says. "I expect important developments within the next few days."

"Isn't that marvelous?" she says.

Rooney snickered. And Alice pipes up, "And I suppose with all this, my birthday will be forgotten."

"Now, now, dear," says Mrs. Fry. "Nobody's saying that."

"Your mother's right, my dear girl," says Rooney. "Don't you believe a word of it."

At which Alice rises from the table and throws down her napkin on the plate. "I'm not your dear girl," she says. "And I'll thank you to stop calling me that." And off she goes in a huff.

Mrs. Fry looked pained. "Now whatever has got into that child, I wonder?"

"The dear knows," says Rooney.

"Pass the sprouts, Mum," says Charley, looking up from his paper.

The next morning Rooney showed me his birthday present for Alice. It was one of those vanity sets with a hand mirror, brushes and combs and the like, all inlaid with colored stones. He told me it set him back a couple of pounds, which was about ten dollars in those days, a considerable sum. I'd always figured Rooney for a tight-wad, but love will loosen the pockets of any man, I suppose.

After lunch I set off for this Knob's Club. I figured I'd ask Findlater if I could accompany him back to America. This place was a narrow stone building just off the Strand near the Covent Garden Market. You went up these stone steps and through a great heavy door with brass knobs and into a dark vestibule. Inside were heavy carpets and big chairs, in which sat several old men reading newspapers. It was just like an old-fashioned hotel. Somehow I couldn't picture Findlater in these surroundings. But I went up to this desk behind which a little hunch-backed fellow was fussing over some papers. He looked up at me with the nervous smile of a man who's been frightened half to death all his life. "Yes? May I help you?" he asks.

"I'm supposed to meet a guest here named Findlater," I says. "The name's Farthing. William J."

At this he went pale around the gills and coughed into this little claw of a fist. "Ah . . . Mr. Findlater," he says. "Oh dear."

Just then this tall fellow in a dark suit comes up to us. "What seems to be the trouble, Harris?" he says. He gave me an icy smile.

"This gentleman," says Harris, "asked for Mr. Findlater."

"Oh, did he indeed?" says Dark Suit. "And what, may I ask, would you like? If this is some sort of confidence game, then let me assure you that we will not stand for it. We've not involved the police thus far, but we shall not hesitate to do so."

I didn't like his tone one bit. "What are you talking about?" I says.

"As if you didn't know," he says. "I gather you're an associate of Mr. Findlater's?"

"I'm his friend," I says. "He told me to meet him here. Now what in hell is going on?"

"Don't you dare use that tone of voice to me! You Americans are all alike. The word is pushy."

"I'm not an American, I'm a Canadian. And I don't know what in hell you're talking about."

"I'm talking about the fact that Mr. Findlater was asked to leave last night before we involved the police, something we at the Knob's Club are always reluctant to do."

"Is that a fact?" I says. "And maybe you'll stop this nattering and tell me why Mr. Findlater was asked to leave last night?"

"As if you didn't know," he says. "The plain truth is that Mr. Find-later was caught cheating at cards. We simply can't tolerate such behavior."

"Didn't he leave a message for me? Farthing's the name."

Dark Suit rolled his eyes towards the ceiling. "He left no messages. Now, may I see you to the door?"

"No, you may not," I says. "I can see the door myself." And I walked out.

I was feeling so miserable and homesick that I stopped at a wine merchant's and bought a bottle of Canadian whiskey. The only thing left was to catch the next boat home.

Back at Mrs. Fry's I locked the door to my room and settled down to feel sorry for myself. A bottle of whiskey is a good friend at such times. He abandons you in short order but while he's around he's good company. Downstairs it was all fuss and bother as Mrs. Fry got things ready for Alice's birthday party. As for Alice, she was at my door several times that afternoon. At first she was coy. "Well, Mr. Bill Farthing. Are you coming to my party tonight?" I might have grunted something but I let it be known that I wasn't in a partying humor. Then after a few more tries Alice's tone changed to that familiar one of sulky ill humor. At the last she said, "Well, if you're going to sit in there all day, you can certainly do so. Just see if I care." And off she went.

In the late afternoon Rooney came home. I heard him next door singing "The Sweet Isle of Erin" while he polished his boots. By and by he was at my door. "What's this I hear about you locking yourself in your room, man? It's Alice's birthday. Come out of there now and enjoy yourself. We're going to have a time. Listen, I've a pint of malt here. I'm treating now. Come on."

"Go away, Rooney," I says. "I'm not in the humor."

"Not in the humor? Well, the dear knows, that's a queer thing to say on a day like this. Listen, I've composed an ode for the occasion. It's called 'To Alice: On Her Seventeenth.' There's some grand things in it. Let me in and I'll treat you to a preview. I'm thinkin' I'll recite it tonight."

"Another time, Rooney," I says, holding up the bottle to note that it was half gone.

"Well, let me give you a little bit anyway. Here now, listen." And damn me for a liar if the man doesn't start reciting his stuff through the keyhole. I got up and walked across the room and stuffed the end of my handkerchief through the hole. "Here, man. What are you up to?" says Rooney.

"I'm trying to shut out the sound of your jabbering, Rooney. That's what I'm doing." I straightened up and was amazed to discover that I was none too steady on my feet. I yelled through the door, "You're a fraud, Rooney. A thick-headed, jabber-mouthed bag of hot air. Now go away and leave me alone."

"Well, the dear knows!" says Rooney. "That's a grand way to treat somebody who's befriended you in a strange and hostile country. I'm forgiving you, Farthing, because you introduced me to Mr. Findlater. But I'm not forgetting your unkind cuts. And your sulking up here is ruining Alice's day too. The girl is close to tears." And off he went muttering.

I remember walking to my window and looking down to the street. A chimney sweep walked by. He was just a kid of thirteen or so, with his long, stiff-bristled broom over his shoulder. I think maybe I dozed a little, for the next thing I heard was Mrs. Fry saying through the door, "I expect you got your reasons for disappointment, Mr. Farthing, but you never mind now. You'll find her yet. A brighter day will dawn tomorrow. Now, why don't you come down and have some cake and beer? Charley's brought home a nice bit of Bass and we're all havin' such a good time."

"Maybe in a little while, Mrs. Fry," I says.

"That's the attitude, and now look here. A hackman just delivered this for you, I hope it's good news. I'll slip it under the door." And she slipped this envelope under the door. It simply said "Bill Farthing" and I recognized Findlater's scrawl. Inside was a piece of toilet paper. It's pretty frail but I still have it, and here's what it said:

Dear Bill:

Say I'm sorry I missed you at that place where I was stayin. Had to get away in a rush becuze of business. Fact is I'm off tonight with this German fellow I was tellin you about. His name's Herr Phlug. He's a bit of a square head but a good fellow just the same. I'm ritin this in the crapper at a train station and Phflug's waitin for me so I gotta go. I'm givin this cabman a couple of pounds to get it over to you and if he don't deliver it, I want you to put the cops on him. His name is Joe Black. I reckon I'll be back in the good old US of A in another week or so. You can always get in touch with me at Mary Kettle's. You remember Mary. She's still goin' strong. Just like me. Ha ha. She has this bar on Fourteenth Street called Mary's. I hope you enjoy your stay in England and let me know when you're coming to Canada cause then we can get together again. Now don't worry about Sal. She's a spirited gal and she'll kill that old fellah inside of a year I predict. Then you'll have yourself a rich wife for I do believe the girl loves you truly Bill. That is, if you can get rid of the wife you already have.

> *Yor frend,*
> *Cass Findlater*

P.S. Tell Rooney that I'm takin real good care of his pomes. And first thing I do when I get home is git them on the open market. I sometimes take one or two out at night and read them. They are inspirin.

Meantime, the party downstairs was going strong. Somebody had wound up the Victrola and they must have been dancing, because there was shuffling of feet and the tinkling of glasses and a lot of laughing. Now, I will try to tell you the truth here as best I can. But the truth is, I'd been pulling on that bottle for a good part of the afternoon and without a bite of food since breakfast, so I wasn't absolutely stable. Thus, not every detail is crystal clear in my mind. I do remember looking at my watch and reading ten o'clock on the face. And thinking to myself, Well, goddamit, I might as well go downstairs and have a drink with the rest of them and let tomorrow take care of itself. Sometimes that's all you can do. For some reason I put on my hat, though why I did this I couldn't tell you. I remember I was about to go down the stairs when, looking over the bannister, I spotted Rooney and Alice. It looked like he'd spirited her away from the main body of the party. Probably trying to steal a kiss, though it seemed to me he was treading dangerous planks, with Charley only footsteps away.

Anyway, there they were and it was plain that things weren't going well, because Alice was crying and shaking her head. Rooney was raising his voice and then I saw Mrs. Fry and Charley and one or two of Charley's friends come into view. I could just see the tops of their heads, mind you, from where I stood. Now Alice was nearly hysterical and I caught some of her words. She was crying, "It isn't true! It isn't true! You're a bloody liar, Martin Rooney, and I hate you."

And then Rooney's voice piped up, "I'm tellin' you it's true, Alice dear. He's a married man. With a wife and little ones."

And then Mrs. Fry's voice. "What's this, Marty? What's this about a married man?"

"Our nabs upstairs, Mrs. F. Our Canadian friend. He's not looking for his mother. His mother is dead. He's been chasing a chorus girl. And he's been having a little set-to with Alice. She says he's taken advantage of her and she loves him. Me heart's broke."

"What's this? What's this? Taken advantage of Ally?" That was Charley, loaded with Bass and smelling blood.

Then I heard footsteps thundering up the stairs. There was nothing to do but escape to my room and run the bolt.

The long and the short of it was that they were soon at my door. Rooney was there first. "Oh, you're a bloody bags you are, Farthing! Why, you've had your way with her, haven't you! Open that door now and put up the dukes."

Then Alice says, "Tell them, Bill. Tell them you aren't married."

"I've told them all, Farthing," yells Rooney. "The bloody cat's out of the bag. Some friend you turned out to be. Taking advantage of me Alice. Open that door now and take your medicine."

Then Charley says, "Out of my way, you little fart. I'll knock it down."

Then Mrs. Fry says, "Don't do that, Charles. I have a key. Perhaps Mr. Farthing can explain. He seemed such a nice man."

"Explain, my arse," says Charley. "He's been having his way with Ally, the dirty blighter. Listen, lads, he may go out the window. You nip around to the courtyard behind."

"Right," says one of Charley's friends.

Then Mrs. Fry screamed, "She's fainted," and I heard a thud. That would be Alice hitting the floorboards.

23. *Trouble*

Now I'll tell you something I remember clearly. As desperate as my situation was, I took the time to pour myself a glass of whiskey, drinking it off at one gulp. It burned right through to the soles of my feet. Then I went to the window and looked down a ten-foot drop to a tool and storage shed which jutted out from the back of the house. Well, I jumped and mercifully didn't break anything. I climbed down to the courtyard just in time to see Charley's friend coming around the house. Although I was then nearly thirty-four I was still able to outrun that fellow, though the exertion damn near killed me. When I finally stopped for breath I was way up near Regent's Park, sitting on the curb under a lamppost. I remember sitting there and then feeling myself keel over. It must have been all that whiskey and running with no food inside me. The next thing I heard was this female voice saying, "Is the poor man dead?" There was a carriage stopped nearby and a pair of highly polished shoes by my nose. I smelled cigar smoke and cologne and then this gent in evening dress was at my side and lifting me to a sitting position.

"I say. Are you all right, old boy?" he asks in this cultivated voice.

"I think so," I says. "A little weak in the knees."

"We nearly ran over you there," he says. I looked up into this pale, handsome face and we studied one another's countenance for a few seconds. Then this fellow says, "Hullo. I know you! Good Lord. It's not you, Bill, is it? What the devil are you doing in London?"

"It's a long story, Percy," I said. And then I think I passed out again.

24

HALLOW'S END

WHEN I CAME TO, it was morning and I was lying on a big soft bed looking straight up at this cream-colored ceiling. At the exact center of it was this huge carved circle with little naked babies blowing trumpets and holding horns and goblets. All of it very intricately done, at least to my untrained eye. And I will tell you that even though my head throbbed, that ceiling proved restful to the nerves, and I lay there trying to put together the events of the previous evening. There was my flight from the Frys' and the carriage in Regent's Park. And then Percy Finchwhistle, my old companion from the woodpile in Dawson City. When I'd left him in San Francisco in '99 I wouldn't have given him six months of life, owing to the deteriorating condition of his consumptive body. And now I was in these rich surroundings, probably belonging to him. The room was full of antique chairs and a dresser with some filigreed work around the mirror. I lay there for a while looking at the sunlight on this ceiling and then the door opened and Percy came into the room. He was dressed in a maroon velvet smoking jacket and dark pants and he was holding a tray with cups and saucers on it.

"Hullo, hullo," he says. "And welcome back to the land of the living!"

"Thank you, Percy," I says. "Where am I?"

He set the tray down on a little table and poured me a cup of coffee. "In my rooms. Here, drink this, old thing. I must say, you tied one on last night. Sleeping in the gutter like that. And you smelled like a grog shop! But listen, I'm dying to know what's happened to you over the past few years. And how in heaven's name you find yourself in dear old England."

"Well, Percy," I began, and he suddenly jumped to his feet and snapped his fingers.

24. Hallow's End

"No, wait a minute, Bill. I've got it. Of course. Why didn't I think of it before? You must still be a bit fuddled. But I've got an idea. Why not come with me to Hallow's End? I haven't seen Mumsy in weeks and I did promise her. It's a beautiful day. We can motor out and you can tell me everything that's happened in your madly exciting life. What say?"

"Well," I began.

"Excellent. Actually Hallow's End is just what I need. I have had such a busy time of it. It began with this damn wedding a week or so ago. An old friend of the family's. He's actually my godfather. Lord Birdlip. The scourge of the House of Lords, with a list of paternity suits as long as your arm. And what does the old goat do? This will amuse you, Bill. He went out to America last autumn on a lark and met this show girl. Pretty enough, I suppose, but common as a garden sparrow. We saw dozens like her up in the saloons of Dawson. Anyway Birdy, we all call him Birdy. Birdy took a fancy to this little redhead. He followed her all over America and in the end didn't he propose marriage. Had her brought over here and they're wed up in Scotland last week at one of Birdy's places. Birdy's a widower and, need I tell you, his family is livid. Wouldn't attend the wedding and kicked up the most awful stink. Birdy went ahead, though. He's most amusingly eccentric. A few years ago he went to Switzerland and had this operation. First of its kind anywhere. It's only a rumor, but some say he had monkey glands put in you know where. He's a wonderful old chap, Bill. You'd love him. But imagine! Cruising somewhere now in the Mediterranean with this little trollop. At his age! But look here! You're pale. You need more coffee. Then after breakfast we'll pop in the Rolls and go over to Hallow's End. It'll be such fun. And I want to hear all about your adventures."

Well, if you have any imagination at all, you can figure out the state of my feelings when I heard this terrible story, for surely it couldn't be anybody but my Sally that married this old degenerate. I was still feeling glum when we set out for this Hallow's End, which was located some seventy miles to the west, near the famous city of Oxford. Percy drove like a madman, scattering chickens and pigs along the country roads, squeezing the *ooggaa-ooggaa* horn as we raced through villages, leaving behind a bunch of gaping locals, for automobiles were still rare sights in rural parts, especially when they were driven in such a crazy fashion. And I was more than a little nervous, it being my first automobile ride since Billy's death.

But it was nice to get out into the countryside, with its green fields and grazing sheep and cattle and the pretty little towns. Percy was full of questions and I concocted a story about how I'd come to England just for the hell of it. Like that bullshit you sometimes hear from a fellow who's just been asked why he lost both his feet climbing some mountain in a blizzard. And he says because it was *there*. This satisfied Percy, you see, because he had this idea that I was an adventuring type. And he had this rich man's grudging admiration for the fellow who appears to follow his nose around the world with nothing more than the pants on his backside. He also had the notion, peculiar to Englishmen, that anybody from the New World must be a rough-and-ready type who'd probably spent some time battling red Indians, as he called them. If he'd only known that a few weeks before, I was in a common general store, laying out boxes of prunes for constipated housewives!

Percy also told me about what happened to him since Findlater and me had left him in that hospital in San Francisco. He said he'd gone on down to Arizona and spent several months living with some Indians. He even brought one fellow back as his personal valet, but the Indian sickened and died because of the climate. But that time in Arizona more or less cured Percy's lungs, though he still couldn't abide an English winter and always left for some warm place like Greece when the first leaves fell. In fact, over the past fifteen years he'd spent most of the time looking for places to go or things to do and he complained that he was running out of geography. Although he was only a little older than me, I figure Percy was just about the most bored and restless person I've ever met, and I suppose that's one of the reasons why he was so glad to see me. I represented some kind of diversion for him.

We arrived at Hallow's End in the afternoon and, God Almighty, what a place! I knew Percy was fairly well off but I hadn't imagined his home would be so big and imposing. It was a great stone house, several hundred years old, set back on this long driveway which was flanked on either side by two rows of lime trees. The house had a history, according to Percy. It had been some kind of headquarters for the King's army during the English Civil War. Percy's people had all fought with the King but they'd taken a hammering from Oliver Cromwell during some battle in a nearby field. In fact, after this battle Cromwell had spent a week or two in the house before sacking it. Later on Percy showed me this old cabinet upstairs with teeth marks on it. The story went that after receiving some bad news of one sort or another Cromwell fell into a fit and took a bite out of this cabinet. I didn't know whether to believe that or not.

As soon as we started up the long drive Percy began to squeeze the horn and the doors of the big house flew open, with servants spilling out of doorways like shelled peas. It all put me in mind of my days with the Easterbrooks, though of course Hallow's End made the Easterbrooks' place back in Toronto look like a cottage. Well, after a good deal of fussing over Percy the servants took our dusters and goggles and we went into the main hallway, which was more like small fancy theater lobby, with a lot of marble heads mounted on mantels and a number of Percy's ancestors staring down at us from dark pictures along the walls. Right off Percy bellows, "Mumsy, dear heart! Where are you?" And these double doors were opened by a gnome-like character in tails and Lady Finchwhistle came sweeping in with her arms outstretched, wearing this long peach-colored chiffon dress. Not a bad-looking old girl either, tall and straight with a pile of white hair and a sharp, beaky look to her face.

As she advanced towards us she says, "Precious one! Where *have* you been?"

Well, they kissed each other on the cheek and Percy explained how he'd got sidetracked but he was glad to be back to "dear old Hallow's End" and was looking forward to the pleasures of rustic life, as he put it. Then he turned to me and said, "But dear Mumsy, look! We have a guest. You'll remember I told you about Bill Farthing and another chap named Findlater. They saved my life up in the Yukon gold fields. Well, by the greatest of good luck, I ran into Bill in London. Over here on a bit of a lark, you see. He travels all over. A genuine adventurer. So I invited him down here for a bit of a visit. I hope this doesn't crush you."

"But dear Percy, of course not," says Lady Finchwhistle, offering me a dry, cool hand, which I didn't know whether to shake or kiss, settling for the shake with a slight bow, which seemed to please her. So then she says to me, "You're most welcome to Hallow's End, Mr. Farthing. You must think of it as your home."

Which as a matter of fact I did as the days went by. They gave me a fine bedroom with a big bay window which looked westward across the fields, and I could see the spire of the village church three miles away. It was about the most restful place I've ever been in. The only trouble was that for the first few days Percy wouldn't leave me alone. He wanted to show me everything and everybody. This is one of the reasons why he got bored so fast. He went after everything with such an enthusiasm that he wore out its interest in no time at all. It was the same with me. For the first week he was by my side nearly all the time, until we just ran out of things to talk about. If he'd have let me alone now and again, we could probably have stretched out things for a couple of months or so. Now, I won't say that he didn't treat me well, because that would be a lie. Being roughly the same dimensions, he fixed me up with clothes, and once again my vanity was flattered as I strolled about in golf shoes and white flannels.

Now, in case none of you have experienced that style of life, I'd better give you an idea of how it was lived. Firstly, nobody was in any particular hurry to wake up in the morning, because there wasn't anything to do, and in fact the hardest job was trying to figure out how to fill your day. It took practice and a certain kind of temperament. So perhaps you'd awake about nine o'clock and there'd be a fellow assigned to draw your bath and lay out your clothes. Under no circumstances were you to do anything for yourself. Percy explained that if you did that, you were putting somebody out of work. It made a crazy kind of sense. On rainy days we had breakfast in the dining room. If it was fine, we sometimes ate out on a little patio. Now I should say that I wasn't the only guest at Hallow's End. There were several of Percy's relatives there, mostly old geezers, uncles and aunts and cousins, and you'd see them now and again tottering along the halls or eating a boiled egg. They could never remember your name and you were always introducing yourself.

After breakfast Percy and me would put on these big black rubber boots and we'd take a couple of thick, knobby walking sticks and set out around the estate, which was several hundred acres in size and employed maybe fifty people. There was always a good deal of bowing and scraping as we met the cowherds and other lower orders. Not that I personally care for any of that, though I can see how it might grow on you. Percy wasn't really interested in farming but I think that like most idle people he wanted to give the impression that he wasn't totally useless. After this stroll we'd come back for lunch, though nobody was really hungry. However, after a few sherries I could usually manage to push down a little cold partridge. In the afternoon Lady Finchwhistle sometimes took a drive in the Rolls, which was an experience, because she was as crazy behind the wheel as Percy and the pheasants and peafowl along the driveway ran for their lives when they saw her coming. If the weather was good we sometimes played croquet or, if it rained, poker. Both Percy and his mother were devoted to games of chance and skill. Dinner was always a dress-up affair, which meant you had to fidget in your room for an hour or so and then present yourself in the dining room in a boiled shirt and all the rest of it. After dinner we generally played billiards. As I say, I was living in the grand style and I could have taken at least a few more months of it, though I could tell Percy was growing bored after only a few days.

Perhaps you've already gathered that the Finchwhistles weren't quite sane. Either that or they were too sane for this world. What I mean is that, depending on how you regard strange behavior, Percy and his mother were either eccentric or just crazy. It wasn't only the way they drove that Rolls around the countryside. There were other things. For example, they had enough money to buy and sell the whole of Elmhurst, Ontario, and they were generous enough too, furnishing me with clothes and board and spending money. But on little things they could be tight as bark to a tree. Such as if you sprinkled too much salt on your morning egg. Well, that would draw a frown from Lady Finchwhistle that would make you feel like two cents. And at the same time she would throw a nice fat chop to one or another of the big red setters that were always padding about the house.

Another queer side to the Finchwhistles' nature was the fact that they cheated. They weren't very good at it either, which made it worse, because there is nothing more pathetic to watch than an incompetent cheat. I know, because I saw plenty of them up in the Klondike, ass-patched, clumsy-fingered fellows who got their heads broken open on dance hall floors. In fact, if you can remember, that's what landed

24.   Hallow's End

Percy on the woodpile and he was lucky he wasn't given a beating as well. Of course, at Hallow's End the Finchwhistles weren't competing in that kind of tough league, but it was an amazing thing to me how they felt they could get away with it. Say we'd be playing croquet out under the trees. Well, just before Lady Finchwhistle would take her shot she might point up to one of the branches and clap her hands and say, "Oh, do look! I believe that's a brick-breasted tit whistle! The first I've seen this season." Naturally we'd all look up and that would allow Lady Finchwhistle to edge her ball closer to the hoop for a direct shot.

Same thing with billiards, which, as I say, we played nearly every evening after dinner. Usually there'd be just the three of us, the cousins and uncles having tottered off to bed with glasses of brandy. Percy and his mother really loved billiards and it was amusing and interesting as a neutral bystander to watch the two of them cheat. It just ran in their blood, I suppose, and I'm not making any kind of judgment here, because I've been known to favor the odds my own way at times. So Percy often made a mistake on the scoreboard and it usually involved his opponent's points. When you brought it to his attention he'd say something like, "Oh, I say, old man. Did you get a carem back there! I didn't see it. Awfully sorry!" Lady Finchwhistle's tactics were just as crude. As she'd go by, she'd pass a wet thumb over your cue tip. What that did, you see, was wipe all the chalk off the tip, causing you to miscue on your next stroke. Now none of this bothered me too much, because I shot a pretty good game of pool in those days, Findlater having taught me the finer points of that sport. So I usually beat them pretty easily and by the end of the evening nobody was saying very much and the mood in the room was grim. Often I'd let one or the other win just to put them in a better humor.

Now, as I've already remarked, I've never met anyone in over ninety years of existence who got bored as quickly as Percy Finchwhistle. So after a couple of weeks at Hallow's End he was just itching to do something different. So he'd say, "Bill, why don't you and I go out to Newfoundland and catch some whales? Or maybe we could go on an alligator hunt in Florida? An American chap I met says it's great fun." And he'd get all excited and go into his father's trophy room, a dark, gloomy chamber with elephant tusks on the walls and leopard skins on the floor. And there he'd settle down with steamship timetables and catalogues from outfitters and gun merchants. But the trouble was that he'd been everywhere and done nearly everything. So in the middle of one of these planning sessions he'd throw up his hands and say, "Oh, dash it all anyway. It'll be the same as that beastly tiger hunt in Rampu last winter." And then he'd get depressed and mope around the house. He'd already more or less lost interest in me because I was turning out to be a pretty ordinary fellow and not the big adventurer he supposed me to be.

But I enjoyed the peacefulness of that place and I liked walking around the estate. It seemed to ease my mind. After the first two weeks I was left pretty much alone, which was a nice change after the nosy atmosphere of the Frys'. I became a kind of curiosity around the place, a conversation piece like the elephant tusks hanging in Lord Finchwhistle's trophy room. I was the person who'd saved Percy's life in the Yukon, and the story took on wondrous turns. Say I'd be sitting in the library. The Finchwhistles had this huge library, maybe ten thousand books, though none of them were read and a good many of them didn't even have their pages cut. But I'd be sitting there browsing through some of these books and I'd hear the door open a crack and then Lady Finchwhistle would be saying to the parish rector who'd come by for tea, "That's the young Canadian who rescued our Percy from the red Indians out in the wilds of Canada." It was all crazy, of course, but I was grateful to be there and the calm and peace was good for me.

Then one day Percy came through the hall leafing through the mail and out onto the terrace. "Oh, I say, Mumsy, listen to this," he says. "It's a card from Birdy. He writes, 'Having a good time with my little American moppet. Food and service absolutely wretched but am keeping a stiff upper. And I might add, a stiff lower as well. Love, Birdy.'"

"Percy, really," said Lady Finchwhistle, laughing behind her fan, for the day was warm.

"Why, that old goat!" says Percy.

"Well, it runs in the family," Lady Finchwhistle replies. "Birdy's father, your great-uncle Lampert, sired a child at eighty-four. Quite remarkable, really."

"Good Lord," says Percy.

I had to leave and go to my room. Anything to keep myself from thinking about Sally and that old carpet knight. Whenever I did think about them, I felt just as miserable as it is possible for a man to feel. It's at times like this that a catastrophe comes in handy, because it takes your mind off your personal problems. In that sense I was fortunate, for a week or so later England went to war against Germany.

25

YES SIR, YES SIR, THREE BAGS FULL

As HECTOR McCOY puts it in his book *All Our Yesteryears,* "The storm clouds were gathering over Europe that summer of 1914." That's Hector's idea of an original line. How he could know what was going on in Europe is a mystery to me, for the only important thing happening to him that August was the news that he was to take over Miss Fillibuster's grade-seven class. But maybe he read it somewhere. All I know is this. If there were storm clouds around that summer, I didn't see them. On the day war was declared there wasn't a cloud in that English sky. The birds were twittering and Lady Finchwhistle and I sat in wicker chairs drinking lemonade spiked with gin and playing poker. She was taking me to the cleaners with one of the crudest examples of card palming I've encountered in a lifetime. Then we spotted a terrible roil of dust along the road and the Rolls came up the driveway scattering the birds and nearly upsetting a two-wheeled pony cart. Percy jumped from the car and came running over all flushed and excited. I don't believe I'd ever seen a man so happy.

"Mumsy," he cried, "I have the most absolutely smashing news. It's too marvelous really." He slapped his hands together like a kid and says, "Mumsy, we're to have a war!"

The old girl dealt herself a seven off the bottom. I could see she was going for an inside straight. And then she says without looking up, "What on earth are you talking about, Percy?"

"A war, Mumsy. There's to be a war," he says. "I was just on the telephone down at the pub speaking to Jack Pottleby in London. It'll be in all the papers. Isn't it the most wonderful news?"

Lady Finchwhistle laid down her hand and saw it destroyed at once by my three kings. She then said with a note of irritation in her voice, "Well, whom on earth are we warring with?"

219

"Why, the Germans, Mumsy!" says Percy. "Old Kaiser Bill is rattling the saber."

"Nonsense," says Lady Finchwhistle. "You must be mistaken. The Germans are civilized people. Why, we have third cousins in Fortelburg! The Queen herself has German blood. It's absurd."

"But true, Mumsy."

"I could understand the French doing something silly," says Lady Finchwhistle. "I've never trusted those people. Always parley-vous this and parley-vous that."

But Percy was too excited to listen. He did a little caper and swallowed some lemonade. "Pottleby says it's going to be a grand show. Oh, I do hope we can get in on the fun before it's all over. Canada will be in it too, Bill, you wait and see. The colonies coming to the aid of the old mother country, and all that rot."

Well, of course, Percy was right about Canada going to war with England against the Germans, but you may be surprised to learn that I didn't join the Canadian army. The reason I didn't was this. I was afraid I might be prosecuted for running out on Merle. She might even have brought charges against me for helping myself to the money in that safe. So instead, I joined the British army.

Now you might wonder why I bothered to join any army, so I'll tell you. The doctors who come into this place to poke at us and look up our backsides are always harping about depression. A lot of people in here are depressed, because they've mostly outlived their friends. And their families aren't that interested in them anymore and just come around on Sundays because they'd feel guilty if they didn't. So these doctors are always prescribing pills for what they call depression, by which they mean sadness. Now, sadness! That's what I was suffering from back in the summer of 1914. Even though Hallow's End was about the most restful and civilized place I'd ever lived in, I was sad beyond measure owing to Sally's marriage to Lord Birdlip. Of course, there weren't any pills to take for sadness in those days, so what you tried to do was involve yourself in something bigger than your own personal miseries. That's where a war become useful, so I joined up.

Percy was after me to enlist in the cavalry. As he saw it, "If you're going to fight a war, old man, you might as well do it sitting down." But although I'd worked around horses a good deal and knew something about them, I had no great craving to ride one. So while Percy went off to join the cavalry, I decided on the infantry and said my good-byes to Lady Finchwhistle, who wasn't really sorry to see me go. I'd gotten tired of her cheating and was doing some of my own, which meant that I was winning all the time at poker and pool. However, she had a nice lunch prepared for me and drove me to the village train station. A few hours later I was standing in line at a recruiting station in London, offering my services to King and Country. They gave me a medical, and while they found me a bit long in the tooth, pronounced me fit for active duty.

25. Yes Sir, Yes Sir, Three Bags Full

I rented a room and for the next couple of weeks reported every day to a schoolyard, where an old scoutmaster and veteran of the Crimean War put a bunch of us through some elementary drilling and marching. We were mostly clerks and warehousemen and we all felt a bit silly marching back and forth with broom handles and garden rakes over our shoulders. I remember one fellow saying to this old scout, "When do we get to fight the bloody Hun, mate? I'm getting married in another month." Looking back now, it's an amazing thing how naïve we all were.

A couple of weeks later they sent us down to Aldershot, which was a big army camp with thousands of soldiers being hollered at by sergeant-majors. At first it was a novelty to wear a uniform and be told what to do every minute of the day. But after a few weeks it became tiresome as hell. When you weren't shining boots or polishing buttons you were out on the parade square, where it was all slope arms, present arms, about-turn, etc., etc. We used to sing a little song about it. I think it went like this:

> Yes sir, Yes sir, three bags full
> Right wheel, left wheel
> What a lot of bull.

There was another song we used to sing on route marches that went "Bored, bored, so bloody bored. And nobody seems to care!" There was also the rifle range, where they invited you to pretend you were shooting at Germans, and then bayonet practice, where you stuffed the end of your gun into a canvas sack filled with straw while this big joker bellowed in your ear. I can still hear him yelling, "Don't look down! You'd soon find the 'ole if there was bloody 'air around it."

The men in our platoon called me Dad because I was older than most of them, the average age being about twenty. But I didn't make too many friends for one reason or another, and then just as I was getting to know a few of them I had an accident which landed me in the hospital. It happened in a heavy autumn rainstorm during this mock battle. What I did was put my foot through this rotten duckboard and break my leg in two places. It made me mad, because our battalion pulled out for Belgium the next week. You have to understand that I wanted to go with them and meet a soldier's honorable death out there in Flanders Fields. At the time it seemed the only reasonable course open to me. But instead, I had to lie in a hospital bed and watch our battalion march past the window, receiving the General's salute.

So there I was, trussed up in a hospital bed with my leg attached to wheels and pulleys and just feeling rotten about everything. Then one day, about two weeks after I'd been there, two nurses came into the ward escorting this little bandy-legged fellow. It struck me that there was something oddly familiar in the way he carried himself along. It was more than just the cocky swagger you often see in excessively short people. He walked along as though he was daring you to stand in his way. In front of him he held up his two arms, completely bandaged and fastened by a strip of wrapping around his neck. He was quarreling with the nurses over something. They seemed to be glad to get rid of him and they left him by the empty bed next to mine. I paid him little heed, though I could tell he was studying me, and after a minute he says, "Hey, mate! How about lightin' me a fag? I can't do a bloody ——ing thing with these mitts of mine." So I reached over and lit a cigarette and stuck it in his mouth. He puffed away for a few minutes and then said, "How did you get wounded, mate?"

I didn't care for the sarcastic tone of his voice and told him as much.

"Now don't get your shit hot," he says. "I'm just makin' conversation. We're better off here than over in bloody Belgium." He blew the ashes from his cigarette. "Yes, General, I did volunteer to fight for the bloody old Union Jack, God bless it. Give the Hun a bloody nose, and all that. And then they tell me I'm too short. Going to put me into some kind of runt battalion guarding the fish wharfs. Well, —— that, I says to them. I can do more good makin' bullets up at Sheffield with the ladies. That draws me a fortnight in the guardhouse, but the sergeant is a decent bloke and when the cook comes down with the runs he gives me this job helping in the scullery. And then first day on the job, what happens? Down comes a whole bloody cauldron of hot beans, big as a rain barrel across my ——ing arms! So here I am, a bloody hero! Wounded in the line of duty! But say!" He sat up and squinted at me through the smoke, the cigarette nearly burning his lips. "You're not English, are you? You sound like a Yank."

"I'm a Canadian," I says.

"Canadian, eh? I got an uncle over in Canada. Well, I expect he's dead now, for we haven't heard from him for years. He was my favorite uncle too, my dad's oldest brother. When I was a kid he was always sendin' me little tin soldiers and things. He was an old army man who'd fought in India with all the bleeding heroes. He went out to Canada before I was born. Got a job with some rich blokes out there."

Then damn me if it didn't all come together! The same swagger to the walk, and when I looked closely, there was a certain facial likeness too. I was talking to the nephew of good old Wilson from the Easterbrooks'. So I says, "Your name wouldn't be Wilson by any chance, would it?"

At this he spat out his cigarette and says, "What are you, anyway? Some kind of bloody prophet? Yes, my name's Wilson. Clement Wilson, though I'm known as Shorty and I've got used to it. But how the —— did you know my name?"

So I told him about working with his uncle when I was just a kid and by the time I'd finished, we'd whiled away the afternoon and Shorty Wilson and me were friends. He was a Londoner, the son of a muffin man. He used to walk the streets with his father yelling, "Hot muffins. Get your hot muffins."

"A bloody awful way to make a livin', Bill," Shorty said to me. "And it's dyin' out as a way of life, with more people goin' to the shops now. My old Dad's legs are bad and he can hardly get around anymore. I joined the bloody army to get three meals a day and send some money home. I certainly bloody well didn't join it to help a lot of rich buggers get richer, for that's what it's all about you know. And believe you me, it's only a matter of time before they start makin' blokes join up. Bloody old Kitchener thinks he can fight this war with volunteers, but I've got news for him. This ain't gonna be the ——ing dance the lads in Whitehall think it will be. Not by a bloody long shot it ain't. The ——ing German may have a square head but he wasn't born bloody yesterday either. He'll sit in his hole and stick this one out while we beat our heads against a bloody stone wall. And we won't get much help from the Froggies either. They shot their bolt forty years ago and got the piss kicked out of them. Oh, we'll have our hands full unless the Yanks come in, and that I doubt. They don't give a —— for anybody but themselves."

Now to tell you the truth, that sort of talk surprised me, because nearly everybody else figured we had the Germans on the run. I remember sitting in the lounge one day around Christmas when Wilson was talking like this. In the middle of it a big fellow who'd lost a leg at Ypres says, "Shut your bloody hole, you little half-arse! One English-man's worth ten Huns any day of the week, We'll have them on their bloody knees by next summer." Shorty only laughed at that.

Now they tried to make life bearable at that hospital with sing-alongs and Red Cross parcels. Lady Finchwhistle sent me a Christmas basket and here was a funny damn thing! Among the woolen socks and books was a box of candy labeled Farthing's Fancies and Assorted Fruit Centers. I don't imagine Lady Finchwhistle connected my name with it, but these candies had been made at my uncle Rodney's factory at Cheltenham. I decided that once I was on my feet and granted a leave, I'd visit the family. And as a matter of fact that's just what I did, near the end of April. It was on that occasion that I learned about my father from my two old spinster aunts, though I never got to meet Uncle Rodney, who was away on business. But my aunts showed me the library filled with copies of my father's book *Pine Smoke at Even-song* and seeing all those books sent a funny shiver through me, for the world of my father and his dreams seemed so remote in time and place.

During this time of convalescence I also wrote a letter to Find-later telling him where I was and hoping he might have news of Sally. I got back this reply.

Mary's Hole
14th Str. N.Y.
April 1, 1915

Dear Bill, Say thanks for yur letter which was inneresting tho I think you picked the wrong side in that little fight over ther. I have a noshion the Germans will win it Bill. They're way ahead of the English in pneumatic tires and they know how to make a good road too. I see a future in iron so another fellah and me have bought a couple of dozen scrapyards. This fellah's name is Phlug. I met his brother over in London. Anyways, business is booming and you can't ast for better than that. I ain't heard from Lady Birdlip in some time now but when I do I'll let youse know. We're goin into full production with Martin's pomes you'll be happy to know. I'm expectin a batch of aprons in today. I already got sizeable orders from Marshall Fields in Chicago and from Gimbels right here in NYC. Martin's over here now by the way. I'm gonna get him out readin his pomes to the ladies. Take care of yurself.

Cass

Meantime, Shorty Wilson's hands healed and he left for further training. My leg took a while to mend owing to the nature of the break, so when I finally got out and around it was nearly summer again. The doctors told me that I could probably get a medical discharge and go back to Canada, but I didn't really want to get out of the army. There just didn't seem to be any place better to go, so I arranged to get transferred to this training unit and endured more marching and drilling. In fact, I spent the better part of the next year at it and I got so used to the routine that it more or less deadened the nerves in my head and I just went about like a robot. I needn't bother to tell you that I had no ambition and remained throughout a private, the oldest one in our platoon.

There were two things that happened in that year, and they were both bad. The first was I saw Charley Fry again. It was during one of my leaves in London and Charley was getting off a train at Waterloo Station. He was dressed in a soldier's uniform and his head was wrapped in bandages and he was being helped along by two pals. Although I didn't ask, I believe the man was stone blind. The other sad thing was a letter from Lady Finchwhistle in which I learned that poor Percy was dead, having died a hero's death somewhere out near Palestine. Lady Finchwhistle was given some kind of important medal by the King. I also got letters now and again from Findlater and he seemed to be prospering in the scrap-iron business. He also sent me newspaper clippings, which I still have in my possession, all of them describing the wonderful reception given to Martin Rooney and his poetry readings.

Then finally I went to war. The outfit I was training with was mostly a rag-bag bunch and about the end of May 1916 we were disbanded and then drafted to various battalions to bring them up to strength. Along with a couple of dozen other men I reported to this battalion which was part of the 29th Division. It was stationed down near Dover on the south coast. We arrived at this camp in the early evening and damn me for a liar if the first man I saw wasn't Shorty Wilson! He was running around the parade square with a rifle above his shoulders. "A little punishment from Chamberlain," as Shorty explained to me later in the evening, for wasn't I lucky enough to be assigned to the same platoon!

Shorty told me we'd be pulling out in a few days for France. He'd already been over a couple of times. "I tried my damnedest to get a blitey, Bill, but no luck." A blitey, by the way, was a minor wound that would get you into the hospital. "I think we're going to be in for it this time," said Shorty, rubbing his arms with gun oil, for they were stiff from holding up that rifle. "Nobody's sayin' too much, but I've heard rumors there's a big push on this summer. And we'll be in it, mate. Right up to our armpits. You've been lucky so far, Billy lad. Now you're gonna have a whole new experience. There's gonna be some nice chaps from the other side of the Rhine River trying to shoot the buttons off your fly."

"What about this battalion?" I asked. "What sort of an outfit is it?"

"Well, all I can say is that you're a lucky man to draw us," Shorty laughed. "We're generally regarded as the hellfire boys, you know. Lead the brigade into battle, and all that. A front-line outfit, and every man shits pure iron bricks. It's a load of rubbish really, but that's what old Leatherballs wants everybody to think. Unfortunately, the staff officers believe him most of the time and we usually draw the dirtiest jobs in the laundry."

"Who's this Leatherballs?" I asked.

"Do you mean to tell me you've never heard of Lieutenant-Colonel Hugh John Leatherby, our battalion C.O.? HJL to the officers and Leatherballs to the rest of us. Always spouting fire and brimstone, smite the Boche at hip and thigh, and all that ——ing nonsense. The funny damn thing is that if you listen long enough you begin to believe him. He's a bloody huge man and you can't ignore him. Been in all the important battles over the past thirty years and has a chestful of medals. Refuses to go beyond battalion commander, because then he wouldn't have a chance to kill anybody. And you have to understand that the man enjoys killing people. He's good at it too, and I'll give him that. He leads his men in the field and has nothing but contempt for the staff boys who sit in the farmhouses five miles behind the trenches and stick pins in maps. The only problem with Leatherballs is the fact that sooner or later he's going to get us all killed. Not that he'd mind one little bit, for he's always going on about the honor and rightness of a soldier's death. He gives these little talks every Sunday after service, when he addresses the battalion. Oh, bloody inspiring they are, though I don't necessarily share his ambition.

"I've been thinking, Bill, that if this ——ing war ever ends and I survive it, I might go out to Canada and make a new life for myself. My old Dad passed away last year and there's nothing left for me here. Maybe if we pull through this ——ing mess you could show me the ropes out there in the New World?"

"I'd be glad to, Shorty," I says. "Now what about the company and platoon?" Shorty lit a cigarette. "Well, A Company isn't the worst by a long shot. Our good Captain Furbelow you'll meet in the morning. In civilian life he was, I believe, a schoolteacher. He's a nervous sort of bloke who'd really rather be somewhere else, as who the —— wouldn't? He's not well liked by the men. Too intense, if you know what I mean. The lads call him Captain Cunt, but you can decide for yourself. Our particular platoon's under young Jameson. A nice enough young fellow but he's only been with us a few weeks and he's raw as liver. Only nineteen and never been under fire. It'll make a difference when we get over there. But the fact is that the platoon is really run by Chamberlain. He's a hard man and he hates my guts but he's far and away the best ——ing sergeant in the battalion, though I'd never say it to his face. He's the only man in the platoon who's regular army and he knows what to do when things get hot, as they surely will, mate. Since you've not been in battle before, Bill, my advice is to keep close to Chamberlain." Shorty told me a number of other things about the platoon before the lights were doused and Sergeant Chamberlain came through to tell us all to shut up.

I got to know Chamberlain and a few of the others over the next month or so. I liked Dick Chamberlain. Shorty was right about him being a hard man, but he was also fair and if you did your work he left you alone. For some reason he took a liking to me. Maybe it was because we were roughly the same age and the rest of the platoon was younger. Whatever it was, we often had a smoke together in the evenings. He could never understand why I chummed with Shorty Wilson and he often used to say to me in this big, deep voice of his, "I don't know how you can abide that little beggar, Bill. He's always complaining and the bad spirit rubs off on the other men. I have to watch him twenty-four hours a day. And he's got the dirtiest mouth in the British army." I believe it was Shorty's swearing more than anything else that bothered Dick Chamberlain, for in his own way he was a religious man. I don't mean to suggest he was a fanatic or anything like that. But now and again you'd see him sitting by himself reading the little Testament he always carried with him. He was a serious man and I never once saw him laugh. The only time he'd even smile was when he got a letter from home, for he was devoted to his wife and five children.

There were one or two others in the platoon that I got to know fairly well. There was Lance-Corporal Watson, a red-headed Scot who was our section leader and a nice lad with a sense of humor. I also liked a tall, horse-faced boy from Leeds named Jenkins. He had the odd habit of chewing cigarette tobacco. Captain Furbelow I only saw now and again. He was usually hurrying to some meeting with a frown on his face. Young Jameson looked worried too, and the only time he seemed to relax was when he sat down to read. Somebody told me that before he joined the army he was at Oxford University studying to become a philosopher. All this reading didn't sit too well with the men under him, though the first hint of protest always drew a black look from Dick Chamberlain.

I saw old Leatherballs for the first time on the Sunday after we landed in France. It was also on that day that I saw the supreme commander of the British army, General Douglas Haig. It was near the end of June and we were billeted in this little village near Amiens. In the morning we were told there was to be an important visitor, and sure enough, who should turn up for church parade but Haig himself, a little gray old man on this big black horse, surrounded by lancers with pennants fluttering in the wind. It all looked like something out of a storybook. Of course, looking at General Haig then I had no idea that within a week I'd be planning to kill him.

After Haig left, Leatherballs jumped up on the back of a lorry and gave the battalion a talk on the privilege of dying for your country. He was a giant of a man, about three ax handles across the shoulders and with the biggest head of any human I've yet seen. This great head was bald except for a fringe of hair around the sides, and when the sunlight struck it you almost had to turn your head away from the glare. I'll tell you, it was a head that you couldn't forget once you saw it, and the other striking feature about Leatherballs was his eyes. Even though I was well back in the crowd I could see these eyes blazing and crackling as though they were lit by some inner fire. Those eyes along with a big set of handlebar moustaches and the bald head made him look about as fierce as you'd want any man to look.

Just a brief glimpse and you could discern that Leatherballs was crazy in that special way that old saints and ancient heroes were. And when he started to talk, believe you me, the men listened. Although I've never been educated in the Latin tongue I can still hear Leatherballs thundering out, "Dulce et decorum est pro patria mori. I want each and every one of you men to remember those words when you fix your bayonets for the next battle. Dulce et decorum est pro patria mori. Noble words for a noble Roman, and they mean as much today as they meant during the glorious days of ancient Rome. It is sweet and suitable to die for your country. Remember that and act accordingly. If any man in this battalion does otherwise, then by God he'll have me to answer to."

To which Shorty Wilson, who was standing at the back, piped up, "Why, I'd rather face the ——ing Hun any day!" That got a few laughs, though if Leatherballs heard him, he didn't let on.

A few days later the word was out that we were moving up to the front. "It's going to be a ——ing big show, Bill," Shorty said to me one morning. "A fellow in B Company told me that ——ing near the whole British army is set to move. I guess this is the big one we've heard so much about. Did you hear those ——ing guns again last night? I've never heard anything like it."

Well, Shorty was right about this bombardment. For nearly a week the artillery kept up this constant bombardment. All day and all night the guns roared and it got so you couldn't remember what absolute silence was like. With a barrage like that it was only a matter of time before a major battle. Then sure enough, on the last day of June, we moved up past the artillery lines where the gunners, stripped to the waist, were laboring over their big cannons, some of them bleeding from the ears. As we moved into position in the trenches nobody was saying much. We all sensed we were about to take part in something big and everybody was a little tense. There were two schools of opinion, and you could call them the optimists and the pessimists. Watson led the optimists, maintaining that after six days of bombardment there wouldn't be a German left to face us.

Naturally Shorty Wilson was the spokesman for the pessimists, and I recall him sitting in the trench that last night, digging at a tin of bully beef and saying, "I've said it before and I'll say it again. The ——ing German is a good bit smarter than the rest of us when it comes to fighting this war. Right this very minute, lads, he's sitting over there in his hole drinking beer and waiting for the guns to stop. I will grant you that this artillery of ours is giving him a slight head-ache, but probably nothing more. When we let up with the barrage he's going to pop his ——ing square head out of his hole and set up his machine gun. And he's not going to be in the best of humor when he does it either."

"Shut up, Wilson," said Dick Chamberlain, who was leaning against the trench wall trying to read from his little Testament in the half-light of the fading day. "You've got too much to say, Wilson," says Dick. "If I hear another word from you, I'll ram this bloody rifle down your throat." It was the first time I'd ever heard Dick Chamberlain talk like that.

So there we were, and I found it difficult to believe that only a few hundred yards away were other men whose job it would be to kill me in the morning. As I've said, our battalion was part of the 29th Division, and we were set to go into the lines at a place called Beaumont-Hamel. The next day would be my thirty-sixth birthday. It would also be the blackest day in the history of the British army.

26

JULY 1, 1916

———————

I'M REFERRING, of course, to what historians later called the Battle of the Somme, or at least the first day of it. On that day, Saturday, July 1, fourteen divisions of the British army, that's nearly a hundred and seventy thousand men, attacked the German trenches along a twelve-mile front in the province of Picardy in the north of France. Mind you, I didn't know anything about any twelve-mile front at the time. Our battalion was responsible for only about two hundred yards of that front, and for once Shorty Wilson was wrong. He predicted that we'd be in the advance wave. "Leatherballs will see to that," said Shorty. "He won't be happy until he knows that we're the first ones to be killed come dawn." But that wasn't to be. About midnight another battalion moved past us into the front trenches while we remained in support. "I don't believe it," says Shorty, shaking his head. "If this is God's will, then He'll have to face Leatherballs in the morning." But the rumor was out that Leatherballs was fuming and spitting, because, of course, it was generally thought that the best battalions always led the attack.

Nobody got much sleep that night, crouched and crowded as we were in the trenches. A few of the older ones who'd been through it all before had the knack of falling asleep standing up or leaning against the trench wall. But the rest of us couldn't settle our nerves and so we waited, watching the Very lights along the line and now and again hearing machine guns rattle or rifle fire. Because the generals wanted the Germans to think this was just another ordinary night, we were sending men out on patrols and raids here and there. But it was mostly quiet along our section and the night was still and the sky full of stars. And I stood there looking at them and wondering what Findlater was doing right at that moment. And Sally! God Almighty, it didn't bear thinking about.

Around two-thirty a couple of store men brought up some big petrol tins full of hot tea and rum, elbowing their way past us and cursing. Their arrival cheered us up, for although it was a summer night it can be cold standing around in damp trenches. But the rum carriers moved on past us, for the boys in the advance wave were entitled to their ration first. After they had it they began quietly to climb the scaling ladders and crawl out to no man's land to await first light. I didn't envy them lying out there in the cold wet grass, knowing they'd be the first to stand up and face the Germans once the attack started. That is, if there were any Germans to speak of after an entire week of shelling.

All through the night our platoon was divided in opinion. There were some like Watson who were convinced it would be a walkover. Whenever Watson went on about how easy it was going to be, the younger ones crowded around him and nodded. Even young Jameson seemed to take heart and would nod his head. I remember Watson saying, "Nobody could survive a week of that bloody shelling. You mark my words. There won't be more than a handful of Jerries to greet us and they'll throw down their Mausers when they see what they're up against."

But Shorty Wilson wasn't having any of that. "The Jerries'll be greeting us, all right," he says. "Oh, you can depend on that. They're nobody's fools, and you see if they don't give us a hammerin' into the bargain." He went on like this until Dick Chamberlain came by and edged his big frame down beside us. Before I knew it, he was squeezing Shorty's arm. Even in the darkness I could see Shorty's face filled with pain.

Dick was whispering so as not to arouse others, but I heard. What he said was, "Listen, Wilson, you little heathen. We've got a job of work to do in the morning and by heaven we're going to do it. Now, you're entitled to your opinion but you keep it to yourself for the next few hours or I'll personally see that you get it out there. And not from the Jerries either." Then he let go of Shorty's arm and got to his feet. Soon he was standing by young Jameson. It did shut up Shorty, too, and he sat there sulking, not saying a word until they issued us rum and tea.

Well, to say I wasn't nervous would be a lie. Yet I was in a difficult position too, being older than most of the others. A good many of these lads were just like Jameson, fuzzy-cheeked kids fresh out of school. Naturally they looked up to older men like me, and then it wasn't generally known in the platoon that I'd not seen any action. When I felt edgy I liked to get close to Chamberlain. He seemed to have a confidence that rubbed off on you. It was hard to figure whether he was on the side of the optimists or the pessimists, and so as we stood around drinking our rum I drew him to one side and asked on the quiet what he thought our chances were. He was drawing on his pipe and sipping his rum, everything done in a slow, deliberate manner. You couldn't hurry the man, and he took his time answering too. Then he whispered, "If you'll pardon my language, Bill, I think it's going to be a bugger. But what's the sense in worrying about it? We've got to do it, don't we?" He sounded bitter to me but I suppose he was thinking of his wife and five kids and of how lucky he'd been so far. Dick knew as well as the next man that you can only tempt the fates so many times and then you're going to get it. Still, I figured on staying close to him come the morning, because if you ever served in an army you'll know that there are some fellows who seem to have a natural instinct for survival and I guessed Dick Chamberlain was one of them.

It was interesting to observe young Jameson, and I admired and felt sorry for that young fellow all at the same time. He was frightened half to death but he was doing his best to hide it, spending most of his time up on the firestep peering into the darkness through his field glasses. There wasn't anything to see but I could tell he was doing that so he wouldn't have to show the way his face sometimes twitched. It was hard to notice unless you were watching but I could see his knees sometimes shook, too. Once Chamberlain took him a mug of tea and rum but Jameson just shook his head and I could tell that Chamberlain liked him for that. To my way of thinking, people who are scared and still go on with the job are always more admirable and more natural heroes than the unthinking fearless types like Watson. After a bit Dick Chamberlain shifted his weight and muttered something about "I wish they'd get those guns going. It'll soon be daylight."

With the rum inside him Shorty was uttering the same sentiments a few yards away. He was moving about restlessly, bumping into people and getting their wind up. "Where's the bloody artillery?" he kept saying. "When are they going to get to work, for Christ's sakes? It'll soon be daylight."

He was jumpy as a racehorse at the gate and it finally got to Watson, who turned on him and startled us all by pointing his gun at Wilson's stomach. "Shut your ——ing trap, Wilson. We've all heard enough from you."

His voice was shaking, but Shorty was quick and brought his own rifle up so hard it knocked Watson's weapon from his hand and Shorty pointed his rifle at Watson's throat. "And we've all heard enough of your ——ing fairy tales about no Jerries being out there too."

They glared at one another, but just then Chamberlain came up. "All right, you lot," he says. "What do you think this is? A bleeding picnic?" He knocked Wilson's rifle aside. "I'll have you both shot within the hour if you don't stop this bickering. I mean that." He did too. You could see by the grim, hard way his jaw was set that he meant it. And I remember thinking to myself, Pity the poor German that gets in his way tomorrow morning! Then Dick whispers, "Attention down the line there." And he went on by us to Lieutenant Jameson and said, "Captain Furbelow's on the way, sir." Jameson looked down and nodded. And sure enough, in a few minutes Captain Furbelow came scrambling through with his little batman behind him. He edged his way past us to Lieutenant Jameson and they exchanged salutes.

By now a thin gray light was filtering through the darkness of the eastern sky. You could see it beyond the barbed wire and no man's land. And the first birds were starting up, and sounding pretty too. Then a drizzle began to fall and this was queer because the sky had been filled with stars all night. That drizzle made us curse, for a wet tunic is uncomfortable and if it rained hard it meant mud and bad footing, so there was a good bit of grumbling but Dick Chamberlain hushed us and Lieutenant Jameson came down from the firestep to talk to the Captain. "All right, Jameson," says Furbelow, looking around him. "You can pass the word along. Artillery will lay down the first round any minute now." He paused. "Zero hour is seven-thirty." Even in the poor light I could see Jameson go a little pale at this, and Dick Chamberlain passed a big hand across his stubbly jaw.

Then Shorty Wilson was there, squeezed up near the front of us to get all the latest news. When he heard this he shook his head as if he couldn't believe it. "Seven ——ing thirty, Captain!" he says. "They must be mad back there. Why, seven-thirty is broad daylight! We'll never get across that ——ing meadow in broad daylight!"

Captain Furbelow squinted into the sea of dark faces around him. "Is that you, Wilson?"

"Yes, sir," says Wilson.

Others stepped aside as Wilson elbowed his way forward. Furbelow shook his head. "I thought as much. You know, Wilson, I'd recommend a visit to the chaplain. Your language is frightful. It simply isn't necessary to punctuate your comments with so many curses."

Just then Dick Chamberlain says, "Excuse me, sir. But is the artillery not going to start up?"

"Any minute now, Sergeant," says Furbelow. "And I want you all to have faith! Not like Wilson here with his poisonous cynicism. That sort of attitude will get you nowhere. Now, I've told you time and time again that this will be a walkover. Why, some of you may not even get to fire your rifles! In all probability the barbed wire will be gone and their trenches will be a shambles. I seriously doubt whether you'll meet a single German this morning. Lieutenant-Colonel Leatherby feels the same way. As a matter of fact, I was just talking to him a half hour ago. And do you know where he is this very moment, Wilson?"

"No, sir."

"At this very moment, Wilson, the head of this battalion is some fifty yards to your left with C Company, prepared to lead his men into battle. And do you know what he will be carrying as he goes over the top, Wilson?"

"Well, sir," says Wilson, "a revolver, sir, I would expect. Maybe one in each hand."

"Don't be insolent, Wilson. Lieutenant-Colonel Leatherby will be carrying a walking stick."

"A walking stick, sir?"

"A walking stick," says the Captain. "That's confidence, Wilson. And that's what you lack. And that's why you'll always be a fifth-rate little man in this army. Do you understand, Wilson?"

"Yes, sir."

Then the Captain turned to Lieutenant Jameson. "Good luck, Jameson. Let's show them how A Company can do the job. I'm expecting a good deal from your platoon."

"Yes, sir," says Jameson, tight-lipped.

And the Captain moved down the communications trench to another platoon. The soldiers went back to their thoughts. Shorty shook his head. "A ——ing walking stick! Old Leatherballs is going out there carrying a walking stick. Did you hear the man, Bill?" He slumped against the trench wall as if the sheer craziness of the world had finally got to him.

Lucky for us the rain was only a shower and just dampened our tunics. The only creatures that seemed to enjoy it were the birds. There were meadowlarks and redstarts swooping and diving among the poppies and long grass, singing as sweetly as ever you'd want to hear. It was a perfect summer morning, cloudless and not a breath of wind. You could tell it was going to be a hot day. It put me in mind of the summer mornings I'd walked down the main street of Elmhurst to the post office to pick up the mail. I'd hated the confining nature of my life then but now, standing in that trench, I thought about how nice and comfortable that homely existence had been.

The sky slowly brightened to the east and then our artillery began. The shells went whishing overhead and puffs of white and black smoke appeared to the east. That tightened my stomach, I can tell you, for I knew that once those guns stopped, we'd be into it. Nobody was saying much now, not even Shorty, who just leaned against a traverse, shaking his head and muttering to himself from time to time. In the morning light I could see young Jameson still up on the firestep, his face pale. He was licking his lips. Dick Chamberlain was beside him. So the sun rose higher and the smoke from the shelling drifted back to us but the birds sang as though there weren't any war going on at all. And somebody says, "Why don't we get this over with?" And Dick Chamberlain, as though glad to have something to do, told him to shut up.

Then about twenty minutes past seven they blew a big mine under the Hawthorne redoubt a half-mile or so to the north of us, and God Almighty, it was a sight to see. This huge column of earth and white chalk rose into the blue sky about a thousand feet, I'd judge. I know I was watching a British scouting plane at the time and I thought sure it would be knocked out of the sky. But it just banked away northward and then this column of earth and chalk seemed to hang up there suspended like a giant umbrella before falling back to the ground. Then Chamberlain yelled, "Mind the shock now, lads." And a few seconds later the whole trench seemed to be swaying back and forth as if we were in some kind of earthquake. Young Jameson was thrown from the firestep and landed on his back on the trench floor. Dick Chamberlain tried to pick him up. "Are you all right, sir?"

Jameson jumped up quickly and the blow seemed to have brought him around. Either that or he didn't want to appear foolish in front of his platoon. Anyway, all he said was, "Of course I'm all right. Tell the men to fix bayonets."

"Right, sir," says Dick. "Fix bayonets, lads, and pass the word."

Now, blowing that big mine ten minutes before we were due to attack wasn't very smart. What it did, you see, was to alert the Germans that something big was coming up shortly. In a matter of minutes they were throwing the stuff at us. Shells whistled over our heads and then I heard the *tac-tac-tac* of their machine guns. It sounded like hail as the bullets whistled through the grass. "No ——ing Germans, eh?" says Shorty. "Just listen to Leatherballs now. He probably thinks that's a ——ing hailstorm up there."

The artillery bombardment increased in fury for the next few minutes. It was deafening and we just crouched down like ground hogs in a hole with our fists over our ears. From time to time I glanced at my watch, and then at seven-thirty the damnedest thing happened. Our guns stopped and oddly enough the Germans stopped firing too. It was weird. This deathly quiet fell across the battlefield and there was only the sun beating down on the grass and the birds singing. Then all along the trenches you heard the officers' whistles blow and rising up from the long grass was the advance wave, a whole line of khaki beginning its long walk across no man's land. Where we were the meadow sloped upward a bit and so I could see them clearly going. Our platoon was in the third wave and already we were moving from the support trenches up to the front line. Now for maybe five seconds nothing much happened. I suppose the Germans were so startled to see these British soldiers strolling towards them in broad daylight that at first they couldn't believe it.

But it didn't take them long to recover and soon their machine guns started up and I'll tell you what it was like, because we were standing there watching and waiting our turn. As the machine guns traversed the field it was like a giant scythe cutting through a field of grain, only it was men being chopped down. Here and there a few kept going but most of them were falling. Then more whistles blew and the boys in front of us scrambled over the top and that awful whistling sound was right above our heads. One poor fellow was hit just as he got on top of the parapet and he fell to his knees with the blood pouring from his throat. He just knelt there with his head down as though he was praying and everybody stepped over or around him. A fellow next to me vomited down Dick Chamberlain's leg and Chamberlain looked at it as if he'd just been handed the worst insult in the world, so he said, "Why, you filthy little bastard!" and slapped the youngster across the face. And the boy started to cry, which was strange because just hours earlier that same boy had been crying and Dick had put his arm around him and told him to buck up.

Then it was our turn. Young Jameson jumped up on the firestep. The whistle was in his mouth and he was trying to get his revolver out of the holster but his hand shook so bad that he had to use both of them. Right behind him Dick Chamberlain yelled, "All right, lads, let's give it to them. Wait for the whistle."

And Jameson blew his whistle and so did the others along the line and the men in front of us were scrambling up and disappearing over the lip of the trench. There was a scaling ladder in front of us and I was behind Shorty, waiting my turn. And Shorty turned to me and his eyes were wild. "Didn't I tell you, Bill? Didn't I tell you? We're just lambs to the slaughter, that's all."

His knuckles were white on the ladder rung and somebody behind yelled, "Let's get on with it, eh! Let's get going, for the love of Christ!" And so we scrambled up and got into it.

Now, once you got up out of the trench the first thing you had to do was to move smartly through the hole in our barbed wire. These gaps in the wire had been cut the night before, and the idea was to get through them quickly. But some of the German machine-gun crews had already spotted these holes and trained their guns on them. Before long they were just narrow alleys of death, with the bodies piling up in a heap. It was awful to see. Our section was luckier than some and we got through our gap and into this big open meadow, which as I may have mentioned, slanted upwards a bit. Even after you'd gone only a few yards you could tell how much of an advantage the Germans had had all along, looking down into our lines. Now what you saw a few hundred yards ahead was the German barbed wire, all of which, we were told, would be blown to pieces by the week's bombardment, but all of which was still in place, at least in our part of the line. Behind those big coils of wire were the sandbags of the German trenches, from which poured out this murderous gunfire.

I'll tell you that in a sense I was fascinated. The fact is I really couldn't believe what my eyes were telling me. The whole attack made so little sense that you couldn't begin to understand how human beings ever thought it would work. There we were in broad daylight, *walking* with our guns at the port to *certain death*. It was an incredible sight and not one I can ever forget even after half a century. Everywhere you looked khaki uniforms were disappearing in the grass, and yet we moved ahead. Nobody was running. That was forbidden by order, believe it or not. Nobody was retreating. Nobody was even shouting or cheering, for that too was not allowed according to the battle plan, and don't ask me why.

A lot of things about that day have never made a particle of sense to me. I remember walking forward and watching with a kind of dazed look as those machine-gun bullets whipped across the field, knocking off poppy flowers and grass and buckling men. And coming closer to me. And then, who knows? Maybe the particular gunner's weapon overheated or jammed. Or maybe he stopped for a drink of water or to scratch an itch behind his ear. On a battlefield your entire fate often rests on something as trivial as that. The man next to you gets hit and you keep on going. There's no rhyme or reason to it.

Anyway, I kept going and some of the men in our section were falling. In fact, Shorty was absolutely right. The battalion was going to its slaughter. I saw the optimist Watson put his right hand up to his face and stagger forward a few feet before falling into the grass. Jenkins went too, dropping like a sack. Remarkably enough, young Jameson was still moving forward, with Dick Chamberlain right beside him. I was a few yards back, with Shorty on my left. He just kept saying over and over, "I told you so, I told you so." And I remember thinking, Well, I've had thirty-five years on the planet. More than most of these poor young buggers. Now I'm going to get it and I just hope it's quick and doesn't hurt too much.

Now what probably saved my life at this point was the German artillery. You may find that a strange statement, but it's nevertheless true. Once the German artillery got the news that we were attacking, they started to shell us. Now you might think that's not exactly the best news in the world, and of course it wasn't if you happened to be anywhere near an exploding shell. But what it also did, you see, was throw up craters and give the men a legitimate excuse to take cover from the machine-gun fire. The attack had already bogged down. You could see that after five minutes, so here and there men began to dive to the ground as the shells whistled down. If they were lucky they jumped into a shell hole. I myself found a shell hole, but I didn't jump into it. I was blown there. What happened was that I heard this shell come screaming overhead and I saw Dick Chamberlain dive for the ground. I was certain that shell was headed straight for me and so as I fell to the grass I remember saying, "Goodbye, Sally. Maybe we'll meet in a better world." At the same time I was back in my childhood. In Jake Snipes' shack with all the light and noise of that freight train bearing down upon me.

The next thing I remember was looking at my watch and trying to figure why it was stopped at ten minutes to eight. I was on my back in this shell hole and above me the blue sky kept spinning around and I lay there watching it slow down and finally come to a stop. On the lip of the shell hole were four lovely red poppies. I felt as though I'd been stamped on and kicked in the ribs and at first I thought every bone in my body was broken. But the strangest thing was that I couldn't hear a damn thing. All around me there were shells exploding and bullets whizzing through the air but all I heard was a terrible ringing in my ears. There was something sticky running down the right side of my face and when I touched it I saw it was blood. Other than that, I seemed to be in one piece.

Now this shell hole wasn't a bad place to stay, for the simple reason that, like lightning, shells seldom strike the same spot twice. Then I got two terrible frights. When I turned my head a little to the left I saw a human hand lying not five feet from my face. I recognized the ring on the little finger and knew that Dick Chamberlain had been blown to pieces. The other strange thing was an enormous pair of boots lying near the hand. When I turned my head some more I saw that there were legs in the boots and indeed a whole body lying on its back. The eyes in the enormous head were closed and the hands folded across the stomach, and old Leatherballs looked as though he was having a Sunday nap. I crawled over to him and felt his heart, which was beating as steadily as a baby's. He didn't appear to have a scratch on him, but for the life of me I couldn't arouse him. It was queer. I figure he was blown into the shell hole along with me and Dick Chamberlain, although I couldn't remember seeing him before the explosion.

So I lay there and watched these poppies sway back and forth as the machine-gun fire passed over the shell hole, knocking the petals off one of the flowers. By being extremely cautious I could peer out now and again and see that the whole attack had stalled. It was weird lying there watching a war without hearing anything. Ahead of me about fifty yards I saw Jameson. He'd reached the first coil of German barbed wire and that's where he got hit. And he fell into the wire and was hooked there like a fish on a line. The German gunners poured it into him, so that you saw bits of uniform and flesh being blasted away. Most of the boy's head was shot off, and for the rest of that day the Germans used Jameson's body for target practice whenever they got bored. And there wasn't a damn thing any of us could do about it but watch.

A few of the men sniped away at the Germans from their shell holes but I didn't even have a rifle. I just lay there like a trapped animal with an awful headache and this ringing in my ears. I knew if the Germans counterattacked, all of us lying out there would be either dead or prisoners in a matter of minutes. The whole thing was a ——up and I remember thinking that somebody should damn well pay for this. It was easy enough to be mad at the Germans taking pot shots at poor Jameson, but what about the fat-arsed generals who'd dreamed up this slaughter? Right at that moment they were probably sitting down to bacon and eggs in some château ten miles behind the line. God Almighty, it was enough to madden a fellow as he lay out there under the sun and was shot at by strangers.

Well, the sun climbed the sky and still the British army came on. They came out of the trenches, a fresh wave every couple of minutes, and were mowed down. They say we lost fifty thousand men before noon that day and I can believe it, for I myself saw hundreds die.

It must have been pushing on towards noon, because it was stifling hot and things seemed to let up a bit. Either the generals had changed their minds or they were running out of men, because the attack seemed to be halted. I was also getting some of my hearing back and now and then I could faintly hear a burst of machine-gun fire or a rifle shot. So I was pinned down in no man's land and about the only thing I could do was lie there and hope the Germans didn't counterattack. And maybe with luck, by nightfall I might sneak back to our trenches. But to tell you the truth, there were periods during that day when I wasn't absolutely certain which way were the British lines and which way were the Germans. And I wasn't about to stick up my head and find out.

Maybe some of the battalions took their objectives that day. I've never been interested enough to read about it. But I know there wasn't a hope in hell of us getting past the German front trench, and you could have seen that the minute you stepped out in that field and took a look around. So I lay there and had a drink of water and then dozed off, not knowing whether I'd be bayoneted in my sleep but not really caring either. I know I had a terrible dream. I can't remember it now, but I woke up staring into the sun and I could hear the *tac-tac-tac* of machine-gun fire and it was whistling over my head, because another poppy flower danced back and forth, with the petals shredded and falling over my face. And that left only two poppies. Now the funny thing is, you get superstitious under these circumstances. And I remember thinking, When those damn flowers are all shot away I'm going to get it too.

Just then the grass behind me parted because somebody was wriggling through it and he plunged down the side of the hole with the bullets spitting all around him, and God Almighty, it was Shorty Wilson! He took one look at me and threw his arm around my neck. He was jabbering away and pumping my hand but I couldn't make much sense of his words. It was as if I was down at the bottom of a deep well, so I pointed to my right ear and he nodded and shouted directly into my left ear.

"Bill, old mate. I'm glad to see you. I been lying out there for hours waitin' to make my move. Jesus, I got a beautiful blitey, Bill. Half my kneecap's gone and it hurts like hell. They'll have to take the ——ing leg off for sure. No more bloody war for Shorty Wilson. And you got yours too, eh Bill? A little shell shock. Ah, that'll go away in no time at all. A pretty little nurse will take that away. Listen, Bill. Can you hear me? Tonight after dark we'll slip away. You've got the legs and at least I've still got my wits. Do you understand me, Bill?" I nodded like a simple-minded person. "In a few hours we'll be out of here. By tomorrow morning we'll be on nice clean sheets. With a bit of beef tea in the morning and all the rest of it."

But to tell the truth, Shorty didn't look well. Although he'd been out all morning under the sun, his face was shrunken and pale under his helmet. The sweat stood out on his brow and his eyes were glazed and bloodshot with pain. He pulled on my tunic. "You can see for yourself, Bill, that she'll have to go. Take a look now." He lay back on his elbows and moved one of his legs. The sight was enough to sicken you, the knee all smashed to blood and muscle and bone.

"My gift to my country," he shouted, and laughed. "She'll have to go, though. It'll be wooden-legged Wilson from here on in. But as long as they didn't get the middle leg, eh Bill?" He laughed again and fell back, breathing hard. Then he got up on one elbow and plucked at my sleeve. I turned my good ear to him. "Bill," he says, "I'll tell you the God's honest. I'm not feeling so good. You wouldn't have a drink of water, would you? My canteen is full of rum. I thought it was a smart thing to do this morning, but that ——ing sun is hot and I could use a drink of plain water now." I held my canteen to his lips and all he did was pat my hand before lying back. Then he sat up and stared at Leatherballs lying there. "Well, for Jesus' sakes, that's not old Leatherballs himself, is it? Am I dreaming, Bill? Or have I died and gone to hell and there's old Nick himself. Is that really Leatherballs?" I nodded and told Shorty how I'd tried to waken him. "Well, —— me," says Shorty, lying back. "This is a rum war."

So we lay there through the hot afternoon, sipping rum and water. Shorty grew a little delirious at times and he'd doze and then he'd come around and laugh, shaking his head and beckoning me to hear. "All joking aside, Bill, I think we must be the only ones left in the whole ——ing platoon! Did you see the Lieutenant get his? I lay out there all morning watching those bastards shooting his head away." There were tears in Shorty's eyes. "I never even liked that snotty little bastard, but that's no way to end your days." Shorty was crying and I guessed it was from the pain of his leg. He wasn't in his right head, I could see that. "And what about big Chamberlain?" he asked. "If anybody could survive this ——ing mess, it'll be him. I told you to stick by him, Bill. Where is he, I wonder."

All the time he was talking I pushed Dick's hand under the soil so he wouldn't see it. But Shorty's mind was jumping all over the place. One minute he'd be talking about how he'd like a glass of beer and then he'd say, "I wonder. I wonder. What do you suppose Mr. Haig is doin' right now, Bill? I suppose it must be just tea time. And I imagine he'll be sensible enough to sit in the shade, for that's a ——in' hot day. We wouldn't want old Dugald to get sunstroke, would we? Why, we might even win the war then. God, I'm seeing about five of you, mate!" And he fell back.

I took a handkerchief and dipped it in my canteen and tried to make him a little more comfortable by dabbing his forehead. He wouldn't let me touch his leg, for it was too painful, and anyway the leg was gone. They'd have to take it off. What he didn't seem to realize was the danger of gangrene. Still, there was nothing we could do about it as long as it was daylight.

In the late afternoon our artillery started up another barrage, which was a silly damn thing to do because it only put the wind up the Germans and they fired back and it was no help to anybody. Finally the sun moved behind us and I judged it to be around six o'clock. I figured we had another three hours or so before dark. Shorty had been sleeping, twitching and turning with pain and talking in his sleep. By and by he'd wake up and pat my arm. "By Jesus, Billy, we're lucky blokes. We must be the only ones left. And we got ourselves a couple of bliteys." He raised himself to a sitting position. "It hurts like hell, but if we can just hang on. Listen to this. I've been lyin' here composin' a song in my head.

> *I don't mind a wooden leg*
> *Or even if I have to beg*
> *So long as I'm in Blighty!*

I gave him the last of the rum, because I could see he was failing fast. It seemed to restore his strength, for he says, "It's awfully quiet now, Bill. I wonder what old Fritz is up to?" It *was* quiet too, with only a little gunfire here and there. Well, I paid Shorty little heed but lay back and thought of how hungry I was, not having eaten since early that morning. So I lay there thinking of that and watching a fly bother Leatherballs' nose. Every so often he'd shoo it away with a hand the size of a skillet. But there was no waking him. Shorty edged up over the lip of the shell hole, and then I heard what sounded like a dull plop. Shorty shuddered against me and slipped back down. That's when I noticed the blood leaking into the white, chalky soil. When I rolled Shorty over he was stone dead with a bullet through the eye. I pushed him into one corner of the hole and began to shake like a leaf because just then there was another terrific burst of machine-gun fire overhead and the last two poppies were blasted away.

At this Leatherballs opens his eyes and sits up, shaking his head and using his fingers to clean the ends of his moustaches. "Look here! What the deuce is going on?" he says. "Who is making that infernal racket? Are those damn Boers at it again?" His eyes were yellow as a cat's and clouded. He looked over at me. "Why the devil isn't your tunic properly buttoned, soldier?"

"Beg pardon, sir," I says. "But we're under fire."

"No excuse, no excuse," he says. "What's the meaning of all this? Skulking in the ground like rabbits? Where's the cavalry? We'll run them into the ground. Damned nuisance." He pointed at Shorty. "Take that man's name. I won't have soldiers sleeping on duty. What the devil has got into this army?" He peered at me again. "You're not Loomis. Where the hell is Loomis? Every time I need that man he can't be found. I could use a whiskey and soda right now. What time is it?"

"I don't know, sir. I'd judge it to be close to seven."

"Seven, eh?" he says. "Well, we're over the top at seven-thirty. Pass the word along. And we'll go with pipes lit and walking sticks too. There won't be a Boer within miles, you mark my word."

It wasn't hard to see that his head had been knocked about, so I says, "You're confused, sir. The attack was this morning. We went over this morning!"

"Of course you're confused," he says. "We're not getting the right men for the job. I don't know how they expect us to fight a war with the caliber of men who join the ranks these days. Well, I'm going back

to battalion H.Q. I could stand a bite of breakfast before we go over."
He took off his cap and there was a red rim around his huge bald head.
I remember the slanting sun catching him full in the face and making
his yellow eyes blaze with a strange light. "What's your name, soldier?"
he says to me.

"Farthing, sir," I says.

"Knew a George Farthing once. Killed at Ladysmith. That was a
bad show." He scratched his head with a forefinger before replacing
his cap. "Do you know what, Farthing?"

"Sir?"

"We mustn't grumble."

"No, sir."

"It's bad for morale."

"Yes, sir."

Then damn me if he doesn't lever himself up with this walking
stick and say, "Well, I'm off, Farthing. And button that tunic, man."
And he climbed out of the damn hole and headed straight for the
German trenches.

"Back, sir," I yelled, but he strode forth, as big and juicy a target
as ever was presented to a German machine gunner. As he walked
across that pitted field the sinking sun caught him in a blaze of light
and he looked like some illustration in an old book, maybe an apostle.
I suppose if the Germans had been smart they'd have let him come
through, for he was a lieutenant-colonel, full of information and
strategies. But some hot-head began to pepper poor old Leatherballs,
who just kept walking for a few seconds as though he was immortal
and no steel could penetrate his hide. But finally he staggered a little
and then fell forward, as full of holes as a Swiss cheese. This started
some sniping over to my right and things got pretty lively for about
ten minutes. Then they settled down again and the long day drew to a
close, with the shadows lengthening across the battlefield. Soon the
German lines were in darkness and here and there a flare lighted up
the sky before coming down with that snaky hissing sound.

My head still ached but most of my hearing was restored and now
I had to think about getting out of there. Now, you have to understand
that I was in a confused state of mind if you're to believe what happened to me next. Probably I was suffering from shell shock. How else
could you explain the fact that lying there next to Shorty Wilson's dead
body and Dick Chamberlain's hand I decided to kill General Haig.
I'd go looking for him back in his château and put a bullet through his
head on the principle that somebody in charge should pay for the day's
events. And if the British army wants to send somebody up to Craven
Falls and arrest me, even at this late date, let them damn well come.
Whether I was responsible for my actions at the time, I can't say. All I
know is that I wanted to put a bullet through General Haig's head,
though I hadn't any idea where he was. This much was certain. He
wasn't in any trench dodging machine-gun bullets.

After a time it grew full dark, a beautiful summer night with the last of the swallows swooping over the fields. Here and there you heard rifle fire as some fellow tried to sneak back to his own trenches. I said goodbye to Shorty and slowly eased myself out of that shell hole. Thus began the long trip back to my own trenches, not marching along on my two pins as I'd done that morning, but belly-down and face in the grass like a snake. I say it was a long trip because it took me several hours, though the distance couldn't have been more than a couple of hundred yards. But it was painful and slow because other fellows were doing the same thing and the Germans were on to us and every so often would rake us with machine-gun fire. I remember the bullets one time just grazing my boots. Also, I had to crawl around several shell holes and bodies, some dead and others still dying. Often the poor fellows just cried for their mothers or a drink of water.

As it turned out, I was nearly killed myself about twenty yards from my own trenches by a trigger-happy young fool who was standing sentry duty. His first shot just missed my head by about the span of your fingers. So I croaked, "Don't shoot, you son of a bitch. I'm a friend." And he squeezed off another one that kicked up the dirt in front of my face and I thought to myself, God Almighty, this is just great. Last a whole day out in that shell hole with half the German army throwing crap at you and then a few yards from safety get plugged by one of your own men. But then I heard voices and one of them sounded sharp and in authority, and I think that was the only time in my life I thanked God for an officer, because this voice asked me to identify myself, which I did. Then I was ordered to crawl towards them. When I reached the trench the lieutenant pulled me in and of course I was some kind of hero, with everybody slapping my back and offering me cigarettes and rum, which was welcome. I told this lieutenant that I'd seen my battalion commander killed and he wrote this down on a piece of paper and told me to report to my battalion headquarters.

The whole thing was in terrible confusion, with fresh troops moving up the trenches and those of us who'd survived the day trying to get back down. But I wasn't about to look for my battalion headquarters. I was looking to get back to that lush country behind the lines where Haig was staying. Along the way I picked up a rifle from a sleeping soldier, which was a dirty trick, because he'd catch hell the next day. But I needed a gun. Now in all this muddle, nobody paid me too much mind. Most could see the blood on my face and the state of my uniform, so they knew I'd had a rough day and usually made way for me to pass. I remember one young fellow anxiously grabbing my sleeve and asking, "How was it out there today, dad?" I just looked at him, and that was all the answer he needed.

I finally got out of the support trenches and onto a road, which was choked with lorries and horses and men. I jumped on the back of this lorry and rode to the outskirts of a village, where they'd set up Casualty Clearing Stations. There I left the lorry and walked down a lane. Nobody missed me in the dark and I wandered through an orchard and went for three or four miles, making a broad semicircle around that village. Then I lay down in a country cemetery, just as I'd done one night years before when my sister Annie chased me away from her door with buckshot. I was so tired I fell asleep right away, with the guns booming off in the distance and the sky glowing here and there with light.

When I awakened, the sun was shining and the birds were singing and I could still hear the dull booming of the heavy guns. I was confused for a while and so I sat against this tombstone and counted my fingers and said my name to myself. Had I gone through the battle or had that all been a dream? Was Shorty dead? And Dick Chamberlain? Had I really seen old Leatherballs stroll to his death with a walking stick in a blaze of heavenly light? It was damned strange, and then I reached into my tunic pocket and pulled out this note for battalion headquarters. Then I remembered why I was there, and I set off across this field.

It was pretty countryside, and you'd never have guessed there was a war going on nearby. After a couple of hours I came to this big country house. A stone wall and huge oak trees encircled the grounds. It wasn't as impressive as Hallow's End, but it wasn't bad either. There was any number of army lorries and staff cars parked in the driveway and a little sentry box was set up near the front gate. The British flag fluttered from a pole stuck into the grass by the front door. Had I by sheer accident stumbled onto General Haig's headquarters? To this day I cannot give you an answer to that question. More than likely, it wasn't. The coincidence is simply too remarkable. However, that doesn't matter, because at the time I thought it was Haig's headquarters and damn it all, perhaps it was.

Anyway, what I did was climb this stone wall and make my way across the grounds, hoping for a shot at Haig. I didn't care who saw me and I marched right across the grass. As I came around behind the house I saw a number of figures in white. They were standing around in little bunches and now and again some of them would run across the grass. Standing to one side and watching these white figures was a group of officers. As I drew closer I could see that they were observing a game of that English baseball. Then one joker yelled out, "Who is that man on the field? Say, you there! Get off the field." Now I turned to look at him and even though he was a staff officer I had a mind to tell him where to go. But I shouldn't have turned my head, because then I would have seen this ball coming. As it was, I looked up at the last second and the ball was dropping from the sky like a dead bird. I can't say for sure but I may have tried to reach for it, but it seemed to change direction at the last minute. Then it hit me flush between the eyes and out went the light of day.

27

REVEILLE

When I awakened the sunlight was streaming through a tall window, raising dust motes in the air. It seemed to be another fine summer morning, with the sun still low in the sky. I lay there taking in my surroundings and noting that I was comfortably looked after, being in my own private room. The sheets on the bed were clean. There was a dresser and a washstand, clothes cupboard, and everything as neat as a pin. On a table in the corner was a small brown box with a glass face on it. It looked to me like some kind of fancy clock. Well, I said to myself, maybe I've taken a harder knock than I first thought and they moved me to a base hospital.

I felt all right, though for some reason I seemed to have put on a few pounds. As an infantryman I'd been lean and fit. Now I had quite a little belly on me and the flesh was gray and soft. However, I swung my legs out of bed and, walking to the window, looked down on a nice residential street. Of course I figured I was back in England, though it struck me as queer that I wouldn't remember arriving. The street below was mostly deserted except for a truck. The driver was unloading a big chunk of ice and carrying it up the steps of a house. The truck looked queer to me, bigger and more streamlined than I remembered. Then a couple of automobiles went by and that struck me as peculiar too, for they didn't sit high on the road and weren't box-shaped.

There was an alarm clock ticking away on the dresser and it said five minutes to six, which probably accounted for the fact that everything was so quiet. Then I thought to myself, If that's an alarm clock, then what in hell is that brown box sitting on the table? It had a couple of knobs on it and some figures on a dial, so I turned one of these and a light went on, with this drone starting up. It looked crazy to me, so I left it and went over to the closet. Hanging on the racks were a couple of sports jackets and a pair or two of pants, which also struck me as strange. Where the hell was my uniform? Then, let me tell you, I glanced in this mirror on the dresser, and God Almighty, I nearly fainted dead away. The reason for this was that my hair was mostly gray, except for a bit over the ears. And my face! It wasn't exactly too seamed with lines, but I looked a good bit older. But what really shook me down to the rivets was I now looked like the spitting image of my father at about the time in his life when he'd run off with Miss Boswell. So I stood there with my mouth open stroking the gray bristles on my chin and holding on to the dresser for support.

Then I sat on the edge of the bed to compose myself when damn me if the room didn't suddenly fill up with the sound of a marching band playing "God Save the King"! To say it startled me would be an understatement, and it took me a while to discover that this music was coming from that little brown box on the table. At first I thought this. The Germans have won the war and I'm being held in some kind of prison hospital where they torture and experiment on people. I'd heard stories in the army about such places. So I got out of bed and gingerly approached this box and turned it off. But the whole experience gave me such a fright that I lay in bed and listened to my heart thumping for the longest time.

Then I must have dozed again, because when I woke up Findlater was sitting on a chair with his legs crossed, playing a game with this wormy old derby hat, rolling it up and down his sleeve. I watched him for a few minutes behind half-closed eyelids. He didn't look too prosperous in his shiny blue serge suit. There was cardboard stuffed into a hole on the bottom of his right boot and what looked like a little shoe blacking had been applied to the holes in his dark socks. His face hadn't seen a razor in days, and the gray stubble was streaked with dirt. His hair was also gray and thinning, though it was still hard to put an age on him. And he was still heavy too, with a good-sized gut, though he looked powerful enough in this tight-fitting suit. Well, I pretended to be waking up and when he saw me coming around he clamped the hat on the back of his head and leaned forward saying, "That's it, old pal. Wake up now! The sleeping fox catches no poultry!"

"Hello, Findlater," I says. "It's good to see you again. How are things?"

He looked at me strangely and then grinned. "Then you recognize me, pal?"

"Of course I do," I says. "Where the hell am I, anyway?"

Findlater grasped my hand. "Praise the Lord, you've come around. Bill, this does my heart the world of good. I've been waiting for this day."

"Findlater," I says, "what's going on?"

Findlater fingered his derby and looked down at the floor. "What's the last thing you remember, pal?"

"Well," I says, "let's see. I took a crack on the head on Saturday.

No, wait. That would have been Sunday morning. That's right. Sunday morning, because I slept Saturday night in that graveyard. And next day I walked a couple of miles to this big fancy house. There were some fellows all dressed in white playing a game of that English baseball. What do you call it?"

"I believe the game's called cricket," says Findlater.

"That's right. Cricket. Well, damn me! I must have caught one of those cricket balls on the head. And that would have been Sunday morning. July the second. What I can't figure out is what in the hell you're doing here, Findlater. Where are we, anyway?"

Findlater sighed a little and said, "You're in the Weary Warrior's Nursing Home, Bill. In Toronto, Canada."

"Toronto!" I says. You can appreciate how this news amazed me. "Well, for Christ's sakes. I don't even remember crossing the ocean!"

"I'm not surprised," says Findlater. "It was some time ago."

"Some time ago, eh?" I says. "What's the date today, anyway?"

"It's July the first, Bill," says Findlater.

"It can't be July the first," I says, sitting up in bed. "I was hit by that ——ing cricking ball on July the second!"

"I'm afraid it's another year, pal," Findlater said, sticking a finger through a hole in his hat.

"Another year!" I says. "Do you mean to say I've lost a whole year?"

"Mind yourself now, Bill. Take it easy."

"To hell with that," I says. "What year is it, anyway?"

"Nineteen thirty-two," says Findlater. It was barely a croak.

"Nineteen what, for God's sakes!"

"You're pale, Bill," says Findlater, standing up. "Lie down there for a while and I'll get you a glass of water."

But all I could do was look up at the ceiling and say, "Holy Christ! Are you telling me the truth? That I've lost sixteen years from my life? Why, that would make me . . ."

"Fifty-two today, Bill," says Findlater, patting my hand. "Happy Birthday!"

I think a tear rolled down my cheek, and Findlater seemed to make some kind of clucking sound in his throat. "You've been a mystery to the medicos all these years, Bill. Why, they tell me they've had famous doctors from all over the world here to visit you in the hopes of bringing you around. And here you come to just when your old pal Cass is making his annual visit."

"Your annual visit?" I says weakly, for I was feeling poor.

"Yes sir, Bill. I've visited you every year on your birthday since 1922 when I found out where they were keeping you. It took a little investigation. You've been here since 1917."

"Holy God in Heaven," I says. "And I don't remember a damn thing."

"Well, you must have taken a nasty crack on the old bean! The doctors in here would like to write a book about you and they been waitin' for you to come around. But, Bill, I was kind of hoping that when you got back in your right head, you might hit the road with me like in the old days."

"Findlater," I says, "what about the war?"

"What about it, Bill?" he asks.

"Well, who the hell won? Or was it a draw? Or what?"

"Oh, we won it. In late 1918. November, I think. The good old American army got in there at the end and we polished off those Germans in no time at all. But everybody is friends again now."

He handed me a glass of water and I wet my lips. "Well, how are things going anyway, Findlater? I mean with you?"

"Well, you can see that for yourself," he says, opening his coat to a patched vest. "My fortunes, you might say, are in temporary decline. But I ain't complainin'. You got to think positive if you want to get ahead in this world. That's the trouble in this day and age. Everybody's bitchin' like hell, while what you got to do is look on the bright side of things."

"You always were an optimist, Findlater," I says.

"You got to be, Bill. Even in these times. I don't suppose, now that you've waked up to your old self, you know anything about this here Depression we're into?"

"Not a damn thing," I says. "What's a depression?"

Findlater pulled out a flask from under his coat. "Have a snort of this, Bill," he says. "Though make it a small one, for it's not the best that money can buy. In fact, it'll take a fair-sized bite out of your throat if you don't pay attention." I swallowed a little of what appeared to be a mixture of iodine and shoe polish. I coughed and handed back the flask. Findlater shook his head and grinned. "Don't smoke for ten minutes or you'll blow us to doom." Then he himself took a good pull of this stuff and put the flask back in his coat. He shook his head some more and says, "Everything's gone kind of haywire in the last couple of years. Business is bad and there's no work around. Some of the banks is closed up. It's a helluva note. What a shame you didn't wake up five or ten years ago, though. That's when the party was going full blast. Now it's hangover time.

"Oh, this Depression is bad, Bill. It's all over America. And up here in Canada too. And the foreigners are having a rough time of it over in Europe. *Heavy lies the head that wears the homburg.* Everybody's mad or complainin'. Why, people were jumping out of windows there for a while. Friends of mine, some of them. Worth a million on Wednesday and wiped out on Friday. But hell's bells, jumping out of windows don't do no good. Take me for instance. In 1926 I owned a string of gravel pits and a good part of a coal mine in the state of Kentucky. I had the crushed-stone market east of the Alleghenies in my right pocket. And most of the road inspectors by the left ball. I had three houses and a penthouse in the Waldorf-Astoria Hotel in downtown New York City. Would you call me a liar if I told you that three years ago I owned forty-two pairs of shoes? I hobnobbed with movie starlets, politicians, sporting heroes. I knew them all. And now look at me! I haven't got a pot to piss in nor a window to throw it out.

"But did you see me jumping from the fifteenth floor of the Cornstarch Building just because the grapes turn a little sour? Hell, no! What you got to do is laugh in the teeth of the gale. Trim your sails accordin' to the direction of the wind and ride her out. I'll make another pile. They can't keep a good man down. And America'll get back on her pins too, you'll see. But people got to think positive. That's been my stock in trade, you know, Bill. Thinkin' positive."

All the time he was talking I was wondering about Sally. What had happened to her over the past sixteen years? Findlater took a deep breath and then suddenly stopped talking. He didn't say a word but sat there, leaning forward in the chair as though he was studying the floor. Maybe he was thinking of all those shoes he once owned. Anyway, I said to him, "What about Sally, Findlater?"

Findlater came out of his studying mood and looked at me. "You know, Bill, I tried to visit you each year on your birthday. Made a little promise to myself. Because we were old pals and you don't desert old pals even when they're out of their head. That's the way I look at things. Oh, there were a couple of years when I missed, to be truthful. Usually I was over in Europe making a deal with those Frenchmen or Eye-talions. You can't always rush things when you're dealing with those fellows, for they'll take the hair right off your backside if you're not careful. But I didn't miss many years, Bill, I'm proud to say. And I always hoped you'd come around to your senses and then you could rejoin me. Hell, with the money I had you could have lived like a king. Told me what books to read and how to speak the right way. I'm still an old diamond in the rough, you know. But lookit here. It's not too late. Now that you got your right senses back, we can clear out of this place. Hit the road together. What do you say?"

"Maybe," I says. "But never mind any of that for now. What about Sally?"

"You know, that's a remarkable woman, that Sally. You can sure pick them, Bill. That girl has class. Me, I never could seem to be attracted to anything but cheap little trinkets. But that Sally. Do you know, at first I thought she was just another of your run-of-the-mill dance hall girls, especially when she hooked up with that peg-legged bastard up in Dawson. But no sir. That woman's had a rough life and she's come up smelling like a flower shop. Course, when I think on it, I might have knowed you'd be a judge of character. That's why I'd like you to come along with me, Bill. I like to travel with an educated man. There's an awful lot of riffraff on the road these days."

"But what about that English lord she married?" I asks.

"Oh, dead and buried, Bill. Years ago. Good God, the man would be nearly a hundred years old if he was still around. No sir, he passed away back just after the war ended. That war was something now, wasn't it? You remember me saying I thought you was on the losing end. Well, I felt that way at first. I was sure the Germans would win. They had the damnedest rubber tires you've ever seen back in 1914. Years ahead of anything we had. But then I changed my tune when we got into it. We gave them a pretty good lickin' in the end. Those were some of the best years of my life. I made four hundred thousand dollars in scrap metal alone in 1918. Old bedposts. Chamber pots. Stovepipe lids. It's amazing what people throw away." He was staring at the floor again.

"Did she remarry?" I asks.

"Who?" says Findlater.

"Sally, for Christ's sakes," I says.

"Oh, Sally." And he roused himself. "Oh, I couldn't say, Bill. I wouldn't like to speculate. But you know. She'd been burned twice with the old marriage poker. And maybe she learned something. The old fellow's family treated her like hell. There was some great big long court case and she didn't get a cent of his money. You can't trust those Englishmen, with their snotty accents and their butlers. They'll steal you blind. Martin Rooney always said that and he was right. You remember Martin, don't you, Bill? Now there was a boy with the gift of tongues! He could have made a fortune if he'd lasted. I made ten thousand dollars net on the pincushions alone. I couldn't begin to tell you what the breadboards brought in. What a shame he passed on. There's some truth in that sayin' about the good ones goin' young. Rooney was a talented man."

"What happened to him?" I asked.

"He was rakin' it in, Bill. Had the world by the short hairs. I brought him over to America for one of these reading tours. By then I had his pomes on half the kitchen walls of America. Canada too. By God, Martin did a cute job on the breadboxes. What was it now? Something about bread being the staff of life.

> *When troubles are plenty*
> *And your worries are rife*
> *Look on this loaf*
> *As the staff of life!*

We had that in varnished pine with a painting of some stacked wheat and the words done up in a kind of fancy scroll. Seventy-five cents, and you couldn't keep them in the stores at Christmas."

"What happened to the man, Findlater?" I asked.

"He died from drink, Bill. I'd never have taken Martin for a drinker, but he was partial to it on the sly. Took an overdose of bathtub gin in Philadelphia one afternoon in twenty-one! And the hall was sold out for that night too! A real shame." He was staring at his boot again, lost in thought.

"You still haven't told me much about Sally, Findlater."

"Who?" he says absently. "Oh, Sal. Well, as I say, that old fellow's family treated her like dirt. Put her through a long court case which she couldn't afford and then left her without a plugged nickel. That's when she turned up on my doorstep one night. That would have been maybe twenty-two. Possibly early twenty-three. Anyways, we was havin' a party. The goddamnedest bunch of people you ever saw! Movie types and sportin' heroes. Jack Dempsey was there, I think. He used to be the heavyweight champion of the world, and a first-class fellow. I used to spar with him just for the hell of it. And Rudolph Valentino. I'm sure he was there. Of course, you wouldn't know any of those people, Bill, but this Valentino was a big movie actor back then. He's dead now, poor fellow! The women were nuts about him. They'd tear the clothes off his hind end if they caught him alone out on the street. He made a fortune in money out in Hollywood. Had all this slicked-down black hair with a lot of pomade on it and was thin as a fence picket. I'll tell you, he put me in mind of one of those river men who pole you along the streets of that Eye-talion city where they ain't got any roads, just these streets of water. What's it called? Vienna?

"Anyways, I met their head beetle Muscleenee a couple of years ago. We was poled down this canal and I sold him five thousand Springfield rifles. Without the springs, of course, and last used in the Spanish-American conflict. He's still waitin' for the ammunition, but I didn't bother to tell him that they don't make that caliber anymore. You got to get up pretty early in the mornin' to beat those guineas. They're a foxy bunch. But then, so am I. Or was! What in hell was I talkin' about?" He was staring at his boot again.

"The party," I says. "And Sally? What about Sally?"

"Oh, yes! That party! Well, we're goin' pretty strong there when along about midnight there comes a rappin' on the door. Usually I had my English butler open the door but he wasn't anywheres to be found, so I opens it myself. And standin' there in this moldy thin old cloth coat is a woman. She's pretty enough but skinny as a garden hoe and faded right out, with no rouge or face paint or nothin'. Right off I took her for a tramp. Somebody tryin' to bust in on the high society. Hopin' to catch a fellow in a good humor. Well, I was all set to send her packin' when she breaks into tears and says, 'Don't you remember me, Cass?' So I looks a little closer and even with her undernourished and peaked appearance there was no mistakin' those eyes, so I says, 'Good Lord in the sky. It isn't really you, is it, Sally?' And she just falls into my arms and cries like a baby. And, Bill, I could feel her ribs right through that coat. She'd stepped off the boat from England a couple of days before and had been wanderin' the streets lookin' for me. Finally located me in a gossip column, where I turned up quite frequently in those days. So there she was, a pitiful sight with those ribs stickin' out. A beautiful woman like that. Here, take this and have a blow." And he offered me this crumpled-up gray rag. But I shook my head and used the sheets.

"Now," he says, "you can turn off the taps, because this story has a happy endin'. All stories have happy endings if you look on the bright side of things. So listen. I took Sal inside. More or less snuck her in, because she did look like she just climbed out of a coal bin. And I hustled her into one of the bathrooms in that place. Hell, I had six of them. And I got ahold of a girl there to get some perfume and bubble bath and fetch out a gown and some jewels. Those girls would have done anythin' for me in those days. I was always tuckin' hundred-dollar bills between their titties or pullin' fifties out of their ears. Just after the war there, I studied a book on magic. Sent away for it, and it learned you how to do those things. I thought it would be a good way to break the ice at parties and generally win friends and influence people. Anyway, I got Sally fixed up and got some grub into her and a glass or two of champagne and by and by that old Sally smile came back. And I took her into the party. Most of the people were fallin' asleep. But when they saw this girl, pale and thin though she was, enter that room, they knew they were in the company of somebody special. And what I did was, I had Sally go and sit up there on the grand piano while a fellow sat down and counted it a privilege to play for her. And it was the same Sally Butters of old! And, Bill, I'll give you the next five dollars I find if you can guess what song that gal sang."

" 'Beautiful Dreamer,' " I says, with tears in my eyes.

"I owe you five, Bill, because that's absolutely correct. 'Beautiful Dreamer,' and God didn't she render it in the sweetest voice a man's ever heard! I'll tell you this much. When that girl finished her song, there wasn't a dry eye in the room. Even Valentino was blowin' his nose with a perfumed handkerchief, which, by the way, he gave to her, along with an invitation to accompany him west on the next train."

I sat up at that. "Did she go? These Italians are fast workers!"

"You're telling me! But the answer to your question is no. However, that evening was the beginnin' of a reversal of fortune for our Sally, Bill. Naturally I helped her get back on her feet. For old times' sake. Cass Findlater never deserts an old friend. I got her a suite of rooms and a new wardrobe and a little spendin' money. Before long she'd put some weight on and was attractin' attention. After all, there was a woman who'd been married to a Klondike gambler and an English lord. It wasn't long before she was goin' to parties and balls and the like of that. I don't want to make your life miserable, Bill, but all the time you were in here playin' checkers that girl was seen on the arms of famous baseball players and movie actors. But like I said, she shied away from marriage. But you know, whenever I'd bump into her at a nightclub or some gala event we'd always talk about you. She always had a soft spot in her heart for Bill Farthing. 'My own true love.' That's how she put it to me one night. So I said to her, 'Lookit here, Sal. Why don't you come up with me to Toronto on Bill's next birthday and see him? Maybe if he sees you he'll get his senses back. And she did come up too!"

"Here?" I says. "Sally was here to see me?"

"Correct. That might have been nineteen and twenty-five. Maybe twenty-six. The years went by in a hurry there for a while. Course, you didn't recognize her and she just sat there with tears in her eyes. She never come back. Said she couldn't stand to see you lost like that. But she told me she'd always love the Bill Farthing of old. And that was spoken by a woman who'd been escorted around by some of the great men of the age."

"But where is she now, for God's sakes!" I asks.

"Bill, I wish I knew. This old Depression caught up with her too, I suppose. We parted company in New York just after twenty-nine. She'd been invited to a big weddin' down south someplace. We said we'd get together before long, but I don't know. Maybe the weddin' party lasted longer than she figured. It wasn't unusual, you know, for some of those parties to go on for months. Anyways, we just never managed to get together again and I ain't seen her since. But my God, she was a beautiful woman, Bill. She seemed to improve with the years." Findlater sighed and stood up and stretched his back. I heard a tearing sound and when he looked behind his left arm, the cloth had given way on about a nine-inch front. "They just don't put the material into clothes these days the way they used to.

"But listen, Bill. I'm sure Sal is makin' out all right. The job now is to get you the hell out of here. Get some clothes on you and start livin' again. I ain't sayin' it's the best time to go about it, but we'll see good times again. Why, they might be just up the street and around the corner. The trick is to be there when it happens. Well, looky here now!" He opened the closet door and looked at the clothes. "This'll get us goin'. And the rest will fetch us a dollar or two at the pawn shop." He looked over at me and then broke into a little shuffle, his tattered boots scraping the floor. He finished his dance by rolling the derby down his arm and catching it with his other hand. "Come on now," he says. "You've already lost sixteen years. You've no more time to waste."

Well, I thought to myself, the man is right. What in hell did I want to stick around that hospital for, answering a lot of foolish questions just to satisfy some doctor's ambition to write a book about me? As though I was some kind of experimental monkey in a cage waiting to be examined. The thing to do was to get out and live. Make up for all that lost time when, according to Findlater, the most exciting thing I ever did was play checkers. So I got dressed and Findlater put the rest of the clothes and anything else of value, including the window curtains, in an old carpetbag. "It'll buy us a potato or two" was how he put it.

I asked him about the brown box. "That's called a radio, Bill. They invented it a few years ago and now you get music and people talkin' all the time. Oh, there's a number of things goin' on that you'll have to learn about. It's a new world. We'll have to get you out and give you a feel of the times. Maybe a feel of something else too, if we're lucky. Sixteen years without a hump is no joke, by God. Let's hit the road."

28

ON THE ROAD

Now YOU MIGHT WONDER about this. Did I just walk out of that hospital after all those years without so much as saying goodbye to the doctors or my fellow patients? Well, I did. After all, they were complete strangers to me. I remember it was a baking hot day and many of the streets were empty owing to the fact that it was Canada's national holiday. As we got closer to downtown we heard band music and then we saw the crowds standing on the sidewalk watching a parade. There was a number of hecklers in this crowd, all holding up placards which said "We're Veterans. Where's the Work?" I couldn't make head nor tail of that. Then some fellow handed us a pamphlet printed in red ink which announced a Communist revolution was taking place and he invited us to join. Then a couple of big cops came by waving their sticks and telling us to move on, which we did in a hurry.

On a side street we went into this restaurant. Findlater ordered a cup of hot tea with extra hot water. Then he shook about eight blobs of tomato ketchup into this hot water. "Makes a reasonable soup, Bill," he says to me. I was looking out the fly-specked window at the street. I couldn't get over the size of the automobiles, which everybody now called cars. The other thing that amazed me was the absence of horses. You saw one here and there pulling a rag-and-bone cart, but when I'd left Canada back in the early summer of '14 the streets were full of horses. Findlater was still thinking about those cops in the crowd. "These bad times have brought out the worst in them, Bill," he says. "I don't know whether it's all these radicals runnin' around botherin' people or whether they're just tryin' to hold on to their jobs, but most of them are as mean as a starved rattlesnake. They'd rather give you a lick with their truncheon than eat a dish of beef stew. Look at that." He took off his derby and, bending over, showed me his head. The scalp through the gray hairs had an ugly purple welt.

"Got that outside Detroit on my way up here. Of course, Detroit is a particularly ugly son of a bitch of a town. But I was mindin' my business. Walkin' along a stretch of highway, which, by the way, I'd actually contracted for ten years ago. Walkin' along this highway, mindin' my own business, when a patrol car comes along. Now, I hadn't ate a bite in a couple of days and was weak as a kitten. So the patrol car stops and these two cops get out and walk over to me. Both of them big bastards over two hundred pounds. I'm sittin' on a stone by the side of the road restin' my dogs. 'What the —— do you think you're doing, bub?' one of them says to me. 'Nothin', Officer,' I says. 'Just restin'.' 'You can't rest on state property,' he says. 'Move it along, you lazy son of a whore.' 'Yes, sir. Right away, sir,' I says, for you got to be polite to them, Bill. You've got to give them the old coolie smile, because one bit of back talk and they'll lay on the wood.

"Then what happens? This guy's partner decides to take a leak. And he looks me over, standin' there with his meat hanging' out, and he says, 'Do you want to earn a quarter, you good-for-nothing son of a bitch?' Other fellow laughs, of course. So I says, 'I'm always in the market for employment, Officer.' They both laugh at this and the fellow waves his pecker at me and says, 'Give this a good kissin' and you got yourself a nice twenty-five-cent piece.' 'Well, Officer,' I says, 'if it's all the same to you, I'd rather not.' Well, he buttons up his breeches, thank the good Lord, and then his partner, just for the hell of it, mind you, gives me this lick over the back of the head with his stick. 'If I wasn't in a hurry,' he says, 'I'd ram it up your ass, you Commonist bastard! We'll be back down this road in about half an hour and you'd better make yourself scarce.' And, pal, I did. Hid in a culvert till nightfall, then lit out across some fields, stayin' off the main roads. But, you know, the thing that hurt me most was them callin' me a Commonist. Me, an American businessman down on my luck.

"But those cops can be rough! I'm just givin' you an idea of what we're up against, so you won't think it's goin' to be any first-class ticket on the *Century* with niggers shinin' our shoes and servin' hot soup in the dinin' car. Speakin' of trains, I might add that those Michigan troopers was just a bunch of boy scouts compared to the cops you'll find workin' for the railways. They're the worst by a country mile. The toughest, meanest, most miserablest man I've ever met in two years of criss-crossing this continent was a feller out in the province of Saskatchewan. Right in this fair land of yours. He worked in the Regina freight yards for the Canadian Pacific Railway. About seven feet tall and half again as wide. Wore boots with spurs on them, and one night I saw him kick a fourteen-year-old boy half to death. Yes sir, there's a lot of meanness around and it's because of this damn Depression." He put the spoons into his pocket. "We better get down to those freight yards. These days it's just like Grand Central Station in some of those places. Half the damn country is ridin' the rods. You'll soon see."

We were down on King Street abreast of the King Edward Hotel when this big Packard limousine pulled up to the front entrance. The chauffeur stepped out smartly and opened the back door. At the same time the hotel doorman came running down the steps. Together they hauled out a wheelchair and then the two of them lifted out this lady. Her hair was snow white, though she didn't look too old, maybe my own age or a year or two younger. Her face was unlined and she had that well-kept look of rich people who don't indulge in too many fleshly pleasures like smoking and drinking and staying up nights. Of course I recognized Esther Easterbrook right away, and not only that but I still had the little gold penknife she'd given me as a Christmas present years before.

Now, if you think I went up and introduced myself and that out of all that she offered Findlater and me a job, then you've been reading too many fairy tales. No sir. I knew it wouldn't be right for a bum and a stranger like me to make myself known to a lady like that. What's the point in embarrassing people? But I'll tell you what did happen. As we passed by Esther called out to us in the sweetest voice, "Excuse me there. You men."

Findlater and I stopped and he looked at me as much as to say, Is she talking to us? What have we done wrong now? That's another thing about those times. You were always going around feeling guilty over nothing. Anyway, Findlater took off his derby and said, "Was you addressin' us, Ma'am?"

And Esther fixed us with those beautiful clear blue eyes and says, "I don't suppose you men have jobs, have you?"

"No, Ma'am," says Findlater, smelling a handout.

And he was right too, for Esther opened the clasp of this little silver purse, took out a dollar bill and handed it to me, as I was closest. "At least that will get the both of you a decent meal," she says.

"Thank you," I muttered, and Findlater made a little bow.

It was hard to tell whether he was mocking her or not. I know I didn't care much for it, but he says, "We're grateful for your Christian heart, Ma'am."

And Esther just shook her beautiful white head and said in the saddest voice, "What a pity that men like you can't find work." Then she waved to the chauffeur and he and the doorman carried her up the steps and into the hotel.

Not very many rich people thought the way Esther did. She was a genuine lady, even if she did have too much money for one person. Of course, I didn't say anything to Findlater about knowing her. I figured he might want me to hit her up for money and I wasn't going to do that. So we stood there for a minute or two, Findlater amazed by our sudden good fortune and me amazed too, but more at the passage of the years and the peculiar things that happen to people during a lifetime. Findlater kept kissing the dollar bill over and over, saying, "Why, that sweet little old lady! With this and what we can get for that radio, I think we might soon treat ourselves to a bottle of decent whiskey. I knew you were going to change my luck, pal."

Just then the doorman came out, his face all red. "All right now," he says. "You two got your handout. More than you probably deserve, too. So just move it along. This is the King Edward Hotel you're standing in front of."

"I know where I'm standin'," says Findlater, "and it may surprise you to know I've stayed in these premises too. Not so long ago I pressed money into your greedy little palm for openin' that very door."

The doorman snickered. "Sure you did, Buster. Now move it along or I'll call a cop."

"We're on our way, Captain," says Findlater. "But there's one thing I'd like to warn you against."

"Like what?" says the doorman, sneering.

And Findlater says, "Just stop sleepin' with your mother, because you're producing a family of half-wits."

Then we got away from there in a hurry and wandered down near the harbor. Some of this area was familiar to me from my first days in Toronto. We spent the rest of that afternoon and most of the early evening sitting on a bench watching the holiday crowds come and go as the excursion boats and the ferries went back and forth to Centre Island. The sun shone and the water sparkled, and though it was hot, there was a mild breeze. In general, I felt glad to be out of that hospital. On the railing of the ferry men in shirtsleeves looked down at the water, some of them wondering whether they should jump, I suppose. I noticed that men weren't wearing as many hard straw hats as I'd remembered and the kids seemed noisier and worse behaved. Of course, that could have been because I was older. Shortly after we sat down Findlater fell asleep, with his arms folded across his chest and the derby over his eyes.

Now Findlater, as you've probably gathered by now, was never exactly normal in the old days. But now nearly twenty years later, he acted even more peculiar at times. I've already mentioned how in the middle of a conversation he'd seem to lose himself and spend the longest time staring at his boot. Nothing too unusual in that, I suppose. But that first day out, a couple of other things happened that made me wonder about Findlater. He sure wasn't his old self. For instance, as he slept he did a queer thing. At one point he sat straight up, pushed his derby back on his head, and shook his finger at some imaginary person. Then he settled back into sleep and started to mutter about devils. I bent closer to listen but couldn't make anything out of it.

The other thing happened just about dusk. That evening the sun went down in flames. The sky to the west was a raw orange and the darkness just folded over everything. There was maybe a dozen of us crouched behind some boxcars waiting for this freight. It kept shunting back and forth, gathering cars, its big headlight traveling up and down the rails. As I stood there, it put me in mind of poor Jack Gillies, who'd lost his life probably not too far from where I was actually standing.

By and by this freight got its load together, and as the brakeman waved his lantern the train slowly started its haul westward, the engine throwing black smoke into the sky. We were lucky because she was not only hauling sealed boxcars but about a dozen loaded coal cars. Not the best ride in the world, as I soon discovered, but better than flying along at fifty miles an hour on top of the train. Well, as these coal cars started to pass us, men broke out running, their feet crunching on the gravel. They were soon swinging themselves up on the side ladders, and Findlater said to me, "All right, let's go, Bill. Here's your first ride on the fresh air express. Keep your legs apart and, mind you, don't stumble or they'll put what's left of you in a shoe box."

I was surprised at how fast Findlater could move, considering his size and age, but soon I was running right along behind him. Findlater took hold of the railing and swung himself upwards, scrambling over the edge. I followed. Being slight and wiry, I've always been a bit on the nimble side, so although I wasn't used to this kind of exercise I made it all right and soon found myself sitting on a pile of coal with the wind in my face. There were half a dozen fellows at the other end of the car. Then the train sent a long whistle into the night and Findlater picked up a piece of coal and hefted it in his hand. "Number one Pennsylvania anthracite, Bill. That's nut coal you're sittin' on. You can bank down your furnace with this stuff and she'll go all night."

"Did you really own a coal mine, Findlater?" I asks. "Or are you kidding me?"

He put up a blackened hand. "As the good Lord is my judge, I did, Bill. A good part of one, anyway. Course, it was mostly bunker coal. For ships, you know. But this stuff is number one. I wonder what it's fetchin' a ton now."

Just then there came the sound of pounding feet on the gravel of the roadbed and, looking over the side, we saw a skinny young fellow reaching out a hand for the ladder rung. The train was picking up speed and this poor fellow was losing strength. I reached down to give him a hand, when Findlater pulled back my arm and shouts down in the gathering wind, "You got a ticket there, bub?"

"Help me," the fellow cries, and says something else that I can't hear. I can only just make out this skinny white hand on the ladder.

"Findlater!" I yells. "For Christ's sakes. Let's give this man a hand!"

Findlater was looking down. "If you just wait till nine tomorrow, pal, there's a special goin' through. Dinin' car privileges included."

"Give him a hand there, you bastards," says one of the fellows in the car, scrambling over the coal towards us on his hands and knees. He knelt beside us and expertly pulled this young fellow aboard. Then he looked at us and shook his head before the two of them crawled back to the other end of the car.

I was so shocked by Findlater's behavior that I just stared at him. He was grinning and digging a little hole for himself in the coal. "I didn't like that feller's looks, Bill," he says to me. "You know, you can't be too careful these days. *A man is judged by the company he keeps.* An educated man like you should know that."

Then one of the fellows at the other end of the car threw a piece of coal, which whistled by us in the dark. "You sons of bitches," he yells. "You could have helped that man."

Findlater cupped his hands to his mouth and shouted, "Keep the peace there, neighbor, and remember you're throwin' away good anthracite. A few pieces like that could keep a poor man warm most of the night."

"Bastards!" somebody else yelled.

They seemed to be all bunched together trying to keep warm. It may have been a summer night, but it can get breezy and cool in the open like that, moving along at forty miles an hour. Findlater didn't say anything for about five minutes and I thought he'd gone to sleep, which worried me a little because I wasn't too sure our traveling companions wouldn't come over and start something. Perhaps even throw us off. Then Findlater startled me by saying, "Don't worry about those fellers, Bill. They won't try anything now. Most men are yellow as a crow's foot. You'll learn that soon enough. They like to talk, but they're short on action." Although I was now fifty-two Findlater seemed to treat me like the kid I'd been back in the nineties. It made me wonder. But another thing appeared certain. Findlater wasn't the same man who'd helped Sam Dowd back in Seattle in '97.

After that he fell asleep and I hunched up my knees and watched the huddle of dark figures at the other end of the car. They seemed to be talking over things. Once I dozed off only to be awakened by a big hand clutching my throat. And God Almighty, it was Findlater's hand! "I ain't forgot what you done to me!" he says. I figure he would have choked me to death if I hadn't shaken him awake. Then he looked around puzzled and when I told him what he'd been doing, he says, "Lordy, Bill, I'm sorry. I must have been havin' a bad dream. Haven't been gettin' my regular forty winks lately. I hope I didn't harm you there." After he went back to sleep I edged a little away from him, for he was still muttering and cursing into his coat collar.

So I sat there looking at his bulky figure and watching the trees and towns and the farmhouses flowing past us in the dark river of night. Sitting there, I wondered whether maybe I'd made a mistake to hit the road with Findlater. Maybe I should have stayed in that hospital and found out more about the kind of man I'd been during that long spell of amnesia. It was hard to puzzle out all that lost time. Findlater had said that during his visits he found me to be a glum, bookish fellow who wouldn't have exactly livened up any party.

Maybe that was how I was. I figure I must have spent some time in the hospital library, and I'll tell you why. Now and again I'd get what you might call an inkling that I'd passed over something before, though I couldn't exactly say where or how. I remember this, for example. During the Second World War when I was back in Craven Falls raising Yorkshires, I went into town one day to buy a bottle of whiskey and some groceries. Just for the hell of it, I decided to go to the movies. From the posters outside the local movie house it looked like one of those pirate shows, for there was a picture of a couple of fellows sword fighting. But what it turned out to be was a movie of Shakespeare's play *Hamlet*. There was only a dozen customers in the theater, including Hector McCoy and his best pupils from grade eight. As the movie went along you could hear Hector whispering from the front row about this being significant and that being important. Till I finally told him to pipe down. But now here's the strange thing! I didn't know what in hell this *Hamlet* was about when I bought my ticket. As I say, I figured it for a pirate show. But it was a story about a young prince trying to get even with his uncle for murdering the prince's father. The people talked in old-fashioned English and mostly to themselves. It was nice enough to hear, mind you, but there didn't appear to be that much going on at times. But here's the ringer! *I knew what was going to happen right down to the last detail.* I could tell there was going to be one helluva sword fight at the end and I also knew that this fellow Horatio would end up saying, "Goodnight, sweet prince. And rest attend your dreams!" Or however it goes. So I figure that I must have read that story when I was in the hospital. The whole thing gave me a turn, and I've pretty well stayed away from moving pictures ever since.

Well, that night on the coal car I just sat there listening to Findlater snore and thinking about my lost years. I had no idea where this freight train was headed, but that wasn't too unusual back in the thirties. Men just jumped on the first moving train. Or you might hear somebody say in a freight shed, "That train's goin' to Kingston. I hear they're hirin' down there at the door knob factory." So a bunch of fellows would climb aboard. Of course, it was all lies and probably most of the men knew it when they jumped on. But somehow a man in those days felt better and more hopeful if he was going somewhere.

But at first light the train we were on slowed and I could see the white whistle sign for Sudbury, a nickel-mining town in northern Ontario. The train stopped there and took on water. Luckily no railway dicks came by to check the cars and we were soon on our way again, passing through bush land with lakes and rocks and fir trees as far as the eye could see. At the other end of the car everybody was sleeping, but Findlater stirred as we rounded a big curve. We were both filthy with coal dust but this didn't seem to trouble Findlater, who reached into his vest pocket and pulled out this little book entitled *Helpful Hints to Success and Happiness*. "Mornin', Bill," he says to me, and opening his book, starts to read. This was a morning ritual with Findlater in the same way that a priest starts his day with a couple of proverbs from his prayer book. After a while Findlater says to me, "Listen to this, Bill. *Plow deep while sluggards sleep. And you shall have corn to sell and to keep.* And how about this? *If your head is wax, don't walk in the sun.* Now that is true!" He settled back and gazed at the trees. "That's as true as the man tells it."

By and by the other men woke up and stretched their cramped

muscles. The young fellow who'd been helped aboard the night before had some baloney and bread in his pockets and he shared it with the rest of them while Findlater and me looked on. This young fellow wore an old suit coat and work pants and had a thin, hawklike face. He wore glasses too, as I recall. I was hungry enough to bite a piece of that coal but I knew we wouldn't be getting anything from those fellows, and you could hardly blame them. Findlater didn't appear to mind but just sat there looking at his book.

Late in the morning it clouded over and tremendous flashes of lightning forked across the sky. Even over the clacking of the train wheels we could hear the thunder rolling through the clouds. Then the rain started and before long we were soaked through. It was a furious and spectacular storm and at one point a bolt of lightning hit this big solitary pine tree perched atop a rock. It split right down the middle in a shower of sparks and smoke. It was awesome to behold and one old fellow said from underneath his coat, "That was the finger of God, sure enough!"

It struck me as a pretty good description of that natural phenomenon, but this young skinny fellow in the suit coat just snorted and said, "Finger of God, my eye! What's God got to do with anything? That's just static electricity and you know it, so let's not bring God into any of this. In this day and age it's simply childish to believe in God. A fairy tale for Sunday school children! Men are suffering, and what's God doing about it? Sitting up there playing a harp, I suppose? Or maybe putting on a little fireworks display like out there now? To take our minds off the fact that he couldn't care less about what happens to us." His sharp, thin face looked tense as a coil. "You'd better forget about these superstitious thoughts of God and concentrate on men. Some collective action by men. That's how we're going to save this country. Look what they're doing in Russia. And God has nothing to do with that. At the university I studied political philosophy before I ran out of money and had to leave. I studied the various ways men govern themselves, and believe me, friends, there is a better method. But people have to be organized. People have to come together as brothers. We can't wait for this fairy-tale father in the sky to do it."

Just then there was another big crack of thunder and Findlater looked up from his coat collar and shouted, "I ain't travelin' with any college-educated atheist."

This was so sudden that everybody looked our way and said not a word for several seconds. We were crossing this river on a wooden bridge and all you heard was the rain splashing off the shiny coal and the *lunkety-lunk, lunkety-lunk* sound of those bridge rails. Then this young fellow pushed his glasses back on his nose and says, "If you're an example of a Christian, then I'd rather be an atheist any day of the week. Why, you wouldn't even stretch out a hand to me last night!"

A few of the others grumbled in agreement but Findlater merely says, "Never mind that. I will not travel with the likes of you people."

"This is a free country," the fellow says. "I've as much right to use these trains. Just because we disagree."

"You can gather up your stuff right now and get off this train," says Findlater, standing up with his legs braced apart against the sway of the train.

"What are you talking about," says the young fellow, looking frightened for the first time. "Right here in the middle of nowhere? You must be crazy."

At which Findlater slowly walks through the coal towards him. "I can't think of a better place for a atheist son of a bitch to meet his Maker and learn somethin' about God." The young man's face was now pale with fear. "Now git," says Findlater, and the fellow looked around.

"Listen, men," he says, spreading his hands apart. "In the name of reason, are you going to allow this man to bully a fellow passenger? We're all brothers . . ."

One or two stirred, but Findlater had pulled out his bottle of bad liquor and he pushed it in front of the roughest-looking character. "Have a drink, pal," says Findlater. "It'll keep the damp out." This tough-looking fellow hesitated for a moment but then took the bottle and had a good pull, wiping his mouth with his sleeve. "Any of you other fellers like a snort?" asks Findlater. "It ain't prime, but it's the best I got." Three or four hands went up for the jug, and then Findlater says to the college man, "You still standin' there, you goddam heathen? This train's not movin' too fast now. You want to go by yourself or you want me to help you along?"

"I'm telling you, this is insane," says the young man. He points a finger at Findlater. "That man wouldn't lift a hand to help a fellow human last night and now you're all drinking his whiskey."

Just then Findlater gave him the back of his hand and he disappeared over the side of the car, falling into some bushes, where God alone knows what happened to the poor devil. He could have hit his head on a rock or wakened up in the night to be chewed by a black bear. The whole thing sickened me, not only because I'd watched it happen but because I'd done nothing. After that Findlater passed the whiskey around again until the bottle was empty, and people cheered up a bit. This rough-looking joker said, "Those educated fellows are always shootin' off their mouths about things they don't know nothin' about."

"That's right," says this old fellow. "And then you know the first thing the sons of bitches do when things get back on the rails again and the factories are open. That's when you find all these guys with this college education and their white shirts and ties lookin' through the glass windows of their offices on the factory floor. Keepin' an eye on you if you go for a piss, or tellin' the foreman to speed things up. I've worked for plenty of bastards like that."

That sort of talk went on for a little while, and one or two fellows then sang. Findlater soon had those fellows listening hard as he told them about his forty-two pairs of shoes and his Pierce Arrow automobile. The storm passed and I sat there watching the ragged clouds skim across the sky. The rocks and the trees steamed in the afternoon sunlight and in the lakes you could see the fish jumping.

29

RUBY

———————

THAT SUMMER of '32 Findlater and me traveled across most of western Canada. We slept in fields and ball parks and freight yards. We put the bite on people from their back doors. I'm no historian and you can read about the Depression in a dozen other books. I suppose Findlater and me were typical of thousands of other men moving around without any special trade or skill. As I've already said, it was just enough to be moving. It beat standing around the drugstore or the post office corner in some backwater hometown, where everybody knew if you were on relief or not. We were a good bit older than most others, but the grime and the disappointment and the pinched looks made men of twenty-five look ten years older. Nothing seemed to matter much except what's for supper and where do we sleep tonight? Those were the questions you woke up to and went to bed with.

I couldn't believe things had got so fouled up in the time since I'd left for England. But then I've never claimed to understand banks and money systems, which, according to most of the men, was behind the trouble. As for Findlater, he was determined to get back his fortune and be once again in the driver's seat, as he put it. How he proposed to do this wasn't clear, though he hinted one night outside Winnipeg that I might consider selling my story of sixteen years' amnesia to a magazine. "Why, we could become celebrities, Bill! They might even make a moving picture out of us." But I didn't want any part of that, and I'll tell you why. I was enjoying the freedom of being my old self again. Things were tough and there was no denying it. But at least I knew who I was and every day I could see hundreds of others worse off than me. There were men who'd left families because they couldn't stand it anymore and were now eaten raw with guilt.

One day about the middle of August we found ourselves on the outskirts of a town called Marion in the southern part of Saskatchewan. Marion was a two-street town south of the Canadian Pacific main line in a part of the west known as the Palliser Triangle. In those days the land in that part of the country was scorched and blasted by the sun and wind. About all you could see was dusty gravel roads, couch grass, and Russian thistle with here and there a boarded-up farmhouse. Findlater and me had about fifteen cents between us, so we decided to blow it on some coffee and pie in this little diner on the highway leading into town. It was called Ruby's and it was just an old faded-red trolley car with the wheels removed and some of the windows painted over. Behind this godforsaken restaurant was a little bungalow that needed a good deal of patching and painting and beside it an old black Star sedan.

We were the only customers in the place, and when the owner came out from behind this little curtain I was taken aback, because for one terrible moment I thought I was looking at Sally Butters. Not the Sally of old but maybe a faded copy. This woman was perhaps thirty-five, with thin arms, a good figure, and red hair. She looked like she'd suffered a few knocks in life and was ready for more. I think Findlater must have also been struck by the resemblance, for he put his tongue in the corner of his cheek and looked thoughtful as we sat down on the counter stools. It wasn't much of a place, with its glass cake covers and fly-blown pies and greasy skillet. So we sat there drinking our coffee and eating our pie while this red-headed woman stood off to one side with her arms across her chest. She watched us while we ate and hummed a tune that was playing on the radio called "I Found a Million Dollar Baby in a Five and Ten Cent Store."

But Findlater wasn't a man to endure silence for long, so after a bit he began to make casual conversation. He told her we were headed for Vancouver, where maybe we'd ship out for the Orient. It was the first time I'd heard that. "They tell me," says Findlater, "that they're lookin' for business executives and former wheels out in Shanghai. And Bill here and me fit that description." The woman laughed at this and went on shooting the breeze with Findlater. All the time I could tell she was interested in me. Anyone with any sense at all can get a feeling about these things. And what you also have to remember is this. While I may have been fifty-two, I was still a fairly presentable-looking man and a good cut above the worn-out-looking jokers that were wandering around in those days. The reason for that may have been simply this. For over a decade and a half I did not have to worry about making a living and raising a family. Thus I looked and felt a good bit younger than most men of my physical years. I still do for that matter, and a number of people in here still think I'm only eighty or so.

Well, this woman's name was Ruby Staedler and after a half-hour she says, "Look, I'll make a deal with you boys. There's patchin' needs to be done on the roof of my house at the back. I got the shingles and

the roofin' nails. I've been goin' to do it for weeks now and haven't got
around to it. But then it hasn't rained around here for weeks and I
just keep forgetting about it. If you do the job, I'll give you your
suppers and a couple of bucks. What do you say?"

Well, it was the best offer we'd had in a long time, so we got the
tools out and a ladder and a couple of bundles of shingles and set to
work. It didn't take more than two hours. After we'd finished, Findlater
squinted across the fields to the gravel road leading into town and says
to me, "That's an awful good-lookin' woman, Bill. She puts me in mind
of Sal. It makes you wonder, don't it? I mean, stuck out here all by
herself! She don't appear to have a man around the place and that's a
damn shame, because she looks to me like she knows what takes place
between the sheets in the dead of night. What do you think?"

"I think you're probably right."

"Yes sir," says Findlater, scratching at the long underwear which
he wore winter or summer. "But you know, this little place of hers has
real possibilities. You could make somethin' of a place like this. As it is
now, it's just a place to stop and take a crap. But you could fix it up
with a string of colored lights. Put in gas pumps and generally attract
a better class of people. If a person could find himself a reasonably
priced bootlegger in the neighborhood. Then slip the local cops a few
bucks to look the other way. Why, in no time at all a person could have
themselves a nice little profitable roadhouse. Nothin' spectacular, but
then Andrew Carnegie didn't start out with no steel mill. Am I talkin'
sense, Bill?"

"Maybe," I says. "But it sounds complicated to me."

"Hell," says Findlater. "Ain't no more complicated than two and
two is four. I wonder if that woman is as smart as I think she is. I seen
her lookin' you up and down, Bill. She's lookin' for a man to help her
out with this place. It could mean a turn in our fortunes."

"Maybe," I says.

We'd just finished when Ruby Staedler came out wearing this
green dress, with her hair all curled and rouge and lipstick on too. She
stood there looking at us, holding a hand up to shield her eyes from the
sun. Then she made us another offer. It was a Wednesday and she
closed down Wednesday afternoons so she could drive into Marion for
supplies. The suppliers wouldn't deliver out to her because her orders
were so small. She didn't mind this, for it gave her a chance to get into
town and look things over, not that there was much to see. What she
proposed was that I come along and help her out. Findlater could stay
home and mind the store. She'd put the CLOSED sign on the window
and what he could do was paint a few chipped chairs and tack on a
new piece of oil cloth on one of the tables. In return she'd add another
dollar to our day's wages.

A few minutes later Ruby Staedler and me were sitting side by
side in the old Star sedan watching the heat waves shimmer off the
hood. Sitting there gave me a good chance to size her up. She had that

kind of toughness or hard edge you find in people who've survived tough times and held on to their sense of humor and not let things totally get them down. There was a bit of Shorty Wilson in her and some of the flinty hardness I remembered in poor Jack Gillies and a little bit of Mrs. Fletcher too. I liked the way she drove that old Star, both hands on the wheel, and confident. I asked her how she ended up working a diner, and she told me she came from a small town in Manitoba. She was an orphan who grew up on her own in Salvation Army hostels. At sixteen she ran away to Winnipeg and got a job selling overalls in the Hudson's Bay Store. This was during the First War, and Winnipeg was full of soldiers. Naturally she fell for one of them. Met him at a dance, a skinny little French-Canadian who shot her a line of bull and put her up the stump before waving goodbye from the troop train. She never heard from him again.

So there she was, pregnant and without a friend. On her feet all day selling overalls! That's when this Staedler came into her life. He was a sixty-year-old farmer, a widower who was having a tough time because of his German blood. He bought a pair of overalls from her one afternoon. After work she stopped in this ice cream parlor for a soda, and there was Staedler eating ice cream and watching her. After a while he got up and came over to her booth. Ruby laughed when she told me that. "That dumb Kraut. You had to hand it to him. It took a lot of nerve. He could hardly speak English, you know. I guess I looked so miserable and red-eyed that he could see I was in some kind of mess. So he asks me, What's the trouble? And the first thing I think is, Now what do you want with me, you dirty old bastard. But I don't know. He sounded so concerned that we got to talking. He had his place up for sale because his neighbors were making it tough on him on account of the war. People threatening to have him locked up. He'd lived among these people for thirty years and it didn't mean a damn. Suddenly he was a German spy or something and they were threatening to burn his barns. So he was selling and moving out here, where he figured he might be left alone."

She blew a stream of smoke out through her nose and looked over at me. "You know, we talked in that place for the longest time. Oh, it looked funny. Him being sixty, a powerful-looking man in his country clothes and his short bristly head and moustaches. He really looked like he just got off the frickin' boat. And me just a kid really. But then he says to me, You need money, I got money. And he pulls this wad from his pocket. There must have been five hundred bucks there. And remember, I'm makin' three dollars a week in that damn store. So he walked me back to this boardinghouse I was staying at and then went on to the train station. A week later I got this letter, see? From old Hermann. With a hundred-dollar bill and a proposal for marriage. What do you make of that?"

"Love at first sight," I says.

"I thought you were a cynical little bastard when you first walked in the door of my café." But she laughed. "Okay, old Hermann wanted to make me his wife. He's selling everything, lock, stock, and barrel. In his funny English he asks me to come out with him to Saskatchewan and make a new life together. 'We'll have peace and harmony.' That's how he put it. Which ain't bad for a guy who doesn't speak the language so well. Well, Jesus, he even includes a stamped self-addressed envelope, like some of those things you send for on the backs of magazines. Well, hell, I'm just a kid. Up the flue and nobody looking to do me any special favors. Except this old German farmer who sends me a hundred bucks for a trousseau. Bride clothes, he calls them. Well, I remember saying to myself, he ain't no Johnny LaRose. That's the name of that good-looking little skunk who ran out on me. But then again, beggars can't be choosers. So I writes Hermann back and says Okay! Why not! I've always been one to take chances. Just to see how things work out. Well, things are going to turn out one way or the other. Right? Hell, you've got to take your chances. You get good luck and then you get bad luck. Everybody does."

She laughed again and flipped the cigarette out the window like a man, using thumb and forefinger. She looked over at me again and said, "I lost the kid. It was malformed or something. It wasn't right, anyway, and I lost it because Staedler had me working. I married him and we came out here and he bought six hundred acres of good land about fifty miles north of here. He was a shrewd old guy. But he was different on the farm. The only two things he understood was screwing and working. And I found out he hadn't had just one wife but two, for Christ's sakes. Both long dead and buried. I figure he either worked them or screwed them to death, because that's what he almost did to me. You wouldn't have believed that man's stamina. We worked twelve, thirteen hours a day. Out in the fields. Just the two of us. Never saying a word but just plowing or harrowing or whatever. He wouldn't hire help except at harvest time, and then he'd bring in the cheapest drifters he could find. And then I'd have to feed them too and carry water out to them morning and afternoon. But most of the time Staedler and me just worked alone, side by side. Then we'd stop for lunch and he'd lay me. Right there, not ten feet from the horses' tails. Then he'd snore for maybe fifteen minutes and get up and expect me to go to work. Nearly every day. Then home to cook his supper. Oh, it was something for a girl, I can tell you!"

"No kids?" I asks.

"No," says Ruby. "It's a funny thing. Staedler loved screwing and for a man his age he was just like a billy goat. But he had no lead in his pencil, if you get what I mean. Told me once he had mumps when he was a kid and they went down to his privates and destroyed his seed. It's a good thing, now that I look at it. I wouldn't want to be saddled with no kids in these times. I got enough worries looking after myself."

We were now in Marion, a dusty little place with half a dozen stores and a grain elevator. There was the usual knots of men standing around street corners. After a bit I asked what happened.

"To what? Staedler?" says Ruby. "He died. Four years ago this fall. We were having a good year, too. It looked like the best crop we'd ever had. We were working our guts out. Just before harvest. I'd even aired out the bunkhouse that morning. Staedler had been up since five o'clock roaming around the fields. The weather looked to stay good and dry for a couple of weeks. Perfect. Then after lunch he had a heart attack." Ruby laughed and hit the old wooden steering wheel with one hand. "He was on top of me when he had it, you know, the old bastard. What a way to go, eh? He was seventy-one that month."

"Jesus," I mutters to myself, and I couldn't help thinking of Sally and Lord Birdlip. "That's some story."

"Didn't I just tell you?" says Ruby, laughing. "I was glad to sell that damn farm and buy the café, though I was cheated. Jesus, but men do take advantage of a woman, the bastards!"

By now we'd turned off this main street and gone down this narrow alleyway and come out behind some stores. Ruby backed the old car up to this loading platform with the gears crunching and grinding. The car still carried the smell of manure and old Staedler's sweat. Then Ruby got out and soon was up on the platform, standing there in her green dress damp down the ridge of her back, and joking with the men who stood around in bib overalls. I loaded the trunk with sacks of sugar and coffee, a crate of eggs, and canned goods. And it was hot! God Almighty, it must have been a hundred degrees that day!

On the way home Ruby suddenly pulled off the highway and went up this dirt road for a quarter of a mile. She stopped in front of this little unpainted frame bungalow with the shells of some old cars in the yard and a tire swinging from a tree. There were a dozen kids, all ragged and covered with impetigo sores, running around the place. "Come on," says Ruby. We crossed this scabby-looking front yard and she rapped on the door. It was opened by a tired, thin woman wearing a housedress and long dirty apron. She nods at Ruby and gives me a blank look while Ruby says, "Jesus, it's hot today, Doreen." And this Doreen leads us through a stale-smelling hallway, shooing the kids away to the left and right.

Seated at the kitchen table was an old man maybe seventy-five, sitting there in his undershirt, swatting flies and leaning forward on a cane. He was fat and bald and white as a slug except for these smoked glasses. Ruby called him Tom and when I shook his soft, limp hand I realized he was blind as a bat. Ruby says, "It's hot today, Tom." He just nodded his head and we sat down. Then the old man banged his cane a couple of times on the floor and a few seconds later this girl about eleven, barefoot and wearing a flour-sack dress, presents us with a couple of bottles of cold beer. God Almighty, it was a treat! Ruby puts the money on the table and the old man felt each coin before putting them into his pocket. This woman called Doreen just stood at the sink and shelled peas. Nobody said a word while we drank the beer.

29. Ruby

The flies buzzed around the old man and he whacked at them with
the swatter, killing one or two every time. Before we left, Ruby bought
a flask of whiskey from him.

Back on the highway we took slugs from the flask while the sun
beat down and the radiator hissed and Ruby sang "I Found a Million
Dollar Baby in a Five and Ten Cent Store." About a mile from the café
she turns down another dirt road and we drove to this spot on a little
river. It was brown and sluggish in the late summer heat. Ruby got out
of the car and threw the bottle into some bushes. Then she reached up
behind her and started to unbutton her green dress, yelling at me, "If
you're a gentleman, Bill, you'll look the other way while Cleopatra
here bathes in the waters of the Nile. But if you're just the same as all
the other bastards I've met along the way, you'll be out of your underwear in two seconds flat."

And I don't need to tell anyone over twelve years old that that is
exactly what I did. And we had a fine time of it too, there among the
reeds. The water tasted flat and brackish, and it passed through my
mind that an old snapping turtle could play a bad joke on a grown man
in such circumstances. But Ruby and me enjoyed ourselves like a
couple of kids out of school. And afterwards, lying there in the water,
she chewed on a reed and looked across at me with that straight,
strong, direct gaze of hers. It was a look that said she was laughing at
you and most everything else in this crazy world. After a while she
says to me, "Have you been doin' time, Bill? It don't matter if you have,
because I've known plenty of men who've done time. Some were good
and some were bad."

"No," I says, "I haven't been in jail. Why do you ask?"

She chewed some more on that reed and laughed. "Why, because
you screwed like a starving man, and a woman can always tell that.
The way you went at me there I could swear you haven't been laid in
years. That's why I asked."

"Well, you've got the wrong man, Ruby," I says. "I haven't done
any time. Oh, back when I was just a kid I got into some trouble down
in the States, but that was thirty-five years ago." I sat up, for I didn't
feel like telling her my life story. In those days I was touchy about
mentioning such things as my sixteen-year amnesia.

On the way back to the café Ruby asked me about Findlater and
what I saw in him. "We travel together, that's all," I replied. "He's
about the only friend I got."

"That's too bad," she says, putting a stick of chewing gum into
her mouth. "I don't think I'd trust him as far as I could throw a load
of bricks."

"Findlater's okay," I says. "He's treated me all right. He lost everything because of this Depression. I don't think he's ever gotten over
that and sometimes it gives him a bad night. But that's understandable.
To have been on top once and now to be down with every other
drifter on the road. It's bound to queer you a little."

"Uh huh" was all she said and just snapped her gum.

When we drove into the gravel parking lot in front of the café, Findlater was standing beside a big dusty Studebaker with North Dakota plates. When he saw us pull up, he hurried over. "What do you say, pal? Listen, Miss Staedler, there's a couple of fellows here who'd like a bite to eat."

"We're closed Wednesday afternoons," says Ruby. "Can't they read the sign? They can go on into the Chinaman's in Marion. It'll only take them five minutes in that thing."

Findlater removed his derby to scratch his head. "Well, they're fairly set in their ways, if you get my meanin'. They claim to be tuckered out and half starved. They're carryin' a firearm too."

Ruby stood there chewing her gum and scratching her arm. "American rum runners," she says. "Up from Bismarck or Minot. We get a lot of them passing this way, though I ain't seen these two before."

Then she started for the Studebaker, but not before she pulled down her dress from behind and squared her shoulders. In those silk stockings and green dress and with her face flushed from lovemaking, that woman had more sex appeal than a Hollywood movie star, though her features were far from perfect. And she snapped that gum and walked over to the Studebaker as though she didn't give a —— for any living thing under the sun. Just watching her walk across that gravel gave me another tremendous pang of horniness.

Meantime, Findlater leaned over and sniffed my breath. "What's cookin, Bill? You and Miss Staedler been havin' a picnic? I hope you got your oil changed. But it seems to me you been drinkin' hard liquor. That one-horse town ain't got a store, has it?"

"No," I says.

"Then you been to a blind pig?"

"Yeah," I says, "I'll tell you later," and followed Ruby over to the Studebaker.

She had one foot up on the running board and her arms on the window of the driver's seat, and though the metal was burning hot, she didn't seem to mind. "What can we do for you fellers?" she asks, smiling and snapping her gum.

The driver was a leather-skinned cowboy type in a broad hat. His partner was just a kid, maybe eighteen, with corn-colored hair and a walleye. He didn't look all there to me. Resting on his lap was a double-barreled shotgun. The driver touched the brim of his hat. "Just some bacon and eggs, ma'am. And maybe a cold cola. We've come a distance."

"We're closed on Wednesday afternoons," says Ruby. "There's a pretty good Chinese restaurant in Marion, just down the road about five minutes. You can't miss it."

At which the driver says, "We don't want no Chinese cookin', ma'am. We like it out here and we'd like some bacon and eggs, if it's all the same to you. Floyd here feels the same way, don't you, Floyd?" This Floyd grinned and raised the shotgun a half-dozen inches.

At this Ruby shrugged. "Have it your way, Buster," she says. "But you better tell your friend to put that thing away, because the Mounties patrol these roads pretty often and carryin' a gun up here is against the law."

The driver touched his hat again. "You bet, ma'am."

So they got out of the car and I was happy to see Floyd leave the shotgun behind, though the driver had a revolver stuck into his pants. They went on into the café while Findlater and me carried the supplies to a little shed at the back. "That's a mighty fine machine those boys got," says Findlater, putting down a case of canned beans.

"Ruby claims they're rum runners up from the States."

Findlater laughed. "Imagine the likes of that runnin' booze across a border! It's enough to make a man cry. Say listen, Bill, what about that place you visited this afternoon? Did the people who sold you the stuff make it on the premises?"

So I told him about the old blind man and the woman and the kids. I said I hadn't seen any still, but come to think of it, there were outbuildings in the yard.

At this Findlater did a little dance. "Oh, he's makin' it, all right! And if he's an old bugger, all the better, 'cause they're usually foxy and take no chances. Now you got to get me into that place and talkin' to that old coot!"

"That won't be easy," I says. "The talking, I mean. He didn't say a word all the time I was there. Maybe he's dumb as well as blind!"

"He'll talk to me, Bill, because I'll be talkin' money, and like the Bible says, the dumb do open their lips for gold."

"Where does it say that?"

"Never mind. It says it. Now listen careful. I can see you and the lady have got somethin' workin' fine between you. Just keep up the good work and don't disgrace the regiment. What I'm gonna do is sell some booze to those two cowboys and we're gonna get ourselves a stake. Get back into the business world, by God, and no more of this travelin' around on the fresh air express. Go first-class or stay at home is what I used to say. Had it monogramed on some of my shirts."

"Well, those guys are carrying guns, Findlater," I says. "Somebody could get hurt messing around with people who carry guns."

"Hell. Don't worry about a thing. Those two are amateurs. A couple of punks tryin' to make a fast dollar workin' for some big shot down in Minot. They don't know sheepshit from cranberries when it comes to exportin' whiskey. Bill, I used to know the best in the bootleggin' business ten years ago. In Detroit and Chicago. This pair is just a couple of hicks. Now the thing is this. We gotta hang around here for a week or so to set this thing up. Now that means you're goin' to have to persuade the lady in there that she just can't possibly live without you. Do you think you can do that?"

"I don't know."

"Well, try, pal, try."

Inside the café these two characters ate their bacon and eggs.

The driver, whose name was Ed, had a hard time keeping his eyes off Ruby, who just leaned against the counter listening to the radio. After a while this Ed asked for directions to Estevan. "Estevan's no problem," says Ruby, rolling herself a smoke. "You just go right on into town and the road jogs to the right. You follow that right through and it'll bring you into Estevan from the backside of town. But then I don't suppose that's goin' to bother you boys much."

It's a corker how that woman could make a man look down to his fly buttons and feel foolish. This Ed just grinned and said, "No, ma'am. I don't suppose it will."

They paid and walked out to the Studebaker, followed by Findlater, who professed a great interest in that car. He stood there talking to them in the dusk while Ruby and I sat in the half-light of the diner, smoking. "Did you see that little bastard lookin' up my dress, Bill? Sittin' there with a hard-on for an hour. Just dyin' for it, those cowboys. They spend most of their time drivin' cars at night or playin' pool. Haven't got a hog's sense around women. All they can do is stand around with a bone-on like a mongrel dog. Can't talk to a woman. Can't say anything, the stupid bastards, except How 'bout it, babe! He'll be back too," says Ruby, standing up. "Him and his creepy little friend."

"How come you know so much about all this?" I asks.

"Oh, hell," says Ruby. "Those bastards come and go as the wind blows them. They'll use this route for a bit. Then the Mounties'll get wind of it and put up a patrol on this road. And some farmer will tip them off for five dollars and they'll look for another part of the province. Maybe farther east. Or they might get caught. They're just bums. I've had others like them here before. They're all bastards." She doused the lights. "Why don't you and me go on to bed, Bill? You might as well stick around for a few days. I'll take in the radio and we'll listen to some music. Your fat friend can sleep on the sofa."

"All right," I says.

When I looked out the window Findlater was waving goodbye to those rum runners in the Studebaker.

30

WHISKEY

So I MOVED IN with Ruby Staedler. Took bed and board from her and in exchange helped run the diner, though there wasn't a lot of running to do, business being scarce in that godforsaken corner of Saskatchewan in the late summer of 1932. But travelers and local folk did drop in now and again and were fed and bought cigarettes and Coca-Cola. Since I had some experience in the general merchandising line, I kept the books, for Ruby was a little slack in that department. And between the two of us we made a pretty good team. The personal side of living together was also pleasant, for it was nice to wake up in the morning with a fine big woman in my bed.

Ruby wasn't keen on having Findlater about the premises but she was one of those persons who takes things in their stride and she didn't make too much of a fuss. Besides, Findlater made himself damn useful, which surprised me. He was always saying, "Now you two kids go and enjoy yourselves and let old Cass look after things." Ruby and I always got a charge out of that, since it was pretty damn obvious neither of us had been kids for some time. But we got used to having him open the diner and we'd just lie in bed listening to him shooting the breeze with some trucker down from Regina. If business was slow, we'd look out the window and watch him burning rubbish in the blackened trash barrel at the side of the diner. He'd stand there in his shirtsleeves, vest, and derby, stirring the flames with a broom handle and watching the oily smoke swirl up to the blue prairie sky.

And watching him, Ruby would say, "Your friend's a queer bird, Bill. I can see how you're fond of him. He's a good-natured cuss and generous to a fault. But there's somethin' mean and ugly inside that man too. I'm not one for turning people against their friends, but I like you, Bill. You're not the brightest in the world nor the dimmest.

You been kicked around a bit just like everybody else but you're still goin' on. But your friend out there. I'd be willin' to bet you hard money he's crazy. I don't mean asylum crazy. He ain't gonna run loose in the streets with an ax or anything like that. But there's something fishy about him that I don't like. I don't really think he gives a damn for anything but himself. Now, I know you ain't askin' me for any advice but I'm gonna say my piece anyways. If I was you, I'd cut loose from that man. If you like, I'll sell this place. I won't get much for it. But it'll be a little to set us up. And I still got a few hundred of old Staedler's money in a bank up in Estevan. Put away for a rainy day. We could maybe go out to the West Coast. Try it for a while. If it don't work out between us, then we call it off and no hard feelin's. Neither one of us is gettin' any younger, Bill."

"You don't even know me," I says.

"I know you all right, Bill. At least I know you well enough. I ain't likely to do any better now, and don't go feeling insulted when I say that. I'm just tryin' to see things as they are."

Well, the whole matter was very vexing to me. On the one hand, I owed Findlater a certain loyalty, because there was no denying he'd been a good friend to me down through the years. After all, the man made a point of visiting me every year on my birthday when I didn't even recognize him. On the other hand, he did act queerly at times, and then there was lots worse than Ruby Staedler when it came right down to living together.

One Saturday night, after a good deal of pleading from Findlater, we closed early and paid a visit to the old blind bootlegger's on the edge of Marion. When we got there, there was about half a dozen couples sitting around on this tacky old furniture in the living room being served highballs and beer by the kids and listening to country music on the radio. The kids took our orders and we went out to the kitchen to pay old Tom. The skinny woman was his daughter. She was sawing up bread for baloney or cheese sandwiches, which she sold for a nickel apiece. It was quite an operation. Most of the couples there were young and single. This was their idea of a big night on the town, I suppose. They knew Ruby but didn't pay us much heed. Now and again they got to their feet and danced. Findlater spent most of his time in the kitchen conversing with old Tom, and we left early because Ruby and I were bored and anxious to get to bed.

The next day Findlater told us old Tom had agreed to sell ten cases of whiskey to these rum runners, with Findlater acting as go-between. Ruby was fairly skeptical of all this and warned Findlater not to harm old Tom in any way, for she was fond of him. Everybody in Marion liked old Tom. "That blind old man," says Ruby. "He's kept that family together now for years. Doreen's useless. Just a brood sow. Not worth two cents, and every one of those kids has a different father. But old Tom just takes everything in his own way and I don't want him mixed up in any kind of trouble."

"Now, Miss Staedler," says Findlater. "There ain't gonna be no trouble. Don't you lose any sleep over Tom. I respect that old fellow same as you. But lookit here. It's like I said to him last night. His daughter's in the family way again, I believe. There must be eight or nine kids already around there. That takes a lot of feedin' and shoes comin' up for school, and winter clothin'. They can't wear those damn flour sacks to school this winter. So what's wrong with makin' a quick few hundred bucks? Who in this day and age can't use a spare few hundred bucks?"

"And I suppose you're doing this out of the goodness of your heart?" says Ruby. "So Tom's grandchildren won't run around half naked this winter?"

"No, Miss Staedler, I'm not," says Findlater. "I'm a businessman, and I see before me a project that will make a modest profit for that poor old blind man. I myself will accept a commission as salesman for the deal. Ten percent off the top. Nothin' wrong with that. Bill here will help us load, and I'll cut him in too. Everybody profits. And then with that little stake, well, maybe it'll be time for old Cass to hit the road!"

Well, I think that last statement is what finally convinced Ruby. If she could see Findlater on his way, maybe the whole thing would be worthwhile. I wasn't so sure.

About a week later the rum runners turned up again at the diner. It was just before dark on a dry, windy evening. You could see the storm clouds gathering to the southeast, bunching up on the horizon. A parching hot wind struck you like a blast furnace in the face. The sign over the diner creaked and rattled, and dust filled the air. Ruby was in a sulk. She didn't want me to get mixed up with this whiskey business, and if she hadn't mentioned it so many times that week, maybe I wouldn't have. But she pushed her point a little too strongly, with the result that I decided to help Findlater. I wasn't about to be told what to do by a woman, and I made this pretty clear. The result of that was Ruby going to the bungalow with a bottle of whiskey.

When Ed and Floyd came into the diner Findlater poured out some drinks, but Ed quickly covered Floyd's glass with his hand. "My brother-in-law can't hold hard liquor, mister. It makes him funny in the head. Now if you just have some cola or root beer, that'll be fine."

"You bet your life, Ed," says Findlater, opening a bottle of cola. "Now you try that whiskey and see if it ain't prime."

Now what this Ed was drinking was not Tom's moonshine at all but government-bonded rye. Findlater and me had driven up to Estevan in Ruby's Star the day before and bought it. Then we transferred it into an unmarked bottle. It was the oldest dodge in the world, but these two jokers weren't exactly the brightest specimens of humanity around.

So after Ed had drunk a glass or two he says, "That's not bad. That's not bad at all. How much of this stuff has your friend got?"

"Well, to tell you the truth, Ed," says Findlater, "he wants to start modest. He can let you have ten cases for a start. If this transaction works, well, we'll go to fifteen or twenty. But Tom's got his local customers to think of too. You can appreciate that."

"Sure I can appreciate that," says Ed.

"I can see that too," says Floyd, working that cola down his skinny throat while his bad eye checked out the fly-specked ceiling.

"Where's the pretty little lady?" asks Ed.

"Well, she's just not up to snap tonight," says Findlater.

Ed scratched behind his ear and says, "Well, what's this feller sellin' his merchandise at?"

"Ed," says Findlater, "this is a man with almost no business overheads, so he can allow you a real good price. Now for this Canadian rye you been drinkin'. That's what you'll get tonight if you're buyin'. Three bucks for a twenty-six-ounce. He ain't interested in mickeys. So three bucks a bottle makes it out to thirty-six bucks a case. So tonight we're talkin' about three hundred and sixty dollars. Are you carryin' that kind of money?"

Ed pulled out a big billfold with all kinds of fancy embroidery on it, including a kicking horse and a lasso. And the damn wallet was choked with bills. "Don't you worry none about three hundred and sixty dollars, mister."

Findlater wiped his mouth with the back of his hand. "No siree, I can see that I don't have to worry about that, Ed," he says.

I went back to the bungalow and Ruby was sitting in the armchair by the window drinking whiskey and watching the sky fill up with lightning. The dust sifted against the window. The radio was playing but there was so much static I switched it off. Ruby said nothing but just drank straight from the bottle. I put my hand on her shoulder. "Look here, Ruby," I says. "I don't know what you're so sore about. It's just a chance to make a few dollars. Old Tom's agreed to it."

"Are you going then?" she asks.

"Well, I thought I would, yes. I said I'd help Findlater. I could use the money. A man gets tired of having no money in his pocket."

"I'll give you twenty bucks to stay here."

"I don't like taking money from women."

She laughed and took another swallow of whiskey. "Shit. How you bastards like to talk!"

"Look," I says, "everything's going to work out fine. We'll sell them the whiskey. They'll give us the money. And then away they'll go. So what the hell is wrong!"

"And maybe your fat friend will go too, eh? He can go a long way, as far as I care. I want him out of here by tomorrow!"

"Does that mean me too?"

"I never said that. Two's company, three's a crowd."

She stopped to smoke a cigarette and we both watched the sky flickering and flashing. I felt some kind of heavy weight pressing down

30. *Whiskey*

inside me. A few fat drops of rain splattered the window. Ruby took another sip of whiskey and said, "Staedler hated storms. Well, he was a farmer, and I guess you couldn't blame him. But Jesus, they made him nervous as a cat. He was always worrying about the wind flattening his fields or lightning striking the barn. He'd fuss like crazy all the time a storm was on. Go out to the barn to check the stock. Then come back and stand at this window and then that window. Never said a goddam word through the whole thing. I'd ask him to come to bed but he'd just walk the house in his wool socks all night, his big rubber boots handy by the door. The funny thing is that during storms I really wanted it. Don't ask me why. All I know is that during a storm I was always just dying to get laid. And there I was married to a man who loved screwing better than fresh air. But when I really wanted it, he just roamed around till the storm passed over. Then he'd come to bed and fall right to sleep. In two minutes his snoring would drive you from the room. Well, what the hell!" She took another slug from the bottle. "Have a drink, Bill," she says, passing the bottle up to me.

I took a good long one and handed it back to her. Just then Findlater yelled, "Hey, Billy boy. We're going now. Come along!"

I didn't say anything for a minute. Then between the long rolls of thunder I heard the Studebaker's motor roar into life. Then Ruby says, "Go on then, Bill. Go on, for Christ's sakes. And lock the door behind you. I'm closed for the night."

So I left her sitting there in her chair, sipping whiskey and smoking. Why I left I don't know, except that a man more than often does something contrary to fundamental good sense. Looking at it another way, however, it seemed to me a simple thing. A few minutes' work and a chance to make a few dollars. In an hour I could be back in bed with her. Then I could decide whether to hang on for a while. Or check out with Findlater. I knew this much. Findlater would have to go in the morning. I could tell Ruby's mind was made up about that.

They had removed the back seat of the Studebaker, so Floyd and me had to sit there on the floor while Findlater gave Ed directions, and the big car traveled down the road, swaying slightly in the loose gravel. All around us the air crackled and sparked. Now and then a few big splashes of rain smacked the windows, but the main force of the storm was pushing off to the south and there was no rain to speak of. Nobody said much. Ahead of us the house and outbuildings were in darkness, but then came a great sheet of lightning and you could almost see the grain in the gray, weatherbeaten boards. Findlater told Ed to flick the headlights off and on three times. Then we stepped out into this black night with its heavy, warm wind and, holding on to our caps and hats, made for the front door, where this Doreen was waiting for us with a storm lantern.

The kitchen was black as the top of a cook stove but when the woman put the lantern on the oil cloth we saw old Tom seated in his chair. "Don't they have electricity here?" asks Ed.

"The power's off," says Doreen. "The storm must have did it." Then she disappeared towards a roomful of children.

Findlater bent down towards the lantern. "You remember me, uncle? I was talking with you Saturday night. So, like I said I would, I brought these gentlemen around for the merchandise." The old man nodded, and taking one hand off his stick, lays it palm up on the table. "I guess he wants to see the color of your money, boys," says Findlater.

"How can he see anything with those glasses on?" asks Ed.

"I believe he can see well enough to do business," says Findlater.

"Well, I want to look at the stuff before I lay out any money," says Ed.

"Perfectly reasonable," Findlater replies. "Don't you agree with that, uncle?"

The old man waved his stick towards a corner of the kitchen. There in the gloom we could make out a pile of boxes. Ed opened one up and, uncorking a bottle, started sipping.

"That's all prime stuff, Ed," says Findlater. "This is a business arrangement, and trust is the order of the day. Old Tom here makes the finest whiskey south of Saskatoon."

"Some of this tastes a little barky to me," says Ed. "It don't taste like nothin' half as good as that stuff you had in the café."

"But hold on," says Findlater. "You've got to give that stuff time. It needs turnin'. That whiskey you had in the café was five years old. That would fetch twenty dollars a bottle. Now this stuff you're buyin' here tonight. You can either put it away for a little while, or I'll guarantee they'll lay out twelve dollars a bottle for that right this very minute in Omaha. Now I suggest we pay the man and then move the goods. That's only a businessman's way of lookin' at things."

"All right," says Ed. "We'll take it. But the rest of it better match up. We don't want to be fooled around with here."

"Nobody's foolin' nobody, son," says Findlater. "You give the man his money and you take his whiskey. It's strict business."

So Ed counted out the money and handed it to Tom, who took it in those soft white hands of his. And now here's an amazing thing! Not only could that old blind man tell the twenties from the fifties and the tens and so on, but after a while he says something in a cracked whisper. It was the first time I'd heard him open his mouth and nobody could make out the words, so Findlater bent over and says, "What's that, uncle?"

"What's he sayin'?" asks Ed.

Findlater straightened up. "He's sayin' that next time you come around he wants you to bring Canadian money. He don't like unloadin' a wad of American bills at the bank. Looks suspicious, he says. You have to admit, he's got a point."

"All right," says Ed. "I'll remember that."

"Now," says Findlater, pulling a flask from underneath his coat. "Why don't we all just have a drink on this deal, then we'll load up."

And that's what we did, with me and that walleyed Floyd doing most of the work while Findlater stood to one side talking to Ed. It was still windy and black, with only a pinpoint of light showing here and there as people over in Marion used coal oil lamps in their parlor windows. After we finished loading, Findlater said, "Damn but we are the fools, Bill. We should have brought along Miss Staedler's car. Now there's hardly any room for us. Tell you what, Ed. Bill and me will hang on the running board and you can take it slow. It's only a couple of miles back to the café."

Well, that was all right with Ed, and we said goodbye to old Tom and climbed aboard. As we drove along, Ed sang a cowboy song, something about lonesome in the saddle. Then presently he yells out, "I hope Miss Ruby's feelin' better next week when we come up this way."

"Oh, she will, Ed, she will," Findlater says, bending down and talking through the open window. "She's just temperamental. That's all. It goes with the red hair."

This seemed to please Ed, for he laughed. "I guess you're right about that." Then after a minute he says, "Hot dog!" and squeezed the horn. "Say, does Miss Ruby like chocolates?"

"Chocolates?" says Findlater. "Why, chocolates is her favorite eatin', Ed. How did you know that? There's nothin' she likes better than chocolates."

"Well," says Ed. "In Minot. In the window of the five-and-dime there? They got this great big five-pound box of chocolates. It's shaped like a heart. With some fancy writin' on it. Prettiest thing you ever saw."

"Is that a fact?" says Findlater.

"It's a fact. And so I got to thinkin'. Maybe Miss Ruby might like that."

"It's a thoughtful notion, Ed."

"I mean, you boys don't mind if I give Miss Ruby chocolates?"

"Now why would we mind?" says Findlater. "But lookit, Ed, there's somethin' funny goin' on back here."

"What's that?"

"Well, I may be wrong but I believe your left back tire's goin' flat."

"Feels all right to me."

"We may have overloaded her, Ed."

"Hell, this car can take another ten cases."

"Well, I'm just sayin' what I'm seein'. In case you have to use some speed later on. A fellow never knows."

"Well, damn, it feels all right to me!" says Ed, but he stops the car and climbs out. "Never had no trouble with flat tires on this car." I jumped off my side, while Floyd climbed out and walked around the car. Ed was already kicking the tire and then he bent down. "This looks good to me," I heard him say.

Then what does Findlater do? He yells, "Jump on, Bill," and slides

right into the driver's seat with amazing agility. I just managed to
make the running board as Findlater stuck it into second and the car
spun away, spitting stones. "Get inside, Bill," Findlater yells across
at me. "You're easy pickin's out there." I could hear Floyd and Ed
yelling something about sons of bitches and I managed to get the door
open, when something whistled past my ear. Findlater sliced her
down to third and we were now swaying over the road at fifty miles
an hour. "They're shootin' guns, Bill. Keep your head down," he yells.

"Are you crazy, Findlater?" I says. "What in hell is going through
your head?"

"Money, Bill. Money's goin' through my head. This is our stake,
don't you see?" I sneaked a look back, but we were out of their range
now and the road was swallowed up in darkness and dust. Findlater
says, "By the time we get rid of this booze and this car we'll have
enough to get ourselves on the road to good times again. This is the
chance of a lifetime!"

"But hell," I says. "Those cowboys are going to be spitting mad.
Where does that leave old Tom? You've put him in a fix back there!"

"Oh, they won't bother old Tom. He's got nothin' to do with any
of this. He supplied the whiskey, didn't he? That was his part of the
deal. Once it leaves his place it ain't his responsibility. I mean, the
goods are now in what is called transit. They won't harm a wrinkle on
his brow. They're just a couple of rubes. Probably workin' for some
big-shot bootlegger. When they arrive home with no car and no booze,
they'll be lucky if they don't end up wearing stone slippers at the
bottom of the Missouri River. If they go home at all. My guess is
they'll head the other way."

"Well, what about Ruby? Where does that leave her?" I was mad
as hell.

"We'll take her with us," says Findlater. "Great opportunity for
her to get out of this place. There's no future here."

"Suppose she doesn't want to come?"

"She'll come, Bill. She'll come. She's sweet on you. Anybody with
an eye in his head can see that."

The diner came up fast on the right, a huddle of buildings against
the darkness. "Well, pull over there, for Christ's sakes," I says. "I'll talk
to her. You might have told me what you had in mind all along." The
car rocked to a stop and my face damn near went through the windshield. Choking dust poured through the open windows.

"Now don't take all night, Bill," says Findlater. "You never know
about those two back there. They look pretty dumb to me, but they
might get lucky and find a car somewheres to steal. In which case
they might be on our backsides in no time at all. I don't like the looks
of that bird with the bad eye."

I was already out the door and running across the gravel. The
place was in total darkness, so I stood there pounding on the door
with both hands. Finally I saw Ruby coming from the back of the

place, holding a flashlight. "Hurry up in there," I yells. She opened the door and stood there none too steady. I figure she must have finished off the whiskey.

"For God's sakes," she says. "What are you trying to do to my door? Break it down?"

"There's no time to explain," I says. "We've got their car and the whiskey. We left them back on the road. You better just leave everything and come along too before they get back this way."

"What in hell are you talking about?" she asks. "Are you drunk, Bill?"

"I'm talking about Ed and Floyd," I says. "Findlater stole their car. That's him out there now. We're heading for the border. I didn't know anything about it until five minutes ago."

At this Ruby just threw back her head and laughed. "Why, you crazy bastards! You'll be dead within a day. Those two cowboys will be on the phone to every bootlegger within two hundred miles. You won't get anywhere in the car by daylight. And you left poor old Tom with this mess."

"Well, it's done now, Ruby," I says. "Believe me, I didn't know what he had in mind."

She laughed bitterly at this. "Sure you didn't. Oh, you're all the same, Bill. There isn't one of you worth the goddam trouble. But a man your age should know better. For a while I thought you had some sense. Your fat friend out there is going to get you into a mess."

"Ruby, I didn't know any of this was going to happen."

"Sure you didn't, Bill. Now run along with your friend. You're both makin' me sick. Now get movin'."

"Are you sure you're not comin'?"

"Wild horses couldn't drag me into that car with your fat friend."

"I'm sorry, Ruby."

"I've heard that one a few times, Bill. Now move along before he double-crosses you too."

So I left her. Just like that. Maybe I should have stayed. I've thought about it over the years but it doesn't do any good. Perhaps if I had, I wouldn't be here talking into this machine. It's impossible to know.

Back in the car we were soon barreling down this black road. "Where's the little lady?" asks Findlater.

"She's not comin'," I says.

"That's a mistake. A serious mistake. Those two boys could make it rough for her."

"You might have thought of that before you pulled this stunt."

"I was only thinkin' of improvin' our lot in life, Bill. I had your best interests at heart." I said nothing to that but sat there watching the black night sweep past us. About a half hour later Findlater stopped and by the dashboard lights studied an old greasy road map. "Well now," he says, "accordin' to this map, right here's where we turn south for the good old U. S. of A." I was still too mad to talk. Findlater reached back and got out a bottle of whiskey. "Have a drink, Bill," he says. "It'll cheer you up. Everythin's goin' to turn out right. You'll see."

"Findlater," I says, "are you sure you know what you're doing? I mean, do you realize that there are custom houses strung out across that border on the highways? Ruby told me about them. I'm sure we'll look just fine pulling up to one of these places with ten cases of whiskey in the car."

"Don't you worry about those monkeys," he says. "I've dealt with a few of them in my lifetime. Bill, you've just got to stop this train of pessimistic thought that's always racin' through your head." I said nothing to that but just drank some more whiskey while Findlater revved up the big motor.

By and by we ran into a brief heavy rainstorm. Rain was rare in those parts during the thirties, but now and again one of these heavy showers would come along. They never lasted long. And this rain, it came down so thick and fast that the windshield wipers had a job clearing it. The road was growing bad too, with the rain digging great rivulets in the gravel. Once or twice we had to stop and then inch forward. I don't know how long it was, but we were just crawling through this downpour when we came to a grade. Findlater gunned the motor but the car slued to the right and just as we gained this little hill we hit a washout and the rear wheels settled into the ditch. Findlater tried to back up and then go ahead but we just spun in the mud. "Well now, that's bad luck," says Findlater. "We better take a look."

So we got out. I've never seen rain come down so hard. We stood there at the back of the car looking over the situation. The nose had made the grade but the rear wheels was stuck solid. We stood there getting drenched until finally Findlater says, "This don't look good, Bill. We'll need help to get out of this. There must be a farmer or somebody around here."

"You think you're gonna get somebody out here on a night like this?" I asks.

"I'll get him out if I can find him. When I stuff a ten-dollar bill in his overalls he'll be out here." Then he says, "Look now. There's a light down to the right of us. You can see it through the rain."

I could too, so I walked around the car and to the top of the grade for a better look. Then I noticed something else. The whole front end of the car was resting on a railway track. I bent down and rubbed the polished steel to be certain. When I stood up, that light seemed to be moving. Well, it didn't take a genius to figure out that there was a train coming down the track. Meantime, Findlater was taking another pull from the bottle, leaning against the rear fender with his back to the light. I just yelled, "Run, for Christ's sakes! There's a ——ing train coming!"

He didn't hear me for the wind and the rain but I heard him say, "How's that?" Then I grabbed him and we fell together into this ditch just as the big headlight filled the air and the engine blew for the crossing.

The engineer must have seen the Studebaker at the last minute and applied the brakes, for there were sparks flying out into the wet darkness. But it was too late, and she hit the front end at maybe sixty miles an hour, driving the car around and past us where she exploded into flames, lighting up the sky.

By the light Findlater's face was gray as lead. "What the Sam Hill was that?" he asked.

"That," I says, "was my train of pessimistic thought passing through."

31

ACROSS THE WIDE MISSOURI

WHAT HIT US that night was a westbound freight out of Winnipeg. Findlater couldn't read a road map any better than he could drive a carload of whiskey in a rainstorm. So, instead of heading south, we'd turned north and were then some forty miles outside of Brandon, Manitoba. When the train stopped, the crew came running back along the tracks and stood around the flaming wreck, holding their arms in front of their faces. We stayed hidden in the roadside and then spent the rest of that night in an abandoned barn. Findlater had some wicked dreams and once sat up to shake his fist at an old sawhorse that stood in the corner like a crouching man.

The next morning the sky was clear, but the summer was over. There was coolness in the air. Findlater woke up sweating and shaking. "Lordy, Bill, I'm not well," he says to me. "I feel a bad grippe coming on. This country of yours is hard on a man of my years." He got to his feet and he was creaking all over, his joints being stiff with the cold and dampness. For the first time he looked like an old man. As I've mentioned before, it was hard to put an age on Findlater and he never liked to mention it. When you asked him, he'd always come up with some crap like "You're only as old as you feel." But on that September morning in '32 he looked and acted about a hundred, though I guessed he was maybe ten or fifteen years older than me.

It was a good thing we had the thirty-six dollars that Findlater got from Ed for negotiating the whiskey sale or we might have starved to death. As it was, we hitchhiked into Winnipeg and spent the entire winter in that city. The reason for that was Findlater's health. He damn near contracted pneumonia from that wet night, and for several weeks he was laid up in bed. When our money ran out I got a job slinging hash in this restaurant owned by a Greek. It wasn't much of a job but it kept a roof over our heads. Findlater spent most of his time lying in bed clipping coupons from the back of magazines. *Have You Ever Seen a Bald Headed Sheep? Sell Our Lanolin Hair Tonic to Your Friends. Fifteen Minutes a Day Can Earn You Real Money Studying Our Radio and Phonograph Repair Kit. Door to Door Super Sales. From Boils to Acne. Send for a Ten Days' Supply of Dr. Jim's Home Ointment. Money-Back Guarantee.* But he didn't have any energy for it. In fact, for the first time he looked downright discouraged about things, but that could have been due to the weather. Winnipeg is a cold city to spend the winter in, and except for the Yukon, that was just about the bleakest winter I can remember, with the temperature down below zero most of the time and the snow seeping under the window sill and piling up in little drifts under the bed.

I'd given up the notion of ever seeing Sally Butters again, though I often dreamed of her as she'd once been on the musical stage, twirling her parasol and singing "Beautiful Dreamer Awake Unto Me." I sent a Christmas card to Ruby Staedler but it came back in February with the envelope marked "Addressee Unknown." I often wondered what happened to that woman. I hope she went out to British Columbia and did all right for herself. A lot of prairie people went out there during those times.

By the spring of '33 Findlater was almost his old self again. It was as though the strengthening sun was firing up his enthusiasm for life. The result of that was we left Winnipeg and struck southward for America. Findlater was homesick for his native country, and I confess I was anxious to see something green and growing after the long winter. So we took to the freight trains again and headed down through Minnesota and Iowa. The spring seemed to rush up and meet us in the fast-flowing brown rivers and the warm winds. As we rattled southward Findlater sometimes stood by the open door of a boxcar and, cupping his hands to his mouth, bellowed like an old bull.

We left a Union Pacific cattle car just below Jefferson City, Missouri, one soft night after a day of rain and we stood by the side of the tracks inhaling the smell of wet grass. It was dark, with a mist rising from a river below us. Down in a gulley by the river was a campfire and we could see dark figures moving around. Normally in our travels we were pretty much loners, steering clear of hobo camps, which were always full of rough customers. But we hadn't eaten anything that day, and sometimes you could get a bite in those camps. It depended. Some was good and friendly and others wasn't, according to the two or three tough guys who ran it. Usually when you walked into those places you were an object of curiosity and you had to be careful not to appear too smart or tough. You had to balance things out.

But as we slithered down this wet grassy embankment and walked towards the fire nobody paid us any mind, owing to the fact that everyone was milling around in a sort of general commotion. There was about a dozen men, all of them tough-looking jokers. In the middle of this circle near the fire were two black men. One fellow, small and somewhat elderly, was poorly dressed in a bad-fitting coat and tan pants. His bald head gleamed in the firelight and his bubble eyes were bright with worry and fear. The other fellow was just a kid, but what impressed you about him was his size. He was a young giant standing there in faded bib overalls with no undershirt and barefoot as well. It was plain these two fellows was in serious trouble. This crowd was grumbling and taunting them. We stood next to this sallow-faced man who was sucking on an empty corncob pipe, not saying anything but grinning from time to time with a mouthful of rotten teeth.

"What's the trouble?" Findlater asks him. "What's going on?"

The yokel takes his pipe from his mouth and points at the black men. "These two niggers come into camp a half-hour ago. Big Jim tells them to git. And gives the old one a boot in the arse for good measure. The young buck there, he ups and takes a punch at Big Jim. Knocks him colder than your wife's ass in January. Those two oughten to know better, comin' in here like that."

"Well now, it makes you think, don't it?" says Findlater. "I mean, some of these people just go too far."

"That's what I always say," replies the string bean, returning the pipe to his mouth. "But that young buck packs a wallop. Big Jim used to fight in the prize ring!"

"Is that a fact?" asks Findlater.

"That's right. And they say he once fought Jack Sharkey. Now that's somethin', ain't it?"

"That's true as you tell it," says Findlater.

"But that nigger there, he took Big Jim out clean as a whistle with one punch. It don't seem right to me. A nigger knockin' down a white man."

"What's this country comin' to, is what I want to know," says Findlater.

"That's what I always say," says the string bean.

"And where's Big Jim now?" asks Findlater.

"Over yonder agin that tree, rubbin' his bristles. That man took a punch."

"Seems to me," says Findlater, "that he could have been victim of a sneak punch."

"I never thought of that. You could be right. He wasn't ready for it."

"That's what I'm sayin'. A man's got to be ready before he can fight."

"That's what I always say."

The crowd had now pushed the two black men down near the riverbank against an old willow tree. You could hear the dark river flowing past and see bits of junk and old logs being carried along.

"We ought to throw them in," says a voice. "Nobody's gonna miss these two."

Another fellow pipes up: "Watch out for the razors. Niggers always got a razor on their person. They like to slice you in the business."

All this time the two black men have said nothing, except the old fellow is looking more and more scared. Then Findlater surprises me by elbowing his way through the crowd, until he's standing right in the middle. "Hold on now, boys, What's going on here?" he yells. He looks reasonably impressive there, with the firelight throwing shadows on his coat and derby. There was a cry or two of "Who the hell wants to know?" and "What's your business here?" but Findlater had a way of attracting notice and respect. Some people have that and some haven't. He was just a hard man to ignore, and before long he'd moved right into the center of things and was standing there pretending to listen as he got a dozen different versions of what actually happened. There was a dozen different proposals for what should be done to the two trespassers, the punishments ranging from hanging to drowning to roasting in the fire. After a bit Findlater holds up his hands and says, "Seems to me like maybe Big Jim got hit with a sneak punch!"

"That's right!" cry a number of voices. "That's what happened. Listen to this man. He knows what he's talkin' about."

"A man should have a chance to right a wrong," says Findlater, and there were yells of "You bet" and "That's right," and somebody clapped.

Meantime, I'd moved over next to the two black men, for I was interested to see how they were taking this new turn of events. The old fellow's eyes glittered in the firelight and I thought I could see suspicion now as well as fear in them. I couldn't see the big fellow's face, for it was lost in some low overhanging branches. He just stood there like a big dark statue. Then Findlater looked over at the two of them and says with a kind of authority in his voice, "This business should be sorted out right here and now. Did you hit that man with a sneak punch?"

"My granson don't hit nobody with no sneak punch," says the old fellow, and his voice was trembling. "He's just naturally strong in the limbs. He was provoked, is all. Now we just wants to be left alone. If Mistah Jim there wants to take a punch back at Sunny, we go along with that. So long as we is left alone."

Findlater scratched his jaws and smiled. "I don't think Big Jim wants any favors from you, Gramps. Isn't that right, boys?"

"That's right," they yells.

"What he wants is fairness here. A chance to right a wrong."

"We ain't studyin' no more fightin'," says the old man quietly. Then he adds, "Black man fightin' white man always end in trouble. We just wants to be left alone now. The boy was provoked and forgot hisself."

"Maybe so, Gramps," says Findlater. "But that ain't the way I see things."

But now this Big Jim had come over and elbowed his way through the crowd. He was a heavy-set blond fellow wearing a work shirt open at the throat. He stood in front of Findlater with his fists on his hips and says, "What in hell's your name? I heard you throwin' mine around."

"He's all right, Jim," somebody yells. "He's standin' up for you."

Jim snaps his head around and says, "Shut your trap. I don't need nobody standin' up for me."

"That's as true as you tell it, Jim," says Findlater, and somehow he contrived to find Big Jim's hand and shake it. "Cass Findlater is the name. I used to be in the fight business once. Oh, just a hobby of mine. And your face looks mighty familiar to me. Didn't you once give Jack Sharkey a rough time of it?"

"I fought Sharkey once," says Big Jim. "They stopped the fight before I got goin'. Said I was cut in the eyes. I was no more cut than that man over there. Just like that nigger caught me with a sneak punch. I should whale the piss out of him for that."

"Well, I knew probably that's what happened," says Findlater, "so what I suggest is that we simply right a wrong here. You got your pride as a professional man to think of. So what I'm sayin' is that we should devise a kind of ring here and you can give this boy the lickin' he deserves. I mean, fair is fair."

"That suits me," says Jim, and everybody cheered.

Then the older black man spoke up. "This only gonna mean trouble," he says. I believe I could see tears in his eyes. "No good gonna come from black fightin' white."

"Make a ring, boys," says Findlater, "and excuse me for a minute." The others formed a ring and began to slap Big Jim on the back while Findlater took the two black men to one side.

"Mistah, I'm not lettin' my granson fight that man. It could be bad trouble."

Findlater leaned a palm on the tree and pushed his hat back on his head before he says quietly, "Listen, Gramps. I'm tryin' to save your skin and the boy's here too. What's his name? Ain't he got a voice?"

"Sunny got no voice. He can't talk. He's a little slow."

"I get the picture, but listen to me now. Tell him to get in there. Hang on the man for a couple of minutes and then let himself get knocked down. That way you'll get out of here alive. I'm tryin' to help you."

"What are you tryin' to help us for?" the old man asks.

"Just do like I say. Make it look good, Sunny boy. Jump around for a while before you let him tag you. You tell him, Gramps."

"I don't like any of this," says the old fellow, shaking his head.

Somebody had stoked up the fire with brushwood and it was blazing high into the sky. The men had formed a circle and Big Jim was in one corner, being slapped on the back by his cronies. He'd rolled up his sleeves and there were several tattoos of naked women dancing and shivering on his arms while the muscles rippled. Jim was doing a lot of snuffling and touching his nose with his fist, an old prize fighter's natural reactions, I suppose. Then somebody yells, "Where's the niggers? Bring on that black son of a bitch and let him git what's comin' to him."

And somebody else says, "This is better than a burnin' I seed once in Kentucky. The Klan burned down this nigger's shack. Roasted them all alive."

"Too good for them," says another.

Then the two black men appeared at the edge of the crowd. By the firelight I could now see this Sunny. He stood there in his overalls and he wasn't smiling, but then again he looked somehow confident. And I remember thinking, It's a good thing you're simple, you poor son of a bitch.

Then Findlater stepped into this ring of men. He was running the show now and nobody seemed to mind the fact that he'd just walked into camp a few minutes before. Findlater held up his hands and says, "Now, fair is fair. This here match is gonna be done right. After all, we're civilized people. We're not runnin' around in skins in Abyssinia or someplace."

"That's what I always say," says a voice from somewhere near.

"Now," continues Findlater, "who's got a timepiece he hasn't already pawned for a bottle of whiskey?" That got a laugh and some scattered applause. You see, Findlater had a sort of magic touch when it came to orating to those kind of people. So one fellow pulls out this pocket watch, an old dollar turnip you could hear ticking twenty feet off in a thunderstorm. "That'll do nicely," says Findlater. "All right now. Pay attention! Three rounds of two minutes each. Come out when I whistle and may the good Lord take a likin' to the best man." "Amen," says somebody, and Findlater put two fingers into his mouth and blasted out a whistle.

Big Jim came shuffling out of his corner like an old firehorse at the sound of the alarm. The black kid came out too, and they circled one another for a few seconds before Big Jim flicked a few left jabs in the kid's face. They were smart blows too, snapping this Sunny's head back and making him blink. You could easily tell Big Jim was no stranger to the prize ring. He continued to pepper the boy's face with these jabs, but the boy just bobbed and weaved around. He seemed to know what he was doing too. The crowd was screaming for the kid's blood but he still hadn't thrown a punch. There were yells of "Come on, nigger, fight" and some catcalls and general insulting remarks, before Findlater whistled the end of the first round. The crowd was growing ugly owing to the fact that the contest was not as amusing as they wanted it to be. Findlater managed to whisper to the old black fellow, "Tell the kid to throw a couple and make it look more natural. This gang smells somethin' bad and they could turn mean. Make it look good."

So the second round began just like the first, with Big Jim moving in and the crowd growing more impatient. "Finish off that coon, Jim," yells one. So Jim gave the kid a few more jabs and then stepped in with the big right hand. At the last second Sunny turned and Jim's blow cracked against the side of the boy's head. I saw Big Jim wince, so I figure he hurt his hand. But now a funny thing starts to happen. Whether it was Findlater's warning or not, but the kid starts to move against Big Jim, who's beginning to wheeze a little. That was probably from years of smoking and drinking and immoral living. Anyway, this Sunny snaps out a few brisk blows. They just looked like taps but they were stinging, for you could tell from the look on Big Jim's face. So then it came to me as I watched Sunny through all this. *He didn't like losing.* Fighting was something he was good at and he wasn't about to fake it. This was something he could do well and he took pride in it.

Now what also happens is this. As Sunny changed his tactics and became a little more aggressive, I sensed a change in the weather of the crowd. Now this was turning into a real fight, and there aren't many things most human males enjoy watching better than fighting. Then suddenly as Sunny snaps Big Jim's head back with a couple of jabs, this fellow beside me yells, "I got two bits says the nigger takes out Jim again."

Now, a few minutes earlier that remark wouldn't have earned that man many friends. But now, in the excitement of seeing a real fight, nobody takes any notice, except another fellow who says, "I'll take that bet."

Well, it seems to catch like wildfire. Opposite us an old man in patched pants yells in a high squeaky voice, "I'll lay fifteen cents on Big Jim!"

And another fellow answers, "You got a bet there!"

At this point Findlater whistles again. "Now listen, boys," he says. "Somebody here has had the good sense to bring up wagering. We might as well make a few nickels while the entertainment is taking place. But lookit here. We got to do it right and proper. My friend Bill Farthing over there will take down the names and the bets while Big Jim and his opponent have a breather. That way we'll have a system. Do you see what I mean?" Everybody seemed to think that was a good idea, though it certainly took me by surprise. Nevertheless, I was soon busy scribbling down names on a piece of paper with a stub pencil and holding a fistful of coins and a couple of greasy dollars, maybe ten bucks in all.

There was money on the line now, and that always brings out the blood in people. I was standing near the black man's corner and I heard Findlater lean down and whisper to Sunny, "Forget what I said,

Champ. Starch that big stupid son of a bitch as quick as you can. Do you understand what I'm sayin'?"

The boy nodded. The old man just looked bug-eyed. "Are you tryin' to git us killed, Mistah?"

"Keep it down, Gramps," whispers Findlater, and holds up a finger in front of Sunny, who's sitting on a tree stump. "Do like I say, Champ. Everything's goin' to work out."

Then Findlater whistled, and the third round started. Big Jim had his wind back and for maybe half a minute he gave Sunny a good mauling, employing all kinds of foul tactics like stepping on his bare feet and kneeing him once. But the kid took it all and gave back more. His punches had more bite in them now. Jim was trying to get his goat by calling him names and making various allusions to his ancestry but it wasn't doing any good. Sunny kept coming on and on and you could tell he was getting stronger by the minute whereas Big Jim was now looking more and more like a blowed horse. His eyes were growing puffy where the knuckles were landing. Everybody was yelling, and then it happened. Sunny just sank Big Jim with a tremendous right hand to the jawbone. *Crack*, and you knew right away the man's jaw was broken. Anyway, down he went like a felled tree, and a hush settled over the crowd.

Then somebody muttered, "Why, that black bastard has knocked out Big Jim again."

But somebody else says just as quickly, "I don't give a ——. I got four bits comin' to me."

"Same here," says another. "Where's the little man with the money?"

Meaning me, of course. Now those who had bet on Jim, maybe two-thirds of the bunch, gathered around him trying to rouse him, but with no success. The others were pressing in on me, when Findlater elbows his way through and says, "All right now, Bill. I'll take that money and distribute to the winners."

I didn't know what he was up to, but I was glad enough to be rid of it. But I also had in mind the grumbling of one of the losers, who was saying, "Well, if that nigger thinks he's gettin' away with this . . ." Others were muttering various kinds of threats, doubly sore now because they'd lost money as well.

Then Findlater, standing in the center of things, yells, "All right now, boys. Why, look at this! There must be close to twenty-five dollars here in winnin's. Help yourself."

And damn me for a liar if he doesn't throw all this money into the air, maybe ten or fifteen feet up. And down it comes, a shower of nickels and dimes, quarters and crumpled dollar bills. Well, the effect was striking and you might say predictable. Not two seconds passed before those jokers realized it was raining money and down they all got on hands and knees, fighting one another and scrabbling around. Even those who had been looking at Big Jim joined in. I saw some fingers going right into the fire after a nickel, and here and there a hand stepped on with a sickening crunch. All this time I stood next to Sunny and his grandfather. We were the only ones left standing. Then from out of this heap of humanity Findlater straightened up and came running over to us, half hunched over like a big dark crab. He grabbed hold of my arm and also the old man's, whispering fiercely, "Let's get the hell out of here now."

Well, it didn't seem like any time for explanations, so that's just what we did, the four of us slipping off into the darkness. In a matter of seconds we were scrambling up the grassy embankment and then hoofing it along the tracks. When I looked back a few minutes later, the campfire was just a dim glow. We crossed the river on this old wooden bridge, nobody saying anything but just moving along at something between a fast walk and a half-run, taking care to watch our step, for that dark water was rushing below the trestle pilings. Now, you would have thought that moving at that kind of a clip for twenty minutes or so would have winded the old man, or perhaps Findlater. Or me, a man in his fifty-third year. But the fact is that when we finally stopped in this little woods at a bend in the river, it was Sunny who was blowing hard. Findlater and me flopped down on the wet grass while the two colored men just hunkered down, resting their weight on their ankles and very sensibly keeping the seats of their pants dry. As I say, Sunny was blowing hard and he just hunkered there with his head between his legs. The old man got up after a minute and stood over him. "Are you all right, boy?" he asks, and Sunny just nodded.

Nobody said anything for a couple of more minutes and then Findlater said with a laugh in his voice, "Well, I think we gave that rabble the slip. They'll not likely come this far now. How are you feelin', Gramps?"

"I'm just all right," says the old man.

"What about you, Bill? Are you still with us, old pal?"

"I'm right here, Findlater," I says.

"And the champ there. He's okay too. I can see that. Has that boy got a right hand or has he got a right hand?" Then he jumped to his feet, rubbing his hands together. "It's getting cold, boys. What we need here is a fire."

The old black man moved right away, glad to be doing something. "I'll git us some wood. Have a fire goin' here in no time at all!" And he was off cracking twigs and bringing back armfuls of brush, which were damp from the day's rain, but this didn't bother him. Before long he'd built a good fire, not too big to attract any passing tramps, for we didn't want company, but big enough to take the chill out of our bones.

Now, I could see that these two black men were shy and distrustful of us. On the other hand, Findlater had got them out of a potentially dangerous situation. It made conversation difficult, even though Findlater tried to lighten things up with his usual horseplay, rolling his derby down his sleeve and catching it and so on. It brought a slow smile to Sunny's face. But there's something about a fire that cheers

humans up and brings out the best in us. It's probably some primitive
thing going back to the time we were savages looking for groundnuts
and wild hogs. All I know is that after we got the fire going that night
the old man lost some of his shyness. "Appreciate what you done back
there, mistah," he says. "I can see now what you was up to. My name's
Noah Day."

It looked to me like he wanted to shake hands but considered it
the improper thing to do with a strange white man. Findlater solved
that problem by reaching out and shaking Noah's hand. "Pleased to
meet you, Noah," he says.

"Back home, folks call me Smokey," says Noah. "That's on account
of the smokehouse where I used to hang my bacon. I cured the best
bacon in Rupp County, Virginia. This here's my granson, like I said
before. His Christian name's Rufus but everybody calls him Sunny.
That's cause he's mostly got a happy nature and don't let things bother
him. He likes to fight, but it's all foolin' to him. Don't know his own
strength. He's just about the most easiest person in the world to git
along with."

Well, Findlater introduced us and began to talk a little bit about
our wanderings and how bad times were, etc., etc. While he was talking I reflected that the only other person I knew called Rufus was my
own brother-in-law Rufus Talbot. And how strange it was that he was
a little slow off the mark too! Rufus Talbot and my sister Annie! They
seemed to be a part of a world so remote. Of course I hadn't heard of
them since that letter from Annie thirty years before. Then Findlater
asked Smokey Day what he was doing traveling around the country.
Soon Smokey was telling us about how he left his tenant farm in
Virginia and how he'd been looking after his grandson for the past
year, ever since Sunny's mother ran off chasing a traveling preacher.
The old man told all this with a proper touch of rue in his voice. It was
a voice which seemed to say that there's nothing but bad news for
anybody crazy enough to bring children into this world.

"The way it was," he says, staring into the fire. "My daughter, she
wasn't too right in the head neither, see. But she could get by and
lived down the road a ways from me. And mostly she wasn't a bad
mother to Sunny here. But forgetful. Just like a cat, she'd wander off
after this hand or that hand. Then she'd spend the night in the ditch
with him. And leave the boy here to hisself. Now this boy's father. We
just didn't know who he was, on account of my daughter went to this
here Sunday school picnic when she was but fourteen and there was
men there to take advantage. So she and me mostly reared the boy till
I couldn't stand her no more and I built her a cabin down the road
from me. So like I say, my daughter was a lonely woman and nobody's
sayin' a woman shouldn't ought to have a man in her bed now and
then. That's only natural. But my daughter couldn't say no to no man
or boy child over twelve." He shook his head. "And folks take advantage of someone like that. It's only natural.

"So last summer this tent preacher come along to Flatt's Crossin' and holds a revival. I don't like talkin' bad about a man doin' the Lord's work. And maybe he was a good man. He could preach. I heard him myself. And I took my daughter and the boy here. He preached good and had people believin'. And my daughter went up to be saved. But that preacher had an eye for the gals. I could tell lookin' at him that he was a lustful man, and I do believe he left a few buns in the oven when he went away too. It don't seem right to me for a preachin' man to be takin' advantage of country people like that. But he done it. And my fool daughter run after him. Seems like she couldn't git enough of that man. And it was the worse time of the year, on account of the tobacca ripenin'. So I went to the man to tell him my troubles. And he says we got to prime tobacca, Noah. I can't let you go chasin' all over the country after that foolish girl of yours. I'll call the sheriff and have him bring her in. Likely as not she'll come herself directly. Mistah Travis, I says, that foolish girl don't know the way home. She gits more than a mile beyond Flatt's Crossin' and she gonna be lost. But the man only says to me, we gotta get that tobacca in, Noah. That tobacca is ready and times is bad. Well, he don't have to tell me times is bad, with him sittin' there in his rockin' chair and white shirt. And me with a daughter run off and this boy here no better than a child when it comes to fendin' for hisself. So I couldn't do nothin' but sell out my pigs and belongin's. And Mistah Travis don't like it at all. He's sore as a ripenin' boil. But I tell him, lookit here, Mistah Travis, I got to find my daughter. I can't let that girl go wanderin' over the countryside by herself. Folks take advantage.

"Now where she be, the good Lord only knows. We been travelin' since harvest time. We crossed the Missouri River as far as Kansas City, where we put in a bad time and got ourselves locked up in jail. Somethin' to disgrace me for the rest of my days. Now we is runnin' out of money. We done our best and now we is goin' home. I'm gonna git down on my knees and ask that man if I can have my home back. He got Eligah Wright in my house now, but Eligah ain't half the worker I was and he can't smoke bacon like me. Miss Travis sure like my bacon. So maybe Mistah Travis take us back, cause we is both good workers. This boy here. Now he a bit slow but put him in tobacca and watch him go. You don't need a sound mind when you go into tobacca. And that's where he oughtta be. Not traipsin' aroun' the countryside like this. There is a lot of badness on the roads in these times. Now this Sunny here! He enjoys it on account of he don't know danger when it's lookin' him right in the eyeball. He jus' don't have enough sense to be scared.

"Like in that hobo camp. Back there a ways this nigger tol' us there was a big camp of colored men down by the river. So that's how come we stumbled into that camp. That nigger played us for dumb. You can't even trust your own in these times. So that's when that big fellow roughs me up a little. But, shoot, that don't bother me. I been roughed up before. A few more licks here and there don't matter none to Smokey Day. And we'd have got out of there too, if this boy hadn't gone and hit that big man. Only the Lord's fool would go and do a thing like that. Why, if you two gentlemens hadn't of come along, I don't like to think what might have happened."

While Smokey was talking, Sunny took this piece of paper from a pocket in his overalls and carefully unfolded it as though it was a treasure map. Smokey looked over at him and shook his head. "There he go again. Daydreamin' over that foolish pitcher. Gentlemens, all this boy ever thinks about is prize fightin'. When he was thirteen years old I brought him home that pitcher. I cut it out of a magazine. Sometimes Miss Travis let me have a pile of old magazines, and I taught myself to read with them too. Now, I took this pitcher down to the boy one day. Show the gentlemens that pitcher, boy." And Sunny handed over this worn rotogravure picture of a bald-headed colored man in fighter's trunks. He was affecting one of those old-fashioned boxer's poses, standing beside some fake scenery in a photographer's studio.

"That there," says Smokey, "is Mistah Jack Johnson. A colored man who was once the best fighter in the whole world. I expect you gentlemens have maybe heard of him. You see now what's goin' through this boy's head most all the time for the past three years. He thinks he could be the best prize fighter in the whole world too, like Jack Johnson once was. At first I thought it was a good idea. It gives a boy an interest when he's growin' between boy and man. It keeps him out of trouble, if you gather what I mean. So I fixed him up with an ol' canvas bag for punchin' at. And he'd shuffle aroun' punchin' at that bag or punchin' the air till he got tuckered out and short of breath and had to lie down. He's strong but he gits winded easy. But all he can think of is bein' a prize fighter."

"But hold on, Noah," says Findlater. "So far as I can see, the boy's natural instincts are right on the money. I watched him carefully with Big Jim back there. And believe you me, this boy of yours is the business when it comes to fightin' in the ring. You can take it from me. I've seen many a champion in my time."

Sunny looked at Findlater like he was king of all creation. "No, sah," says Smokey. "The place for that boy is in tobacca."

"Now excuse me again for interruptin'," says Findlater. "But has Sunny here never fought in the prize ring before?"

"Just a few times last year," says Smokey. "He didn't half pester me to death to let him go. Oh, it was just foolin' aroun' stuff at Sunday school picnics and the county fair over to Richfield. He fought growed men and whipped them even then. But I stopped him from doin' it on account of he don't know his own strength and somebody could get hurt bad. And then the way I looks on it, he's bound to take some punishment on the head. And I can't see that doin' his slowness of mind no good. So I put a stop to it. Just like I didn't want him to fight the man back in that hobo camp. He might have hurt him bad and then where might we be, two black men hundreds of miles from home?"

"Well, you can take it from a man who knows," says Findlater. "This boy has got the makin's of a champion. I've seen lots of fighters in my time, includin' the best. Now, what the boy here has is natural talent. What he needs is a little trainin' and a few warm-up preliminary matches. Then watch out. You might just find yourself related to the next heavyweight champion of the world. Sittin' in a hotel and askin' on the telephone for room service. Yes sir, Noah. And you phone downstairs and say, Lookit here, I want two porterhouse steaks. Not just any porterhouse steaks either, but the best you got in the kitchen. And I want them here in my room in twenty minutes. And you fry some onions with the steaks and you pour the gravy over them. And put a couple of hot baked potatoes alongside. And then an apple pie and a whole brick of vanilla ice cream and a pot of fresh coffee. And the man will bring that up and say, Here you are, gentlemen. And you throw a buck to him and say, Keep the change, Buster. Now that kind of livin' is not out of the ordinary for a man like Sunny here who's got natural talent."

Nobody said anything for nearly a full minute. We were all too busy gazing into the fire looking at our porterhouse steaks. Mine was just about done and I was set to pull it out of the flames when Findlater says, "Yes, sir. It seems to me, Noah, that athletics is one of those wide avenues down which you people can travel to fame and prosperity. Sleepin' between clean sheets with your bankbooks under your pillow. You can't beat it." Smokey didn't say anything to that, just poked and stirred the fire enough to send my porterhouse steak up in a shower of sparks. Sunny was still looking at his. "Now," says Findlater, "if I was you, I'd just go about looking for my daughter in a different way, that's all."

Smokey looked over at him and says, "How do you mean, Mistah Findlater?"

"Well, simply this. Look, to me it don't make much sense to go runnin' off over half the country. Why, it's like looking for a needle in the haystack. Seems like what I'd do is put an advertisement in all the big newspapers clear out to California. Because there's no tellin' where those travelin' preachers will end up. Now if you put an advertisement in the newspapers somebody's bound to take notice when you inform them that there's a reward for information." Findlater scratched at his forehead. "Let's see now. 'Information leading to the successful reunion between myself and my daughter.' Well, the newspaper people could help you with the exact wordin'. Then you'd put your name, see. And your address. So interested people could get in touch with you. Why, you'd be surprised how a hundred dollars will make people look smartly about their neighborhoods for missing persons. Why, if it was my daughter, I might even consider broadcasting it on the radio. Millions of people listen to Rudy Vallee and shows like that."

"You'd do all that?" asks Smokey, with a touch of wonder in his voice. And some sadness too, I suppose, for he seemed to realize what a poor strategy it was for him and Sunny to go on the road in search of his daughter.

"You're damn right I would," says Findlater. "That's exactly how I'd go about it. Of course, you'd need money for that kind of approach." He paused and spat into the fire before saying, "But you know somethin', Noah. Bill here can tell you. I've been a businessman all my life. Know a little something about profit and loss. Fell on hard times a few years ago, but who didn't is what I say. Now the way I look at things is this. The good Lord gave this boy a gift. Why deny him a chance to use what the good Lord saw fit to provide him with? Why, with the kind of money this boy can make, in no time at all we'll find your daughter!"

"Are you sure 'bout that?" asks Smokey, raising his head.

"No question about it, Noah."

Smokey poked the fire again. "Well, I don't hold with prize fightin'. Don't seem like a proper way to earn a livin'. But if it would help me find this boy's mother . . ."

"That's what it will do," says Findlater. "Sure as this hat's on my head. And after we find her, then you can decide for yourself whether you want the boy to go on. Of course, by then I expect you'll have enough money to buy yourself a patch of ground over there in Virginia and grow your own tobacco."

"Me? Owning my own land?" says Smokey, looking up as if you'd elected him for the President's chair.

"Why not?" says Findlater. "There's no tellin' where a man can go if he don't get discouraged by the times."

"Well, maybe we'll sleep on that, Mistah Findlater," says Smokey, pulling his coat collar up around his ears. "Throw another stick on that fire, Sunny."

So we all settled down and soon Findlater and Sunny were snoring. I just dozed. From time to time I opened my eyes and saw Smokey. He was just sitting there staring into the fire.

32

RINGSIDE

THE NEXT MORNING we wakened stiff and creaky from the damp gray mist clinging to everything. Across the river the red eye of the sun was burning away the fog and now and again you'd hear a boat hooting. Beyond the tops of the trees there were patches of blue sky. Smokey jumped up like he was twenty-five years old and began to stretch and arch his back till he was supple again. Then he set off for the river with a piece of line and a hook. By and by Findlater got up and stood around beating his arms against his sides and sniffing the air. When Sunny got to his feet, he started to limber up, shadowboxing here and there, feinting jabs and hooks and looking altogether professional to me. Findlater put his arm on Sunny's shoulders. "Sunny boy," he says, "I'm gonna do my best to see that you step out on the road to the championship of the world. You just keep thinkin' about that hotel room and that big porterhouse steak."

The boy smiled and ran off down the tracks, doing his roadwork, I suppose. I said to Findlater, "You don't really think you can get fights for that boy, do you? I mean, he'll need a license and training gear and what not? And he doesn't seem to me right enough in the head."

"You worry too much, Bill," says Findlater. "It's one of your faults, if you don't mind advice from an old friend. There'll be no problem gettin' that boy fights. Just leave the business side of things to me. And say, lookit there now." He was pointing to Smokey, walking from the river through the mist with a string of catfish. "The Lord provides the righteous with sustenance," says Findlater. "God save you, Noah! What would we do without you?"

Then Sunny came back from his running, sweating and puffing, and by then Noah had opened his satchel and brought out this little iron skillet and with a bit of lard fried the fish. It was one of the

32. *Ringside*

tastiest meals I can remember. The conversation of the night before was not resumed but I could tell Smokey had made up his mind to let Sunny fight in the prize ring. It wasn't hard to figure. When you're desperate and broke, it's awful tempting to let someone else take charge of your life and work things out for you. And there is nothing Findlater loved better than being in charge of things.

So the four of us set out on that spring morning in 1933, walking eastward along the railbed with the Missouri River stretching out and glistening under the sun. Later that morning we took a gravel road bypassing Jefferson City. It didn't look natural for two white men and two black men to be traveling together and so sometimes Findlater and I walked on ahead some hundred yards, with Sunny and Smokey coming up behind. Sometime around noon we came to the edge of this fair-sized town, which I can't remember the name of and it doesn't matter anyway. Between the four of us we had about a dollar, but in those days black and white couldn't eat together in that part of the world, so Findlater walked into town for some food.

While he was gone Smokey and me took our boots off and just lay in the warm grass. Smokey told me something about himself. He'd worked up in Detroit, Michigan, for a few years sweeping floors in the Ford Motor works but he came back to tobacco because he didn't care for city living. The old man had a philosophical cast of mind and was interested in how things worked out between God and human beings. Of course, like most people he had his own theories, and one of them was that there was a curse on the land. Mind you, during the thirties everybody had an opinion as to what was wrong. It was the bank's fault or the government's or foreigners buying gold or what have you. But none of that could explain dust and grasshoppers and the god-damnedest series of natural calamities since the Jews left Egypt. Well, Smokey said he'd never discussed these matters with a white man before but as far as he was concerned it was all payment for wrong-doing. "I believe the white man is gonna have to pay for my grand-father bein' forced to come to this land against his better judgment. For it ain't natural or right to force people to go to places where they don't want to go."

Through all this Sunny had fallen asleep and now he lay there snoring gently. "Just look at that boy," says Smokey, shaking his head. "Who's gonna look after him when I'm gone? Why, that boy can't hardly peel a potato, let alone draw and quarter a pig. And his momma nowhere to be seen on the face of the earth. Why, I suppose after I'm dead and buried the sheriff will come around and they'll just take this boy away and lock him up in one of those lunatic asylums where the people runs around naked." He shook his head again. "It's just natural for folks to take advantage of a boy like that. Mistah Billy, I ain't never ast for much. If that boy and his mother was back with me and I had a dozen pigs, call me a happy man. Why, pigs is the best friends a man can have. Pigs been bad-mouthed more than any other animal. They is not as dirty as folks make out. And they is loyal. Once you get on the good side of a pig he ain't never gonna let you down. He got a dog beat every which way when it comes right down to that. It used to be I'd hate killin' time when it came round. You see, you've known them since you pulled them from the old sow and they're jus' baby pigs. Now, a baby pig! There ain't nothin' gonna bring the heart out in you faster than a baby pig. No sah. No pup dog nor kitten can get you feelin' the way a baby pig do. Then you watch them grow, rootin' aroun', and each has habits to itself. There ain't no two pigs the same, Mistah Billy, and that's a fact.

"I been aroun' pigs all my life. My daddy had pigs before me. Why, I can remember the blue-coat soldiers comin' through our place. They was comin' down from Pennsylvania on their way south. And they killed my daddy's pigs. And took what bacon he had hung. Yes sah! They told us they was comin' down to free the slaves, because my daddy was a slave then. But it seems like all they did was kill our pigs. Oh, I remember that, though I couldn't have been but a little child. I was borned the year that war started, Mistah Billy, but I can still remember those blue-coated soldiers killin' our pigs with their long guns." Smokey stopped for a minute and then said, "How do they treat black people up there in Canada, Mistah Billy?"

Well, I said that so far as I could tell there weren't that many black people to treat, so I couldn't exactly say. However, it seemed to me that human nature being as it is, they'd probably be treated just about the same as anywhere else. Smokey said he figured that, even though he had this great-uncle who, according to family legend, had run off to Canada. That's why he had this notion that maybe Canada was different, though he'd never really believed it deep down and now he was relieved to know the truth.

Then we saw Findlater hustling along in his quick-footed way. He was carrying a paper bag. Before long he flopped down beside us, fanning himself with his hat. "Lord in the sky, that's gonna be a hot day, boys. Lookit here now, I brought you some eats." And he laid out hamburgers and a couple of pint bottles of milk. Stirred by the smell of the food, Sunny arose and stretched, and we all tucked into this. Findlater was excited. "Boys," he says, "I've got some great news. Met a feller in the local pool hall and started to shoot the breeze with him. Before you know it, we're talkin' prize fights and does his ears pick up when I tell him I got a future champion! He tells me there's prize fightin' tonight over at Stephensville, a few miles further on from here. It's free for all stuff, but they pay well accordin' to this feller, whose brother-in-law takes tickets. He says they're always lookin' for new faces. So he's gonna phone his brother-in-law and try to get the promoter of this here thing over to see us. We're supposed to meet him at that poolroom by two o'clock."

"But this boy ain't hardly had no trainin', Mistah Findlater," says Smokey. "What kind of man they gonna put this boy up against over in this place?"

32. *Ringside*

"Listen, Noah, old friend," says Findlater. "This is strictly amateur foolin' aroun'. Why, land sakes, the way Sunny handled that big fellow last night, he'll have no trouble against those hayseeds, you mark my words."

Just before two o'clock we walked into town, picking up, as you might expect, a number of curious stares from the locals. Sunny, Smokey, and me waited in the alley beside this Bluebird Grill and Billiards while Findlater went in. A moment later he was back in company with two men, one a scrawny, gray-faced little character with cue chalk on the end of his nose and a pair of shifty, blinking eyes that stared around as if daylight was something altogether strange and unseemly. The other fellow was heavy-set, with the face of a wart hog and a wide behind. He wore a shapeless suit and a Panama hat. He stood there chewing a toothpick and looking Sunny over. Then Findlater says,

"This boy is the real goods, Mr. Hooper. Twenty-three fights with only one loss, and that was a foul. This boy's got natural ability."

"How old is he?" says this Hooper.

"The boy turned nineteen last month."

I looked at Smokey, who seemed to be on the point of opening his mouth but for some reason thought better of it.

Then Hooper pulled out a wallet and peeled off a ten-dollar bill. "All right," he says. "Have him right here in this alley at ten o'clock tonight." And he tapped the ten-dollar bill against Findlater's hand. "And mind now, friend. No foolishness or tricks. Don't get no ideas about leavin' town with my money. I don't want to hear nothin' about that. I got friends all over this county."

"Ease your mind of a fear so vain," says Findlater. "We'll be there with bells on."

"Never mind the bells," says Hooper. "Just make sure your boy there puts on a good fight. That's what we're payin' you for."

"Oh, he'll put on a good fight, all right. Wouldn't be surprised if he showed some of the locals how it's done."

Hooper didn't say anything to that but just got into a sedan and drove away.

This whey-faced little fellow told us we could stay in the back of the poolroom till nightfall. "Personally, I'd suggest that," he says. "Course, it'll cost you a dollar, but then I figger that's cheap on account of folks around here don't take it lightly when they see coloreds and whites minglin' together." So we followed him to this smelly little room at the rear of the pool hall where the air was bad owing to the fact that it was right next to the can. And all that day Smokey, Sunny, and me sat there listening to the clack of the balls and the flushing of the toilet. For a while Findlater amused Sunny with some card tricks from this old greasy pack he always carried around with him. But then Findlater went out to shoot some pool with the locals and, as he put it, "pick up some gossip and loose change."

They came for us at ten o'clock that night. It was pitch black and we groped our way down the alley towards this small red light which I couldn't make out until I nearly bumped into the tailgate of a stake truck. Then somebody grabbed my arm and I recognized Findlater's grip. "That you, Bill?"

"Yes," I says.

"Good," he says. "Go around and get in the cab. Where's the boy and the old man?"

"Right here," says Smokey, behind me. "We right here, Mistah Findlater."

By now my eyes were getting used to the darkness and I could make out Findlater and behind him another man, a large figure smoking a cigar. He seemed to be in charge. "Okay," he says. "Get the niggers in the back there. We're already late." Then he opened this canvas flap and shone a flashlight in there and damn me if I didn't see maybe a dozen young colored men sitting on two wooden benches. "All right," the man says to Sunny. "Get in and take a seat. And don't make no fuss." Sunny appeared to be enjoying the novelty of all this and eagerly scrambled aboard. Then the cigar smoker shone the light in Smokey's eyes and says to Findlater, "Who the hell is this old crock? Hooper never mentioned nothin' about no old nigger."

"He's the boy's grandfather," says Findlater. "Acts as his second in the ring. This here's one of the best cut men in the business. He used to know Jack Johnson."

The man looked doubtful but he was in a hurry. So he says, "All right, get in."

"Yes, sah," says Smokey, and I helped him climb aboard.

Then we got into the cab of this old truck and drove off, this surly-looking cigar smoker grinding the gears as we headed down the main street out of town. We drove a few miles along the highway and then came to a dirt side road where we stopped before a man waving a flashlight. The driver got out and talked to this man with the flashlight. Then I heard this fellow say, "All right now. Git on in the back there and mind yourselves."

In the flickering headlights I saw a couple of dark figures in overalls run around to the back of the truck and climb aboard. At this I turned to Findlater and whispered, "What in hell's going on, Findlater?"

"Don't start worryin' your head over nothin'," he says.

"This isn't legitimate prize fighting, is it?" I asks.

"And where in hell am I gonna get us a legitimate prize fight in the middle of the night in this hogback country?" he says. "We need some money. I'm gettin' us some money."

I was going to say something about that, when the cigar smoker climbed in again and we started off down this dirt road. As we drove along, being tossed about like peas in a sack, I asks the driver, "Where the hell are we going?"

He looked over at me and grinned around his cigar. "Ain't your

partner there told you?" he says. "Why, we're goin' to a quiltin' bee."
And he snorted and snuffled away to himself.

Nobody said anything for about ten minutes and then we came to
this farm where all the buildings, including the house, was in darkness.
But as we drove up the lane there were automobiles on either side of
us and parked around the house too, dozens of them, all with their
lights out. There were men leaning on fenders and smoking pipes and
cigarettes. As we passed some of them I heard a voice say, "Here they
are now. Let's get on in."

We drove down into the barnyard and Findlater and me followed
the driver around to the back of the truck. There he let down the tailgate and pinned back the canvas flap. "All right now," he shouts. "Come
on down out of there and git on through that side door. A man there'll
look after you and tell you where to go. Hurry it along now."

Behind us and off to one side somebody had thrown open the
main doors of the barn and bright light flooded out onto the dark
ground as the crowd of men hurried inside. I heard a dog barking from
somewhere near and I watched the colored men, mostly young and
husky like Sunny, jump to the ground and walk on in through this little
side door. Near the door was a man holding what looked to me like a
baseball bat.

Sunny and his grandfather were the last ones off the truck and
soon as he spotted us standing there Smokey grabbed Findlater's arm.
"What's goin' on, Mistah Findlater? What they gonna do to my
granson?"

"Now don't worry about a thing, Noah," says Findlater, patting
him on the back. "You just go in with Sunny and help him into his togs.
Everythin's provided free. There'll be sandwiches and beer after." But
Smokey was rooted to the spot. "I don't think we oughtta go in there,
Mistah Findlater." And then he looked at me. "What do you say, Mistah
Billy?"

"I don't know," I says.

Findlater put his arm around Sunny's shoulder. "Listen, Noah.
I'm doin' this for Sunny here. Now maybe this ain't Madison Square
Garden. But you got to make a start somewheres. This is how Dempsey
got started. He told me so himself. A few of these here battle royals
and you build up a reputation. First thing you know you're fightin' in
main events in all the big towns."

Then Cigar Face came over and told us to get a move on. Smokey
shrugged and the two of them set off for the side door of the barn.
Findlater says to me, "We better go round front, Bill, and find this
Hooper. He's the man with the money." As we walked along I asked
him what was going on. He stopped for a moment and then says,
"Well, I'll tell you, Bill. It ain't the best arrangement but it'll get us
some pocket money. Let's see now. There's sixteen niggers. That'll
make eight fights of three rounds each if they don't get a knockout.
Then the winners have a crack at one another until there's only one

left. Twenty-five bucks a fight and fifty bucks to the winner. That is, to his manager. So if Sunny there does his stuff, we stand to make, well, let's see now. A hundred and fifty bucks, ain't it?"

"But he's only sixteen, Findlater," I says. "Maybe younger, for all we know. Some of those fighters are grown men."

"The boy's strong as an ox, Bill. You saw how he handled that big hobo last night."

"He's hardly had a decent meal all day," I says.

"Don't preach to me, Bill," says Findlater, with a touch of anger in his voice. "We need some pocket money!" And he quickly walked away.

Now, more than forty years later, I can still picture that barn in rural Missouri. They had a sort of makeshift ring in the center and about a hundred folding chairs placed around it. The barn was filled with men, all of them white. Most of them looked like hayseed farmers, though from conversation I heard, there was also a good sprinkling of small-town merchants and what some folks call professional people, by which I mean lawyers and doctors. A number of them bore a remarkable resemblance to my late father-in-law, Lawford Pickett. They had the same long, dry-eyed horseface and wattled chin. The thin-lipped mouth and the calculating blue eyes.

There was a blackboard chalked up with numbers in one corner of the barn, and a couple of men were taking bets. The place was noisy, with the seats soon filled and maybe another hundred standing behind. A number of the patrons passed jugs of homemade liquor back and forth, and I will say that I myself took a few good pulls from one that came my way. Then this Hooper climbed through the ropes, fanning himself with his Panama, for it was warm inside and smelled of manure and chewing tobacco and sweat. He waved his hat to the crowd to settle them down and then says, "Welcome to another evenin' of festivities, gentlemen. We got ourselves a fine bunch of bucks tonight, includin' a newcomer from out of the state managed by a Mr. Cass Findlater, who's sittin' right down there in the second row. And we welcome him to our little get-together. Mr. Findlater comes from the big city of Chicago, and so I'd ask him to remember that we're just folks down in these parts and we may not be sophisticated, but we have a lot of fun."

At which Findlater jumps up and shouts, "Well, I think you're the salt of the earth. That's what I think! Where would this country be without its rural and village citizens? I'm just glad to be here among you good people."

There was a nice bit of applause following that. The jug passed our way again, and to tell you the truth, that was my undoing so far as that night is concerned. I felt ashamed and sick at what was going on, and to cover up that shame I got drunk. Or mostly drunk. Some things I remember. I recall, for example, Hooper saying, "I'll just remind you that there'll be cock fightin' here on Sunday night after evenin' service, so all youse who got roosters ready, bring 'em along. And now without further ado, I'll turn you over to Mr. McNeil."

This McNeil was an enormous man. He must have weighed three hundred pounds, sweating in dark pants and white shirt. He was referee and general ringmaster, so he bellows out, "Number nine and number three. Get on out here now." And coming through the crowd were these two black men wearing faded and blood-spattered boxing trunks and ragged gray undershirts with the numbers painted on the backs. The fellow next to me was a good-natured idiot hillbilly, as freckled as a turkey's egg. He was there with his father, a red-faced dirt farmer. Between them they had about a gallon of whiskey, which I helped them get rid of.

The first fight was pretty even and I remember Findlater's choice won after a good deal of fouling. There didn't seem to be any rules, and the fat referee's only job was to keep the two fighters from clinching and slowing down the action. They didn't even give the combatants a stool to sit on between rounds, so they had to squat in a corner of the ring or sit on the floor. After the first fight two more were brought in, and fought their hearts out until one fellow got knocked silly. Sunny came out for the fourth fight, I believe it was. He was matched against a big, light-skinned fellow with a head as bald as a chocolate egg and a long-waisted, muscular body. Now, this fellow made Big Jim look like an angel, and what with butting and gouging and hitting below the belt, he took the first round. In the corner Smokey sponged Sunny's face with dirty water from a wooden bucket and whispered in his ear I know not what, except that the boy shook his head angrily.

Well, I can tell you that when Sunny stepped out for the second round he put on an exhibition of boxing that even had some of those jokers standing on their feet. He weaved and wove his way around the big fellow like a hornet tormenting a bull, jabbing and hooking and frustrating him half to death. Then early in the third round he knocked his opponent cold as well water. I remember jumping to my feet and cheering with vague notions of climbing up into the ring to congratulate the kid. But whether I tripped or was pushed or was just plain drunk I cannot say, because I fell flat on my face and passed out.

When I came to, Smokey was sitting by the bedside, pressing a cold towel against my forehead. I was in some dingy room with peeling wallpaper and sunlight pouring through a window and birdsong nearby. Smokey just looked at me with amusement in his eyes. "How you feelin' now, Mistah Billy?" he says.

"I'll live, Smokey," I says. "What happened? And where the hell are we? Where's Findlater and Sunny?"

"They gone to buy an automobile," says Smokey, shaking his head and grinning as if going out to buy a car was the greatest mystery known to man.

"A car?" I says. "Where did Findlater get the money to buy a car?"

"Mistah Billy," Smokey says, "you missed all the excitement on account of you got into that country liquor. And that's the worst thing a man can get into if'n he's not used to it. So now while you was sleepin' that granson of mine, blame me if he don't win the jackpot. Yes, sah! He won every fight and that Mistah Hooper is so pleased at the show that he matched him up at a place called Hayville, for the night after tomorrow. And lookit here. That Mistah Findlater, I gotta hand it to that man. He give me ten dollars for what he call walkin' aroun' money. Look at that now!" And he held up this crinkled ten-dollar bill. "An' Sunny. He got some too. And you got your share comin', Mistah Billy. And now he gone to buy an automobile. Just imagine now. Noah Day ridin' round the countryside in an automobile. Well, what next, is what I say. But lookit here, that ain't all! That Mistah Findlater say when we gits over to Hayville he's gonna put one of those advertisements in the newspaper offerin' a reward for the findin' of my daughter. Blame me if I've ever seed a man the likes of that Mistah Findlater!"

"What is this place, Smokey?" I asks. "Where are we?"

"We is in a farmhouse not far from where the fightin' took place. It belongs to this Mistah Hooper. Mistah Findlater, he thought it best we stay here on account of if we moved into town we'd have to live separate. This way nobody gonna bother us. And Mistah Billy, I'm gonna fix you a meal of ham and eggs. And now we got bread and coffee and all kinds of good things."

I asked him if he'd changed his mind, then, about Sunny fighting.

He looked thoughtful. "I don't know what to say to that, Mistah Billy. I don't like the boy fightin'. It ain't a fit thing for boy nor man to do. But blame it all, look here. This mornin' we got the first good meal inside us since we left home. Not only that, but we got some spendin' money in our pockets. Now Mistah Findlater gonna get those advertisements into the papers. There don't seem no other way for me to find that gal of mine. Besides which is this. That boy is now so admirin' of Mistah Findlater that I don't believe I could get him back home without I tied him up and dragged him. No, I don't like it, Mistah Billy, but I don't see how I can do nothin' about it. I just hope that after them advertisements in the newspapers somebody comes up with the whereabouts of my daughter. Maybe then we can all go home. And like Mistah Findlater says, maybe we'll go with some money in our pockets."

A couple of hours later Findlater drove up in this old Chevrolet touring car with Sunny standing up holding onto the windshield and waving at us. The boy was deliriously happy. Then Findlater climbed out and let us all admire the vehicle for a moment or two. He winked at me and said, "You look a bit better than you did last night, Bill. Too much of that old barn juice ain't good for you!"

"That's what I told him, Mistah Findlater," says Smokey.

"Well! What do you think of her, boys?" says Findlater. "It's not in the same class with what I'm used to drivin', but she'll have to do!"

He stopped and hugged Sunny's neck. "Just keep those mitts of yours in good shape, son, because they're gonna make us all a fortune." I walked down to the end of the verandah and listened to this spring bird warbling in the trees. Findlater came over and said, "You look a bit down in the mouth there, Bill. But say, I got somethin' here that'll cheer you up. A little taste of the old green. There you are!" And from his pocket he withdrew this tremendous roll of bills and peeled off twenty-five dollars. "I'll drive you into town later and you can get yourself some new duds."

"Why do I get twenty-five when you only give Noah ten?" I asks. "He worked Sunny's corner. I didn't do anything but get drunk."

"But we're partners, Bill. You and me, old pal. Why, we've known one another for years. And Cass Findlater always looks after his friends."

"It seems to me," I says, "that you've done pretty well there."

"A little wagerin' on the side, Bill. I knew the boy would win."

"How much does Sunny get?" I asks.

"Don't you fret. He's looked after."

"Like ten dollars?" I says. "It seems to me that's not much money for fighting four grown men in one night."

Findlater's face darkened. He spoke slowly and I could tell he was holding back a good deal of irritation. "Bill. I am looking after that boy. I am managing his interests. These are just poor ignorant country people and they need tendin'."

Now don't get the idea that I'm any humanitarian, but I handed back fifteen dollars and says, "I'll take the same as them."

Findlater looked at me and then plucked the fifteen dollars from my fingers and applied it to the roll, saying, "Ain't you just becomin' so saintly, though?"

That afternoon we drove into Hayville and Findlater placed an advertisement for Smokey's missing daughter in the local newspaper. I wrote it out for him. I don't believe I've ever seen a man so happy as Smokey. I didn't bother to tell him that the newspaper probably didn't circulate more than twenty miles or so.

33

FAREWELLS AND DEPARTURES

DURING THE NEXT few weeks—well on into the summer, I guess—we toured the states of Missouri, Illinois, Indiana, and even into the southern part of Ohio. Always we pressed on to another town where Findlater had been given the name of some joker who organized these fights. He might be the local hardware merchant or the county judge. Sunny fought a couple of times a week and mostly he won, though he lost a few too, particularly if he was tired. One night in a town south of Gary, Indiana, he took a bad beating from another kid about his own age. We drove from place to place in the Chevrolet and sometimes it wasn't bad, with Findlater behind the wheel and the rest of us eating ice cream from a cardboard carton, the wind stirring our hair and rushing past our faces, waving to the hitch-hikers and watching the long freight trains with men being chased along the tops of the cars by railroad cops.

Findlater was sleeping better, with no bad dreams, and I put that down to the fact that he was making money again. He solved the problem of accommodation by buying a big tent, and now that it was early summer we'd pitch that tent by some river where we could fish. Or up some country road where no one would bother us. And I have to say, it was all right. Findlater would drive into the local town to make the arrangements, leaving Noah and me to sit and talk while Sunny slept. The boy was tired a good bit of the time and it was like a shadow over our good moods, because we knew that every bite of food and thread of clothing on our backs was owing to Sunny. All he seemed to do was eat and sleep and fight. Every now and again Noah would fret over him, and the whole way of life, and he'd say to me, "What do you think, Mistah Billy? It don't seem like we're gettin' nowhere lookin' for my gal." And I'd promise to talk to Findlater about it, and

308

he'd say, "Sure, pal, sure. We'll get on that tomorrow." And he would place another advertisement, which cost maybe forty cents.

Now all these fights, as you might imagine, were illegal. Nobody was licensed, and the rules were set by the local organizers. Some places were rougher than others. Nor did these battle royals always take place in barns deep in the country. Now and then they were held right under the noses of respectable citizens in the middle of town. Maybe in some lodge hall where they were part of what they used to call smokers. These were gatherings of men who would sit around smoking cigars and drinking whiskey, carrying on like college kids. Sometimes between fights they might have some old burlesque dancer come out into the ring and do a few bumps and grinds. Or perhaps they'd show a dirty moving picture, which generally no one could make out because it was always faded and blurred and after a couple of minutes flickered and broke down. Those smokers nearly bored me to death. In fact, the whole way of life began to bore me and I started thinking seriously of returning to my own country.

Then one day I saw Sally Butters. And if you think she turned out to be one of those burlesque girls and that I rescued her from making an exhibition of herself in some cheap show, you are wrong and should be reading cheap romances. Actually, what happened was much simpler. We were stopped at a railway crossing early one evening on the outskirts of a town not far from Cincinnati, Ohio. A passenger train slowly creaked by and we sat there in the Chevrolet gawking at the passengers. As the dining car passed, damn me for a liar if I didn't see Sally. She was seated at a table, being fussed over by a waiter. She looked like a queen, cool and regal in this maroon dress. Her hair was still red, though a shade darker than I remembered. There she was, not ten feet away, behind window glass studying the menu. If she'd have glanced out that window she'd have seen a strange sight—a small man in tan work clothes, nearly fifty-three, standing in the back of a Chevrolet touring car with two black men and a large figure wearing a derby hat. And that small man would have been waving his arms and yelling, for that is exactly what I was doing.

"Findlater!" I yelled. "That's Sally!"

"Sally!" says Findlater. "Where?"

"Right in front of your eyes," I says.

"Why, I believe you're right."

And then the train went on down the track and left us sitting there with cars honking behind. For a minute I thought it had just been some kind of vision or a plain case of mistaken identity, but Findlater said no. "That was Sal all right, Bill," he says. "And that woman looks like she's livin' in biscuit city." Then he explained to Noah how Sally had been an old sweetheart of mine.

"I knowed a gal once," says Noah. "We was children playin' aroun' and she was sweet on me. But I had no time for her on account of she was such an ugly little devil in those days. Her whole family up and moved away. That would be nearly sixty years ago. Well, do you know that years later, when I am lumbered down with family and troubles, I sees that gal's pitcher in an old magazine. And if she ain't a famous lady down in New Orleans these thumbs ain't on my hands. With her friends all jazz musicians, and her runnin' this here bordello. And the hurtin' part is this. From the looks of the pitcher that gal had turned into a mighty attractive woman. And she came from Flatt's Crossing and at fourteen she was sweet on Noah Day. Now beat that."

"Life is queer all right, Noah," says Findlater. "A friend of mine named Martin Rooney used to say that. And he was a genuwine poet and philosopher, so he ought to have knowed."

Sunny was supposed to fight the next night at a smoker in a little fly spot on the map called Chapter Hill. But that morning he complained of feeling poorly. He was dead tired, though he'd slept for twelve hours. Noah felt the boy's head but there wasn't any fever or unnatural signs, only this great fatigue. I'd noticed more and more that Sunny was suffering from general tiredness, so I suggested to Findlater that we forget about that evening's match. Findlater said a good beef-steak would cure Sunny's ailment and he drove on into town, returning about noon with a big steak, which he personally cooked over the fire. But Sunny only picked at the food, pushing down a few mouthfuls, more to please Findlater than anything else. I believe that boy would have walked through hellfire for Findlater. You never saw such housedog devotion. When the afternoon wore on and the boy was still listless, I suggested we take him to a doctor. Findlater didn't put any store by medical science. "They're all a bunch of quacks," he said. "I've never seen one yet who could do anything right."

"Maybe so," I said. "But I'd feel better if that boy saw a doctor."

"Mistah Billy's right," says Noah. "My granson don't look good. An' he's had these faintin' spells before. When he was a little child, he'd play too hard and faint dead away somewheres. Then he'd come aroun' and be good as new."

"You never said anything about that, Noah," I says.

"It ain't happen now for years."

It was a hot and sultry day and about four o'clock we drove into town, with Findlater still grumbling about there being no need to involve doctors. We asked where the doctor lived, and it was a white frame house surrounded by a picket fence. It was a pretty little place, with a colored man mowing the grass. He stopped to mop his brow with a handkerchief and watched while Findlater and Sunny and me walked up to the front door. We were in luck, for the doctor, a tall, stoop-shouldered fellow wearing those old pince-nez glasses, was just back from his hospital rounds. Findlater explained that we were strangers passing through. "Sunny here is mute, Doc, so he can't tell you nothin'. He's probably just got a touch of summer flu. Give him a little drop of camphor and he'll be right as rain."

The doctor looked at us with a cold eye and says, "You can wait in the hall, gentlemen."

33. *Farewells and Departures*

I thought he was a little heavy on the sarcasm and I suppose you couldn't blame him, for I caught sight of us in the hall mirror. We looked like we lived in tents and skulked around in the middle of the night. Findlater had bought himself one of those white linen suits for summer but it was baggy and dirty and there were food stains down the front. I might have been some mean-assed little foreman on a chain gang. The colored maid gave us a look of terrible scorn. She was busy flicking imaginary dirt away with this feather duster, though I don't know why she bothered, for the place was spotless and reminded me of my own home in Elmhurst, Ontario. There was even a couple of canaries singing in a cage somewhere.

Well, about twenty minutes later the doctor came out with Sunny, who was buttoning up his shirt. The doctor looked serious. "What's the problem, Doc?" asks Findlater, standing up.

The doctor looked us both over as if trying to decide which of us was the most trustworthy and coming to the general conclusion that neither of us was. "What's this boy do?" he asks. "Does he go to school or work or what?"

"That boy, Doc," says Findlater, "is on his way to becomin' the next heavyweight champeen of the world."

The doctor looked like he couldn't believe his ears. "You mean to stand there and tell me that this boy has been prize fighting?"

"That's a fact, Doc," says Findlater. "And he's a natural. Another Jack Johnson!"

"And maybe," says the doctor, his voice trembling, "you can tell me how you got a license for this boy to fight? He's not physically fit. How did he even pass a medical examination? I'd like the name of the doctor who looked him over!"

"Not physically fit?" asks Findlater, with a touch of bafflement in his voice.

"Not physically fit," repeats the doctor. "And now I'll ask you again how you got a license for this boy."

"Well now, Doc," says Findlater. "These are just amateur fights, you understand. A little bit of cuffin' aroun' here and there. You don't really need a license."

"I've heard of people like you," the doctor says in this low, quavering voice. "But I didn't really believe what I heard. You are the scum of the earth." Behind him I could see the maid looking at us like we were a couple of bugs. "That boy," says the doctor, pointing at Sunny, "has a bad heart murmur. He shouldn't be doing anything more strenuous than a short daily walk for the next six weeks. You've probably already put a strain on that heart that will shorten his life. Do you understand what I'm saying?"

"Well sure, Doc," says Findlater. "We didn't know, you see. Why, Sunny there, he's like my own son. I wouldn't see him hurt for the world."

"The boy needs rest," the doctor says, going to the door and opening it. "I don't know what you two characters are up to, but I'm warn-

311

ing you, if I hear of any harm coming to this boy, I'll have you both locked up for good. That'll be five dollars."

Findlater took out his roll. "That seems a little steep, Doc. Just to tell us the boy's tired."

The doctor took the five-dollar bill. "Now get the hell off my property."

We walked quickly down to the car and I felt as full of shame as I've ever felt in my life. Noah watched us come down the walk with worry in his face. "What's the man say, Mistah Findlater? What's wrong with my granson?"

"Nothin' much wrong with him, Noah," says Findlater, starting th car. "He's just a small-town quack. I've never met a doctor yet I believed."

"Wait a minute now, Findlater," I says from the back seat. "The doctor looked Sunny over and said he had a heart murmur. There's no two ways about it."

"A heart murmur?" asks Noah. "What's that?"

"It's nothin'," says Findlater. "Nothin' at all. Five bucks to tell you nothin' at all." He slammed the car into gear. He was boiling mad. "I say the boy is right as rain. All right, he's a little tired. Anybody with eyes in his head can see that. And after tonight we'll take a couple of weeks off and go fishin' or somethin'. You'd like that, wouldn't you, son?" he says to Sunny. The boy just grinned and nodded his head. "You're feelin' better already, aren't you?" The boy nodded again. "There now, you see!"

We were on our way out of town, going back to camp. "You're not going to let that boy fight tonight, after what the doctor just told you?" I says.

"The boy will be all right, Bill."

"The boy is sick," I says. "You're not going to put him on the card."

"He's already on the card, Bill. I promised the man. They're lookin' forward to Sunny here. He's gettin' himself a reputation."

"Mistah Findlater," says Noah. "I don't want my granson fightin' no more if he's sick."

"He ain't sick, Noah, believe you me he ain't. You're not gonna take some quack's word for it! Listen! I've never let you people down."

"That's true as you tell it, Mistah Findlater," says Noah, leaning forward. "And we appreciates what you've done for us. But if the boy here is sick, I don't think . . ."

"The boy ain't sick, Noah, I'm tellin' you."

"But Mistah Billy say the doctor . . ."

"He ain't sick, goddamit," bellows Findlater. "I'm tellin' you, he ain't sick. And that's the end of that."

By the time we reached the camp I'd already made up my mind to leave. I suppose I could see it coming for a long time and just needed a shove and a push, as they say. But now I knew for sure that my traveling days with Findlater were over.

33. *Farewells and Departures*

I was packing my bag in the tent when Noah came in and said, "Is this heart murmurin' business serious, Mistah Billy?"

"It could be, Smokey," I says. "I don't know much about it, to tell you the truth, but I wouldn't take any chances. The doctor said the boy needed rest."

"And you is pullin' out, Mistah Billy?"

"Yes," I says. "I'm pullin' out. Going back home." We never said anything for a minute or so and it was damned awkward. Then I said, "Are you going to let him fight tonight?"

And Noah says, "There just ain't nothin' I can do about it, Mistah Billy. I can't sway that boy's mind. He don't want to disappoint Mistah Findlater on account of there's a big-shot fightin' man from Cleveland, Ohio, supposed to be there tonight. Mistah Findlater says this be Sunny's chance to make the big time." I didn't say anything to that. "I could tell you been thinkin' deep on somethin' over the past little while," says Noah. "You and Mistah Findlater ain't friends no more, is you?"

"I don't know," I says. "We just don't see eye to eye on things anymore. Maybe we never did. I don't know."

"Sometimes that's the way things happen. Now, I'd like to take that boy back home. I don't want him fightin' no more. I didn't want him fightin' in the first place. But I thought it would help find his momma. Now I see it ain't gonna do no such thing."

"I'll talk to Findlater again," I says. "I'll try to persuade him not to go through with this thing tonight."

"I'd appreciate that, Mistah Billy."

Findlater was sitting under a tree looking as sullen as I'd ever seen him. When an abnormally cheerful, optimistic man like Findlater gets in a foul humor you've got an abnormally sullen man on your hands.

"Why don't you forget about this fight tonight," I says. "You got enough money in your pocket there."

"Can't do that, Bill," he says, chewing on a piece of grass.

"Why not?"

Findlater reached into his pocket and pulled out his wad, which was secured by a thick rubber band. He undid it and showed me. Under two tens there were just about fifty or sixty one-dollar bills.

"Well, where did it all go?" I asks. "Sunny's been winning a lot. What are you doing with the money?"

"Lost in wagers, Bill. And expenses are heavy. I got to outfit this gang."

"But if you're wagering," I says, "it means you been bettin' against that boy. Expecting him to lose."

"Don't talk to me, Bill. I got things on my mind."

"I've a good notion to tell Sunny and Noah what you've been up to."

"Go ahead, pal. They won't believe you."

Probably that was true. "What about this big shot from Cleveland

313

who's supposed to be there tonight? I suppose that's another lie?"

"A *true friend is the best possession, Bill.*"

"I'm pulling out, Findlater. I'm going back to Craven Falls."

Findlater looked up at me and there was a sneer on his face. "Well, that's up to you, pal," he says. "At one time I thought you was a friend of mine. I thought I could learn a few things from you too. Cultured things and what not. Now I don't believe you know half what you're talkin' about. I don't believe your daddy was a genuwine poet neither. Martin Rooney told me that once. He said he looked in all the big liberries and none of them ever mentioned your father's name."

"I never said my father was famous. I just said he was a poet."

"I'll bet he shoed horses or somethin' like that. No, sir. You ain't half the man I thought you was. It turns out you're just a touchy little bugger who don't know which end is up. You could have made a fortune in money back there when you got out of that hospital. Sellin' your life story. Instead of which you rode freight trains and ate cold beans. That was pure foolishness."

"Goodbye, Findlater," I says. "If you're any kind of man, you'll cancel that fight tonight."

To which he says, "A *false friend and a shadow attend only when the sun shines.*"

I walked away from him just as Noah and Sunny came out of the tent. Noah must have told Sunny I was leaving, because he looked a little puzzled. But then, I suppose, me going away was no stranger than everything else that had happened to him during the past few weeks. He just smiled and walked over to Findlater. Noah and me shook hands. "I'm gonna miss you, Mistah Billy," says Noah.

"Same here, Smokey," I says. "You're a good man to travel with."

"You take care now."

"I will do that."

We both looked at Sunny and Findlater sitting under the tree, and Noah shook his head. "It sure do explain some things," he said sadly.

"What does?" I asks.

"Oh, this heart murmurin' you been talkin' about. Like I told you once, I figured the boy for bein' lazy. Say he was primin' tobacca. Well, he'd go like the wind up and down the rows for half the mornin'. Then along about the middle of the mornin' he'd just lay down and go to sleep. I used to scold him for that. Now it turns out he wasn't lazy at all. He was just tuckered out on account of this heart murmuri..'. I did the boy wrong."

"Well, you didn't know," I says.

He took my hand again. "Goodbye, Mistah Billy. I don't know what you're aimin' to do with your life, but if I was your age agin I'd go into pigs. Pigs won't ever let you down. Contrary to general thinkin', pigs is about the best friends a man can have."

"I'll remember that," I says. And I did.

314

34

HOME

FOUR DAYS LATER, on July 1, 1933, my fifty-third birthday, I was walking along the main street of Craven Falls, Ontario, having just jumped
off a flatcar near the railway station. The place hadn't changed much
since I'd been there over thirty years before. The government was
building a new post office, and that seemed to be the only work around.
It attracted the usual crowd of gawkers. They were sons of the men
who used to stand at the long dark bar of Plumb's Hotel helping my
father drink up his remittance check. Plumb's Hotel, which I remembered as a sporting establishment, was now just run-down, with only
a few old-timers sitting in wicker chairs on the verandah. I walked
right on through town and no one recognized me, which was fine,
because I wasn't in any humor to pass the time with those nose-picking
yokels.

Now you might wonder what I had in mind to do with my life at
this point in time. Well, what I thought I would do was this. I'd take
Smokey's advice and raise pigs. I had a few bucks saved and I thought
that if Rufus Talbot was still alive he might help me get the old homestead in shape.

It was a blistering hot day and a mile or so out of town I stopped
by a creek and filled my hat with water. Just then this vehicle comes
down the road from town, with steam pouring out from under the
hood. The driver finally pulled over and stopped. This vehicle turned
out to be an ancient Packard hearse, one of those big old square numbers that looked like a stagecoach without the horses. Well, the front
door opened and damn me if the driver isn't a woman! And a fine-
looking woman too, tall with reddish hair. She was wearing a long,
dark dress, with a little cap and veil sitting on her head. She stood
there for a minute looking at all this steam and then she whips off this

315

little bit of a hat and tries to wrench loose the radiator cap. All she manages to do is scald her fingers and say a few things you wouldn't normally expect a lady to utter. But then it isn't every day you see a lady driving a hearse, either. She was just going through her fourth or fifth "son of a bitch" when I walked up and offered to do the job. She stepped aside, and my old felt hat, soaked through with creek water, was just the business to get that radiator cap off.

We stood back for a few seconds and watched the old Packard steam. It also gave me an opportunity to study this woman, standing there with her hands on her hips. Her face looked familiar to me, I can tell you that. There was a severe cast to her features but a full lip softened the general impression of bad temper. She had a longish straight nose and, as I've said, her hair was red but streaked with a kind of gold that caught the sunlight. She was an admirable-looking woman, maybe thirty years old, and taller than me by a good three inches. We didn't say anything for a while, though I could tell she was giving me more than a passing look too. And if I do say so, there were worse-looking men around at the time. I was trim and fit and tanned nearly brown as a walnut.

So after the radiator cooled down I says, "Now, if you got some kind of jug I'll draw water from that creek and fill up your radiator. You'll be good as new again."

"This is very kind of you," she says, in this cultivated voice.

The old Packard had a big tool chest with all sorts of stuff in it, including a gallon pail, and after a couple of trips to the creek I had the radiator full. While I worked we gave each other another careful scrutinizing. I could see that this woman had some kind of breeding. On the other hand, she'd uttered a few choice oaths when she didn't know I was around. It was damn strange. After I finished, she snapped open a leather purse and extracted a fifty-cent piece. "I hope," she says, "you won't be insulted if I give you this."

Then it came to me in a flash. Maybe it's already come to you, if you're sharp. The way this woman opened her purse was just the way Esther Easterbrook had opened her purse in front of the King Edward Hotel the summer before when Findlater and me were on the bum. I could see it all in her face. The hair wasn't as golden but the chin and eyes were the same. Nor was she nearly as refined as Esther, though she carried herself with remarkable grace for a big woman. I was puzzling all this out and mumbling something about payment not being necessary when she asks me if I want a ride. Well, I certainly did, and we got in and started down the road.

"How far are you going, mister?" she asks.

"Farthing's the name," I says. "Bill Farthing. And I'm going down the road a couple of miles to our old homestead."

At this she damn near ran the old Packard off the road. I thought she'd had a fainting spell or something, for she suddenly looked pale and pulled over to the shoulder. "I'm sorry, Mr. Farthing," she says.

"You just took me by surprise. No one was expecting you. You must be the youngest son. People thought you were dead."

"What people?" I says.

"I don't suppose you know, then?"

"Know what?" I asks.

"I'm on my way out to Rufus Talbot's to pick up your father's body."

"My father's body?" I says in some amazement. "Why, Christ Almighty! Excuse me, but he'd be a hundred years old."

"He was ninety-eight, Mr. Farthing. The oldest man in the township. He died this morning. I'm sorry."

"I thought he was dead years ago. I never did find out what happened to him."

"He came back to Craven Falls about fifteen years ago and lived with his son-in-law. It was just after the war. He was a cultivated old gentleman. I used to see him in town now and again. He had manners, which is more than I can say for most of the local inhabitants. I understand he once wrote poetry. I always liked him for that."

"Ninety-eight years old," I says, shaking my head. "Well damn me, but that is a corker."

Then she offered me her hand. "I'm sorry you had to find out this way. My name is Jessie Fletcher."

We shook hands. "And you'd be related to Phineas Fletcher?"

"He was my father," she says. "He died a few years ago. He was a very old man too. I've been running the business ever since."

"Life is queer," I says. "I used to work for your father. When I was just a kid."

"Is that so?" she says. "It's funny he never mentioned it to me."

Well, I could see why. This woman sitting next to me was once the baby that old Fletcher talked about in the cemetery that morning when he was burying his wife. If you remember, Mrs. Fletcher died in childbirth, leaving behind a little girl. And this was her, now grown to womanhood. And from her appearance, I'd have bet the best hat in town that her real father was Mr. Easterbrook. Old Fletcher must have raised her as his own and naturally he wouldn't mention my name, because he believed I was the cause of his wife's fall to perdition. That's why I scratched my head at the queerness of it. Of course, knowing old Fletcher, this woman would have been raised in total ignorance of the truth, which in many ways is a good thing.

We started down the road again and I asked her about herself. She told me that she had spent most of her girlhood in a fancy boarding school down in Toronto and at one time she had plans to be a schoolteacher, for she was fond of English poetry. That didn't surprise me a bit, for you'll recall how Esther Easterbrook was partial to literature. And even Mrs. Fletcher was fond of reading, even though it was trashy romances. But after her schooling old Fletcher got sick and she came home to help, being a husky young girl and not minding corpses and coffins. Well, she just stayed on, hinting here and there that there were other reasons, which I took to mean a man was involved. Then her father died and a few years later the Depression came along and there wasn't anywhere to go. It seemed to me that she was a lonely person who was just dying to talk to somebody.

"So it's still Miss Fletcher, is it?" I asks.

"Yes," she says. "And I thank my lucky stars I didn't marry a particular party. He was a regular good-for-nothing."

"Well, we've all been stung once or twice in that department, Miss Fletcher," I says.

She looked at me with a wry smile. The woman could handle herself. You could tell that looking at her. "So you've had some experience, have you, Mr. Farthing?"

"Some," I says.

"Marriage too?"

"Yes. But that was a long time ago."

"Did you love her?"

"No," I says. "I didn't love her. I married her for a general store."

That brought a great bark of laughter from her and for a minute I could have sworn I was back forty years before with her mother.

When we got to Rufus Talbot's, he was standing in the doorway waiting for us. I found Rufus much the same, though he was now a prosperous farmer in his late fifties. His corn-colored hair was now white and his powerful frame slightly stooped but he was still the big, easy-going, mildly slow man who used to sit in our kitchen watching Annie fry a half-dozen eggs. He was a naturally sweet-tempered man and he greeted me like a long lost friend. "It's a funny thing, Bill," he says to me. "Your poor old Dad told me at breakfast that he had a dream last night. And in this dream your brother Tom walked through that door. Maybe it was you he was dreamin' about."

"Maybe," I says, following Jessie Fletcher and Rufus into the house. There was a short, pie-faced woman standing there. She was as big around as a rain barrel, with a bun of white hair. It seemed to me that Annie had shrunk about six inches over the years, so I says, "Hello, Annie. You've changed a little."

"Heavenly days, Bill," says Rufus. "This isn't Ann. Poor Ann passed away in 1912 during a fit of apoplexy. You remember that poor girl's temper. This here's my second wife. She used to be Flora Buckley. You remember the Buckleys down on the tenth concession, don't you?"

I didn't but I said I did, and we went on into the parlor, where my father was laid out on the sofa. He lay there in his old frock coat, green at the collar. Instead of a Bible he was clutching a copy of *Pine Smoke at Evensong*. "He died right there in his sleep," says Rufus. "He lay down after breakfast with his book and when Flora came to wake him for lunch, he was gone, poor old fellah."

Jessie set right to work and I helped her, being no stranger to that occupation. Before long we had him in the hearse and were set to go.

"Rufus," I says, "I'm grateful to you for looking after my father all these years."

"He was a good old fellah, Bill. We didn't mind havin' him around one little bit. He turned up on our doorstep one night. It was dark and stormy. He was soaked through. It must have been fourteen or fifteen years ago. He used to help my boys with their writin' and readin'. I was never much for that, you know."

"What ever happened to that Miss Boswell?" I asked.

"Your father once told me she came to a bad end. Took to drink and ended up in one of those houses of ill repute."

"I'd never have guessed."

"Me neither. Your father took to religion at the end, Bill. And he swore off liquor. There wasn't a drop of liquor passed his lips all the time he lived in this house." Just then I heard a terrific whoop and a shout coming from the barn. The door opened and three old men in dirty, ragged clothes staggered out, waving bottles. "I wish I could say the same thing about your two brothers, Bill. That's Ned and Fred down there with Everett Snipes."

"What in hell are they doing drinking in your barn, Rufus?"

"They're wakin' your father."

I remembered them drinking in our barn when poor Tom was laid out forty years before. "Why don't you kick them off the property?"

Rufus pushed the hair out of his eyes and looked pained at the suggestion. "I hate to tell them to leave when their father's just died."

That's the kind of good-natured fellow Rufus Talbot was. Well, I ignored my brothers for the moment, feeling I had very little to say to them, as they were now lying face down in the barnyard with the chickens walking around them. So I helped Jessie Fletcher, and next day we buried my father with his beloved book of poems. It was a simple ceremony, to which no one came except Rufus and his wife and Jessie and me. My brothers were too drunk to attend.

After that I settled in at the old homestead. When Ned and Fred sobered up, they came around looking for a handout and professing to have changed their ways. I'm not and never have been the good-natured man Rufus Talbot was and I sent them packing to their cabin, next to the old Snipes's place. They remained there in a state of total depravity until Christmas Eve in '42. That night they lay down on the tracks for a sleep and were sliced in half by a freight train.

As I've said, Rufus was slow but he was a hard worker and prosperous by Depression standards. His sons now had their own farms and he had two daughters by his second wife. One was away at a teachers college and the other married to a young farmer in the township. Rufus not only gave me back the homestead but helped me to rebuild it. The original log house had fallen into ruin and there was a good deal of work to make it livable. I bought twenty Yorkshires and became a pig farmer of sorts, supplementing my income by helping Jessie Fletcher at the funeral parlor.

Jessie and me became intimate friends, and that was the beginning of the most contented years of my life. I could tell that Jessie liked me right from the start. You see, she was bored with small-town life and I came along just at the right time, because she was getting over this fellow named Frank Tanner. She didn't go into many details about him, except to say that he worked for her father and cheated him out of money. It's an amazing thing how women with looks and brains and breeding will go crazy over an absolute skunk, which this fellow turned out to be. When I came along this Tanner was receding into Jessie's memory and her wounds were healing.

Jessie was a strange woman and it used to amuse me to study her. Not in the way that those gimcrack psychologists try to take a person's head apart, but just to see her as a combination of two things. There was old Easterbrook's blood and her boarding-school life on the one hand. And then there was the undeniable fact that she was Mary Jane Hinks' daughter. All these things turned out an interesting human, as full of contradictions and puzzling behavior as you're ever likely to encounter. As I say, she was a handsome woman, and she carried herself somewhat aloof. She had this air of quality about her and could put the cold eye on the ladies from the Women's Institute. Where her mother might just have thrown open the window and told some old gossip to go to hell, Jess would just cut her cold in the butcher shop. There's nothing that will intimidate small-town women more than starchy manners. I figure all that came from her Easterbrook blood plus the fancy school. Wherever it came from, it caused men to tip their hats and women to smile and look away, because they hated her in their hearts. On the other hand, Jessie was a lot like her mother. When things didn't go her own way, she had a rough temper. She was also uncommonly fond of the carnal pleasures. We liked each other, though I often used to wonder what she'd think of me if she knew that I was once on intimate terms with her mother. She showed me Mrs. Fletcher's picture once. It was a little cameo with Mrs. Fletcher wearing a high-collared dress and her hair piled up in the old-fashioned style of the nineties. That's all Jessie knew about her. Once she'd heard a little unsavory gossip but she put that down to jealousy among the town ladies because her mother was so much prettier. Which was certainly true.

After we got to know one another a little better we came to what you would call an arrangement. I worked for her whenever there was a funeral. I also became her paramour. And here's a funny thing too. She enjoyed being read to. Not the trashy romances that her mother had liked, but first-class stories such as young Esther Easterbrook liked. I must have read books like *Vanity Fair* and *Pride and Prejudice* three or four times to her. It seemed damned strange to be reading to her in the very same room where I once read to her mother. And as in the old days, we'd go up the stairs and have a couple of tumbles and I'd leave early in the morning, usually before first light, walking back

home. Naturally the neighbors were outraged to see the likes of me
leaving the funeral parlor at four o'clock on Sunday morning! Being a
Farthing, I was generally held to be a useless fellow and probably
dangerous. Many of the old-timers remembered my father as a mad
drunken poet, and of course Ned and Fred hadn't exactly distinguished
themselves in life. The other thing about me that bothered people was
that I raised pigs and lived by myself. If you live by yourself, you'll
drive a lot of people crazy, for they don't think it's natural. And then
there's a general prejudice against people who raise pigs. When I'd
pass by on the street the kids would often say, There goes old Billy,
the pig man.

So people just couldn't understand why a woman of Jessie's breeding and refinement could spend her Saturday evenings with a fellow
like me. Some of the more malicious ones put it down to her being fast,
and they pointed back to her involvement with this Frank Tanner. And
others thought it peculiar that I had once lived there with Jessie's
mother and father, though Mary Jane and I had been discreet enough
and nobody in this town had the imagination to suppose that we'd
actually had an affaire de coeur, as the French say. That would have
given half the women in town a stroke.

Jessie was keen to know about my various travels and I told her
quite a bit. Not everything, for you must never tell a person you're
fond of everything about your life. I told her about Findlater and the
Klondike and traveling around, though I didn't mention my long spell
of amnesia. Speaking of which, I have to say this. It's true that there
was a sizable chunk of my life taken out by that damn cricket ball, but
on the other hand there were compensations. Take sex as an example.
Now, I was fifty-three when Jessie and I decided to become good
friends. And fifty-three is a time when a lot of men's juices are starting
to dry up. Mine, however, were flowing like spring sap and it was a
good thing too, because I was confronted with a strong young woman
who had twenty years on me.

When the Hitler war came along, the price of pork rose and I
increased my herd and did well enough for a couple of years, adding
a few furnishings to my home and buying a second-hand Model A
truck. But a man has got to expect trouble in his life, and it usually
comes when he figures he's got things under control. My troubles
began the year before the war ended. For a start Jessie began to decline that winter of '44. She just seemed to go on losing weight no matter how much she ate and she was always complaining of being tired
and having no strength. She could no longer help me with the heavy
work and I had to hire an old fellow, because most of the young men
around town had joined the service. And then we had competition
from a man named Palmer who came up from Toronto with a fancy
new hearse and all the trimmings. But it was Jessie's health that concerned me more than Palmer. It was pitiful to see a big, strapping
woman begin to decline. She just lost her appetite for life and would

sit around looking glum. Her skin took on a yellow, waxy color and her
hair was dry as summer grass. She was too stubborn to see a doctor
about it.

On the day the war ended they had a parade in Craven Falls, with
the local bugle band leading the school kids, who waved little Union
Jacks. Hector McCoy marched along with them, wearing his lodge
medals. I watched them go by from the front window of the funeral
parlor. Jessie was so weak she couldn't get out of bed and so I called
the doctor. He came that afternoon, took one look at her, and was
madder than hell because we hadn't called him sooner. He figured it
could be hepatitis, but he was looking pretty sour and wasn't about to
say much to me anyway. He could smell the liquor on my breath, and
like most folks in town, he had me down as a bum who was probably
hanging around Jessie for her money. I packed a few of Jessie's things
and over her protests we got her into the doctor's car and took her to
the hospital, where they more or less slammed the door in my face.
When I phoned the doctor the next day the bastard couldn't even be
polite. All he said was that they were taking blood samples and she
would be better off if left alone. So I stayed away for a couple of days
and then phoned the hospital. Jessie sounded more cheerful than she
had for months and wondered where I was and would I mind coming
around and reading to her. She asked me to bring *Return of the Native*,
for she was partial to that high-spirited girl Eustacia Vye. So I went
around and read her a few chapters and at the end of it held her hand
and kissed her dry cheek.

As I was about to leave she told me they were going to operate
on her the next day. "Just a routine thing. I'll be up and about in no
time." As I rose, she grabbed my wrist and smiled weakly. "You old
goat, you're not fooling around with any of those township girls, are
you?"

"Jessie," I says, "I'm saving it all for you."

"Go on. Get out of here," she says. "You're a bad influence on me."

The next day they operated and they found the cancer that was
destroying her. For the next six weeks Jessie lingered, growing more
feeble with each passing day. It was midsummer and hot, and all I
could do was sit by her side and wipe the perspiration from her brow.
I left the pigs in Rufus's care and I slept at the funeral home.

Sometimes when I visited Jessie she was angry at me being there.
She was a proud woman and she knew she didn't look good. And once
she said, "Go away, Farthing, and leave me alone." She never called
me anything but Farthing or old goat or maybe pig man.

"Now, Jesse," I'd say, "don't start that."

"I smell," she'd say. "I give off a bad odor."

"Oh Christ, never mind that," I'd say. "Here, let me read to you."
But after a while she couldn't concentrate on what I was reading and
her face was so twisted with pain that I'd have to leave.

The night before she died she told me that she'd sold the funeral business to Palmer. She looked up at me with those big, hollow eyes and said, "I've got to tell you something else, Farthing. I made my will today. I left you a thousand dollars and my books. Maybe it doesn't seem like much, for the rest of it is going to charity. But you'll be able to hold your head up when you come into town. People will never be able to say that you were there for the money. I'm not trying to be spiteful. Do you understand?"

Well, I understood, and anyway it had been many years since I'd put that much store by money.

Then she said, "I've got to tell you something else, Farthing, for we've been good friends now for many years. But that's all we've been. Just friends. We've had some good times and I've always liked you. I've liked you more than I've liked any other person I've known except maybe my father." She stopped to get her breath. "But I've never loved you, Farthing," she says. "The damnable thing is that the only man I ever loved was that good-for-nothing son of a bitch, Frank Tanner." She smiled sadly and tried to squeeze my hand but she lacked the strength. My big Jessie. Who could once almost arm-wrestle me to the table! "I don't know if you loved me, Farthing," she says. "It isn't something we talked much about, and I sometimes think that's the best way. If you did love me, I'm sorry I couldn't return it. But you were a good friend and I hope you loved somebody once. It would make me happy to know you loved somebody once."

"Well, I did, Jess," I says. "I was foolish in love most of my life with a dance hall singer. A beautiful woman. I haven't seen her in years. She had red hair like you."

Poor Jess. She reached up to touch her dry hair, and she was trying hard not to cry. "Go on now," she says. "Go back to your pigs. I'm tired."

The funeral home was locked and my key didn't fit anymore, so I bought a bottle of whiskey and slept in my truck that night. It was parked across the street from the hospital. Jessie died the next day about noon. I drank some beer at the hotel and then drove out to the homestead. There I found Rufus down in the pigpen, bending over a couple of my pigs. They looked sick and were spotted near the rump. Rufus looked up as I came in. "You got trouble here, Bill," he says. "We tried to get you on the telephone. You got some sick pigs here. They won't take their feed. I've doused a couple with castor oil, but it don't look good. See these here spots. I had a couple of sows back a few years ago with spots like that. They just sickened and died. There's a name for it. I think I better go for the vet."

I was half drunk and I stood there swaying in the straw and mud looking down. Then Rufus says, "You shouldn't drive that truck when you're drinkin', Bill."

"Miss Fletcher died a couple of hours ago, Rufus," I says.

"Ah, say now, that's a shame, Bill." He looked like he wanted to say something else but thought better of it. Rufus was never able to figure out my relationship with Jessie. He'd heard people talk. But the whole idea of a man and a woman having a relationship outside of marriage was just so remote to him that he couldn't fathom it. "Well now, Bill," he says at last, "I better go fetch the vet for these here pigs. Maybe you'd like to go on over to my place and have Flora fix you some dinner." And he left me there, standing in the pigpen with those sick animals.

Jessie was buried on a sunny day with a light summer wind stirring the leaves on the maple trees. It was just the sort of day when we might have laid together in some pasture after picking up a body out in the township. Just to say screw you to the fates. A good number of people turned out for the funeral and I stood at the back of the cemetery near the fence drinking whiskey. People talked about me not having any respect, but they didn't know anything about it. That night I visited Jessie's grave and said goodbye.

All my pigs died that summer. One by one they sickened and died just as Rufus said they might. It was something called erysipelas and it was contagious to humans, producing a kind of skin disease that turned parts of you blotchy and red. I understand that in the olden days it was called St. Anthony's Fire. I don't know why, unless this St. Anthony kept pigs like me and caught the disease too. In any case, it didn't help my general appearance. Most people believed that I had contracted a social disease. It fit nicely into their notion of how I'd lived my life.

I can tell you, I was a long way from the young dandy who had once stood outside the Bijou Theater looking for Sally Butters. That fall and winter was my last decline into what you might call general degradation. With the thousand dollars Jessie left to me, I was pretty well fixed for booze and tobacco. So I didn't do much that winter except drink several dozen bottles of whiskey and smoke a few thousand cigarettes. If Rufus hadn't come along now and again with a meat pie or a pot of beans, I might have expired.

Then on an April morning in '46 I came out the front door of my house, a little shaky in the legs and skinny and stiff as a spring bear. I sniffed the mud and heard the running water and watched the snow wasting away in the sunlight. Then I went into the shed and put the wheels back on my truck and drove into town. My skin disease had nearly cleared up but I was still regarded as an object of ridicule, especially by the kids, who used to run after me down the street singing:

> *Pig Man, Pig Man*
> *Tell us all the news*
> *Pig Man, Pig Man*
> *Won't you clean your shoes?*

Saucy little buggers! But I'm sort of proud of that song. They still sing it around this town when they're skipping their ropes on spring evenings. And I'll bet you there isn't one of them who knows that little song is about me!

On that particular day I bought some supplies and then visited the post office for my winter's mail. And there among the seed catalogues and old copies of the *Swine Breeders' Digest* was a letter from Cass Findlater!

35

THE LAST CHAPTER

HERE'S THE LETTER:

Castle Eldorado
Florida, U.S.A.
April 1, 1946

Dear Bill:

Well old frend. How are you anyways? I hope you have let bye gones be bye gones and don't hold no grudge against your old pal and travellin partner. I am fine thouh I ain't the spring chicken I once was. But say, I wanted to tell you that I'm very rich. I made a fortune in money during the recent war with Tojo and Hitler and Muscleenee. I knew Muscleenee once. Did I ever tell ya? Anyways I'm now ritin a book about my adventurous life. I'm ritin on the benefits of positive thinkin and of how if you keep your sunny side up and believe in God, you'll come out on top of the other feller. I rote a man in New York City and he told me his company would put it out for ten thousand dollars. That strikes me as steep thouh as I say there's no shortage of the old mazoola down here. In the room I'm sittin the doorknobs is made of gold. What do you make of that? Not bad eh! For a feller who once travelled on the fresh air express. But say, I was thinkin this old frend. You was always an educated man and I admired you for it. Your own daddy was a poet. You told me that once and I believe you. I wonder if you'd help me rite this here book which I know will benefit humankind if they read it. I will put you up here and pay you five hunnert dollars in cash money to put the rite words in their place. And here's some-

326

thin else which I've saved till the last. Who do you think is
here but your old sweetheart from the stage, Sally Butters?
Yes sir, she is down here with me, as beautiful as ever and she
would dearly love to see her old admirer and frend Bill
Farthing. I am sendin a map to show you how to reach me.

Yur old pal,
Cass Findlater

To tell you the truth, it surprised me to learn that Findlater was
still alive. And thirteen years after we parted, he seemed to be back in
the money again. But the most startling news had to do with Sally
Butters. Why, she would be in her sixties like me! How had she survived the years? It was something I had to find out, so I went over to
Rufus Talbot's and borrowed his new Fargo pick-up truck. Then I set
out for Florida.

It took me four or five days to get there, because the truck was
new and I had to break it in. And then I got lost a few times on back
roads, for Findlater's map wasn't exactly the most precise document
ever drawn up. According to this map the nearest village was a place
called King River, which I finally found in the late afternoon of a
cloudy, hot day. Now, if you think of Florida as sunny beaches and
fancy hotels, you are only partly right. There are sections of that state
that are more like darkest Africa. Swampland, crawling with snakes
and alligators, and big birds skimming over the tops of trees. Maybe
they've drained it all now and it's different, but in those days you half
expected to see one of those old prehistoric monsters lift its head out
of the mud to watch you pass. This place King River was just a dozen
unpainted shacks and a general store. The inhabitants all looked
roughly the same, being gangly and pale with hair so blond it looked
white. None of them appeared correct in the head to me. They lounged
around the verandah of this general store or sat on the stoops of their
shacks staring at the truck as though it was the first motor vehicle
they'd ever seen. Nobody said a word and when I asked one fellow
where this Castle Eldorado was he just pointed down the road and
held up two fingers. Then he gave me a vacant grin and there wasn't
a tooth in his head, though he couldn't have been more than twenty.
I was glad to get the hell out of there.

So I followed this narrow dirt road for about two miles. Although
it was still afternoon it had got so dark I had to switch on the headlights. There wasn't a breath of wind. The air was thick with heat and
a kind of rotten swampy smell. Then as I came around a slight bend in
the road, I saw Castle Eldorado. It was the damnedest sight you ever
laid eyes on, and if the whole atmosphere hadn't been so creepy I might
have laughed. What it was, you see, was a reproduction of an old-time
castle such as you might find in a kid's book of fairy tales. It was made
of pink stucco with turrets and a drawbridge over a moat. I drove right
across this drawbridge and it didn't comfort me any to see the bumpy

heads of alligators gliding through the dark water below. All around me I heard the rumble of thunder. Next to the main gates of this castle was a little door and I opened that and shouts, "Anybody home? Findlater? It's me. Bill Farthing." I was in a hallway and there was an open door off to one side where a bit of feeble daylight seeped through.

Then I heard Findlater's voice say, "Is that you, pal? Come right on in."

So in I went through this open door and I found myself in a long room which was mostly in darkness. The only light, and it wasn't much, came from a pair of French windows which looked out on a patio and a couple of chairs near these windows. And seated behind the desk was an enormously fat man. "Bill, old pal," says Findlater. "Welcome to Eldorado. Say, I'm sorry I can't arise. I've put on a little weight these past few years and it's troublesome to get around. But come closer and let's have a look at you."

When Findlater said a little weight, he wasn't exaggerating. The truth was that he now weighed at least three hundred pounds, all of it squeezed into a yellow checkered suit of the sort I remember him wearing on the boardwalks of New York fifty years before. On his head was a straw boater. His face was gray with bristles, and although there were three or four rings on his fingers, his vest was stained with food. "Bill. It's been a long time," he says. "And you're no spring lettuce either, are you? Silver threads among the gold, I see."

"I don't know how you can see anything in here," I says. "Why don't you turn on a light?"

And then another rumble of thunder rolled across the sky and Findlater says, "There'll be plenty of light once the storm arrives. I've worked through many a good electrical storm. The lamps of heaven. What's new, anyways?"

A terrible gust of hot wind blew open the French windows, scattering dozens of yellow papers from Findlater's desk and knocking the boater off his head. He didn't say a word and I walked over to fasten the windows. In the lightning I could see the swimming pool covered with a green scum. A huge turtle sat on the diving board and a moccasin snake, at least five feet long, slid across the cracked patio into the water. I walked back to Findlater's desk.

"You should have stuck with me, Bill," he says. "Things picked up there about ten years ago. I knew they would. I told you that."

"So you did," I says. "Whatever happened to Sunny Day and his grandfather?"

Findlater thought for a moment. It looked like he was rummaging around in his memory for the right article. "That boy could have been another Jack Johnson. What a right hand he had! Fast on his feet too. Moves that would astound the normal bystander."

"What happened to him, Findlater?"

"But he couldn't take a punch in the old breadbasket, that was his weakness. Too bad. But nobody's perfect. He lost his life in an unfortunate ring accident, Bill. I gave the old feller five hunnert. That was big money in those days. You could buy a nice stone for that kind of money." He said something else, but it was lost in the noise of the storm.

I felt suddenly sick to my stomach. It wasn't only hearing about Sunny, but something physical. The air was filled with the stink of burning sulfur. I wondered if maybe the lightning had hit something close by. Then in the half-light I saw Findlater reach for a gallon jug on his desk. "Twenty-one days now," he says, tipping up the jug and drinking.

"What?" I says, feeling the sickness climb towards my throat. The back of my neck was clammy.

"My bowels," says Findlater. "They haven't moved in twenty-one days. It's an affliction to grow old, Bill." He took another long swig from the jug. "Not even this damn castor oil does the job anymore."

I wiped the perspiration from my brow. "How did you make your money anyway, Findlater?"

He canted sideways in his chair. "Various enterprises," he says. "Mainly involving the wheel. A wonderful invention, the wheel. Especially if you put four of them under a chassis and attach an internal combustion engine."

"You made your money in automobiles?" I asks.

"And other things, Bill. Other things. In 1914 the Germans had a rubber tire that was years ahead of anything we had. A piece of pavement isn't a bad investment." He was gathering together these yellow papers on his desk. "What I have here, old pal, is the secrets of my success as a human person. Never give up the ship. Keep your sunny side up. That's the way I like my eggs. Ignore the long faces of those around you. Smile through the tears and you'll come up smellin' like the flowers in May." He looked over at me and winked. "Five hunnert dollars, Bill. Half now and half when you're finished. Just sign here on the dotted . . ." He pushed a piece of paper across the desk at me and laid a fountain pen on it.

I said to him, "I remember the days when you and me didn't need to sign anything between us."

"It's just a matter of spellin' and grammar. Fix up the sentences but don't monkey with the thoughts. The thoughts are okay." He paused. "You can stay here to do it. The bed and eats are gratis and free. You look like you could use a square meal. You're just a shadow of your former self."

But the thought of food nearly made me sick and I held my stomach, sitting half crouched over. "You mentioned Sally in your letter, Findlater," I says.

Lightning forked across the sky and the windows vibrated with thunder. A few drops of rain fell on the patio flagstones. "What year is it, pal?" asks Findlater.

"Nineteen forty-six," I says.

"A new age is dawnin', Bill, and good times are right around the corner. Canned baby food will be a big item in the next few years."

"What about Sally, Findlater?"

"But in the long run you can't beat the Chevrolet."

"Is she here?"

"Reliable family transportation. Everybody should have one, and will."

There was a red-hot coal lying in the pit of my stomach. Then Findlater reached behind him and pulled a piece of rope hanging from the ceiling. "It's show time, pal. Turn your chair around there and enjoy yourself." On the wall behind me an old-fashioned curtain rolled up and there was a little stage lit by flickering candles. Behind the stage was the painted screen of a blue sky and an apple tree, just like you used to see in the old music halls. From somewhere a scratchy record began to play. Then damn me for a liar if a skinny, red-headed old woman didn't come out on stage twirling a parasol. She was dressed in a purple velvet dress and high button boots and she was singing "Beautiful Dreamer" in a high, squeaky voice that quivered and shook with every word. Her legs weren't any bigger around than a hoe handle and her hair was all frizzy. Sally blew me a kiss. I stood up, hoping maybe the pain in my belly would ease. I'd eaten a ham sandwich at a roadside diner that afternoon and now I shouted, "I believe I've been poisoned."

"Down in front," says Findlater. "Don't interrupt the act."

"I need air," I says. "I can't breathe." I moved a few steps forward and Sally blew me another kiss.

"You could pick them, Bill," says Findlater behind me. "Sal's a winner."

"Maybe it's my appendix!" I shouted to no one in particular.

"It's just like old times," says Findlater. "The three of us together again."

Beyond the window terrible lightning opened up the sky and the thunder nearly deafened me. The rain hammered the lily pads in the swimming pool. Sally continued to sing, her mouth opening and closing like a fish. Behind me Findlater took another pull from his jug. By some miracle, the pain in my gut eased a little. And then, although I was sixty-five years old at the time, I ran.

EPILOGUE

————

A REMARKABLE STORY! A remarkable life! But what, you may well ask, happened to this extraordinary man between the years following his precipitous flight from Castle Eldorado in the spring of 1946 and my initial meeting with him in the autumn of 1974? Well, unfortunately, nothing of any particular significance. The incredible drama of the first two-thirds of his life was over: the principal actors had left the stage; the lights had dimmed; the curtain had fallen, so to speak.

Mr. Farthing returned to his farm and resumed his previous occupation of raising swine. He grew inordinately fond of this cloven-hoofed mammal of the genus *Sus*, and indeed once confided to me that in his later years he preferred the company of pigs to people. It was not the first time that I detected a somewhat cranky, misanthropic strain in the old gentleman's nature.

On 1 July 1955, while attending the funeral of his friend and brother-in-law, Rufus Talbot, Mr. Farthing collapsed. He claimed it was only "a bad case of the bellyaches," but the county health authorities disagreed and diagnosed a mild coronary. Mindful of the author's advanced years and reclusive life style, they forcibly admitted him to Sunset Manor. And here he remained until his death twenty years later to the very day!

Other readers may well question whether what they have just read is the truth, or only the fantasies of a colorful imagination. As Mr. Farthing's publishers, we too were anxious not to be victimized by mere fabrication. Story spinners are a dime a dozen in these times but *real* people who have encountered *real* life experiences and can write interestingly about them are rare indeed. With this in mind, we set about to authenticate the material so vividly described in these memoirs. Needless to say, there is much that cannot be verified and here we must take the author at his word. Our investigations uncovered maddening incongruities. After an exhaustive search through the literature of the Klondike gold rush, for example, we found *not a single word* pertaining to the alleged "onion roast" which Mr. Farthing claims attracted a substantial portion of Dawson's citizenry on that bitterly cold January night in 1899. On the other hand, records, kindly made available to us by the Royal Canadian Mounted Police, clearly show that a Wm. Farthing and a C. Findlater were incarcerated by the Dawson Constabulary on 3 February 1899 for "common theft of goods to the value of sixty-eight dollars ($68.00); said goods belonging to one B. Spraat of Philadelphia, Pa. U.S.A."

When we turn to the author's military experiences we find other interesting documentation. The office of the British War Records, for instance, lists a William Farthing, Canadian by birth, as having served as a private with the Royal Piccadilly Rifles, one of the battalions of the 29th Division. The Records also indicate that Pvt. Farthing was wounded *honorably* near Beaumont-Hamel on Sunday, 2 July 1916. But infuriatingly enough, no details of the injury are given. The office of the British War Records still lists Pvt. Farthing as convalescing in the Weary Warrior's Nursing Home in Toronto. And it is here that we unravel yet another interesting thread in the fabric of this unusual man's life.

The Weary Warrior's Nursing Home was demolished in 1948 to make way for a spaghetti factory. But some diligent literary detective work in the archives of the Ontario College of Physicians and Surgeons revealed the following: William Farthing was the *subject* of a partially completed monograph entitled *An Unusual Amnesiac.* The author was a Dr. Lemuel Hugg, an English specialist interested in eccentric cases of amnesia and narcolepsy. Dr. Hugg accompanied Farthing from England to Canada in the spring of 1917 and indeed from that point on seems to have become obsessed with Farthing's condition. The treatise, incomplete as it is, affords us a carefully detailed account of Farthing's day-to-day activities over the next fifteen years. I fear it makes unhappy and rather tedious reading, for Farthing appears to have done very little during this interregnum except read the occasional book in the hospital library and play checkers with a Boer War paraplegic named Arthur Furbelow. And here again the finger of coincidence which probed and prodded the author all his life is once again in evidence, for who should his opponent in checkers turn out to be but the great-uncle of his former company commander, Captain Furbelow!

Dr. Hugg records that between May 1917 and July 1932 Farthing and Furbelow played 18,556 games of checkers, though why the specialist thought fit to keep such accurate records of this seemingly harmless pastime is not vouchsafed the reader. But here again, as we perused this dusty monograph we encountered mystery and paradox, for *not once* does Dr. Hugg mention that Farthing ever received a visitor! Dr. Hugg, by the way, seems to have suffered a period of prolonged nervous prostration following Farthing's nimble exit from the Weary Warrior's Nursing Home on 1 July 1932. In fact, the specialist died some months later under "unusual" circumstances involving a bathtub of water and an empty light socket.

In sum then, what can one say? The author lived an extraordinary life, and even allowing for the sixteen-year patch of amnesia, he had, if I may employ a little irony and borrow a phrase from the English game of cricket, "a good innings." Over the past several months he declined noticeably, and indeed was near death's doorstep when last I visited him. As I placed the proofs of his life's story on the thin old chest, the eyelids fluttered and for a brief moment those startlingly vivid blue eyes were filled with what I can only describe as angry light. "What you got now is the ——ing truth," he whispered hoarsely. Then he lapsed into "the final sleep." Crude words indeed with which to take leave of this life! And is his story the truth? Who can say? Let us only keep in mind the words of a sage who once observed that truth sits upon the lips of dying men. And then, with charity in our hearts, let us take leave of a gallant old soldier who did his best and fought the good fight.

RICHARD B. WRIGHT

Richard B. Wright has published two previous
novels, both highly acclaimed: *The Weekend
Man* (1971) and *In the Middle of a Life* (1973),
which won the Faber fiction award in England.
He lives with his wife and two sons in St.
Catharines, Ontario, where he teaches English
at Ridley College.